I AM ARMAGEDDON

THE ARMAGEDDON TRILOGY
BOOK ONE

C L CABRERA

Copyright © 2023 by C L Cabrera

All rights reserved.

No part of this book may be reproduced in any form or by any electronic or mechanical means, including information storage and retrieval systems, without written permission from the author, except for the use of brief quotations in a book review.

To my developmental editor, Fahmida, and anyone who read I Am Armageddon in its infancy. Thank you for helping my childhood dreams come true.
To my daughters. May you be as compassionate as Wylie, as brave as Lex, and as ambitious as Laoth.

CONTENT WARNING KEY

Your mental health is important to me. Please review the content warning key. You will find corresponding symbols at the beginning of each chapter.

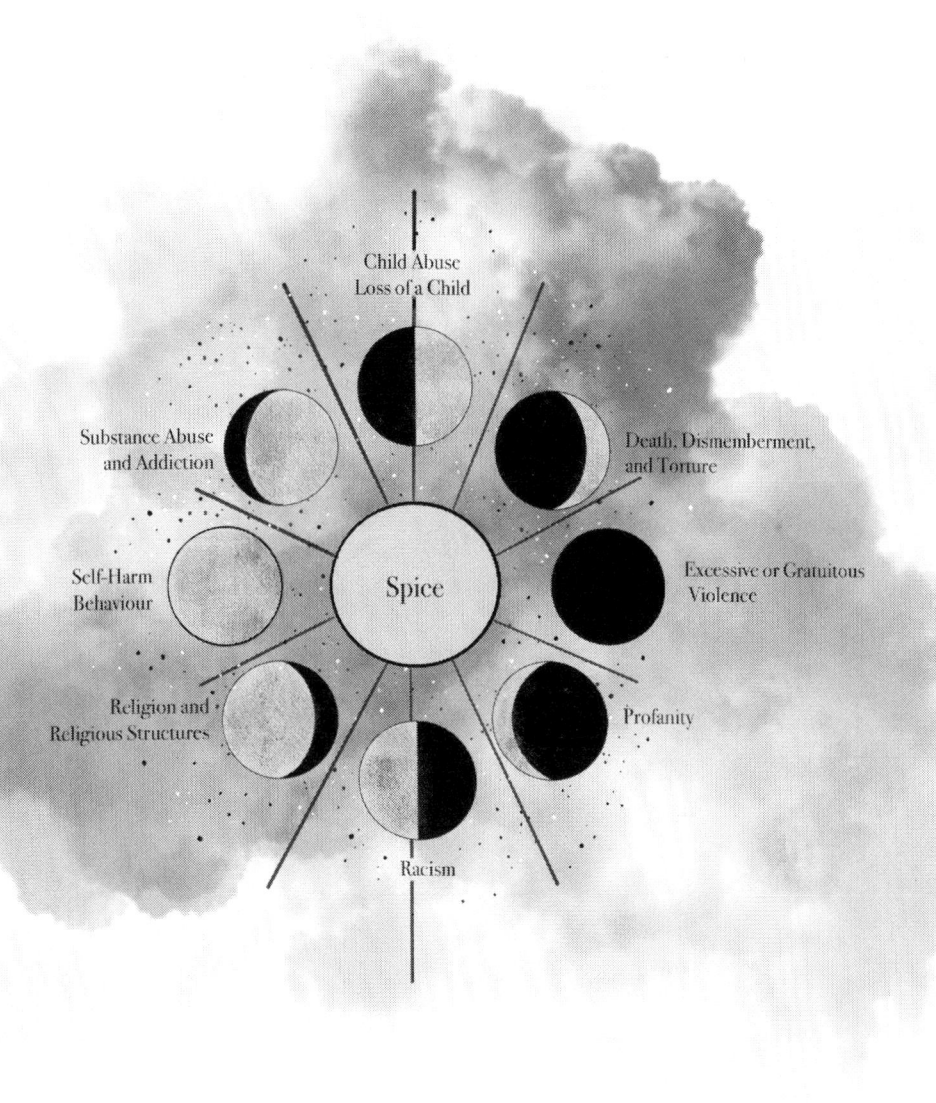

- Child Abuse / Loss of a Child
- Death, Dismemberment, and Torture
- Excessive or Gratuitous Violence
- Profanity
- Racism
- Religion and Religious Structures
- Self-Harm Behaviour
- Substance Abuse and Addiction

Spice

THE PROPHECY

From the water, she will rise
Born of Death
Raised in Love
Above her, her white horse
He will find her
She will break him
Beside her, the red one
He will wake her
She will hate him
Before her, the black horse
He will protect her
She will save him
Behind her, her pale one
He will betray her
She will forgive him
Angel, Fallen, human, muse
They will gather
For she is Armageddon
The entrance to heaven

BONUS CONTENT

To find an I Am Armageddon playlist, angel lore, audiobook samples and more, click or scan below:

PSALM 91:11

For he shall give his angels charge over thee, to keep thee in all thy ways.

Prologue

Samael

A wave of power burst from North America. The impact left hidden scars under the earth's surface. Every angel lifted their head, their hidden wings threatening to flicker to life. Samael searched his memory for a similar surge, but in the last few millennia, no such Scientia had graced this planet.

Angels have cared for humans since they crawled from the primordial stew God grew them in. Samael needed a win, and today he would get one. He tied back his sandy hair before pulling his halo out of his chest and resting it on his head. His armor and wings emerged as he leaned against a wooden platform. The Heavenly Plane —where angels trained—had not seen a new trainee for centuries. The place sat empty and useless as it waited for its final student.

His fellow Dominions joined him before he requested their presence. They came dressed in a spectrum of finery and rags. Their eyes and skin represented lands both far and near. Each donned their halos like crowns. Their clothes were replaced by the armor of their station. Raphael appeared last, already dressed for battle, his black hair contrasting with the silver of his halo, the fluorescent lights casting angry shadows on his face.

Samael growled deep in his chest, capturing the attention of his fellows. "Did we all feel an exchange of power?" Heads nodded. A power exchange this large could only mean her source of Scientia died and was replaced. Samael had waited so long for this sign, any sign she'd come to fulfill her destiny. "My fellow Dominions, we have found her."

The generals in God's army held back their smiles. Only one questioned the truth of the revelation. "How do we know Armageddon caused the surge?" Raphael sat on the metal bleachers facing the platform, his legs splayed and fingers steepled with his usual egotism.

"I've searched for her since God thrust Adam and Eve from the Garden of Eden." Samael stepped before Raphael. His square jaw tightened. He had no space for patience in this moment of exhilaration. "Do not doubt me, brother."

Raphael got to his feet, his height becoming evident as he looked down at Samael. While the black-haired angel stood inches taller, his shoulders were inches narrower. Their chests bumped, their wings dancing with annoyance. "Then retrieve her, *brother*."

"I will." Samael lifted his hand, not wanting to sully the day with a disagreement, leaving an offering that stood the test of time.

Raphael's sneer fell away as they shook. Their hands creaked under the pressure of their grips, their lips pulling up into what a Dominion would call a smile and humans would call satisfaction. "Then go."

Samael turned to the other Dominions. "I shall return."

He projected himself to San Diego State University, appearing against a palm tree. His angelic nose breathed in the ocean salt humans couldn't sense from this distance. The sun blinked against the horizon, hanging onto the last dregs of color. A couple sat framed by the painted purples and pinks of the sky. A clean-cut young man held a curvy woman, both dressed in church clothes.

With the female's back to Samael, he took in her black curls and the couple's matching ochre skin. *Armageddon?* He reached out with his Scientia, his essence brushing along hers. The electrifying bulk of it welcomed him. It overflowed, leaking out of her and touching everything around them.

The man kissed her forehead. "Shhh, *mi Amor*."

This must be her new muse. The sweet aftermath of a major transfer in power lingered around him, matching the spring smells of sage and lilac.

The woman's shoulders shook with sobs as the man stroked her unruly hair. Armageddon, the angel of the prophecy, crying, caused a tremble in his hand. He glared at the offending appendage until her voice interrupted his wandering thoughts.

"Roberto, he's never going to meet him." She untangled her arms from her lover and leaned back on the bench. "My dad, he'll never know our baby." Her round belly moved as the baby adjusted itself. The man set his hand on her stomach. Hers stacked on top of his. The sight sent Samael stumbling back.

"Your father will watch us from heav—"

Samael returned to the Heavenly Planes; his eyes wide.

"So, what did you discover, brother?" Raphael steadied him.

"She's pregnant." Samael's form vibrated with excitement. "Armageddon is pregnant."

Murmurs crescendoed into cheers as tears met grins. Samael's green eyes found Raphael's blues. "We're going to have a baby. The angels are going to have a baby!"

"This is wonderful news." Raphael's forced smile matched the stiffness with which he patted Samael's shoulder.

"I'm her white horse." Samael's smile skipped from Dominion to Dominion, unconcerned with Raphael's sour mood.

"You must be," Raphael spoke through clenched teeth. "You found her, didn't you?"

Samael waved the angel away and moved on to his siblings, ready to share in his good cheer.

Over the next few months, the Heavenly Planes came to life with celebrations as angels returned home for the first time in centuries. Light and color filled the empty spaces. angels smiled and laughed as they remembered other such joyous times, and for once, true happiness warmed the desolate halls and barren rooms.

The angels who didn't see the forthcoming birth as a blessing stayed silent, remaining distant. They stayed earthside and traded whispered words anytime they dared, hoping God would not hear them. San Diego received many a heavenly visitor as the birth grew ever closer. These visitors came from both camps, curiosity luring them.

Two such angels met at the University just weeks before Armageddon's due date, their eyes scouring the crowd for a woman with long black curls and a child ready for his birth in her belly.

"She feels strong," said the younger of the two. His open posture and confident gait matched the popped collar of his wool overcoat.

"She's strong, but she doesn't know how to use her strength." The ancient angel folded his arms, looking no older than his counterpart.

"There's an advantage to that."

"True. You're far more prepared than she'll ever be, son." The two appeared to come from opposite sides of the equator but carried themselves similarly.

"So, what do we do now?" The dark-skinned youth's chin rose with his question.

"You build your army. And when we have enough of a following, we'll take her out."

"So, war?"

"Yes, son. War."

Three years later...

Marut's black wings flashed iridescent against the obscurity of the shadows. Samael's pace quickened. The gray sky reflected his mood.

"Put those away." Samael gestured at the wings, his jaw tight with frustration. The space behind him showed his self-control. His wings were invisible.

"Yes, brother." Marut's shoulders arched as he stretched his wings one last time before they disappeared. Darkness replaced the raven feathers.

"How long have you waited?"

"I came this morning. Laoth told me to expect an attack." Marut pushed his mahogany hair away from his neck and rubbed at his taut muscles with his knuckles.

"You must be tired." Samael's head tilted toward Wylie's apartment.

"I have my job, and you have yours." Marut straightened. "Pro summon bono."

"Pro summum bonum, brother."

"I've seen nothing suspicious thus far. Here, follow me." Marut led Samael out of the alley. "I've warded the apartment against the rebel angels, but I don't think Wylie will be here much longer. She'll get called into work soon. Protecting her at the hospital is more of a challenge."

Cars rushed by, rumpling Samael's sandy hair. "What makes you think she'll go to work?" He admired the shimmering wall which encased Wylie's apartment. The barrier would keep her safe. Marut had locked it so tight, even sound couldn't escape. Samael grimaced. At least a millennium had passed since an angel needed to conjure such walls.

"She's a creature of habit. They will call, and she will go."

Samael raised his brows. "You know her well."

"I know her better than she knows herself."

"You've always been good at keeping your wards safe."

"So, when will she end the world?"

"God only knows." Samael opened his mind and reached for her magic, her Scientia. His power feathered across hers, and his wings threatened to appear in response.

Chapter 1

Wylie

Wylie lay under the covers, wearing only her lace panties, her ebony curls fanned out on her satin pillow. Date night in the Hernandez house started in the bedroom tonight. She arranged her limbs to showcase the definition of her muscles and hide her cellulite. She pulled the blanket over her thick thighs and to her small breasts, readying herself to surprise her husband.

Her phone vibrated, and *'Cherry Hill Charge Nurse'* appeared across the screen. She rolled her eyes and tossed it on the side table as she settled back into her original position.

"Roberto?"

"Coming, mi amor."

The door creaked open. "Dean's asleep." Her husband's hair shone bronze where the dimmed light touched it. "I told you, the no-nap-trick works. He was out by the ti . . ." a wolfish smile crept across his face as his eyes landed on her. "You." He unbuttoned the collar of his polo. "I hope you're naked under there."

She brandished her most seductive smile as her eyes ate him up. "Time to tuck me in, *papi*." She tossed the blanket off, letting the cold air work its magic on her nipples. A marriage, a career, and a child later, Roberto's copper skin and high cheekbones still brought warmth between her legs.

"You got all dressed up for me?" He pulled his shirt off and tossed it. The lines of his chest and shoulders, his abs, his hips—left her mouth-watering.

She cupped her breast. "Come help me make a baby."

He lifted a knee onto the bed and paused as he leaned into the mattress. "A baby, huh?" He crawled to her, his tongue and teeth finding her neck. She groaned as the cedar smell of his cologne engulfed her. "I thought we were waiting until Dean turned four." Her skin hummed with the hint of a growl in his voice.

His eagerness melted her self-doubt into need and abandon. His deft hands made her feel small and beautiful.

A buzz sounded from the side table. Wylie ignored it, weaving her fingers in Roberto's hair. His hand found her cheek, and his mouth found her earlobe as the phone started its dance again.

Roberto sighed. Leaning back, he grabbed the thing and pushed it into her hand. "It's killing the mood." He kissed her forehead, imprinting his frown into her skin. "Make it quick." And then he licked her cheek.

"Gross." She wiped her face, a giggle bubbling up as she pressed the phone to her ear. His silliness helped her forget the twin disappointments battling in her head. One represented her husband, the other her family of nurses who suffered without her.

"Wylie's phone." She pulled the blanket up to her breasts and bit her lip, wishing it was his teeth. Their eyes connected, and his half-lidded gaze told her he wanted the same.

"Thank God you answered." Wylie recognized Mary's voice. They'd survived some terrible nights in the emergency room together.

Roberto hooked his fingers in the blanket and pulled, kissing the swell of her breast.

"What's up?" She shivered as Roberto's tongue sent a shock wave into her belly.

"We need you. I —" Someone interrupted Mary with an inaudible request, and Wylie did her best not to moan. *"Call security then."* Pause. *"Sorry. Wylie, we need help. Can you come in? Management approved extra pay."*

"I can't tonight." Her words came out breathy.

"But you'll get that extra weekend pay. And double-time."

"I . . . I . . ." His tongue circled her peaked nipple, and she struggled to form a coherent thought.

"*I meant to say triple-time.*"

She stiffened, and her husband sat back on his heels, recognizing her I'm-about-to-cave face.

"Triple-time?" She did the math in her head and raised her brows at Roberto.

He nodded, his hand massaging the furrow in his brow.

"Okay, I can be there in two hours, and I only want the easy stuff tonight. I didn't sleep at all today."

"*Sure thing.*" Mary chuckled. "*See you soon.*"

Wylie tossed her phone onto the carpet and frowned, preparing an apology.

"It's okay, Wylie. I'll make you breakfast in the morning, and maybe Dean will take an early nap."

"I'm sorry; they can't survive without me." The wrinkle of his brow caused a lump in her throat. "And, you know, I won't survive without you." She opened her legs and her arms. "You've got two hours to put a baby in me."

His smile returned, an eager light in his chocolate eyes as he answered her with thirsty hands and a hungry tongue. She met him with the fire of a woman on a time limit, her fingers clumsy as she fought with his fly.

Wylie arrived at work flushed, her mind preoccupied with the buzz Roberto had left under her skin. The tidal wave of a full moon at Cherry Hill Emergency Department sucked her in. All free thought was taken by patients and coworkers. She spent her breaks on her phone calculating due dates, and when the shift ended, they made their way out in groups of two or three war-worn survivors.

She sent Roberto a text:

> I can't wait for breakfast!

She wanted to gush, spilling all her thoughts from the shift into text after text, but he didn't respond. She turned her windshield wipers on high to battle the annual Seattle spring downpour and kept the phone in her lap, waiting for a buzz.

"Good morning, boys," she sang. The front door closed behind her. Wylie sniffed the air, frowning when she didn't smell bacon. "Roberto?" No answer. He must have run to the grocery store.

She hung her coat in the entryway closet. Her clogs came off with a moan, bouncing against a pair of toddler shoes. They lit up the space. The smile slid from her face. *Why did they leave Dean's shoes?*

"Boys?"

Her breath became a sliver in her lungs as a frozen breeze brushed past her. The chill against her skin focused her mind in a way only work could. She rushed down the hall. The microwave lay upside-down on the floor, the sliding glass door open behind it. The disarray continued into the kitchen. She dug into her pocket for her phone. Pressing '911', she hit send.

Wylie's world ended in three heartbeats.

Ring.

Thu-thump.

Ring.

Thu-thump.

Ring.

Thu-thump.

"Nine-one-one, what's your emerge—" she dropped the phone.

"No." Disbelief tightened her throat around the word. "No, no!"

Her husband's body leaned into the unlit fireplace. His back faced her as he hunched over, something she couldn't see in his arms. Blood saturated the tan carpet, an island of red. Her legs propelled her forward even as her mind stuttered. She needed to put pressure somewhere. She needed to don gloves and call a code.

Blinded by desperation, she tripped, landing on her knees. Blood clots broke apart under her palms. The smell of pennies filled her nostrils.

"I can fix this. I can fix this."

Her hands climbed his back, discovering with touch the things her tear-filled eyes couldn't. Bullet wounds. There were holes. *Someone put holes in my husband.* Her fingers found his neck. No pulse. She leaned her ear into the cold wetness of his back, listening. His breathing failed to rock her with its familiar rhythm. The heartbeat which always sang her to sleep at night was gone. Her body trembled, and everything between her mouth and her stomach froze, waiting for his song to return.

It never did.

"Why?" Wylie's voice shook with her sticky hands. "God, why?" Her eyes blinked and blinked, bargaining for a different outcome every time they opened. Keening cries ripped through her throat like contractions. Her arms wrapped around him, and though his unnatural stiffness grated against her denial, holding him felt right. They fit together perfectly.

But our whole has three parts.

Sliding to the ground, she curled around Roberto. She found Dean's foot first, her hands following the curve of his calf up to his chubby thigh. "No, no, no. Please, God, no." Pain split her in half, stealing her breath along with her heart. Dean's hickory eyes stared into the heavens, empty of their boyish wonder.

With numb hands, she reached into their tangled embrace and took hold of those little shoulders. "Dean, baby!" She shook him, the nurse in her gone to the primal part of her that wanted to wake him through touch. "Dean!" Her face found its way against his cheek. "Dean, it's okay, baby." Her fingers. His chocolate curls. "Mama's going to make it better." Too cold. Too still. "Mama's going to . . ." Ringing in her ears. "Oh, God. Dean?!" She rocked them, her words unrecognizable between howls of pain. "Baby! My baby!"

𝒫arenting was more about instincts than Roberto and Wylie ever admitted. They read books, watched videos, and planned playdates, hoping the investments would turn them into the mother and father their child deserved.

But . . .

But when it came down to it . . .

When the shit hit the fan . . .

Roberto grabbed their child and held Dean close, shielding their future from the bad.

If only flesh could stop bullets.

If only backs could be shields.

Chapter 2

Samael

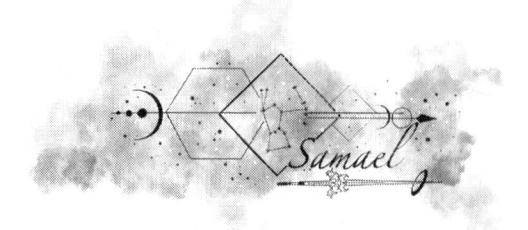

Cleaning up the aftermath of Dean and Roberto's death left a pain in Samael's chest. Seeing Wylie grieve haunted him. And so, he returned to the Heavenly Planes to see his elders. He sank to his knees before the Seraphim, knowing something inside of him was wrong. The soft grass of Elysian wet his shins, defying the lingering frost of the early morning he'd just left behind. He lifted his forearm to his eyes to represent his blind faith in God and waited for permission to speak.

"You've come to tell us what we already know," the God's Guard spoke all at once, four boys with a single voice. Forever children. Forced never to leave the Heavenly Planes.

"I have." Angels required very few emotions to do their jobs. They rejoiced. They avenged. They wept. He shouldn't feel this dull ache, this hollowness.

The Seraphim's unkempt hair shone auburn in the sunlight. Their crimson eyes narrowed. "And you have a question." One voice broke off from the others. Samael strained to recognize its owner with his face still covered. "Speak."

"Armageddon's muse and child are dead." Samael did not lower his arm as he spoke, in fear the Seraphim would remove him from existence. He lowered his mental defenses, showing them the father and son tangled together. Wylie's body curled in on itself as her wide eyes reflected the emptiness of loss.

He closed his eyes and let the orchestra of wind through the leaves steady him. He set his jaw and continued. "Now that she has been untethered from her humanity. We want to introduce Armageddon to angelkind. And so, the Dominions have called a Tribunal."

"And every angel will attend?" Their voices became one again.

"There are some angels that rebel against us." Samael lowered his arm, focusing on the God's Guard's most striking feature. Their wings rose above their heads and around their shoulders. Multiple sets sprung from their backs, making them more feathers than children. The sight of the boys did not reflect the power of their presence. Their Scientia boiled up at his response, hitting him like a tidal wave. He bowed his head. His hair rose from his shoulders, and his skin tightened against its onslaught. Samael threw himself forward, letting his cheek rest against the dirt.

"So, there are," said one boy, his inflection more childlike than the others. "However, fate demands their presence. We have an announcement, and you will invite them." He leaned his head on his taller brother. "They will come."

"It will be so."

"And now your question." Their words weaved together again.

Samael remained silent. He searched for words to describe the flashes of humanity he'd experienced while watching Armageddon create a family. He should have protected her.

"You do not know what your question is."

Samael shook his head, his eyes lowered.

"It is not your fault, Samael. None of this is your fault."

Chapter 3

Wylie

"I don't give a flying fuck! It's been eleven months." Wylie hunched over her phone. She held it in both hands, her fingers knobbier than they'd ever been.

"Ma'am, I understand —"

"You understand? The. Fuck. You. Do. My husband is dead. My child is dead. I think Seattle needs to know the good ol' PD is happy with letting a—" The breakroom door swung open, and Dr. Godwyn walked in. She turned off the speakerphone and curled into the room's corner, effectively putting her back to the intruder "—baby killer, run free."

"I'm sorry for your loss, but this does not change the fact we're out of leads."

"So, you guys give up?" She expected better news. Maybe a miracle. It was Dean's fourth birthday, after all. Justice would make the perfect present.

"Ma'am, we solve fifty percent of cold cases. There's still a chance. We'll continue to do the best we can."

She cupped her hand over her mouth, side-eyeing the white coat as he reached into the refrigerator. "That's not good enough. None of this is good enough. All I've seen you guys do is sit around with your thumbs up your asses." She stole a shaky breath. "Is it because we're brown, 'sir'? Is that why you guys are giving the fuck up?"

Silence answered her. She looked at her phone. The bastard had hung up on her. Rageful tears splattered down her cheeks, and she brushed them away with her palms. She needed to hide her frayed edges before her break finished. She roughly pushed away her emotions, and instead of throwing her phone across the room, which felt like the best option, she closed her eyes and counted, visualizing her favorite place. The breeze, the smell of grass, the wide-open sky.

"Do you need company?"

She focused on Dr. Godwyn's maroon scrubs, embarrassed and unsure she could maintain eye contact with anyone and not tear their head off or start bawling. "I'm good. Thank you."

"Okay." He waited for a beat as he white-knuckled his paper-bagged lunch. "Okay."

She opened her notes app and finished noting the officer's name as the break room door clicked shut behind Dr. Godwyn. A few more words made it in before her alarm went off, signaling her break had ended. She glared at the half-eaten retirement cake sitting on the breakroom table. *Happy birthday, Dean.* Flashes of the smash-cake Dean had destroyed on his first birthday danced in the back of her head. Those round little cheeks, covered in frosting. His cute little cake-covered fists punched the sky as his belly laughs shook his whole body.

She filled her lungs and willed her eyes to dry.

She exited the break room, her shoulders heavier than when she entered. "Code yellow. Fifteen minutes, code yellow emergency department in fifteen minutes." She shoved the feelings away and followed the team into the trauma room, ready to use her pent-up energy to do something good.

Mary took control when she entered the room. "Wylie, you run blood. Shannon, you grab meds. Jared, you record."

"What are we expecting?" Dr. Godwyn's white coat fluttered behind him as he entered.

"It's a thirty-two-year-old Hispanic man with five GSWs to his . . ."

Her ears buzzed, drowning out the report. It took her a second to see the patient instead of her husband, but the man looked older than Roberto, with a few gray hairs at his temples and creases around his eyes. She pulled on a lead vest, logged into the computer, and finished pulling supplies as the gurney crashed into the room, and a cacophony of noise erupted.

"One, two, three." They lifted him onto the bed as an EMT passed her his wallet. "His name's Eduardo Gomez," he said before returning to the gurney.

Wylie pulled out his driver's license and made him a wristband, her fingers flying across the keyboard. She returned the ID to its place alongside a picture of Eduardo with two little girls sitting on his lap. She needed him to live. Next year, she wanted him to take a photo with those girls. Her hands hummed with the want of it.

Band placed and blood drawn, she squinted at the alarming monitor. His blood pressure had dropped below normal. "Are we giving blood, Dr. Godwyn?"

"Yes." He rattled off more orders.

"Shannon, can you take these to the blood bank for a type and screen? It needs your signature first."

Shannon took the tubes of blood, checked them against Eduardo's wristband, and signed. "Got it, heading to the blood bank."

Wylie prepped and hung the tubing, ready to run blood when it arrived, her eyes on her patient. The rest of the world became a flurry of orders and interventions. Eduardo had the same raven hair as Roberto, and she couldn't help but rest her hand on his. The alarms sounded again with even lower pressures.

Shannon appeared with the blood and, after double-checking everything, left to help someone else. Wylie ran the blood fast. Her hand found Eduardo's forearm as she leaned in close and did what many medical professionals forgot to do when a patient was in a crisis. She talked to him.

"We've got you. You're not alone." Before her mind could race her into a paralyzing comparison of the man and her husband, she started a visualization exercise, but this time, she focused on him. She used her mind to staunch his bleeding, picturing blood clotting in all the right places.

Alarms grew silent, and a calm fell over the room. Had everyone in residence joined her in her meditation? She lifted her eyes to find Dr.

Godwyn watching her. She rubbed her chest, which suddenly ached as if she'd sprinted across the icy parking lot.

Dr. Godwyn cleared his throat. "Can you give him another unit?" The chaos returned with his question, and Wylie returned to work, her hand still on her sternum.

Eduardo headed to surgery, and Wylie gave her report to Jared before stumbling out of the room. That's when she noticed how her red footprints followed the trail of the others. Dizziness punctuated the chest pain, which worsened as she gloved up to clean her shoes.

A strong hand caught her elbow as she straightened. Its warmth reminded her to breathe and somehow eased the ache. Dr. Godwyn walked behind her. "You look a little pale. Do you need a minute?"

She'd hoped no one would notice. The sight of blood never made her dizzy, but she saw more than blood when she looked at the red puddles on the ground. "Yeah, I think I should probably sit down."

He guided her into an empty room.

Wylie laughed at herself as she sat and lowered her head between her knees. She'd gone from holding her breath to panting in the space of a few minutes. She shoved her palms into her eyes, willing herself not to cry. "I'm sorry. I'm a mess today."

Dr. Godwyn crouched down in front of her. "Don't be sorry." She caught him frowning as she peeked through her hair. "That patient was lucky you were here today."

Both his voice and his demeanor soothed her. His hands rested on his knees, and she imagined them stroking her back. She wondered why, for the first time in eleven months, she wanted to be touched. Something about Dr. Godwyn spoke peace to her heart, and she realized why their frequent flyers asked for him by name.

The clock on the wall ticked at a steady pace. Her breathing slowed, and the dizziness faded away. She sat back. "Thank you, Dr. Godwyn. I feel much better now."

"It's David." Creases shone at the corners of his amber eyes as he smiled. "I'm glad you feel better." He stood and winked. "I'll see you out there."

She remembered how good it felt to exchange a smile as she returned to her other patients.

Five discharges later and she changed into her street clothes.

Wylie drove to her sister-in-law's house, where she lived in the guest room. All she wanted to do was curl up into a ball surrounded by a pile of Dean's old clothes, but she wouldn't be able to wallow today. Roberto's older sister had planned a birthday celebration for Dean. Rosa had hosted all of Dean's birthday parties, and she said she planned to do so for the rest of her life.

From Roberto's mother to his cousins, they drank and shared stories in the sloppy way drunks did. They all shared his nose and chin, the way the pitch of his voice grew higher when he said something funny. Tears and laughter merged into a rollercoaster of emotions. Their Spanish jabs and English jokes grew louder by the minute.

"Remember the time when he pooped at the pool?" Nacho's round cheeks shone red as he pointed at Rosa. "And you made me pick it up so Tía Lupe wouldn't find out." Laughter garbled his words, but they'd all heard the story enough times they didn't need a translation.

"Yeah, you plopped it in my shoe, and I —" Rosa scrunched her nose as she mimicked, shoving her foot into a shoe full of shit. "I'm still mad about that."

Wylie sat on the arm of the couch, listening. The sprite and tequila Rosa's husband had made for her grew warm in her hands, smelling like sweet agave and hand sanitizer. Wylie winced as the laughter reached a crescendo. Her eyes connected with Rosa's as she frowned. Coming to Wylie's side, Rosa linked arms with her. Rosa palmed a fifth of tequila from the table, and they ventured into the cold. Snow dusted the streets.

The white glow made the harsh world seem smaller. The drop in temperature had written its crystalline signature on every surface. Winter grays and blues surrounded them, reflecting Wylie's thoughts.

Wylie imagined Dean's hands on her cheeks. Even as a baby, he loved holding everyone's faces and staring into their eyes—*my serious boy*. Time had already blurred those happy moments. It turned her memories of playing in the snow from a movie reel to a vignette. *Dean's rain boots drew circles as he spun, catching fluffy flakes in his mouth.* Her knees popped as she sat on the porch step.

"We miss you." Rosa sat close enough to share her body heat, smelling of cumin and chipotle, the lingering scents of the *albondigas* that still warmed their bellies.

She passed the bottle of Don Ramon. The brown liquid filled Wylie's mouth with the taste of date nights and being held in Roberto's arms. "I live with you. You see me almost every day." The frigid air turned her words into clouds.

"No, *chica*, you've been gone since they left us."

Wylie closed her eyes to the pain. "You look like your brother." Her vision became muddied with tears as she rested her hand on Rosa's face. The darkness of night and the spirits warming her throat freed Wylie to speak this truth, and she savored how Rosa's cheekbone fit into her palm just as Roberto's had. Even the way Rosa leaned into Wylie's touch brought back memories of his wiry arms wrapped around her. "He left me. They all left me. I have nothing and no one." Wylie leaned forward, resting her forehead against Rosa's. "Someone smiled at me today, and it felt like the greatest gift. How is it I expect so little out of life?"

"Berto wouldn't want this for you."

She lowered her hand and shrugged. "What's he going to do about it? I'm fucking alone in the world now."

"What am I? Chopped liver?"

"I'm not blood. I love you, but when you have your own family, you'll understand. You won't have time for me anymore. I'm dead weight."

Rosa rubbed her temples. "*Dios mio*, you're giving me a headache."

"Here, let me." Without a second thought, Wylie's fingers found Rosa's scalp and rubbed. Her muscles remembered their job as she massaged in circles. She closed her eyes, and the image of Roberto flickered, it superimposing over Rosa. A connection snapped into place between them as together they imagined a world where brothers, husbands, and sons did not die. Where heads did not throb. A spike of pain drove into Wylie's heart, and her hands dropped.

"Ah, better." Rosa sighed, her shoulders relaxing. "I missed you, *mija.*"

The alcohol caught up to her as the thickening blanket of snow lured her away. "Do you know what Dean would do if he were here?" Her footsteps left uneven bald spots in the snow.

She dropped to the ground, oblivious to the cold as wetness pierced her pants. She fell back, spreading her arms like wings. The snow silenced her laughter as she kicked and flapped. Four-year-old Dean would have fit perfectly inside her snow angel.

Chapter 4

Lex

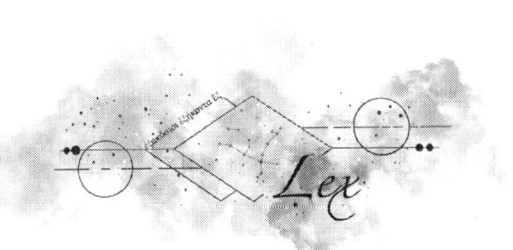

Oregon State Hospital's ornate belfry dominated the air above its façade. The mentally ill haunted the frosted casement windows, their eyes glinting with various stages of longing.

Inside, the chemically restrained, laden by their daily dose of tranquilizers, roamed by day, while the squeaky shoes of psych wardens marked the night.

Olive lines trimmed every surface, turning Alexis' golden skin a sickly green hue. She shuffled down the hospital hall, the grips on the bottom of her socks rolling and bunching against the over-polished laminate floors, releasing the smell of wax and Pine-Sol. She gritted her teeth against the sensation. Her tongue duplicated the feeling in her mouth. She didn't know if she should blame her new medication or the Narcotics Anonymous meeting she'd just attended.

Alexis O'Conner's name read in gold letters across the plaque on one side of her door. Emily Godwyn was typed out on the other. Emily's son committed her due to mental breaks and subsequent hallucinations after her husband died. Lex talked about angels when she roamed the streets, high on whatever she could get her hands on. They had nothing in common but their belief in real-life angels and their confinement in this hospital.

Lex entered her room and pulled off the offensive socks. She plopped onto her bed, disturbing the hospital corners folded into her blanket, and situated herself against the wall. Knees to her chest, she rolled her hair between her fingers. Her mother had given her the thick, black hair of their Vietnamese ancestors and the strands resisted the twisting.

"So, he's coming tonight?" Emily asked from her side of the room. "I'm uncomfortable with him being here."

She glared at the lump in the bed across from her. The woman burrowed deeper under her covers, with nothing of her body visible. "Has anyone told you you're a creep?"

At first, a hiccup moved the lump, and then a low whine filled the room as the woman moaned her dead husband's name. "Jacob. Jacob. Why did you trust the angels?"

"Perfect. I like you so much better when you're crying." Lex covered her ears.

The Xanax hit her hard, and it became difficult to keep her eyes open. She curled on her blankets, ignoring the cold as she set her alarm. She'd sleep for a few hours until the medication wore off.

Abaddon didn't arrive at midnight as expected. Neither did he show at one or two, and an unwanted relief lightened her chest. After hours of waiting, her back running parallel to the wall, sleep drying her eyes, and filling her ears with buzzing, she gave up. Her Angel's tardiness didn't surprise Lex. He always came the moment she lost hope. He'd arrive with his wings on display for her, his face twisted in both a smile and a glare, smelling of rain.

She hated these games as much as she loved them. She craved his attention as much as she craved poison in her veins. At least she knew what to expect when she shot herself up. When Abaddon graced her with his presence, she lived in a swirl of tension and sweetness. Maybe he wanted her to think she was crazy. Maybe he wanted her to watch the clock, wondering if she'd imagined him all these years.

But Lex knew she wasn't crazy. Her mother taught her songs about him as a girl. Their bloodline chose her. This angel belonged to the Doan family for generations past human memory. Her mother had whispered Abaddon's collective oral history in Lex's ear from birth.

Doan Thị Dung prepared Lex for this duty and nothing else. Believing her mother's stories of winged men and angel obligations became insanity when her mother died, leaving Lex to carry the burden alone. A *tianshi*, a muse, Lex collected titles but not much else. The names for her kind seemed endless: Eternal Witness. Prophet. Sky Walker. It all meant the same thing. Language and geography were the only differences.

In her slight frame, she carried the soul of an angel. On her thin shoulders sat all the responsibility which came with such power, as had her grandmother and her great-grandmother before her. Through some strange genetic lottery, Lex received the power to fuel Abaddon with the energy he needed to do his angelic duties. Each Doan generation brought forth another walking, talking angel battery pack.

"Wake." A hand caressed her face. The smell of a storm surrounded her, all rain, earth, and electricity.

She blinked several times. Her body slumped sideways. "Abaddon? Is that you?"

"I'm here, *Cưng*."

Lex rolled her eyes at the endearment her mother always used. "Don't call me 'dear' after showing up—" She looked at her watch. "—almost four hours late."

Abaddon tutted as he sat beside her, an arm pulling her into his side. "A meeting ran late. I'm trying to set us up, *cục cưng*, so we don't have to do this anymore. Isn't that what you want?"

"I don't believe a thing you say."

He cuffed her ear with an angry hand. "Don't be disrespectful."

Ringing muffled his words, her eyes stung with tears she refused to shed. "Asshole."

He smacked her harder the second time, and her head snapped back, hitting the wall. She blinked against the flash of pain that blinded her, tasting blood.

He pulled her back into his side and patted her hip, using his angel magic to soothe her pain and calm her down.

"I so hate having to discipline you," he said, his annoyance obvious in how his brows met. He kissed the top of her head, and shame replaced her anger.

"I'm sorry." She locked her fingers with his. "I just hate it here."

"Now, let's get going." He pulled her to her feet and spun her around before wrapping his arm around her. "You're always such a good girl."

Lex's breath caught as warmth filled her. She stared up at him. These moments reminded her of why she loved him. His peace and his touches made it easy to forget Abaddon's inconsistency. His propensity to leave her questioning herself. The angel always remained a mystery, from his mood to his features. She couldn't predict how he'd look, but as long as he gave her these moments, she'd put up with anything.

Right?

Today his eyes were round, his nose flat, and his skin the color of rich earth. Lex knew better than to trust it. His appearance became a volatile expression of how much he would require of her. The more pleasing, the higher his expectations. She'd seen him at varying heights, with innumerable shades of skin, hair, and eyes. But he knew this was her favorite.

They swayed for a moment as he held her. Lex let herself enjoy the fleeting kindness. "Where are we off to?" she asked. Abaddon opened the secured window, and the fresh smell of night air filled the room.

He turned back to her, his white teeth shining against his dark skin as he spoke. "Ethiopia, and you're in for a treat—we're going to fly."

Abaddon called flying a treat, but Lex disliked it, especially in the winter. It took her days to stop shivering after long flights. The speed frightened her as much as the height. She screwed her eyes shut. They crossed a continent and an ocean, but she refused to open her them as the temperature changed. Lex's hospital gown whipped about as the icy wind cut her. She clung to her angel, absorbing as much of his heat as possible.

Flying also meant he would soon have expectations of her. Nervousness cramped her fragile gut as she distracted herself with the preparation she needed to tell Abaddon 'no.' Upon landing, she stumbled, her knees weak and stiff. Her hands came to her stomach, holding everything together as she lifted her head. She squinted at the sun and then at her angel.

Abaddon smiled, reaching into his pocket. He held out a rubber tourniquet and a capped syringe full of brown fluid. "I brought you a gift, *Cưng*."

Lex shrank back from the proffered goods. Her teeth still chattered, the desert heat not yet piercing past her skin. She shook her head and dried her sweaty palms on her gown, her body craving his approval and the high.

"C'mon." His hand wrapped around her wrist, cutting off circulation, as he waved the paraphernalia in her face. "We can't have you breaking down and running away like in Fukushima."

"Please." Lex caught her breath. "I'm done with that stuff." Her eyes widened. "I've been clean for almost a year. Please, Abaddon, don't make me." Even with her hands shaking. Even as her body teased her with mock sensations of the high, she didn't want it. "I can do this without it." She didn't think she could stop again if she started. She took a step back. "I'll be good."

Abaddon frowned, releasing her wrist. "If you don't do this, I will do it for you."

She studied the miles and miles of flaxen sand, missing the shelter of trees and buildings to hide behind. Panic gripped her. The craggy surface stuttered over rust-colored rocks and nothing else. The flatness stretched forever. She ran, her bare feet screaming as sand and pebbles burned her. She scrambled to the skeleton building. The concrete base announced the slap of her footfalls. The bare bones of a building bore testament to the long-forgotten home around her. One wall stood, with a concrete base and an erect door frame remaining.

She spun around. A dozen feet behind her, a ridge dropped into a basin. White tarp tents lined the bottom. Ant-sized people milled about under the midday sun.

"Abaddon, why? I want to stay clean. Why won't you let me stay clean?" She looked down at his hand again. "Trust me. Fukushima was so long ago."

"Because, Alexis, you've done nothing right in your life."

A blow landed on her head, silencing the panic in her mind. She crumpled to the ground and her world became a dial tone.

When Lex's eyes opened, Abaddon stood before her, the smile back on his face. "There, there."

Lex shook her head, puzzled.

Her hands clenched into fists as the pain hit her, and something else consumed her thoughts. Something as familiar as breathing.

She looked to either side, her head hazy, fire burning up her arm.

Centered in the door frame, she turned towards the sensation, her body moving slower than her mind. She tried to find her feet. Her shoulders screamed. Her body weight pulled against the bindings which held her wrists above her head. Her vision blurred and then focused on the blood that dripped down the crook of her left arm.

Though she meant to scream, she moaned in ecstasy. Peace pulsed through Lex's chest, and she wondered why she was angry.

"You wait here." He smoothed her hair away from her face, her head bobbing to the side with his rough gesture. "Good girl, remember I can't do my job without you."

Lex snickered as Abaddon opened his wings and shot into the air. He climbed high, and then, folding his wings, he spun, his arms out like a helicopter. Lex squinted at his acrobatics; the sun turned him into a man-shaped emptiness in the bright blue above her.

Each blink revealed a new moment in time. At first, rainbow colors flashed through Abaddon's wings as they fanned wide. Lex breathed in deeply, sucking the sky into her lungs.

Eyes closed. Eyes opened—partial cloudiness. Puffy clouds bounced against each other. Lex batted them with her eyelashes, flirting.

Eyes closed. Eyes opened. Millions of gray cotton balls clung together, and she giggled as she tried to blow them away. And then the rain came.

Abaddon danced in the sky, conjuring up raindrops the size of golf balls. Lex's eyes drooped, and a river rushed beneath her feet, speeding toward the white city below. The flood caused screams, her lullaby as she nodded... and nodded... and nodded.

Lex woke with a shiver as a shoe pressed into her ribs, the sounds of the city amplified by disorientation.

"Rough night?" Lex recognized Nurse Justin's voice.

She pushed the clog away, cursing every nurse she'd ever met as she turned her face and rested it on a new cold patch of the stone she lay on.

"I've got to clock in, and then I'll send security out for you."

Lex closed her eyes as her itching skin reminded her of what Abaddon had done. Curling onto her side, she cradled her arm to her chest, hating Abaddon for ruining the most important achievement of her life and herself for letting it happen.

The door opened. The smell of outdated medical equipment and urine cut with lemons wafted out on a gush of warm air.

After a long pause, Lex covered her ears as Nurse Justin spoke. "I'm disappointed. One more month, and you would've had a year clean." The door swooshed shut behind him.

Lex stumbled down the steps and toward the street. Her hands rubbed her belly as she thought of how she could get her next hit. Abaddon was right. She needed it.

Chapter 5

"But, Mom, I want to fly." Jinx's voice woke Wylie. She recognized the dialogue. Episode eight of Dean's favorite cartoon played.

"Jinx, magic isn't a toy," said his stern single mother.

Those voices brought back memories, faces and actions which swam around her foggy mind. Dreams beckoned her with bittersweet promises. Images of her son as he smiled, his giggles. Those times when she'd look down and the thought, "my child's a genius," flashed in the darkness. Those moments she dreaded, those moments she worshiped. She'd never hold him on her lap again, lay a kiss on his forehead, or smell his hair.

Rolling to her side, on a bed that wasn't hers, she tried to find sleep. But a child-sized hole beckoned with remembered investments in labor pain and unconditional love—a current which tugged her down and turned her waking into drowning.

She opened her eyes and reached for the remote. Sleep would not return tonight and she didn't want to wake her sister-in-law with the sound of the television.

"But, look . . ." Jinx held out a broom as the TV flashed white and powered down. Hearing the child speak physically hurt her, as did turning the show off. Gritting her teeth, she flicked the remote off the bed, afraid she'd turn the show back on if she didn't. Would this pain stay with her forever?

She blinked back tears and wished for closure. *We solve fifty percent of cold cases. There is still a chance.* Last month she spoke to the police.

The officer had called her family's murder a 'cold case.' *12:15 a.m.* read the alarm on her bedside table. It had officially been twelve months since she'd found her husband cradling their son in his death grip. Twelve months.

"Who would do this?"

The popcorn ceiling refused to respond. The police had no answers. This left Wylie to imagine how a child killer would look. She pictured the black outline of a man. He would be tall, wide-shouldered, and smelled of hellfire. He'd have black wings sprouting from his back like a demon because only a monster would shoot a toddler. In this scenario, she placed herself behind the shadowy figure.

Hey, you! Asshole!

He falls to his knees, afraid of her. *Please, forgive me.* He begs.

Never.

Wylie reached out with her mind and hit him like a truck. The blow lifted him off his feet. He flew backward, landing in a heap on the ground, his wings crumpled under him. His hand came up to block his face, but she didn't care. She drove her imagined magic into his veins, following the trail to his heart. The heat of her wrath curdled his blood, leaving strings of clots in its wake.

When he stopped writhing in pain, she wiped his agonizing death away like shaking an Etch A Sketch—four times total, once for every bullet in Roberto's back.

An agitation boiled in her chest as her world spun. Chocolate filled her mouth as her dinner, Roberto's favorite ice cream threatened to come back up. Her breaths became sputters. Her blanket suffocated her. Panicked and dizzy, she clutched at the ache. Fate, God, or some higher power stabbed her in the heart. She wondered what she did to deserve this.

Alone, in Rosa's guest room, she missed her husband's warm body and craved the way her toddler's limbs used to cling to her. She covered her mouth as a sob escaped. What did she do to deserve this?

She rolled away from the emptiness, landing on her knees. The carpet burned her skin as she slid. Blind in the dark, she crawled to the closet. She needed to run. She needed her body to work as hard as her mind. Shoving her naked feet into running shoes, she pulled on Roberto's Toreros hoodie and left the house, her head in a fog.

Water splashed as Wylie ran down the unlit sidewalks of Rosa's quiet neighborhood. With their booster-seat-laden cars, these rows of houses represented everything she no longer had. The rain pounded the pavement, and she welcomed the iciness of it, wanting to be numb.

Two men shouted at each other in an alley. Trotting around on Pill Hill in the dead of night was a bad idea, but she needed the runner's high more than she needed oxygen. What could they steal from her? She ground her teeth against the pull to stop and shout at them, to run in front of a car, to make one leg follow the other until they were gone, the pain was gone, and Roberto could hold her in his arms.

She moved toward traffic. Headlights sped past, and water soaked through her shoes as her run became a sprint.

Is it possible to outrun sorrow?

She pumped her legs, feet splashing through puddles. Her mouth gaped as she gulped down rainwater with her air, catching dirt and tasting grime.

"Wylie." The man's voice worked like a clothesline, stopping her in her tracks.

"Ro-ber-to?" Her heaving breaths separated the syllables. Her head turned toward a voice her soul recognized.

Dr. Godwyn stood at the bus stop in his cycling shorts. He held his helmet under one arm, and a backpack hung from the other, the rain shelter keeping him dry. His bike leaned next to him, one of its tires flat.

The streetlight above them cast shadows over his chiseled face, turning his dove skin mint. His bald head shined with raindrops as he tossed his things on the bench behind him.

"Dr. Godwyn?"

He stepped out of the shelter and placed his hands on her shoulders. "Are you okay? Is someone chasing you?" He searched the space behind her.

"I'm." Gasp. "I'm." Sniffle. "I'm fine."

"Breathe." He steered her out of the rain, transitioning into doctor mode. His eyes searched for signs of injury. He spoke the first question they asked confused patients. "Wylie, do you know where you are?" His hands brushed stringy hair from her face, lifting her chin. Between her sobs, her head bobbed in the affirmative. She stepped back, bumped into the shelter wall, and slid to the ground. Her arms wrapped around her knees as the tears overcame her.

Dr. Godwyn sat on the bench beside her and stared out into the rain. Several buses passed before Wylie spoke. "You don't have to wait here. I won't cry forever." She managed a grimace which would've been a smile in any other circumstance.

"No way I'm leaving you here," he said, showing her his palms. "Would you like to . . ." his voice trailed off, and he averted his eyes, giving her privacy. Understanding creased the corners of his mouth, his gaze cold with the loss her sorrow reminded him of.

"It's been a year . . ." A moan escaped her throat with the confession.

She felt the weight of sharing space with another person fall away when he rested his hand on her back. "There are no words." He wouldn't make her talk. They sat in silence and Wylie began counting cars to keep her mind away from the darkness inside her. "My father died when I was a teen. I tried to run away from home at least once a month for the first year."

His confession halted her counting, and she missed a few before starting over. Six. Seven. The eighth car passed them in a blur of splashes and brake lights. Her tears slowed, and her breaths evened out. His presence calmed her. "How old were you?" She rubbed her nose. "You know when your father died?"

"Sixteen." He shook his head. "I haven't thought about it in a while." His hand went from her back to covering his forehead. "It's all so shitty."

Wylie realized her discomfort when his touch disappeared; the cold, the wet, the hardness of the ground, the ache in her back. She lurched to her feet, reaching for the shelter when the world swam around her—crying punished her physically, echoing her mental anguish.

"Thank you." She sniffled. "I . . . I'm okay." The words were a dismissal.

He missed the memo. "So, where are you going?" His chin tucked in, and he looked at her through his lashes. "What's your plan?"

Her head swiveled as she looked back the way she came. The rain came down harder in response.

He stood, his hands finding her upper arms. "Wylie, look at me." She met his warm gaze. "You don't have to do it alone." He pulled her to him. His hug pinned her arms to her sides. His cheek rested against hers.

She stiffened as the wetness of her tears transferred to his skin. A strange part of her brain recognized that David was taller than Roberto. That his arms were more muscular. Even the way he fit against her felt unfamiliar. But the warmth and the weight of his touch were the same. She closed her eyes and rested against him. He smelled like cinnamon and didn't falter when her arms came up and returned the hug.

Peace. She'd forgotten this feeling of being held. "Roberto was thirty-eight. Dean had turned three the month before." Wylie spoke into the darkness of her eyelids, her forehead pressing into his chest. "Someone came into my house and shot them. No one heard anything. No one saw anything." She fisted his shirt in her hands, his silence encouraging her to say more. "They beat Roberto before they shot him. They found sixteen bullets in my house. How? How could this happen?"

His breaths rocked them as Wylie worked on composing herself. They stepped away from each other, the smell of the city replacing his spicy scent. "Thank you." She wiped her eyes.

"Anytime." His frown flattened out. "I know how difficult it is to share."

She nodded, not trusting herself to speak yet.

"Now, where are we headed?"

We? The word warmed her, reminding her she wasn't alone. She reached for her cell phone, thinking of her sister-in-law, who'd been at her side throughout this tragedy, but found her pockets empty.

"Shit. I forgot my phone."

He checked his watch. "A bus is due in ten minutes. This feels unprofessional, and I don't want to put you in a tough spot, but you could come home with me?" He ignored Wylie's raised brows. "My sister's also there, and she'd love to have a visitor. I just want to make sure you're safe." He rubbed the top of his head and looked up at the bus schedule.

She should walk back to Rosa's. The hug on its own, if seen, could cause major damage to her reputation. But could she walk away from this serenity? She'd felt more in Dr. Godwyn's presence than she'd felt all year. After this, the thought of returning home burned her throat. She couldn't return to a bed she'd once shared with her husband. Her feet turned to concrete. She couldn't look at the pictures of her boys on her wall, reminding her—constantly reminding her of what she'd lost.

She turned back to Dr. Godwyn. "Okay."

"Okay?" His lips twitched as if holding back a smile. "Good. Great. Outstanding."

"Can I use your phone to text my sister-in-law? I don't want her to wake up and be worried."

"Sure."

"Thanks, Dr. Godwyn."

"It's David."

She tapped in a quick message and handed his phone back.

"Thank you, David."

The squeal of brakes accompanied the purr of an engine as the bus arrived, offering warmth and soft seats. The rain had turned into a chilly early spring mist. Painting the bus and the landscape around it in the same surreal mystery her night had become.

He paid for them both. She slid into the front row while David ran back into the rain to roll his broken bike around the front. The accordion door shut, and he settled in the aisle seat, leaving a space empty between.

Out the window, her city's beauty bewildered her. The grays and browns of buildings ran together—streetlights and 'open' signs crossing them out with neon streaks. An hour rolled by as slowly as the bus.

"This is our stop." The gentle shadow of confidence David wore at work filled his tone.

She followed him off the bus, and he collected his bike. "You live here?" she asked as she gawked at the mini-skyscraper sandwiched between Downtown and Belltown. Her head tilted back, her hand coming up to block the rain as she counted the windows.

"I do." He chuckled at himself. A soft sound that didn't impose on the heaviness of the night but lifted it. "My sister picked this building."

Rent must cost a fortune. No wonder the man rides a bike. His cycling shoes clicked on the marble as they crossed the tiles floors of the lobby. The crystal chandeliers and chic post-modern paintings caught her eye and slowed their walk to the elevator.

A wall of windows turned David into a silhouette as they entered his apartment. Her hand found her chest. Like a masterpiece, the Port of Seattle and Pike's Place sparkled with their nighttime glory. For a moment, everything else disappeared, leaving the view and peace she now associated with David. "Your view is stunning."

"Yeah. It's the reason my sister chose it." David took a moment to admire the view with her. "C'mon, let's get you settled."

Passing through the entryway, Wylie discovered a woman in scrubs watching TV on the couch. A man and a woman kissed in a soap opera. The word 'MUTE' shone, a red statement in the bottom corner. The woman turned when they entered, her eyes going from David to Wylie and narrowed. She imagined what she looked like standing there in her soggy PJ pants and an oversized hoodie, a swamp monster with college pride. She probably smelled like one too.

"You're home so late. Who's this?" She reached for the remote and shut off the television. "Jane's asleep." The room continued as if the answer to her question didn't matter. "Poor girl had a hard day." She got to her feet, pushing her corkscrew curls back over her shoulder. "We ended up canceling physical therapy."

"We haven't done that in a while. Anything specific going on." David peaked at the first door coming off the entryway. "Should I take a look at her?"

"No, no, no." The woman waved a dismissive hand. "It's the contractures. You will not fix those tonight."

David nodded and gestured to Wylie. "Martha, this is one of my coworkers, Wylie." He leaned his bicycle against the wall. "Martha helps with my sister." He hung his raincoat and backpack.

"Nice to meet you." Martha crossed the room with her hand out. The shadows made the jeweled undertones of her skin show blue. They shook, and Wylie wished her palms weren't moist from the rain.

"Likewise." Wylie looked away when the caregiver wiped the wetness from her hand on her scrub pants.

"I better head home. I'm tired." Martha yawned as she pulled a scarf around her neck and picked up her purse. "Sleep well."

"Have a good night. I'll see you tomorrow."

Martha left without giving Wylie a second glance.

Maybe her hand was as gross as it felt?

David listened at the door he'd almost rushed into earlier. "Sorry," he whispered. Worry creased his brows before he gestured for Wylie to follow him to the living room proper. "Would you like anything to drink? Water, Coke, something warm?"

"Hot chocolate?" She blushed, wishing she would take back the request the moment it spilled from her lips. She looked away, her breath catching. "It was Dean's favorite."

David offered a kind smile. "Coming right up. Let me grab you a towel first." She leaned against the kitchen island and lowered her hood, smoothing the sweatshirt, her fingers catching on the peeling logo. David pulled a towel and some blankets from a closet, tossed them on the couch, walked through the open layout, past a dining table with six seats, and disappeared into the room on the other side. She studied the view framing his dining area and noticed her reflection in the window. Her hands went straight for her hair, which stuck out in every direction.

Finger-combing her mane, Wylie let the warmth of David's home wash over her.

He returned with a pile of folded clothes and a pillow. "The bathroom is over there if you'd like to shower and change." He pointed. "I'll have your hot chocolate ready for you when you're done." Picking up the pile of clothes, she spared him a shy glance. His back was to her as he dug through a cabinet.

After a scalding shower and changing into David's baggy clothes, Wylie felt half-human again. She joined him in the kitchen. He sat at the island, head resting on his arm, his eyes closed.

"Are you awake?" she whispered.

He lifted his head, the side of his face creased by his sleeve. "Yes, just resting my eyes." His voice came out husky with sleep.

"Thank you. This means a lot." Wylie wanted to apologize too. For taking up space and time, but instead, she sat in front of the steaming mug next to him.

"Not at all. Like I said, Jane would love the company." He yawned and reached for his mug. "Also, I don't get a good excuse to drink hot chocolate very often."

Taking a sip, Wylie closed her eyes and savored the chocolaty goodness, remembering the sound Dean made with every mouthful. She opened her eyes to find David smiling at her. Wylie couldn't help but smile back, the gesture lightening the load on her chest. They sat in companionable silence as they drank.

"I couldn't help but hear Martha mention your sister having a bad day. Is she okay?"

He didn't answer immediately. "My sister has Guillain-Barré."

The cup froze by her lips.

"She's been breathing independently for about three months now," he continued, "but she's still struggling with her motor skills. That's why I have Martha here during the day."

Wylie thought back to her nursing textbook. She remembered studying this disease in a neurology unit. She could still taste the coffee she'd placed next to her book during that early morning class—the picture of damaged nerves and a caption describing the autoimmune disorder on one page. An image of an intubated patient lay on the next, overlayed with a mutilated nerve cell. David rubbed his scalp.

"That's horrible. How old is she?" She frowned, regretting inconveniencing him.

"Jane's sixteen." He cleared his throat. "She used to be so active. But progress has been slow, and it happened so fast. One day she's a freshman in high school talking about homecoming, the next . . ." He looked down at his nearly empty mug. "You know how GBS works. I'm hoping she's out of the wheelchair by the end of the year."

"Oh, wow. When you said your sister lived here. I assumed it was a roommate situation until I met Martha." She pictured the sleeping girl, preparing to bolt. "You have so much on your plate. Maybe I should go." One foot landed on the ground before David grabbed her hand.

"No, it's fine. Please, stay. She's lived with me for seven years now." The sudden scent of laundry soap and cinnamon reminded her why she'd come. Him.

"Are you sure she won't mind? She must be so uncomfortable."

"The two of you are going to get along so well. I promise." His hand squeezed hers. "She's so bored of me."

Wylie nodded, her eyes on his hand, where his touch thawed some of her apprehension. His hand fell away.

"Would you like to use my room? It has an ensuite."

"Where would you sleep?"

"The couch. I've slept on it before. It's nice."

"I'll take the couch." At that moment, she didn't want to sleep in a bed again. Too many memories. Too much awkwardness.

"Okay." He smiled. "Just give me a knock if you need anything. I'm going to sleep. Speaking of, we work the same shift tomorrow, right?"

"I think so. Seven to seven."

He nodded, looking at his watch. "Martha gets here at five-thirty."

"Thank you," she said again. "For the hot chocolate and the company. You're a lifesaver."

"I hope so." He winked.

"Goodnight, David."

"Goodnight."

Wylie checked in with her body as his door shut. The chest pain and dizziness had dissipated somewhere between Rosa's guest room and drinking hot chocolate with David. She stared out the window at the black water that cradled the sparkling port. The sight spoke to her.

Can I keep my lights on as this darkness swallows me whole?

Wylie woke to find a teenager staring at her. Drool collected at the corner of her mouth, her curled hands resting in her lap. Her hazel eyes shone sharp and curious.

Wylie rubbed her face and sat up, yawning. "Hi."

Jane worked her lips, the sounds she made not quite forming words. Her blond messy bun bobbed as she shook her head, wiping her mouth with her forearm. She stretched her soft-blush-colored fingers against each other before waving. Half of her face formed a smile.

Wylie waved back. Jane's charisma pulled Wylie from the couch, beckoning her to follow.

"I see you've met Wylie." David wore flannel pants and a white tee that stretched across his shoulders. "Wylie, this is my baby sister, Jane." A grin he never wore at work softened his face as he clapped his hands. "Are you two ready for breakfast?"

Jane rolled back and swung the wheelchair around. It was a tough move, and Wylie grinned as the girl showed her another maneuver. Jane winked, looking like a miniature of her brother, before rolling to the kitchen island.

David opened the fridge, searching for ingredients, and she found a seat, feeling out of place as she leaned onto the cold marble counters. Jane pulled a phone from her pocket, her fingers dancing along the screen in a strange adaptation of stiffness and speed.

Jailhouse Rock broke the trance, Elvis' soulful vocals removed Wylie from her doubt.

Jane narrowed her eyes at Wylie, daring her not to smile. The teen's shoulders bounced, her foot tapping to the beat. Wylie couldn't help but laugh, influenced by her happiness. They giggled as the song started over. The crackles of cooking joined the smell of butter.

David placed a plate in front of each of them. "Thanks." Speaking with enthusiasm, Wylie wore a smile which mirrored Jane's. She speared the bacon with her fork and took a bite before remembering a year had passed since the last time she'd sat down with a family and eaten breakfast. The thought zipped by as she jammed to Jane's music without interrupting her meal.

"You're lucky." He leaned against the counter, his breakfast untouched, as he turned from his sister to Wylie. "Jane told me I'm not allowed to dance."

Jane rolled her eyes and waved David away as the front door opened and the whirlwind of Martha marched in. She went straight to Jane and kissed the top of her head. "Good morning, honey." She tossed her purse on the counter.

"Good morning." Wylie forced a smile.

"Mhmm." Martha's eyes slid from her head to her toes. "You're still here." She raised one side of her mouth, her cheek bunching. The look slid off her face when David came around the island with a plate of food, but Wylie heard the warning loud and clear. She wondered what gave the older woman the impression she was a danger to the pair. Not for long, though. Jane turned the volume up and rolled up to Wylie with an expectant grin.

An hour later, Wylie pulled on a pair of David's scrubs. She had to roll the pant legs and waistband, but it sealed the deal on her opinion of the guy. He was a saint that would give the shirt off his own back to make someone's life a little easier. Wylie exchanged numbers with Jane and left the apartment with David at her side.

He stared at his phone as they took the elevator to the ground floor. "I downloaded the app for Zipcar yesterday before I went to sleep. Did you know those things are everywhere? We have three within walking distance from my apartment." He threw her a glance, a sly smile sneaking across his lips. "Are you ready for an adventure?"

Wylie blinked, feeling her cheeks warm. "Um, sure." Her heart fluttered, and she placed a step or two between them. She was with Roberto the last time she'd been alone with a man in a car. Yes, she'd just slept on David's couch, but all the firsts piled up, brushing against Wylie's frayed edges.

"You don't seem very confident in my Zipcar skills." His clean-shaven jaw worked as his finger ran up and down the screen.

"I just feel bad. How much is it going to cost?"

"I'd be doing this either way. My bike needs to go to the shop. That's my third flat in a week. I think there's something wrong with my wheel." The elevator chimed, and he waited for her to exit first. "It looks like there's a car right across the street. They named it Christiana."

On the other side of traffic, a Mini Cooper flashed her yellow paint job at Wylie. She glowed in the morning light peeking between the clouds, and Wylie forgot about the cost. She wanted a ride in that car.

David drove with his eyes straight ahead. Wylie suspected David turned up the radio loud enough to keep the conversation at bay. He seemed like a man who needed to get in the zone before work. The NPR announcer chattered about flash floods in East Africa displacing fifty thousand refugees.

They left Christiana in a lot under the hospital. "I'm going to give that car five stars. What do you think?"

Wylie nodded as heads turned and eyes narrowed. Walking in with the youngest, most eligible ER doc on staff would be gossip for months. She ignored the looks and hoped no one noticed the squelches of her wet shoes.

She stopped at the women's locker room. "Thank you." She took a cleansing breath. "I wouldn't have survived last night without you."

David's hand rested on her shoulder. "Anytime you need a friend,

I'm here." His knuckles stroked her upper arm once before he continued down the hall. "Have a good day." He held his head high as onlookers got busy doing other things.

She leaned into the break room door. "Bye," she said as she watched him walk away. The magnetism she'd felt the night before was stronger than ever.

Wylie went straight for the spare pair of socks stashed in the corner of her locker, kicking off her soggy shoes. She dropped a sock when a hand landed on her back.

"Wylie?" Susan, a fellow nurse, crowded into her bubble.

"What's up?"

"Where have you been? I've been trying to call you all morning." Susan picked up Wylie's sock. "Have you heard from the police yet?"

Wylie raised her brows. "I haven't had my phone since last night. Is everything alright?"

"You should talk to the police, but I can tell you." Susan ate drama like Popeye ate spinach. And she only hulked out like this when she had something devastating to share. It must be juicy, juicier than Wylie disappearing and her walking in with David. "You should sit."

"Just tell me." Wylie fisted her sock to keep herself from strangling Susan.

"They found him."

Wylie frowned. "Who?"

Susan pounced on the confusion, gesturing for Wylie to sit again. The grimace on Susan's face masked her excitement. "I saw him last night."

"Who?" Wylie sat, pulling on her dry socks. "What are you talking about?"

"Robert and Dean's murderer."

"What?" The sensation of cold blood between her fingers sent chills up her arms.

"A truck hit him." Her voice came from far away, her face a blur. She shook her head. *I hit him like a truck.* "No." Her daydream of the night before blended with the images conjured by her PTSD.

"The man who killed your family came in last night. He's here."

Wylie shot up. "Where is he?"

"In the morgue."

"What? Why?" Wylie paced alongside the bench, her socks slipping on the tile.

"That's what I'm trying to tell you. He died. He's dead."

"That makes no sense." Wylie pressed her knuckles into her lips, breathing in the scent of David's lavender handwash and wishing he were there. "If he died in a car accident, how did anyone know who he was?"

"He confessed." Her lips flattened, and she pushed at the gray wisps of hair escaping her surgical cap. "He begged an EMT to write it down on the ambulance ride."

"The EMT wrote his confession?"

Susan nodded. "You want to see it? I took a picture with my phone."

"You took a picture?" Wylie's eyes narrowed as Susan pulled out her phone. "That's messed up."

"Just in case you couldn't see it once it became evidence." She sat and thumbed to the image. "Here."

A scrap of paper sported bloody handprints and the illegible writing of a healthcare worker.

Wylie Hernandez. I took your husband. Please, forgive me.

"I was there when he died, Wylie. Whenever we thought he was in the clear, he'd crash again. We resuscitated him three or four times before he croaked." Her lip quivered. "It was a terrible death, and he deserved it." Her tear-filled eyes met Wylie's.

"It can't be true." It must be a coincidence. Last night, she'd imagined cyclical deaths. One for each bullet in Roberto's back, but an actual vehicle hit this man. Not her imagination. She's a healer, not a murderer, no matter how frustrated she could get with Susan.

"Girl, you need to sit back down." Susan patted the space next to her and pulled Wylie into a side hug when she joined her. "Should I ask Mary to give you the day off? I'm sure you want to talk to the cops."

Wylie shook her head and gripped the cold metal beneath her as three words flooded her mind: *I did this*. The notion made her want to laugh and cry and punch a wall.

Susan walked away and returned with a cup of water. "Here, drink this."

Wylie took the cup with a shaking hand. It tasted like regret, or revenge, or a little of both.

Chapter 6

Samael

Wylie stumbled from her break room with a pale face and wide eyes. She entered a stairwell.

Samael waited for a beat and followed. Her Scientia burned to the touch. A leaking bag of dark emotions, her contradicting moods, clung to the concrete steps behind her. He'd seen examples of these. He'd trained to read them. Grief, anger, satisfaction, and more. He'd never seen them all together? Or he'd never paid close enough attention.

Samael advanced through the trail of sickly-sweet Scientia in her wake, following her to the ground floor. She walked with purpose, though her gait faltered as she neared a set of elevators. Samael ducked into the shadows as Wylie looked around. She pulled off her badge and tapped it on the security device at the door that read 'Morgue. A light flashed red. She jiggled the handle and tried her badge again. The rattle ricocheted down the hall.

"Fuck!" She tried the door once more. She stood there for several breaths, and when she turned around, her red-rimmed eyes remained focused on the ground. Her hand grazed the wall as she returned the way she came, pausing every few steps and covering her face. The strangled sounds cut him to the bone. Her hand caught a closet door handle, and she stole inside. A muffled scream escaped.

He leaned into the door and listened. Those weren't cries of pain or the keening of sorrow but muffled shouts of battle. A fire stirred inside him, awoken by her fierceness. He backed away from the sensation, shaking his head as he left her protection to one of Laoth's archangels, who awaited Wylie's return to the emergency room.

Having heard enough of her sounds, he projected himself to the morgue. The smell of formaldehyde stung his sinuses.

Samael found Marut in a white body bag with his ankles and wrists tied together, a knot at the top of his head, holding his jaw closed. He knew humans did this to keep their dead from flopping about. Their limbs and mouths took longer than their minds to figure out their life had ended. With his thumb, he wiped the crusted blood from the corner of Marut's mouth. He closed his eyes at the coldness of his lips.

"I didn't know this could happen." He spoke in Marut's ear, the words an apology. It tasted like ash. Wylie used her newfound Scientia to calm people, to take away their pain, and then she'd done this? He looked down at Marut. "How will I tell your brother?"

Samael pulled the zipper lower, placed his hands on Marut's chest, and sent him back to the Heavenly Planes. The angel's body vanished, and the bag fell flat. Samael made his way to the rooftop. He denied himself one more stop on the first floor to see Wylie in her natural habitat. A long flight lay between him and discovering the truth of the unrest that bloomed among his brothers and sisters. With information trickling in, they knew more now than they'd known the year before.

He took to the skies, breathing in the smell of storms, his wings hungry for wind, his mind racing through the clouds. Every time he closed his eyes, he felt. The tawny-skinned angel, with her obsidian eyes, transfixed him with her humanity.

He wanted to return to Seattle, reveal the angelic world to Wylie, and show her how to use her abundant Scientia. He wished to tell her what she would become. Guide her as she discovered her fate. But he needed to be in New Orleans to stop these rebel angels before they destroyed everything she was meant to fix. He shook his head, freeing himself from distraction as he landed in St. Louis Square.

Footsteps echoed around the lofty ceilings of St. Louis Cathedral as Samael found a pew near the back and knelt, his head falling into his hands. Though his lips prayed, his mind wandered north.

Two angels joined him. The rustle of clothes preceded a male's voice. "My brother is dead?" The question came as much a prayer as the words Samael spoke in hushed tones.

"Amen." Samael sat up, reverence making his movements slow. Though all angels were made by Thrones and considered siblings, Harut and Marut came from the same piece of clay. They were more brothers than any other angel claimed to be. This weighed on his heart as he pushed the kneeler forward with a clunk. "I'm sorry." His lips parted as he read the simple anguish on the Archangel's face, so different from Wylie's. "Marut gave his life to God."

"No." His arm swiped the air, cutting off Samael's response. "You will not spin my brother's death into something of glory." The blatant insubordination caused Samael's eyes to narrow and the other archangel to wince. "His life was taken, not given, and I demand retribution."

The second archangel leaned into her seat. "Harut, sit before you say something that cannot be unspoken." Her handmade shoes tapped in time to the second hand of the Rolex at her wrist.

Samael's back straightened. "You speak to me like this? I was there when you came into being." His hands opened, his palms facing the archangel as he pushed his Scientia against him.

Harut stumbled back.

"Your brother died in service to his God. The same death we all hope for."

Harut lowered his eyes. "Yes, brother."

"I've sent him home so our Throne can rejoin him to the earth. You will be reassigned, but you may visit him anytime." The last Throne proudly merged angels to the soil she'd made them from once they died. The cycle began and ended with her hands as she built angels out of the earth they resided over, returning their husks at the end of their lives.

Harut nodded. "May I take leave?"

"Yes."

He disappeared.

Laoth sat in her male form, her half-mast eyes on the wooden carving of the crucifixion at the end of the nave. The varnish gleamed, highlighting the wound across his side and the crown on his head.

"This won't be over until we're all gone, will it?" She scratched her beard.

"You know our motto." Laoth had been one of Samael's closest friends and advisers for over a millennium. Her fierceness in battle preceded her. Her legendary warpath during the days of the Vikings won her a place in the fabric of human history. Valkyrie, they called her.

Her legs stretched before her, crossed at the ankles. Anyone who saw her would think she was a middle-aged businessman. She once explained to Samael that she used her male form for specific jobs because men could get away with things a woman never could. This must be one of those occasions. But her mood plunged when she was forced to wear the body of a man. Her nails brushed over the wooden pew like a wayward branch against a window. "This is the third death. When are you going to step in? A child is dead, a father is dead, and now we've lost an angel?"

Samael grunted, his voice a low growl. "Are you implying I'm doing nothing?"

"The bodies are piling up, Samael."

"I helped Marut clean up the mess after Roberto and Dean died. I sent Marut home. I'm very aware of the lives lost. Therefore, we are here. What have you learned?"

"I've learned little. These angels are tight-lipped." She cracked her knuckles. "I've found that those who offer free will aren't new angels. They've been hiding amongst us, gathering followers for years." Laoth showed her teeth. "But I'm less concerned with their plans than I'm with Marut's death. No angels have died in Louisiana."

"When did we stop agreeing with each other, friend?" Samael breathed in the smell of his fellow angel's musk-scented cologne. It reminded him of office meetings in skyscrapers, not the hardened angel who knew better than to question her duties. "We have one duty. Pro summum bonum."

"Greater good, my ass." Laoth's lined lapels rumpled as she leaned forward. "What does that mean anymore?"

"Enough." Samael slid to the edge of his seat. His hands found Laoth's shoulders. "The days of mythology and playing at being gods are over. We're almost done here."

She shrugged her mouth. "Our brother is dead, Samael. Let us mourn."

Samael's hands dropped. "Marut knew the risks. He loved his ward and was ready to give his life for her."

"He was ready to give his life to protect her." Laoth's voice echoed through the cathedral. "Not to have her take it from him."

"He died knowing she can now protect herself." Samael's reply was little more than a whisper, his brows low.

"He died in pain." Laoth swallowed, her voice once again growing louder. "I've seen nothing like this. How did she even do it? You and I couldn't have done it, and we're old."

Samael shook his head. "There is a reason the God's Guard calls her Armageddon."

"The God's Guard rule in their Heavenly Planes. They've never stepped foot on earth. How can they understand?" Laoth slapped her thighs, her insolent sneer a step over a line that their friendship could allow. "Marut was older than I. Can we let a thing with that kind of power exist in the world?"

Samael stood, his hands fisting at his sides. "Her name is Wylie, and the world has waited for her since Adam bit the apple."

"I'm not the only one upset, brother." Laoth straightened her tie.

Samael gritted his teeth. "I came for information, not to argue about our duties."

Laoth shook her head. "But Samael, we must . . ."

"Not another word." Samael waved, and Laoth's word froze in her throat, his Scientia reminding her of her place. He stood. "Let's go."

The smell of incense followed them. Frankincense and myrrh clung to their clothes.

His chin tilted up as he spoke over his shoulder. "Now, tell me what you've learned."

"I've discovered the name of their leader." Laoth's contrite voice landed on Samael's back.

"And?" A single brow lifted.

"Gabriel. His name is Gabriel."

Samael stopped. "So, he's not an angel?" He knew of no angel named Gabriel. humans used this name in their legends, but no angel Gabriel existed.

"He's like your Wylie. As far as we know, he was born to a human mother."

"The prophecy only spoke of a female." Samael felt his wings straining to join him on this side of the veil. His frustration with Laoth and the shock of this revelation hit him hard. His brow lowered in concentration as he kept his human form.

"This is the one consistent confession I've gotten. His name is Gabriel, and he was born to a human mother. And then there is the nonsense of free will."

"Free will?"

"It's something they've all brought up, but I'm not sure what it refers to. They are pretty far gone by the time it comes up, so . . ." Laoth shrugs. "I can only guess."

"We have no clue about their numbers?"

"That is why you're with me. Some have said he collects muses. I hoped you'd help me test the theory."

"Are you going to act like a belligerent ass the entire time?"

"When don't I?"

Samael pushed the door open, suppressing a smile. "How many of his angels have you spoken to?"

"Three and a half." Laoth smirked.

Samael lifted his eyes heavenward, sending a plea for patience. "Where did the half come from?"

"He started as a whole but had a mouth on him. He's a half now."

Samael grunted, his head shaking slightly. "This is why angels don't tell jokes."

"You're just mad mine are better than yours." Laoth clapped Samael's shoulder. "You wouldn't know a good joke if it kicked you in the balls."

"Hmph." Samael paused at the end of the courtyard. "Where to now?"

"I've spoken to an angel, Astins, who plans to join him. She's shared little, the slippery thing, but her muse is local. I've monitored him for weeks." Laoth led Samael up Newstead Avenue, one of the first balmy days of the year closed in on them.

"And that's where we're headed now?"

"Yes. His place of employment is close by."

They came to a stop outside of a stucco-walled building. Laoth pulled open the arched door to *Milagro*. "After you."

The place smelled of cigarettes and stale beer. Spanish jokes and conversations quieted as the regulars lifted their heads. "We aren't being very discreet." Samael looked down at his white painter's overalls and Laoth's suit. They didn't belong together. They didn't belong here.

Samael lifted his chin. As God's general, he belonged wherever he went. He let out a cloud of his calming Scientia, and eyes lowered before they met his, suddenly uninterested in him. The two angels took a seat at the bar.

"I'll take a Jameson neat and a Budweiser. He'll take the same." Laoth pointed his thumb at Samael.

"Sure, sure." The bartender tossed his rag onto his shoulder and went to the other end of the bar.

"That's Brandon, the muse I was telling you about." Laoth leaned back on the bar, scanning the customers, her eyes settled on a slight woman who sat alone in a booth. "Do you think there are too many people here?" A wolfish grin touched her eyes.

"The humans are of no consequence." Samael ignored Laoth's flirtation, ready to meet Astins. Brandon's angel should arrive soon. He would've already shown up if he'd sensed strange angels around his muse.

The drinks arrived.

"Cheers." Laoth held up her Jameson and drank the two fingers of the brown stuff in one gulp.

Samael did the same, his tongue burning with the citrus and spice. His thoughts wandered to the rebels and their goals. He'd expected dissent among the angels. Unemployment lurked in their future. That and extinction. But free will? Angels didn't need another human burden.

Laoth fixed her hair in the mirror above the bar. She stood, her eyes still on the woman. Her red dress matched her lipstick. "Excuse me. I'm going to go say 'hi.'"

"Every time." Samael shook his head with a grunt. He didn't see the point in flirting with humans. Angels weren't sexual beings, but he assumed what Laoth craved was worship. He gritted his teeth and scanned the bar's patrons. Two Lesser Angels intermingled with the humans. The Shadow remained as visible as Samael, standing at the pool table with a group of men. A Messenger placed himself just beyond human sight. Both worked, and neither missed a step when he and Laoth entered. They released a wave of Scientia to show their reverence as Samael's eyes met theirs. Their power splashed over him with the intimacy of an embrace.

Samael finished his beer and basked in the sweet headiness of the alcohol. He wondered if this rebel angel would show up. Laoth's low laugh accompanied a hand on his shoulder.

"'Every time.'" Laoth tossed a napkin with a phone number written on it.

"You're a fool."

"No, those two are fools." She gestured at two men who sat at the bar, mesmerized by a football game. One crossed his fingers, and the other checked and rechecked his phone. The Messenger sat between them, unseen, balanced on his stool. The tips of his wings rested against the ground, and he leaned back, jotting a few notes on a glowing stone tablet.

"I can never understand this human habit." They showed the consequences of free will. The Angel Ruling Class, or the ARC, didn't have time for the capricious nature of choice. As a Dominion, Samael did everything with absolute clarity, even as he drowned in heavenly labor. A general in God's army, he never strayed from his assignments . . . until Wylie. She unearthed a fierce protectiveness in him.

He waved at the bartender. "Another whiskey, please."

"Sure thing." The man filled his glass.

"Where's your angel?"

Both Laoth and Brandon's heads jerked up in surprise. Samael's cup received an extra three fingers before Brandon remembered himself.

"Who are you?" The bartender slid Samael's pounder to him, and a trail of spilled drink followed.

"I'm worried about Astins." Samael brought his whiskey to his lips, the aroma now stronger than the taste.

"I don't know why you're here then." Brandon returned the bottle to the shelf. "I haven't seen her in weeks."

Samael closed his eyes and searched the man's thoughts. He spoke the truth. "Every angel needs their muse."

"Not my angel. Not anymore." Worry lines marked the young man's face, the corners of his mustache dipping into his beard as he frowned.

"She's here now," Laoth said, standing from her seat.

The bell above the entrance rang as a female walked in. Her Scientia smelled of fear and poison. Her powdery Anglo features were weighed down by the same emotions burdening her shoulders.

She leaned against the bar, her eyes on her muse as she lay her open palm on the counter. "Brandon."

"Astins." The bartender dropped his rag and took her hand with both of his. "I thought I'd never see you again." Tears splashed into his facial hair. The men watching sports both turned their heads, curiosity guiding their eyes.

Frustrated, Samael stood, his wings becoming visible. He paused time. Conducting angelic business would be easier without human interference, so the magic of a human reprieve thickened the air. They all froze under the spell of Samael's Scientia. Unseeing and unhearing, the humans remained motionless as his power continued to fill the room. Compelled by his strength, all angels present came to a knee on the dirty floor of *Milagro*, their forearms lifted to cover their eyes in reverence.

Astins got to her feet first. Her champagne-colored wings unfolded. This female would not cower before him.

"Leave." Samael looked at the Messenger and then the Shadow. "Laoth will watch over your humans, and I will summon you when you may return." Both angels looked to Laoth, who nodded with an eye roll. With that, they disappeared.

Laoth walked around the bar and stood next to Brandon, who remained frozen in time. "What do you think? Could I pull off a beard like this one?" She pulled the hair and laughed when the man's lips parted, repeating the action several times. "Look, I'm a human and a tool. Check out the stupid look of surprise on my face," she said in a low voice, using the man as a puppet.

"Leave Brandon out of this." Astins untied her halo from her belt and placed it atop her head. Light leather armor stacked itself over her torso and limbs. Her hands came together, the cruciform hilt of a long sword forming between her fingers. This angel had seen the middle-ages. Her choice of weapon gave her age away.

"Whoa." Laoth raised her hands. "We just want to talk."

"Leave, now." Astins stepped into a fighting stance.

"You want to fight me?" Samael asked, raising a brow.

"No. No, she doesn't." Laoth pointed at the blade. "Hurry, put that thing away."

"It's too late, Laoth. Drawing a sword before a Dominion is punishable by death." Samael rubbed his face. "You know it. She knows it. All that's left to decide is how much you'll tell us before you die."

She raised her sword to her shoulder, her stance widening.

"Oh, shit." Laoth stepped behind Brandon.

Samael's brows rose as he finished his whiskey and set it on the bar. Astins rushed forward. He eased a big frame revolver from his back holster and fired, punching a hole in the woman's chest.

She stumbled a step, crashing down on a bar stool, which splintered under her. Her sword fell, useless, at her side as she rolled to her back. Blood and spittle flew as she coughed.

"They made this gun to take down big-game." Samael re-holstered his sixer.

"Damn, Samael, that was unnecessary." Laoth slapped the bar with both hands, a grin on her face, a laugh in her voice.

Samael ignored Laoth. "I'm not in the mood to fight, sister." He crouched over Astins. His eyes lifted to survey the paused humans. Satisfied no one had been affected by the violence, he continued. "Tell me where Gabriel is."

Astins sputtered as she drowned in her blood. Centimeter by centimeter, the wound knit itself together.

Samael reached through her tattered leather breastplate and into the hole before it closed. The back end was much larger than the front so he had to work hard to get more than his fingers into the wound. He grabbed a rib. "Where?" He pulled, and her body lifted from the ground.

Her eyes widened in renewed pain. "Baton Rouge."

"And how does he provide free will?" He shook her when she didn't answer.

"He separates us from our muses." She gripped his forearms and pulled, attempting to wrench herself free.

"He takes your souls?" he whispered. "But why?"

"So, we can take the earth as our own."

"Thank you, sister." He removed his hand, and she cried out. "I've heard enough."

Astins wiped her mouth. Her teeth clenched against her pain. "We have an army." She grimaced as she sat. "The ARC will not destroy all angelkind with their blind faith."

"You're pathetic." Samael reached under his shirt for his halo. Ready to end this fight.

"At least I'm free."

Samael scrunched his nose in disgust as his halo became a long sword. "And you're ready to die for defying us?"

In slow stages, Astins returned to her feet. "I'm ready to be free."

The sword reformed in her hands. Her blue eyes shone with fervor. "And it'll be my choice. Can you say that about anything you do, Dominion?"

"Ouch, low blow." Laoth leaned against the frozen bartender, once again playing with his beard.

Samael rose to his full height. "Die knowing I'll pull everything you didn't share with me from your muse's fragile human brain."

"He's no longer my muse. He knows nothing." The Archangel lunged forward. Her sword met Samael's. Sparks flew as metal clashed. His blade slid across her shoulder as he stepped past her. She moved with him, striking. He parried and countered, drawing blood again, this time across her abdomen.

"Enough." He spun around, his sword parting Astins' head from her body. The image of her last thought burned in his mind.

"Great job. Now we have to clean this all up." Laoth wiped a drop of blood from Brandon's cheek and, grabbing a bottle of water, joined Samael. She crouched next to Astin's body and poured the water over the stump of her neck. "Just in case." She held up the water in a toast.

Samuel rolled his eyes, bending over the decapitated head and settling his hand on her cheek. "Goodbye, sister." He sent her home with a single word.

"Show off."

"Laoth, do you ever shut up?"

"No." She returned to the bartender, her eyes once again tracing his form. She straightened his apron. "What do you think, Samael? Can I keep him?"

Samael grunted his approval. "Let's have one more whiskey before I end this reprieve." Samael tilted his chin toward the bottle on the wall. "I want to celebrate."

Laoth uncapped it and grabbed a fresh glass. "You're smiling. That must be good news. Tell me what you saw."

"I saw Gabriel, and I recognized him."

Chapter 7

Lex

*M*onths passed in a haze of pole dancing and lights flickering in disgusting bathrooms as Lex pushed poison into her veins. Now, withdrawals chilled her body, freezing her from her toes to her ears. All but one hand—her left hand. It burned in a cocoon of soft flesh. Someone held it. John? It felt like him. Strong, yet gentle. Caring, yet aloof. But he'd died three years before. Lex's body grew heavier as she thought of her big brother. The only other person in the world who looked like her. She'd thought of him often over the last few months. Especially those nights when she'd slept outside in the fog of a high, staring at the sky, hoping he was in heaven—hoping there was a heaven.

She tested her limbs, ignoring the squeal of the alarms which surrounded her. Her legs and arms refused to move. Tight bands secured her wrists and ankles to the bed.

"Lexy?" The familiar roughness of her father's voice slowed her racing heart.

"Daddy?" She licked her lips. "Where am I?"

"Yeah, gal, I'm here." He squeezed her hand, rubbing circles with his thumb. "You're at OHSU. The nurse told me to come."

"Daddy, I'm sorry. Please don't send me back to that place."

"Never again. Lexy, you're coming home with me."

A low moan accompanied her shiver as her father swam through her blurry vision. Gray stubble covered his chin. It wobbled, though his round crystalline eyes remained clear. Lex filled the gaps where crying should be with memories of the last few months. Of highs and sitting in circles. Of sleeping outside and being hungry and dancing in clubs for money. All the hate, hating Abaddon, hating herself for wanting him. *O'Connor's don't cry.* She tucked her face into her shoulder.

From how her body ached, it'd been three or four days since her last hit. Invisible tremors vibrated under her skin, and perspiration sullied her bed.

Lex's stomach cramped as her mind dove further into her past. She'd lived for Abaddon for so long she couldn't remember a time without him. Her mother raised her to know her angel. All of his history, all of his abilities. Abaddon was a Virtue, an angel who could wield earth and weather. He functioned as a critical driver of population control.

While other girls dreamed of Prince Charming, she'd lay in bed and imagine what her angel would look like. Her mother raised her to love him, so when Lex met him, he became her world. On her seventeenth birthday, her mother gave her to him, and she remained his until now. With wrath as quick as his affection, Abaddon spoiled Lex and punished her arbitrarily. Yet, she still believed in the perfect creature she'd imagined as a child and loved him as only a muse could. But love must have its limits.

The Gujarat earthquake became Lex's first natural disaster. Over twenty thousand people died that day. She bore witness. Watching everything crumble. Buildings turned inside out as people died. So many people, just gone. Americans think R-rated movies and bloody video games hardened them to death. They were so wrong. She knew the stark difference between seeing the light leave a person's eyes and watching an actor stare off into space. There was a smell to it: ozone. There was a taste to it: ginger.

Abaddon had let her wander the ruined city with the survivors for several hours before he took her home. She stumbled over rag-doll bodies and stairways that now lay horizontal on the ground. The quake crushed cars like soda cans. Quiet followed the sound of the world breaking, muting alarms, and cries of pain. As if reality took a gasp before humans could voice their sorrow.

Moans of pain filled the silence. Since that fateful day, she'd survived the European heatwave of 2003, Mumbai floods, Hurricane Katrina, and Cyclone Nargis. Haiti gave way to Japan. She lost the entire year between the two. Somewhere during that time, her mother died. In her late twenties and hardened, she no longer played the good Vietnamese girl who made altars to remember her ancestors. She'd seen more deaths in a decade than any man in history. She'd be one less asshole in the world. Her mother groomed her to serve death. Why would Lex deny her master his prize?

In Fukushima, Lex decided she could not go on. Closing down, she walked to the water. She'd seen every kind of natural disaster. She'd seen the sky open and hell fall, she'd seen wind tear the world apart in a spiral of teeth and nails, and she'd witnessed the earth gallop and shift. Nothing could compare to a tsunami.

The glorious wall of water and white noise rose like a mountain. She would never forget her insignificance as the vibrating rush surpassed the sound of her heart in her ears.

Looking up, and up, and up, her neck had strained. She found no top to the forty-foot surge. She savored the caress of wet death, welcoming it, arms opened wide, a sacrifice to an apathetic God. Peace; she would have peace.

Abaddon swooped down, his massive wings brushing along her blue death like a rock skipping on the ocean's surface. "You will not die today," Abaddon said as he held her. "*Cưng*, if it's peace you want, then peace you will have." His bone-breaking grip tightened. She'd felt bruises form as he clutched her to his chest.

That night, he taught her how to use a needle. She found the peace he promised every time she filled her veins with poison. From the streets to the hospitals to Abaddon's arms, she continued her life as if it were an unspoken challenge for the universe.

Frank's hand slipped from hers, bringing her back to the present. "Daddy?" His hand returned the instant she spoke, and the kindness sparked a new form of bravery in her chest. She found him through the bed rail. His ashen face stared down at her. "I'm so sorry. John should be here instead of me." Her perfect brother had joined the army and died in the desert. Someone broken like her had no right to a legacy like his. "I'm going to make this right. I'm going to make this all right."

Her father blinked. "No, Lexy." He shook his head. "I would not trade you for anyone or anything, gal." He squeezed her hand and, leaning over the rail, kissed her forehead.

"Daddy, I want to come home. I'm done with this."

---

*L*ex woke with a start, her dream of drowning replaced by an intense urge to free herself from her childhood bed. The ceiling and the heat suffocated her. She kicked off the pink covers, her legs flailing as they stuck to her sweat-slicked skin. She couldn't remember leaving the hospital, but her body begged to be outside in the sunlight with a needle in her arm. The drive home from Portland had drained her, and her elderly father had to carry her up the stairs and plant her in bed.

Her insides tightened, and her arm flopped over the edge of the mattress, where her hand fell on the unopened letter. Both curious and bored, she pulled it to her face, recognizing the name *David Godwyn. Isn't that Emily's son?* She ran her fingers along the paper. The texture brought her back down. Moving her fingers helped her focus. Her first time at her new NA meeting was in the morning. She just had to get there. She turned the letter over. What could Emily's son want to say to her? She ripped it open and unfolded the page.

Hello,

My name is David. My mother, Emily, asked me to contact you. She said she believes you're a muse and may be in trouble. I recently discovered that I'm also a muse. I want to offer support. Being a muse isn't something we ask for. I have my own questions. Like how does a muse get assigned an angel? How do we become muses? You know, things like that. Anyway, I wanted to let you know you're not alone in this. See my contact information below if you'd like to reply.

Sincerely,
David Godwyn

She turned on the desktop computer she'd used in high school. If it were worth anything, she would've pawned it years before.

David,

Okay. So, I've never talked to another muse before. And you live so close. This feels weird. It doesn't help that your mom annoyed the shit out of me.

I have questions I'm looking into too. I want to figure out how to block my angel from using my power. Because let's be honest, that's what it is—my power. I've given him too much of my life, and I'm ready to cut him off. Any chance you know how that shit works?

This brings me to my next question. How did you 'just find out' that you're a muse? Because, dude, we're born this way. It's genetic. It runs in my family, and I'm sure it runs in yours. We have an angel that has been with us for generations. He built my line to house Virtues. Yours might be for Archangels or Guardians. I've got some info I can send you about angel classes if you'd like.

Okay, so now, to answer your second question. How do we get assigned? I think it's dumb fucking luck. When a muse expires, their angel's soul pops into the closest compatible vessel that can hold that power.

God, it feels good to get these thoughts out. I'm not much of a talker, and even if I were, who would believe me? Speaking of, I'm not ready to meet or talk on the phone, but emails, I can do emails.

L

Lex hit send. The email took hours to write. Maybe because the tail-end of withdrawals wouldn't let her go. Maybe because she'd written nothing in years. The ping of a response sounded before she powered down the computer.

Alexis,

Thank you for your response. I'm on a lunch break, so I'll make this quick. No, I have no clue how it works. But you've given me more information in one email than I've ever been given. Please send me more! I know it's weird finding out I'm a muse as an adult, but my angel IS weird. Believe it or not, she doesn't know she's an angel yet. This will take an in-depth explanation, but I promise to send more information later today. Thank you again. Are you safe?

Talk to you soon,
David

Chapter 8

Wylie

"When I first moved here, I wondered if my feet would ever be dry again," Wylie said after they skirted a puddle. The clouds broke apart above them, and the sun peaked out, reminding the city that it was summer.

"I missed the rain while I was in med school. I hated living in the desert. I don't know why everyone moves south when they retire." David laughed, his hand resting on her back as they crossed the street. Wylie and David had grown close over the last few months, and she cherished each story about his past he shared.

Wylie's heart squeezed at his touch, settling once they reached the sidewalk, and it fell away. Today would be her second day in her new apartment, and he planned on helping her move some furniture. What she didn't tell him was she'd stocked her fridge with him in mind. They'd taken their breaks together enough times for her to know what he liked.

Wylie cleared her throat. "I was thinking of making you dinner tonight. If you're interested."

He beamed. "You want to cook for me?" They entered the apartment complex, the decades-old carpet soaking up the wetness from their shoes. She searched her bag for her keys.

"Yes, I found this *phad thai* recipe and . . ."

He stopped mid-hallway. "You want to make me my favorite food?"

She leaned against the wall, enjoying how his whole body grinned.

How his thumbs hooked in his belt loops, how the miles of cycling uphill looked on his forearms.

"I can't remember the last time someone cooked for me." He stepped in front of her, braced the wall on either side of her shoulders, and kissed her cheek.

She breathed in his cinnamon, her eyes fluttering closed, ready to kiss him back. But the moment was over faster than it'd begun. When she opened her eyes, he'd moved toward her apartment again, only slowing enough for her to take the lead.

Wylie fumbled with the lock. Her nerves made her hands shake. They'd hug to say hello or goodbye. But they'd never kissed, even though she imagined doing it at least once every time she saw him. The door opened. She bit her lip to help her return to the present as she hung her bag. The hallway lights came on next, and she resisted the temptation to turn around and kiss David properly. But was she ready?

"Surprise!"

She jumped, stumbling back into David, who caught her waist with his hands. And even with the warmth of his chest against her back, her mind rushed to the darkest places before her eyes caught up. Friends and in-laws filled out all the walking space in her new studio apartment. Someone had unpacked many of the boxes. Her furniture was organized just how she described it to Rosa when she'd come to tour the place.

"Oh." Her hand came to her mouth. "Guys." She couldn't speak.

"Welcome home." Rosa pulled her into an embrace.

Charge nurse Mary squeezed her hand.

Blabbermouth Susan patted her shoulder.

Giggles boiled up from some hidden place inside her as everyone took turns embracing her and showing their love through touch. The 500-square-foot apartment couldn't fit another soul inside.

"So, what made you move here?" Mary asked.

"You know. I already live in the hospital. Living across the street only makes sense." The truth of it sent her on multiple late-night runs over the last few months, but when Rosa and her husband started infertility treatments. Wylie knew she needed to move on. God denied her another baby, which may be selfish, but she couldn't take a front-row seat to her sister-in-law blooming with pregnancy.

She found Roberto's mother last. Guadalupe wiped her eyes. "*Mija*, you'll always be my daughter. I promised your mother that a long time ago." She pulled Wylie down and planted a kiss on both of her cheeks. One glanced over the spot David branded with his lips earlier, and Wylie blushed, her head lifting. On the other side of the room, David shook hands with Rosa's husband. His honeyed eyes found hers, and he smiled, his brows lifting. "He seems nice."

Guadalupe's voice brought Wylie's attention back to the present. Wylie smiled. "He's nice."

"Good." Her soft hand rubbed Wylie's back. "You deserve it."

Wylie smiled. "Thank you, Mama." Her eyes shined as she distracted Lupe from Dr. Eye-candy. "Now, let me introduce you to my charge nurse, Mary. You'll like her. The two of you are a lot alike."

After an eternity, Wylie sat next to Jane at the kitchen table. She let out a long sigh. "That was exhausting."

"It looked exhausting." Jane gave Wylie a little shove. "I've never heard of a surprise housewarming party. What a genius idea. Your family is the best."

Family? She loved them like family, and Lupe called her daughter. But she didn't know if she deserved it now since her husband no longer connected them through marriage. Now that her son no longer connected them by blood.

The living room opened to a shared lawn where the BBQ smoked and visitors clustered. Rain clouds continued to thin out over guests. The brightness of the sun reflected the smiles on their faces. The smells of *carne asada, jalapeños,* and onions wafted in, following guests as they came and went. Wylie's coworkers found their niches as they filled their bellies, sitting in lawn chairs and enjoying a cool beverage.

Lupe stood six inches shorter than her three daughters, but her stature did not distract from her charisma. Wylie could hear the woman from where she sat. She commanded her troops like a general. "Maria, set that here." The water ran for a minute. "Listo, Rosa, can you peel these?" Her daughters fell in line. Laughter and mariachi filled all the spaces between their working bodies.

Wylie piled three plates high with meat and *Oaxaqeuño* cheese, bringing one to Jane and Martha, and for once, Martha didn't scowl at Wylie. Steam rose from the fresh corn tortillas Lupe had placed at the center of the table. The tang of homemade *salsa verde* danced on Wylie's tongue. No one could starve with her mother-in-law present.

"Please come watch the last episode. I'm dying to find out what happens," Jane articulated each word perfectly. She'd started speaking clearly after a late-night Netflix binge with Wylie. Jane had fallen to sleep, and Wylie, in a hazy half-awake state, rested her hand on Jane's. Wylie delved into her nursing school memories. Thinking of brain anatomy and speech pathways. She fell asleep with an ache in her chest and woke up with the sun. David sat on the arm of the couch, watching them.

"Wylie."

Her name broke her out of her thoughts. "What?"

"Should we rewatch the Outlander finale next time you come over?"

Wylie smirked, waggling her brows. "No way, that one is too sad. Let's watch episode seven."

Jane giggled, her cheeks burning red.

"Are you old enough for that show?" Martha asked, narrowing her eyes at Jane.

"The show says it's for fifteen-year-olds and older." Jane stretched in her wheelchair. "So, yes." Jane had somehow become Wylie's defender against Martha.

"I see." Martha folded her arms. "Let us know if you have questions."

"Questions about what, Martha?" asked David as he walked by. Wylie and Jane burst into giggles as Martha's face flushed. His fingers ran along Wylie's back, and her laugh turned into a shiver.

Martha waved the conversation away, and without easing up on her critical tone, she raised her brows at David. "I'm glad you're here.

Did Jane tell you her goal for physical therapy?" It sounded like she was continuing an argument from earlier in the day.

"No, what's the plan?" David ruffled his sister's hair, and she slapped his hands away, irritation sparking in her eyes.

Jane lifted her chin. "I want to walk."

"I just don't want you to get your hopes up, honey." Martha set down her fork.

David rested his hands on Jane's shoulders.

"I can do it. I know I can." Jane turned to Wylie. "Right?"

"You can do anything you set your mind to. What does your physical therapist say?" Wylie's eyes met David, her lips flattening into a silent question as if to ask him what he thought. He frowned in response.

"He thinks I'm setting myself up for failure." Jane's nose wrinkled. "But he's been wrong before."

A warm enthusiasm piqued in Wylie's chest. She wasn't about to argue with three medical professionals about a disease she'd barely researched, but she felt a sudden confidence in this new thing inside her. Whether it was positive thinking, God answering her prayers extra well, or magic, she didn't know, but it worked. "Your body is the only one who knows," Wylie said, convinced she could help. "Does anyone want seconds?" Standing, she gathered their plates.

Wylie placed the dishes in the sink and leaned forward, closing her eyes. She imagined Jane's spine, the spidery nerve cells igniting as they received long-awaited communication from her brain. She brushed imaginary fingers against the fireworks that highlighted the chaos and then touched the inflammation with a cooling hand, soothing the nerves and reminding them of the best avenues for dissemination. A familiar burn filled her chest, and she knew the healing would work.

"What happened?" David's furrowed brows brought her back to the present. His hands steadied her.

Wylie rubbed her chest, resisting the urge to lean into him. It hurt a lot more than usual. "I don't feel well." She squinted as he swam in her vision.

A shout from Jane tore him away from her. Wylie held tight to the sink. Begging her legs not to betray her and give way.

"I'm gonna be sick." Jane gagged.

David grabbed a bowl as he covered the distance between them, leaving a trail of chips behind. He made it just in time to catch Jane's half-digested *carne asada*. He held her hair as she vomited and wiped her mouth when she stopped. *"Better?"* he asked.

Jane leaned back in her chair and nodded.

"You look pale," David said as he passed by Wylie with the bowl of vomit. He didn't wait for a reply. Down the hall, she heard the toilet flush and the faucet run. He returned with an empty bowl. "I thought nurses had iron stomachs."

Wylie gave him a small smile. "I thought we did too."

"Maybe it's a stomach bug?"

The silence of the guests pressed in on her. "I need to sit down."

David took her arm and helped her stagger to her new twin-size bed. The plastic on it crunched under her weight. This cued the guests that the party was over. Everyone took turns patting her back as they excused themselves.

Soon the studio emptied, and Lupe and her daughters attacked the aftermath of strewn camping chairs and balled-up wrapping paper before leaving.

Jane refused to move. She gripped her wheelchair. Her head lolled to the side.

David stroked Jane's ginger hair with his fingers, his voice a low hum from where Wylie sat. She watched his gentleness, noting how he leaned in to hear his sister better. The way his smile eventually reflected on her face. After a long while, Jane nodded, and he stood, handing his keys to Martha.

Martha waved as she disappeared down the hall.

David returned to Wylie's side, squatting beside her, his hand on her forearm. The moment his skin touched hers, her dizziness slipped away, and her heart stalled, the pain turning to warmth.

"Martha is pulling the van up." His eyes met Wylie's. "Jane is going

home with her, but I can stay here for a bit. You know, make sure you're okay." His hand found her forehead. "No fever."

"I don't think she likes me." Wylie leaned her shoulder against the wall. Her forehead enjoyed the coolness there.

"Who, Martha?" David searched her face. "She's been through a lot with us. I think she's just protective."

"I see." Wylie unrolled her sleeves, wanting to invite him to stay as long as he pleased, and picturing Martha's scowl had her conflicted.

David's phone buzzed. "I need to take Jane to the van. Do you want me to stay?"

Wylie nodded.

His knuckles brushed her cheek. "I'll be right back."

Something she thought she'd lost forever fluttered in her belly. She would soon be alone, in her apartment, with a man. She risked getting up. With the chest pain gone, she felt back to normal. She headed for the bathroom, brushing her teeth and patting down the frizz in her hair.

The crinkling of her bed announced David's return.

"You guys surprised me with this party."

"It was Rosa." His smile graduated to a grin when she sat next to him. "You look like you feel better." His shoulder bumped hers.

"I do. I feel much better." She weaved her fingers together, thinking of how this man had spent his entire life caring for people. "How did Jane end up with you?"

David leaned forward, his elbows on his knees. "My mom didn't handle my dad's passing very well, but it got worse when I went to college. She, uh . . ." He shook his head. "She had to be committed. It wasn't safe for Jane to be alone with her." His knuckles brushed her cheek. "Today is a day for celebration. No more sad questions."

Her hesitant smile reflected his as he pushed her hair over her shoulder, his eyes studying her face. Wylie's heart pitter-pattered in her chest. She felt silly, like a teenager. But she was a grown-ass woman, so with hope emboldening her, she took the plunge. Her hand rested on his knee. "Thank you for staying."

He shivered as they watched it glide up his thigh.

"Wylie." David weaved his fingers with hers and lifted her palm to his lips. "I've wanted to do this for a while."

"Me too." She brushed her lips against his cheek, and his free hand caught her chin. His nose slid against Wylie's. His cheek rested against hers. Their breaths rushed to catch up with each other. "David, I'm scared." The pressure of the hard planes of his body against hers made her wild.

"There's no rush." His hands came to her cheeks, his forehead leaning into hers. "You're in control here."

Using his forearms to stabilize herself, she crawled into his lap, her legs straddling his, her chin resting on his shoulder. She was not in control.

Warm arms wrapped around her. His face found her neck, his lips imprinting their shape into her skin.

She tilted her head away from him, making space for his mouth. "Kiss me."

He did.

Again and again.

His lips were both hot and cold against her skin, teasing intense vibrations just beneath the surface. He made a trail from her jaw to her lips. Their mouths found each other. Their tongues met. He tasted of cinnamon, and she was lost. Lost in tenderness.

Her eyes closed, and her hips moved against his. The friction between her thighs drew a whimper from her lips. He captured the sound with his kisses.

Her hands slid from his shoulders to his chest, her fingers recognizing something her mouth had ignored. They rejected his unfamiliar posture. Noticing how life had sewn his muscles for opposing uses to the ridges known by her touch. This chest belonged to a cyclist and a healer, not a father and a laborer.

David's chest. Not Roberto's. Not Roberto's thick lips or his poetry against her skin.

Right became wrong in an instant.

It happened in a smooth, single motion: David welcoming her passion, became him, pulling her tear-covered face to his chest.

"I'm sorry." She loathed how she wished he were someone else, even as she wanted more from him. How could she kiss one man and think of another? "I'm sorry, I'm so sorry. You must wonder if I'll ever stop crying."

"Hey." He ducked his head, finding her eyes with his. "There is nothing wrong with crying."

Wylie breathed through her shakiness. "I enjoyed kissing you." She sniffed. "I did."

"I liked it, too."

"Can we try again?" Wylie's finger came up to rest in the cleft of his chin.

His lips met hers in a soft question, and Wylie kept her eyes open. Her body trembled with the effort of dismissing Roberto from her mind.

David pulled back. "You're shaking." He rubbed the outside of her arms.

"I don't know if I'm ready for this." She gestured between them. "Whatever this is."

He nodded. "Not everything needs a name. Let's just take it slow." He pulled her into a hug, the kind he'd first given her. The one that made her feel like he could read her mind. "I'm your friend. I also think you're sexy. Let's just start there."

Grateful for the hug, she hid her blush in his shoulder. "Friends?"

His smile touched her temple. He moved her to arm's length. "Friends." His pocket buzzed. "That must be Jane. Do you mind?"

Squeaks and squeals made it to Wylie's ears, and David's demeanor changed. He sat straighter, his eyes clearing with excitement. "You did what? —No way— send it." He turned Jane on speakerphone. "Wylie is here too."

"*Hi, Wylie!*" She said more, but the high pitch made the words unclear.

David's phone pinged, and he lowered it so Wylie could see him open Jane's text. Soon a video played of Jane taking two steps on wobbly legs.

Wylie gasped, her vision blurring with tears. It worked. It really worked. She made this happen.

David stood, his eyes on her as if he'd come to the same conclusion. His hand settled on her shoulder and squeezed. "Jane. This is amazing."

"Yeah, bro, I told you. Can you come home now? I want to show you in person."

David nodded at the phone, his eyes still on Wylie. "Yeah, I have to get my bike first, but I'll head home. Love you." He hung up.

"You're giving me a strange look." Wylie smoothed her hair, guilt filling her belly. She'd just magicked his sister. What if she messed something up instead?

"It's just you called it earlier." He shook his head with a chuckle.

"Yeah, I called it."

"I can't wait to see it in person. Oh, but before I go, I didn't forget about your plan to cook for me." He winked. "How about tomorrow, so the food doesn't go bad?"

She squinted through the dark. The sun had set while they were *busy*. "Tomorrow's great." Wylie needed to unpack some thoughts before proceeding head first into kissing and where such activities could lead.

"Goodnight." He hugged her, his hands running down her upper arms, leaving her breathless and alone in her unlit apartment.

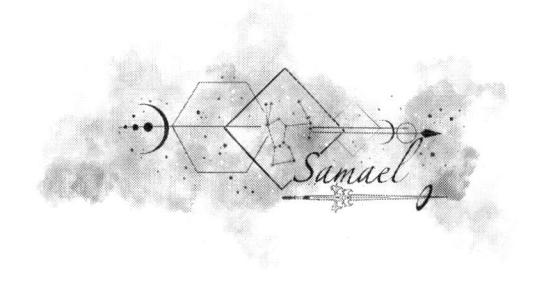

Samael settled down in front of Brandon's TV. The muse's cigarette hung from his lips. Under an ashtray lay a pile of scattered photos. A newspaper clipping was strung between both of his fists. A man with short black hair and ebony eyes stared at him from the page.

In the picture stood a billionaire benefactor of multiple orphanages in and around Baton Rouge. His hand rested on the shoulder of a scraggly boy. The child stared up at the man in his tailored suit with the type of adoration humans often reserved for angels.

Samael tossed the page on the pile. Most people in the area knew Gabriel. He'd posed for magazine articles with titles like 'The Hottest Billionaires in The World' and interviewed with Sixty-Seconds for an episode about philanthropy. Samael had watched the program, and now the news mumbled in the background between gunshots as live footage of a military coup played out across the screen.

Light bounced off his white tank top, his muscled chest becoming a projector screen as it reflected the quick flashing movements of the soldiers ducking behind barricades to avoid being shot.

He picked up his phone and dialed. "David." Wind and heavy breathing answered. Samael held the phone close to his ear. The gadget felt small and fragile under his grip.

"I'm. Going. Up. A. Hill." David's gasps clipped his words. "Samael?"

"I've been waiting to hear from you."

"I'm on my bike." David's breaths evened, but the wind became louder. "She did it. Is that what you wanted to hear?"

"I know." He'd felt her Scientia expand and contract earlier that day. She'd been toying with healing Jane for months, but this was the most Scientia she'd used since killing Marut. "How is your sister?"

Light weaved in and out of his sandy hair. Like a wall of ivory, his wings stood taller and wider than him. Thousands of glistening feathers twisted to the sounds of the muted gunshots emanating from the television.

"She's fine. She seems better. But Samael, there must be a safer way. Jane is lucky. Things could go wrong." David's exasperation scratched through the phone speaker.

Samael's wings ruffled in response. "I won't let anything happen to Jane."

"You won't?" David's voice rose, his temper clear. "Look at her. She's in a wheelchair. Tell me what you've done to prevent that?" Samael waited out David's pause, letting the child speak his mind. "I spent months next to her hospital bed, and here you're letting Wylie experiment on her."

"Wylie is learning, not experimenting."

"And how can she learn if she doesn't know what she is?"

"This is the last time I'll say this. It isn't your place to tell her."

"I feel like I'm lying to her."

"I didn't send you to Seattle to feel. I sent you there to become Wylie's muse." Samael's words received no response. He lowered the screen. He frowned as it lit up with its home screen. The boy had hung up on him.

With a grunt, he stretched his neck, rolling his head on his massive shoulders. He reached for the pack and pulled a cigarette out, placing it between his lips. He wanted to tell her, but he needed to keep her safe first. Brandon had been helpful so far, but Samael grew impatient. He wanted to know where Gabriel and his angels were based. And the bartender was his best chance of finding out.

Leaning back, his wings wrapped around him. "*Aduro*," he said through the side of his mouth. The cigarette bounced with each syllable of the word. A bright cherry flashed to life at the end—a spot of red framed by angel wings.

Chapter 9

David,

I'm about to do a deep dive into a shit-ton of my family's records. I'll let you know later this evening what I find. For now, check out these attachments. This is all I know about angel classifications. There's a lot, so don't fuckin' hurt yourself trying to get through it all before you write me back.

L

Lex sent her email, her mind wandering over the last few months of correspondence. She hadn't learned much, but there was something about it which made her feel less alone. She returned to the kitchen, where her father made a fresh pot of coffee every morning. She couldn't drink the bitter stuff. Her drug use had destroyed her insides. Nothing acidic passed her lips without hours of suffering. But she loved the new routine of coffee, newspapers, and grunted conversation. Frank would then escort her to an afternoon Narcotics Anonymous meeting.

The better she felt, the more obsessed she became with separating herself from Abaddon. If she wanted freedom, she would have to make it happen herself. Either way, she would need to leave. It was the only way she could protect her father from her angel.

"Hey gal, the VA's preparing a breakfast buffet this morning. You wanna go? We can go to NA after." Frank washed and dried his mug, putting it back in the cupboard.

Lex cringed. The Veterans Affairs calendar, with its saluting elderly men, grabbed her attention. His drug-addict daughter wouldn't impress his POW buddies. "Go have fun. I can do some shit around here."

Frank narrowed his eyes, and Lex remembered how much he disapproved of her cussing. He shook his head and grabbed his keys. "I'll be home for lunch. Maybe we can go get you a cell phone?"

"Sounds good."

"Bye, gal."

Lex waved him away, listening as he closed the door and locked it. She stood from the table. Dung put the oral history of angels to paper when Lex was a kid, often employing her to dictate the memories. As a child, she only heard the exciting parts of the stories. Now she looked for something different.

Lex settled into her search, skimming text after text. She spent time in each room looking for clues from her mother. She found herself in her brother's bedroom, looking through a stack of his old homework, letting her memories of the boy warm her. But now he's gone forever. What broke her heart the most was that she'd been so high she didn't remember anything about the last time she'd seen him.

Mid-morning, she climbed into the attic, finding a box of journals. What she found was meaningless to her: pictures of people she didn't know, random notes, a Bible, dog-eared and highlighted, a copy of an English translation of the Quran, and other religious books, all with notes about the apocalypse shoved into their pages.

Lex looked up from the journal with widened eyes. She sat up in Frank's recliner, his reading glasses balanced on the tip of her nose. Shaking her head, she reread the last few paragraphs as she nervously played with her septum ring.

> *In the year 1881, Abaddon became wounded during the Haiphong Typhoon. It became the third deadliest natural disaster in history. 300,000 people died, beginning with Doan Thi Khiêm, his muse.*
>
> *Abaddon lost control of the typhoon with the loss of his muse. His Scientia separated from him. He wasn't able to regulate nature with his usual precision. He could not stop the typhoon on his own.*

Drained and without a muse to provide power, Abaddon found himself spent and imprisoned by water.

She reread it.

. . . imprisoned by water.

Lex clutched the book to her chest and headed up the stairs to browse the internet and make phone calls. She'd found a solution, which would be easier than she'd thought. Painful but easy.

David,

You won't believe this, but I just scheduled an appointment for a facial tattoo. I found some interesting notes. I'll send pictures of everything. Hopefully, the damn thing does the job. It should prevent my angel from drawing energy from me. If this shit works, would you get a matching tattoo? Just fucking with you. I can't imagine you getting away with a facial tattoo at your job.

Anyway, did you tell your angel what she is? It seems unfair for you not to tell her. I'd be pissed. Such a shitty story, though. I've met a few angels, and there is no way they can pass as a human for an extended time.

Also, explain why your sister doesn't know she's a muse. God, you guys have so many secrets. It can't be healthy. I'm planning to do more research when I get home.

Talk to you soon,

L

A bell rattled as Lex stepped into Dragon Ink, a tattoo shop, a bus ride away from her house. A gust of icy wind followed her, along with her muddy footprints. Two tattooed men stood talking at the front desk. Her legs resisted moving further into the building, her skin crawling with the need to leave.

The taller man turned around. "Lex?"

She nodded, taking in the crimson walls and posters from random places in Asia. She felt assaulted by the red and gold paper lanterns with their dusty tassels. They hung too low.

"Welcome." The man put out his hand. "I'm Seth. We talked on the phone."

"Yes, we did." Shyness tied her tongue. Other than her father and sitting through NA meetings, she couldn't remember the last time she'd spoken to someone. She ignored Seth's hand.

"Can't wait to see this emergency tattoo." Annoyance dripped from his words, and his buddy at the counter rolled his eyes. "This way."

Ready to argue, she followed him into a large, partitioned room. "I'm the second one on the right."

She stepped inside, her hands sweating as she pulled the black-and-white picture she'd found wedged in her mother's Bible. The headshot of a stoic-faced man held the key to her freedom. The name Liu Quan, written on the back, led her to believe he was Chinese.

Quan glared through his spectacles, his cheeks round, his black hair parted. Liu Fu, Quan's cousin, the famous poet and linguist, took the picture in the early 1900s. Lex had found a copy online after searching the name and the year.

She held the picture up for Seth to see. Her finger ran over the tattoo on Quan's forehead. The letters scrawled just below his hairline. It spanned from one side to the other. "This is the tattoo. Can you do it?"

Seth tilted his head, stepping closer to the picture. "It looks simple enough. Where do you want it?"

"Same place."

Seth grimaced. "Are you sure?" He squinted at the picture. "I mean, you have such a pretty face."

"Do I look confused?" Her eyes narrowed.

"You're the boss." Seth shrugged, walked to the red toolbox in the room's corner, and pulled out the bottom drawer. He shifted through a stack of papers. "The studio requires all customers to read and sign this disclaimer."

Lex took the proffered paper. "In case I'm too dumb to realize tattoos are permanent?" She held out her hand for the pen.

"Pretty much. Oh, and I'll need your ID." Seth smirked. "So, those letters, I'm sure I've seen them before. What language is it?"

"Greek." Lex pressed the paper against the cushion of the table. Her heavy hand pushed several holes into the page. "Make it burnt brown instead of black." She looked up at him, and he nodded. "Sorry, I'm being a bitch. Can it be the color of henna?" She handed him her ID.

He ignored her confession and answered her question. "I can do that. I can play with it. The font can be fancy if you'd like." He paused as he focused on the tiny text.

"You think it looks like shit." Lex shrugged, already resigned.

Seth shook his head, giving the card back. "The tattoo looks hand done and rough, which is fine for him, but you've got a pretty face and should have a pretty tattoo."

Lex looked away. "Thanks, but the tattoo isn't for decoration."

Seth picked up the form and the picture. "I'm going to borrow this for a minute. I'll be right back. Make yourself comfortable."

Lex watched him go. Once alone, she climbed onto the massage table and balled her hands into fists. She felt so angry, angry that fate forced her to mark her face. Angry, her freedom would cost her so much.

Revelation 13:16-18. The highlighted scripture lay on the page saved by the picture. She whispered the scripture to herself:

> 16: And he causeth all, both small and great, rich and poor, free and bond, to receive a mark in their right hand, or in their foreheads. 17: And that no man might buy or sell, save he that had the mark, or the name of the beast, or the number of his name. 18: Here is wisdom. Let him that hath understanding count the number of the beast: for it is the number of a man; and his number [is] Six hundred threescore [and] six.

The hurried notes made in the blank column clinched the deal. The mark gave man the ability to *buy or sell*. It wasn't that simple. Someone scribbled the Greek words for *buy* and *sell* in the margins, and beside those were English translations. Next to *buy: redeem and ransom*. Next to *sell: exchange* and *barter*.

> Quan's mark allowed him to ransom and exchange his Scientia with angels. He decided how he would use the Scientia and who he would share it with.

She'd read and reread this scribble. The riddle of the passage was not clear, but the translated pages of her great-grandmother's journal describing Quan's abilities left Lex a believer.

"So, what does it say?" Lex jumped at Seth's voice, her eyes flying open. "Oh, sorry, were you sleeping?"

"No." She sat up and watched Seth gather his tools and paint. "It means six hundred and sixty-six." She held back her standard sarcasm.

"Wow, so you're . . . uh . . . like a devil worshiper?"

Peals of genuine laughter filled the air as she remembered what this tattoo represented. "It's the mark of the beast. And there is no devil."

"So, it's a family thing?" he asked, half smiling.

"He's Chinese. I'm Vietnamese." She crinkled her nose and knotted her fingers together. "The numbers symbolize a name."

"The Devil's?" He lifted his brows, his smile brightening as he ignored her eye-roll.

"I told you, I don't believe in that shit."

"So, what name does 666 symbolize?" Sarcasm dripped from his tone.

Lex watched Seth's face for a moment before answering, searching for interest. His eyes met hers, and she shared the weight that threatened to crush her. "Greek letters each have a corresponding number. Both Nero Caesar and Mohammad are equivalent to six hundred and sixty-six in Greek."

"That's cool." He sat down. "Can you lay back?"

Lex relaxed on the massage table, and soon she stared into Seth's brown eyes as he leaned over her. He placed a thin, white transfer paper over her brow and rubbed it against her skin. Pulling off the paper, he passed her a hand mirror. "What do you think?" he asked. "I made it a little smaller, a little girlier."

Lex caught her breath. It turned out better than she'd expected. "It's perfect." She handed the mirror back.

The buzz of the tattoo gun filled the air.

"So, why are *you* getting this number tattooed on you?" The pain of the needle punctuated his question, the exquisite burn of it filling her eyes with tears.

"Well, it's also the number of the Beast. It's said that his name lets people make their own decisions . . ." she paused for a moment, searching for a word to describe Quan's abilities as her teeth buzzed with the tattoo gun. "To have freedom."

"I see," he said, his voice relaxing as he worked. "So, this represents freedom."

Lex closed her eyes and pictured the script.

ἑξακόσιοι ἑξήκοντα ἕξ.

She smiled.
"Fuckin' freedom."

The cold air stiffened her toes and fingers. The wind chafed her face. Orange and red leaves tumbled past her feet. Her forehead burned, and every eye followed her as she approached her bus stop. The stares didn't put her on edge as much as the crunching of leaves under heavy footfalls behind her, mimicking her pace. Someone followed Lex. She pulled the hood of her jacket up and rounded a corner, walking straight into a man's chest.

She glared up and pushed against his body. He towered over her, his muscles visible under his polo shirt. His chiseled face twisted in rage. "Abaddon?" she whispered the question.

He yanked her hood down. "You bitch." He turned her around, forcing her down the sidewalk, away from her bus stop.

"Let me go, or I'll fucking scream." Her feet dragged along the concrete as tried to stop their movement.

"Scream, and I will bring every building in this city down on its occupants."

She pulled away, and he rewarded her by squeezing her against his chest until she couldn't breathe.

"Run, and I will erase the place of your birth." They continued down the sidewalk with Abaddon partially carrying her.

"Holy shit, why don't you just kill me?" Lex whispered as he jerked her across a street and over to one of the tallest buildings in the city.

"You're the last of your bloodline. Why would I trade a muse from an ancient family for anything less?"

He pushed her into a bank. Money counters flipped through bills, and whispering clients stood in lines. Abaddon pushed her to the back of the large, marble-floored room, dodging tall, white columns as he went. He stopped at the elevator and shoved her inside so hard she smacked into the back wall and crumpled to the ground. She cradled her injured head.

When the doors opened, he grabbed Lex's collar and dragged her into a room made of windows. A woman stared out at the panoramic view. She didn't turn around.

"She doesn't feel like a muse." The woman's accent made Lex think of the deep South. That and the way cowboy boots peeked out from under her Levi's.

"Binah, I have a problem." Abaddon hauled Lex forward, smashing her face into the glass. "My muse took to reading the Bible." He forced Lex to face the female. "As you can see."

The woman's hazel eyes turned to Lex. "She must have read an old Bible." She tossed her braid over her shoulder, her eyes and hair several shades lighter than her skin giving her an angelic glow. "You know she's useless now. I doubt he'd trade anything for her."

Lex took the opportunity to send her elbow into Abaddon's nose. Under her blow, she felt it crack. She ran, making it to the door. She wrenched it open. The wind cut through her.

The woman waited on the other side. She grabbed Lex's shoulders and spun her around. "I won't let him hurt you anymore, but honey, you need to be a good girl. You're pissing him off."

Abaddon wiped the blood from his nose with the sleeve of his jacket. *Fuck, it already healed?*

"Would he take her if her face wasn't as pretty?"

The woman kept Lex in her arms. "I think he'll want to meet her first."

"You're lucky she's here, Alexis." He joined them outside, his wings appearing as he closed the door. "It seems like the perfect time to drag you back to the gutter." And with a running start, he jumped off the roof. Wings spread wide as he soared.

With Abaddon gone, Lex tested her captor's grip.

"I guess that means I'm carrying you." Binah's arms tightened. "Don't make me drop you." With that warning, Binah dragged Lex off the roof and waited to open her wings until they'd dropped a few floors. "Woohoo! That was fun."

Lex closed her eyes and hung limp, hating every second. Sharp pains twisted her guts as the landing jolted her. Abaddon waited in the gravel just steps away.

Binah shoved Lex toward her angel. "Take your mess, brother."

Lex grimaced as Abaddon took hold of her upper arm. She hadn't expected him to find out about her tattoo so soon. She'd planned to disappear long beforehand, but she should have known that he would feel the change the tattoo caused. She straightened her shoulders, readying herself for anything, as Binah opened the door of a neo-gothic monstrosity of a castle.

"Abaddon. We've been expecting you. Please, come in." A man in a black wife-beater opened the door, allowing them to pass. He caught her staring at his gun, and he turned so his other side was facing her.

"Thanks, Todd." The angel left her wings out as she walked down the hall, the white feathers contrasting with the maroon walls. "Good luck, little warrior." She waved over her shoulder.

"Gabriel will meet you in the library. Follow me."

The marble tiles and walls blurred into reds and whites as Abaddon dragged her down the hall. Every few feet, a stand held a vase of flowers. She didn't know what they were, but the smell overwhelmed her. The bitter taste choked her.

In the library, books covered the walls, and lavish wingback chairs formed a sitting area in front of the fireplace. Lex counted the exits in her mind, knowing she wouldn't get far in any direction. Abaddon stayed on her heels as she broke away from him and settled on a bench beside a window. She pulled back the curtain and searched the horizon for clues about their location. A soggy green rolled out before her for the length of a football field surrounded by a belt of skeleton-like deciduous trees. She rubbed her tummy, feeling her panic rattling around like glass.

Abaddon waited until they were alone to speak. "Why?"

"Why do you think?" She turned her shoulder to him.

"I've been nothing but good to you."

He ran a gentle hand down her arm, and she ignored him as the bodyguard and a stranger entered.

"You're dismissed." The man took a few steps. His hands clasped behind him. "Oh, and Todd, thank your wife for the beignets."

"Yes, sir," Todd replied before shutting the door.

The light shined on the stranger's slicked-back raven hair, causing a halo to form around the curls. The muscular male joined Abaddon and Lex near the window. Her eyes traced his pinstripe suit, from leather shoes to unbuttoned collar.

Lex shivered as his obsidian eyes landed on her.

His gaze didn't falter as he put his hand out to Abaddon. "Hello, brother. I hear you have bad news for me." A French accent hid under his careful enunciation.

They shook.

"You must be Alexis." He turned to her, hand outstretched. "I'm Gabriel."

She stared down at his hand. She glared, biting her upper lip to hold in the string of profanities she wanted to share with him.

Abaddon cuffed the back of her head. "Take his hand, Alexis. I know your mother taught you better."

The smile disappeared from Gabriel's face. He caught Abaddon's wrist, and his eyes narrowed on her angel as he winced. "We don't put our hands on our muses without their permission."

"I … I … I'm sorry." Abaddon stepped away from Lex, removing the temptation to hurt her.

The apology brought Lex's heart to a gallop. No one spoke to Abaddon with an upper hand like that.

Gabriel turned back to Lex. His smile returned as he sat on the bench next to her. "Don't worry, I won't keep you here long." Gabriel leaned back and gestured for Abaddon to sit. "Abaddon, your muse is of no use to me in her current . . . condition." He leaned toward Lex. "I'm interested in how she performed such a trick."

"I'm not doing shit for you or any other angel." She wanted to punch his smug face but decided anyone who put Abaddon in his place wasn't worth messing with.

"There you have it," Gabriel said. "Abaddon, I'm not sure why you came."

Lex's angel scowled. "What if I removed her tattoo?"

Gabriel shook his head. "This is a strange position you put me in. The gift I'm offering is not for angels with broken tithes."

Lex shivered with this pronouncement. "I'm not a fucking tithe."

"Of course, you're not." Gabriel waved her words away, still intent on Abaddon's response.

Abaddon slipped out of his chair and onto his knees. "I can fix this. She's one of the oldest unbroken lines of muses in the world. She can have children. I know you see her potential. She's a dying breed. If I had free will, I could make a tremendous difference for your side. I could—"

Gabriel held up a hand. "I'm not God, Abaddon. I don't need you to kneel before me." His smile did not falter as he turned to Lex. "*Mon cher*, would you be interested in getting that tattoo removed?"

"I'd rather die, you flying sack of shit." She glared down at Abaddon.

Her angel shot up from the ground, fury in his eyes. His fingers found her neck, cutting off her breath.

Gabriel's wings appeared, their uniqueness on display. They breathed and glistened. Made of ice and mist. Water flowed heavenward in vein-like paths as they shifted with his movement. "Sit." The simple command from Gabriel sent Abaddon sliding backward, his knees giving way and his bottom landing on the carpet. The gallop in her heart returned. She'd never seen an angel like him. She touched her throat. Something inside her recognized his strength and longed to see what else he could do. Namely, kicking her POS angel's ass.

"I suggest you treat your muse with more kindness. It's much easier to reach agreements that way. She's welcome to stay if she comes willingly, but unless that tattoo is removed, there is no free will for you, brother."

Gabriel stood. "It was a pleasure, *cher*." Again, he reached out for Lex's hand.

This time Lex took it after finding a sliver of respect wedged in her heart. He kissed her knuckles, sending a zing up her arm.

She managed to maintain her dignity as she walked out of the mansion, straight into whatever doom Abaddon had waiting for her.

Her angel's fingers tangled in her hair the moment they stepped outside. He pulled her against his chest and squeezed her so hard her ribs crowded her lungs. "You will regret this."

Lex smiled and closed her eyes. *Fuckin' freedom.*

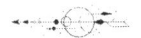

The carpet Lex sat on had fibers thickened with mold. Tammy, a previous occupant, maybe, had written her name with a brown substance on the wall. Lex turned from the smell. No sheets covered the stained mattress in the middle of the room. Neighbors ignored screams in motels like this.

Abaddon had handcuffed Lex to a rusted pipe and left. She discovered the limitations of her reach as she tried to chew through her gag.

She remembered a note from her great-great-grandmother's journal. Something about 'water solidifying the angels' static forms;' or at least, that's what Google Translate said. Unsure how best to use this information, she tucked it away and thought of an easier way to solve her problems. Her skin crawled with the urge to find a fix. Flashes of bliss sparked between her ears, and her heart pounded with longing.

God, grant me the serenity to accept the things I cannot change. . . Lex's prayer stopped as the motel door swung open. The darkness of night made Abaddon's outline glow.

Lex flinched away when he turned the light on. Her eyes adjusted as he set several grocery bags on the ground. Remaining silent, he marched back and forth in front of the bed, his chin in his hand, his brows meeting, his eyes intense.

. . . the courage to change the things I can, and the wisdom to know the difference. God grant me . . .

Her silent tears marked the passage of time as the words repeated themselves in her mind.

Abaddon's pacing stopped with an abrupt turn in her direction. He squatted before her. She avoided his gaze, looking up at the popcorn ceiling.

"I've never been this angry at you." His hand pulled at her chin. "Look at me, Alexis."

Hickory eyes met hickory eyes. He wore her favorite mask. The face of her mother's homeland. She looked away, and he growled in response, returning to the bags he'd brought with him. Lex watched him dump the contents on the bed. Honey, salt, some green gel, bleach, and a few other items that didn't bounce high enough for her to see.

"I'm going to remove your tattoo." He grabbed the salt. "This is going to hurt."

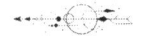

*B*lood dripped down Lex's forehead. She slumped against the wall under Abaddon's weight, her head moving back and forth with his scrubbing. He'd scrubbed off the skin on the top half of her face.

Her attempts to breathe burned like sandpaper. The pain of flesh tearing and skin peeling reverberated to her toes. Screaming . . . and screaming . . . and screaming. Her throat was shredded by her pleas for help. Salt dug into her eyes, blinding and burning. Her neck creaked with the jolting friction of his scrubbing motion.

Abaddon leaned back to see his handy work. "Shit!" He threw the salt across the room. The canister exploded on impact.

Salt rained down, and Lex flinched. She couldn't open her eyes; they stung too much. *I can't see! I can't see!* She shrank into herself, joining the stains on the motel carpet.

Abaddon returned to pacing the length of the room.

"No more." Her pleas smelled of lemon and bleach. "No more, no more. No. More."

She heard him stop and then the sound of sniffling as he gathered her into his arms. "Why? Why did you do this?" He pressed his face into her chest. "I loved you."

"No more. No more." She chanted the only two words she could find in the fog of pain, saturating her thoughts.

Abaddon's hands wandered over her. "Shh." He uncuffed her wrists. "Hush." He lifted her, and she sagged against him, hating him. He carried her to the bathroom and turned on the shower, stepping in with her in his arms.

"I loved you," he said again, sitting with her under the warm water. "This is the only way. I'm sorry." The sharp edge of a blade against her forehead marked his last word.

Screams left trails of acid as they escaped her mouth. She vomited, and then she choked on the vomit, sputtering. Sight, sound, and touch evaded her. Leaving only the burning line he carved into her face.

Abaddon's hand faltered as his canvas suffocated. The knife slipped from her eyebrow to her nose, engraving the "S" of his "sorry."

Her limbs went wild as one last surge of adrenaline filled her. Pushing and kicking, a rattle in her chest crescendoed with her screams.

Abaddon striped her hands and face with lacerations.

Her mouth and nose flooded with water and blood.

Each new hurt, a bright white flash in her mind, like stars brawling for space.

The Scientia he wanted back expanded.

Her pain stretched, stretched, and snapped.

An explosion rocked through the motel, creating a crater in the earth.

Chapter 10

Wylie

Jane's head rested in Wylie's lap. The girl's soft snores matched the rhythm of the orchestra playing on the television. Wylie had spent almost every day off with the pair since her housewarming party four months before.

"Is she asleep?" David asked from his end of the couch.

Wylie nodded.

He stood, resting her feet in his spot before pulling a blanket over her. "Let's go." He whispered, passing Wylie a pillow.

She did her best not to wake the girl as she replaced her lap with a pillow. David took Wylie's hand and, kissing her forehead, pulled her to his room. When the door shut, he pushed her against the wall, his mouth landing on her neck. She moaned.

"Thank God, she's asleep." His teeth found her earlobe as his tongue played.

"It was your idea to have a *Lord of The Rings* movie marathon." Wylie willed herself not to wake Jane, who slept on the other side of the door.

"I didn't realize she'd stay awake until three in the morning." He braced his hands against the wall on either side of her. "It's been too long." The last words came out of him in a grumble.

His lips found hers, and their tongues met. Her hands lifted to his shoulders, where they remained. Fully dressed, they'd made it horizontal a handful of times over the last few months. She blamed work, Jane, and life for never making it further. And while it was hot and passionate, it had become a slow burn, lest her skittishness took over.

David's patience and Wylie's hunger brought them a little further each time, but then she'd hit a wall, and they'd end up cuddling. She needed to learn how to be touched again.

She knew she was too stuck in her brain, but since meeting David, she'd found some happiness. Color snuck back into Wylie's life, one lovely hue at a time. It started with him and Jane, then work, and finally in the mirror. Vast shades stared back at her now. On a run last week, the blur of the sky grew vibrant as if God had lifted a filter. The green of the plants became vivid markers of how far she'd come.

"I should go home and sleep. We work tonight." She spoke between kisses.

"You're always working." His words vibrated against her skin.

It was true. So far, the holidays had filled her studio with ghosts of memories. She volunteered for doubles the entire month of December, and not just because she'd make bank. The structure of her job helped her as much as the Godwyns' did. She preferred the clean halls and constant cacophony of machines. Seeing David there was a bonus. If she didn't want to date, the hospital was the safest place for them to be together.

"But it's Christmas Eve." David smiled against her lips. "Why don't you stay?"

She laughed. "I want to, but we'd get no sleep."

"I know." He nipped her lip, his hand coming to her cheek. "At least promise to come over for breakfast tomorrow." He leaned back to show Wylie an eye roll. "My uncle will be here, and I plan to use you as my human shield."

"Oh, that sounds fun." She smirked. "Not. Why do we hate your uncle?"

"First, he's not my uncle. Just a friend of my father's." David cleared his throat, his eyes focusing on something behind her. "I know you've wondered how Jane came to live with me."

Wylie nodded and rested her head against his chest.

"You know about my mother being committed, but we've never discussed why. My father was murdered the night she went into labor with Jane." David played with one of Wylie's curls. "He was out with my 'Uncle' Sam when it happened. If my uncle hadn't asked for my father's help with whatever nefarious thing he was up to, Jane would have been raised by two parents instead of me and a broken mother." He leaned back, locking eyes with her. "I blame him."

Wylie wrapped her arms around his center. "That's awful, David. I hurt for you."

He rested his chin on top of her head. Their bodies aligned as he stroked her back.

"I know what it's like to feel alone in the world. My parents adopted me at birth. They were the best parents. I never wanted anything. When I turned six, I realized they weren't my biological parents, and even though I loved them, I always wondered what I was missing." Wylie's hand rested against David's cheek. Like pearls and gold. The contrast always surprised her because, on the inside, she didn't feel any different from David or her parents. "You know what it would be like to see myself in their faces. There's nothing more important than blood relatives. I love that you want to protect them. They're lucky to have you." She kissed his neck. "I'm lucky." Then his shoulder. Her hands danced down his back to his ass. Soon the pair were moving together.

"David?" Wylie said with a gasp, her hands made up for all the touch she'd denied him. "I need you."

He gripped her hips, pushing her into the wall. His amber eyes trapped Wylie's. She supposed this was how amber worked, luring its victims with its sweetness and holding them forever.

"Are you sure?"

Wylie looked into herself and touched the healing scar that represented Roberto. No pain. No fear. Just hunger. She smiled and nodded.

David laughed and spun them so Wylie's back faced the bed. She giggled, clinging to him as they kissed. He walked her backward, and she fell the controlled fall of a woman being draped in front of a man. He crawled on top of her—a grin on his face as he cupped her cheeks.

"Is this okay?"

Waves of need moved her hips. She was more than okay. She

wanted their clothes off. She wanted the hardness she'd felt through his jeans inside her. How had she waited this long?

"David." Her fingers tore at his belt. "I need you now."

He kissed her until they forgot to breathe. She pulled at his clothes as he traced her curves.

"You're killing me," Wylie gasped as David freed her breasts from her bra. "You're better at this than me."

He smiled against her lips. "Don't you do this at work all the time?"

"I usually have a pair of scissors."

He rolled to his back next to her, and she followed his lead, taking off her shirt first and then her pants. She went for her panties next.

"No, leave those for me." David stood and pulled off his boxers. His cock sprang free.

Wylie's heart pounded against the wall of her chest. She'd forgotten how big they could be. She reached for him, but David had other plans.

"Scoot up the bed." He watched her move with a wicked grin, palming his length. "You're beautiful."

Wylie blushed, covering the parts of her she'd only shown her husband. David went to his nightstand and pulled a condom from the drawer. He opened it and left it there—a promise.

He sat next to her and lifted his palms, waiting. "Hands, please."

She raised her brows as she placed her hands in his.

"These belong on me now." He winked. "Not covering you." He kissed her knuckles and then her hip, his lips half on her pink panties and half on her skin.

She trembled as he climbed onto the bed and kissed her other hip. His eyes went from her breasts to her pregnancy-scarred tummy. A finger traced her stretch marks and then kissed the pink lines. She wiggled under him. Tentatively, her hands found his shoulders, defining his muscles with touch.

"Mm." He kissed the apex of her legs. "Someone's eager."

She moaned. His voice made the muscles in her core tighten and relax in turns.

He bit his lip, and his fingers curled under the band of her panties.

The sight consumed his full attention. He ran the fingers of his other hand over her slit, watching as her wetness bloomed on the cotton. Wylie's toes pointed, her entire body reaching for more.

David smiled at her as he slid the panties to her knees, where he had left them. He fisted the fabric between her legs and, using them as a handle, pushed her thighs up and against her chest. With her bent knees trapped against her breasts, she was more vulnerable with him now than she'd ever been with anyone else.

David lowered his head and ran his tongue along her core.

"David!" she cried out.

"Shh, you don't want us to get caught, do you?" Air brushed her pussy as he spoke, then he pressed his mouth against her again, his tongue entering her as she rocked into him. Her hands clawed the bed, but she ate her moan, turning it into a rasping, muffled question. *"Please?"*

He cupped her sex. "Not yet." He kissed her thigh, the back of her knee, and her ankle, creating a path for her panties to follow. His hand found her breast as he tossed the garment aside and climbed her body.

"David?" Wylie's hands lingered on his chest. She turned away from him. Her eyes closed with embarrassment. "I've only done this with one person."

His fingers found her chin. "Look at me, Wylie." He ran his thumb over her lips. "Right now, you're the only person." He moved his hips against hers, and her body trembled as his velvet head slid across her leg. Her fingers admired the ridges of his abs as they traveled south, searching for the one thing that would satisfy the ache between her legs.

Her hands grasped hold of him. "Am I putting the condom on, or are you?" She smirked when he reacted to her touch with a low growl.

"I think you should."

She slapped the side table a few times before she found the thin package. He held himself up, a hand on either side of her as he watched her cover him. Once done, she smiled up at him with a proud glint in her eyes. Her legs opened, and her hands found his ass, pulling him to her.

He buried his face in her neck. "You're perfect." He fisted his cock and traced her slit. He rocked against her but didn't enter. "Tell me what you want."

"You inside m— yes!"

His breath shuddered as he pressed into her slowly. Inch by inch, stretching her.

"Wylie, look at me."

She lifted her eyes to his, and he buried himself to the hilt.

Her head fell back with a moan. She lost control of her hands and her hips as he thrust into her again and again, wanting to touch every part of him, hold every inch of him inside her. His thighs slapped hers, opening her wider. She thought she'd found heaven until his hands gripped her ass and lifted it from the bed. The change in angle sent her over the edge, her body shuddering with release. Three more thrusts, and he joined her.

"David." She couldn't find any other words. Her whole body buzzed. "Fuck." *Oh, look, I found one.*

He dragged his teeth over her collarbone. "Are you sure you don't want to stay?"

"They were jumping on the trampoline. I didn't see the ax until it was too late." The elderly woman covered her mouth with a tissue. Her fingers stained red from holding pressure on little Ben's wound. "I was doing the dishes, and that's when I saw them from the kitchen window. I couldn't tell what they were playing with. He and his brother were pretending to be characters from that movie."

She shook her head in frustration and rubbed little Ben's back. The kiddo seemed more shaken by his grandmother's crying than the blood-soaked towel wrapped around his hand. "Oh, you know, the one with the swords made of lights." She dabbed at her eyes with a tissue. "He's only four. He shouldn't even be watching those kinds of movies."

Wylie rested her hand on the woman, her floppy Santa hat and dangling Christmas present earrings reminding her it wasn't any other day of the year. She felt bad for patients who had to spend their holidays with her. "We've got him. You're in the right place." And then she crouched in front of the child, making eye contact with the boy. "Hey, buddy, what's your name?"

"Ben." He wiped his nose with the back of his free hand, his lips the same color as his face. Dirt had smudged a line down his jaw. He smelled like outdoor play.

"Can I see your owie?"

The way Ben looked at his grandmother for permission broke her heart. Wylie wished her son could ask her questions with his eyes.

"Baby boy, you need help right now, and this nurse will do that. Show her your hand."

He held up his hand, and Wylie took it, the smallness of it making her palms tingle with recognition. Memories of counting little fingers brought back a bittersweet warmth in her heart.

Blinking away the thoughts, she pulled back the crunchy towel. The laceration on his palm needed about four stitches. Yellow beads of fat appeared under the oozing blood, but not smooth muscle or white bone. The ax hadn't done its worst.

Putting a sterile gauze against the wound, she turned to Grandma. "I'm thinking this will be an easy fix. Can you just hold pressure here while I get a Doc and start our paperwork?" She moved over to the gurney where Ben sat. "Here, I'll show you." Wylie took Ben's little hand and placed it in hers. "Like this." She pressed her thumb over the wound with just the right amount of pressure. "We've got you. Both of you." Wylie's throat tightened as she spoke. She allowed her eyes to water, but no more. This was their sadness. Wylie would not take it from them.

She paged David, who responded quicker than some providers in the ER, and opened the computer. "Do you mind if I ask you a few questions?" She clicked all the buttons, aware of the grandma's dwindling confidence. "He's not the first kiddo to get hurt on a trampoline." Wylie rested her hand on Linda's free one and made eye contact.

She nodded, managing a small smile as David walked in. The way his white coat stretched across his shoulders, his stoic work face dropping the moment he saw Wylie always sent her into daydreams of a Grey's Anatomy-style rendezvous.

He smiled as Wylie introduced him to the pair. Soon Linda giggled as David charmed her tears away. Next, he turned to Ben, his honey-colored eyes narrowed as he peeked under the gauze. "Linda, you must be so proud of how brave Ben is." The boy beamed.

Wylie loved how patients responded to David. He made people feel safe, including her. He did other things to her too.

She shook the image away as Dr. Godwyn pulled the bell of the stethoscope off the boy's chest. "Thanks." He handed Wylie her stethoscope back. "Let's get Ben here, 12.5 milligrams of Benadryl. I'll also take some—" His directions came out in quick succession.

When he stepped out, Wylie sat on the rollie chair to translate the plan. "As Dr. Godwyn said earlier, we're going to try some medicine that will help you stay calm." She showed Ben her hand. "It's hard not to move when you're scared, so I'm going to have a friend come help. She'll hug you while I hold the hand with the owie. Is that okay?" Ben looked at his grandmother again, and she pulled him to her side. Wylie excused herself, ready to do David's bidding.

"Hey, Cindi." Wylie waved at the tech jamming out to a fast-paced Christmas song at the nurse's station. "Can you grab the papoose?"

The smile dropped from her face. "Shit, you have the toddler with the ax wound, don't you?" She rolled her eyes when Wylie grinned. "If he kicks me, you owe me a drink."

"Deal."

"Merry Christmas to us."

Wylie blew her a kiss and headed off to get her supplies. After triple-checking, scanning, and doing the hokey pokey, as required by the fastidious Medication Cart, she returned to Linda and Ben.

Cindi leaned against the papoose as she eyed the child on the bed. The hooks and loops connected to the board stuck to her scrubs.

"Linda, will you be okay staying for this?"

She nodded, wiping her nose. "When is Dr. Godwyn coming back?"

Wylie held back a smile. "Any minute now. Before we start, can we practice holding your hand still?" Wylie held her palm out for the boy, and he rested his uninjured hand on hers. *Now.* Like filling a vase, Wylie poured in all the happiness and peace she'd found over the last few months. A burn built in her chest as she imagined Ben's neurons releasing the hormone equivalent to calm. The response was immediate. His breathing slowed, his muscles relaxed, and his hands settled in his lap.

"You guys ready?" David's voice brought Wylie back.

She straightened her shoulders and took a deep breath. "Yeah, what about you, Ben?"

Ben didn't respond. Instead, he snored.

"Wow, the Benadryl worked fast." Cindi left the papoose against the wall, and Wylie shoved the unopened pill packet in her pocket.

Twenty-minutes later, Cindi and Wylie followed David out of the room as if *Eye of the Tiger* played in the background, their heads held high. Her chest pain stopped halfway through the procedure, and Wylie left the room with a skip in her step.

"That was too easy." Cindi clapped once. "Did you see Dr. Godwyn's face when the kid woke up to say 'Thank you?'" They laughed, and Wylie headed to a computer station to gather discharge paperwork.

She'd just logged on when David leaned against the nurses' station, his thumbs hooked in his pocket. Wylie smiled, and he smirked.

"Three things;" he said. "One,"—he paused for emphasis— "can you find out if any pharmacies are open today or tomorrow? I want Ben to get those antibiotics?"

"Sure thing."

"Second, are you sure you didn't give him a narcotic? That went way too smooth." He winked.

She snorted her cheeks warming.

"And third." He cleared his throat and lowered his voice, making it rumble in a way that made her breath catch. "Lunch?" He rested his hand on the top of his head.

Wylie licked her lips. "Yes," she said, excitement bubbling inside of her. "Same place as usual?"

David winked. "I'll meet you there after the discharge."

Chapter 11

Wylie

An after-Christmas-sale had exploded in David's living room. Each door had red plaid wrapping paper covering it with a giant bow in the center. Gold garlands connected every corner. Jane's laughter met them as they entered. A tree dripping in ornaments and blinding lights assaulted her eye from the dining room.

Jane, in an apron and her usual messy bun, jumped on Wylie, squeezing her tight. "I'm so glad you came." She smelled of pine and cinnamon. "Uncle Sam and I were about to make a treat for you." She grabbed Wylie's hand and led her to the kitchen island.

An older gentleman, with gray strands feathered through his sandy hair and lines around his moss-colored eyes, came around the island with an outstretched hand. Wylie stifled a laugh. He wore a pink frilly apron matching Jane's.

David took Wylie's coat. "This is my Uncle Sam." His reaction to the man couldn't be more different from his sister's. He frowned, his voice lowering with his eyes.

"Nice to meet you." Sam took her hand and kissed both of Wylie's cheeks, Italian style. With his button-down shirt and slacks, Wylie couldn't help but wonder if he were part of a mob syndicate.

"Likewise." She squirmed under his green gaze. Unsure if it was his rolled sleeves and muscular forearms or tied back shoulder-length hair that made him feel dangerous.

"Excuse my appearance. I can't seem to say no to my niece." His calloused hand sent shivers down her spine, and though he must have been twenty years older than Wylie, a dark magnetism sparked between them.

"I doubt that." David's hand found her back, steering her past his uncle to a platter of doughnuts. The action would have charmed her if it didn't feel like he'd done it to dismiss his uncle.

"I'm so glad you came. We were about to make that Mexican hot chocolate you said you liked."

"You and Sam?" David pulled a seat up next to Wylie and chose a lemon-filled doughnut. "I guess our *Uncle* Sam is a man of many talents." She cringed at the sarcasm, and David gave her an apologetic frown.

Jane missed the slight as she returned to the stove and stirred the milk she double boiled. "Okay, Uncle Sam, I think it's ready. Will you pour it for me?"

"Hmph." Sam poured the milk into the blender container and returned it to its place.

"Wylie, I even got the brand you mentioned."

"Oh, so that's what I was smelling on you?" Wylie inhaled again and grinned.

"Yep." Jane pulled the chocolate circle from her pocket and unwrapped the yellow and gold foil. She handed it to her uncle, who broke it into wedges without being asked. "Thanks."

She dropped a few wedges into the milk, covered the container, and hit blend.

The liquid swirled. The fluid rose higher and higher until the lid blew off.

Boiling milk sprayed.

Sam yanked Jane away, spun, and hunched over her. The hot chocolate splashed the counter and his back, leaving brown dots against the canvas of his white shirt. From a distance, David pulled the plug, and it turned off, then hurried to his sister. Jane's sobbing broke the silence as both men looked her over. They found two quarter-sized burns on her wrist where blisters bloomed over bright red splotches.

"Okay, missy, let's run that under cold water." David walked her to the sink.

"What about you?" Wylie touched Sam's shoulder.

He stepped away and rubbed his arm where she'd touched him. "Hmm?"

"Your back."

"It's nothing. Take care of Jane." The gruff command sent Wylie forward.

She found herself at Jane's side. Their shoulders touched before she realized what she was doing.

Jane sighed, and her whimpers ceased. "It's better." She turned off the water and lifted her wrist to her face. "It doesn't hurt anymore."

Wylie grabbed a dish towel and wiped the counters, ignoring how the Godwyn family watched her. "Do you have enough ingredients for a second batch?"

No one answered.

"I think we could make it without the blender."

Jane wiped her eyes. "I should have tightened the lid." She pulled another towel out of a drawer. "Are you okay, Uncle Sam?"

"Fine." He folded his arms. "It wasn't hot anymore by the time it got me."

Wylie's eyes narrowed, but David stepped between them before she could ask more questions.

"I think we should just skip straight to gifts. Wylie and I had a long night." David squeezed Wylie's shoulder, his head dipping. "I can clean this later."

Sam grunted. "I should go."

"No, Uncle Sam." Jane jumped on her uncle, and he stiffened and then patted her head.

"I'll be back to visit soon." He ruffled Jane's hair. "Your father would be proud of you."

She kissed his cheek. "Thanks."

The man turned to Wylie. "It was nice meeting you." She shivered as their eyes met. Her finger ran up her forearm, soothing herself as the thing between them intensified.

"I look forward to meeting you again."

She nodded.

The man exited without acknowledging David.

Jane tossed her towel in the sink, her eyes sleepy. "Let's do this." She coasted into the living room and dug under the tree, making piles. The adults sat on the couch. Wylie was grateful she'd brought her gifts the day before.

"These are yours." Jane pointed at a ridiculous stack of presents.

"All of that's for me? Jane, you shouldn't have."

"Just shut up and enjoy." Jane dumped the pile at Wylie's feet.

David's hand brushed Wylie's thigh, and the pair smiled at each other. Jane's enthusiasm warmed Wylie's heart. The girl had gone from wheelchair to messy teenager since they'd met, and Wylie couldn't help but feel pride. She'd helped. She knew she'd helped.

The morning sun peaked around the tree, making the room glow orange. David clapped. "So, how should we do this?" His cyclist's arms reached for the sky as he stretched, his fists raised against wakefulness.

"Let's do a free-for-all, like Mom used to."

"Sounds good to me," he said. "Oh, and that reminds me. We should call her before I go to sleep." He grabbed a present from the ground. His finger curled into claws, intent on ripping the wrapping paper to shreds.

"Wait." Jane slumped on the ground in front of her presents.

Wylie froze, her hands around the gift.

"Music." She pulled out her phone.

Love Me Tender played, and Jane winked at them. David and Wylie leaned away from each other at the same time.

"Go!" Jane eyed Wylie's gift, pulling it to her lap first.

David joined his sister in a rapid-fire unwrapping spree, creating a chorus of ripping paper and silly grins.

"Don't be shy, Wylie." Jane didn't look up from her busy hands.

Wylie had yet to open a gift. She was too busy enjoying this family. A warmth filled her, and through the happiness, she remembered her last family Christmas. This would be her second without them. Little

Dean's two-year-old language ricocheted off the walls of her skull—Roberto's hand in hers as they watched their little man laugh from the belly and play in a pile of wrapping paper.

A large ball of paper connected with her forehead, breaking her trance. "Earth to Wylie." Jane had her hands cupped around her mouth. "Don't make me take those back."

Thankful for the wake-up call, Wylie smiled. She hoped her eyes didn't glisten with tears as she opened her first gift.

The room went from orange to red as the sun crested the horizon. It burned away Wylie's hesitancy to feel joy. She leaned back and looked at her pile of gifts. She'd done pretty well for a person who hadn't planned on celebrating Christmas this year.

Jane plopped onto the couch next to Wylie, resting her head on her shoulder. "So?" Jane turned the vowel into a question mark.

Wylie raised her brows.

"What did you think of the scarf my brother got you?"

She opened her mouth to respond.

"He's a pretty great guy, isn't he?" Jane eyed Wylie in a way that only a teenager could.

Wylie knew how this worked, and she wasn't about to admit to David's little sister that she wanted her brother because she wasn't ready to have him yet. Jane needed a distraction, so Wylie grabbed the scarf and rubbed it on Jane's face. "You mean this scarf?"

Jane giggled, cuddling closer as her eyes drifted shut. "What was that for?"

Wylie pushed back Jane's hair from her face. "Are you tired?"

"You know he's single, right?" Jane mumbled.

Concern stretched over Wylie's face.

"What are you two talking about?" David asked as he strolled out of his room wearing his new plaid pajamas.

"I was telling Wylie what a dork you are." Jane yawned and nuzzled closer to Wylie. "I think I'm going to take a nap."

David frowned. "Are you feeling okay?"

"Just tired." Jane didn't move from her spot, resting against Wylie's shoulder. "Will you carry me?"

David shook his head, but not in response to Jane's request because he scooped his little sister up and carried her to her room. Wylie wondered if the frown was for the disease threatening to take Jane's childhood away or if something else was happening in David's head.

He left her room minutes later as he rubbed his forehead.

"Is she going to be okay?"

"She's tired. She gets like this sometimes." He rubbed at the sleep in his eyes. "You ready to head home?"

"Yes." Wylie wrapped her gifts in the fancy scarf and used it as a bag. "Ready."

Seattle took her time waking up. The city gave them light traffic as a Christmas gift. Wylie stole a look at David's jawline, studying the features which had her fellow nurses giggling in the break room. For a moment, Wylie considered inviting him in but remembered Jane and decided it would be best for David to be with her. They kissed a long, slow kiss that fogged up the windows. The promise of sleep was the only thing strong enough to tear them apart. Wylie ran through the rain and into her apartment building. She waved goodbye before making her way to her door and twisted the key in the lock. The last of her energy drained away as she pushed it open.

A chill traveled up her spine as she stepped inside. The darkness of her apartment repelled her, the air thick with her loneliness. She hung her soaked jacket, realizing her gifts were still in the car. She'd call David when she woke up. Grabbing a cup of water, she headed to bed. Her body froze when she noticed a dark form sitting on her couch. A squeal escaped her lips, and she jumped back, dropping her water. The cup bounced on the carpet, splashing her and the intruder.

Somehow, she recognized the figure. She'd conjured him up whenever she thought of her husband and son's murderer. But he was missing the black wings. His face twisted in anguish as blue eyes found hers, and tears streaked his face. He stood, stacking his bones atop each other with the hesitancy of a person in pain.

"Who are you?" She stepped back.

"You killed my brother." One of her steak knives flashed in his fist as he lifted it to point at her. "You." He shook his head, his other hand tangling in his black beard. His worn steel-toed boots and torn jeans matched his haggard appearance.

"You killed him, and all he ever wanted was to help you." His teeth flashed as his eyes slid up and down her body. "What a waste. You're nothing. Just another mound of flesh." He appeared before her, though she didn't see how he got there.

Wylie's legs became lead, but her hands came up.

"Easy, buddy, you've got the wrong person." She backed away wide-eyed. "I'm a nurse. I heal people, not hurt them."

He scoffed. His face glistened with the evidence of his sorrow. "You lie." He lifted the knife, and the pointy end slammed into her shoulder, the serrated blade ripping more than cutting.

A warmth splashed between her breasts as blood escaped the wound. Wylie's mouth gaped open. Pain shot up her neck and down her arm.

His empty hand connected with her face. She flew into the wall. He stalked toward her, his hands finding her throat, he pushed her onto her toes. He spat on her face and then his skull crashed into her nose as he released her.

Blood gushed down her throat, and she slid to her bottom. Her ears rang. Searing pain threatened to suffocate her. White dots danced in the foreground of her sight, turning the man into a monster.

He paced before her, his hands in his hair as he mumbled.

Pain and blood, and fear projected the horror in her son's eyes, flashing the image in time to the beat of her throbbing wound. The dial tone effect in her ear matched a three-year-old boy begging. Her world darkened, and in that blackness lived her scrabbling husband, clinging to a dead child.

Dead husband.

Dead child.

They died like this.

The world refocused, and the terror dissipated, replaced by rage. It burned through her veins, turning her pain to ash. Defiance pulled air into her lungs. She reached for him. One hand caught his pant leg. She pulled until her other hand found flesh. Instinct took over as she seared a picture of his lungs filling with fluid into his ankle. She pulled the sound of harsh breaths from her memory and forced them into him, willing crackles to punctuate each of his inhalations.

She pushed and pushed until she felt as if her heart might explode.

His boot landed in her gut. "What have you done, Armageddon?" His hand clawed at the collar of his shirt.

He kicked again. She vomited with the second blow; the carpet burning her cheek as she slid onto her belly. Her lips opened and closed, but no air moved in or out.

With a thud, her assailant landed on his knees next to her. His fall jump-started the wheeze that entered her chest. His face mirrored her panic. The need for air made his eyes round. Pink, frothy fluid ran down his chin. They stared at each other as they gasped, his eyes accusing her of a second murder.

His eyes widened and their connection broke as he slumped forward.

The throbbing, sharp ache returned as her heart wavered. She couldn't curl in on her pain. His wide-open eyes held her captive. She'd killed him. She didn't have to check his pulse to see life had vacated the form before her.

"Wylie, your door's open." David's voice came from the entryway. "You left your gifts in the car." Footsteps. "I thought I'd bring them by before you fell asleep."

"Wylie?" His voice broke on the name as he rushed to her. "Oh, my God!" He knelt at Wylie's side, and she spat blood on the ground, attempting to speak.

David braced either side of her head to steady her neck as he turned her. Wylie groaned as she lost sight of the dead man.

"Fuck. What did he do?" David's eyes scanned hers.

"I killed him." The confession blistered as she birthed it with a gasp.

"Hush." He pulled off his jacket and wrapped it around the knife handle. He pulled his phone from his pocket. "Yes, I have a medical emergency." He paused. "Dr. Godwyn here—I'm a friend of the victim —Yes, I have a twenty-seven-year-old female with a four-inch knife embedded in her left shoulder and multiple head injuries. It looks like a home invasion. I just got here."

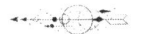

A deep ache reverberated through her face. Her right eye refused to open. One sliver of sight revealed nothing but brightness. She kicked her legs, her fingers curling as her last memory came back to her.

"Wylie, you're safe."

A hand on her cheek.

"I can't see." Wylie turned her head from side to side. Her frantic heartbeats muffled the pain which had woken her.

A hand took hers. "Wylie. It's David. You're safe. I'm here. You're at the hospital. You're safe."

Her brain caught up with his words as she pulled his hand to her chest. She remembered the knife first and then her shoulder. The fingers on her injured side twitched, sending shock waves of pain crashing through her. She moaned.

"Here." David replaced his hand with a handle. "Push this. It's morphine."

Her thumb pushed the button again and again, impatient for relief. Her body grew heavy, and dreams dragged her back to her apartment, back to the man's dark gaze.

Cyan pools swirled in his eye sockets, splashing onto the carpet from his face, leaving stains like ink on the floor. The splotches expanded and lengthened, eating up the ground beneath them until they floated in an endless abyss.

They spun, waves of nausea hollowing out her belly. The man's arms flung about; his head dangled on his chest. The storm threw him around like a doll.

"Armageddon." It started as a whispered chant. "Armageddon. Armageddon. Armageddon." His voice crescendoed from his lifeless form as the waves pushed him further and further away from her.

Alone in the chaos, his screaming mantra became her truth.

"Armageddon!"

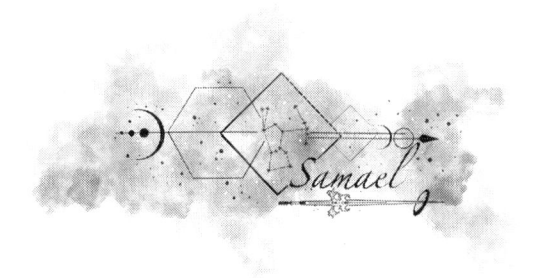

Samael paced before the Emergency Department's entrance; brooding set his jaw. The neon sign flickered as if responding to Samael's dread-anger cocktail. Wylie had been whole. He'd seen her, touched her, and now . . .

David stumbled out of the sliding glass doors wearing a haggard frown. Several blood stains covered his torso. He folded his arms against the cold as he approached Samael.

"What happened?" Samael bit off each word, his fists ready to hurt something.

"I dropped her off after we opened gifts. She walked into her apartment with no issues. I was on my way home when I noticed her presents in my car and turned around." David leaned forward, his hands shaking as he rubbed the naked skin on top of his head. "Harut was dead when I got there. She's hurt. She's hurt bad."

Samael grunted; his jaw so tight human teeth would've crumbled.

"How did you know to come?"

"I felt it." Samael smacked his shoulder. Wylie's Scientia went off like a bomb, followed by the death of an angel. But something new had happened. He'd felt her pain. He looked at his hand, which had held hers just a few hours before.

"Tell me you didn't do this," David whispered.

"I didn't do this." But he should have seen it coming. Samael thought back to the last time Harut and he had met. He imagined the brothers. Harut and Marut couldn't survive without each other. But even if he blamed himself, this human had no right to assume such guilt. "Harut helped the Persians into Babylon. He'd been nothing but loyal."

David followed Samael away from the hospital entrance and lit a cigarette. "Jane and I care about Wylie. Tell me you didn't introduce her into our lives just to take her away."

Samael read the anger on David's face. The way his teeth showed and his chin dropped with his brow. The boy hated him. Samael inhaled his nicotine. "She's not yours to keep." He cleared his throat. "I gave you to her, not the other way around."

"Fuck you. I'm tired of playing charades. You come into my house in your old man costume. You're a joke."

Samael grabbed David by his shirt and yanked him forward. "I promised your father I'd protect you; otherwise, I'd have strangled you years ago, you foolish child."

David shoved at Samael, but he might as well push a mountain. "I don't care. Just stay away from her."

Samael's forehead crinkled as he let go of David's shirt, the boy stumbled back. "You want her? Don't you?"

"I already have her."

Samael advanced, nostrils flaring.

David took a step back.

"I forbid it. *Un-have* her." His hands hovered in front of David's chest, itching to harm. "Don't touch her." Samael's voice dropped to a deadly growl. "Never question me again."

David lifted his chin. "Or what? I'm human. You can't touch me."

"I'll take her away." Samael didn't wait for an answer. Instead, he projected himself to Harut's apartment, afraid he'd hurt the boy if he stayed longer.

For a moment, he closed his eyes and let the darkness wash over him, preparing himself for the worst. Humans should worship Armageddon, not touch her. Roberto came with Wylie. He didn't know who or what he was. David could poison her mind against angels. Leaving her as afraid of Samael as David was. He didn't want that for her. He wanted nothing but peace for her.

Centered again, his footfalls echoed off the walls as he entered the living room. He did a three-hundred-and-sixty turn, searching for any evidence of Gabriel. Harut kept his place as sterile as heaven. Only emptiness greeted him; no furniture, no decorations, no sign the place had an inhabitant.

He touched a few surfaces, reading their histories with his fingertips. Nothing. He'd yet to see Harut, but he'd hoped his brother found the free will to harm Wylie through his enemy instead of the alternative.

All hope gone, he walked to the bathroom. He steeled himself. With a creak, he pushed his way in, flipping on the light.

Dried blood drew vertical lines up the white-tiled walls. Two pools thickened on the lowest points of the uneven floor. A soiled hacksaw leaned against the wall. The shattered mirror left pieces of glass around the sink like frost. The closed shower curtains showed blotchy patterns through which light couldn't travel. Samael pulled it back.

"*Merda.*" He cursed under his breath as he sat on the toilet.

A pair of wings lay in the tub. The tips folded up inside the porcelain. The feathers lay crumpled and tangled, their gilded spines soiled by clotting blood. He gripped the saw's handle and looked into its past.

Harut genuflected. "Please." His hands shook as he pressed them into the ground.

"No, I don't trust you." The man from the newspaper clipping glared down at Harut from a wing-backed chair.

"But I'm ready to fight for you."

"Being angry and being willing to kill your brothers and sisters are two different things. I'm raising an army here, not babysitting winged toddlers."

Harut shot to his feet, and Gabriel lifted a hand, freezing Harut mid-stride. "Don't." Gabriel waved over the man posted at the door. "Please give Harut his gift and see him out."

Harut growled, his feet sliding on the ground as he pushed against Gabriel's Scientia.

Gabriel stood. "If I see you again, Harut, I will end you." He left as the guard he'd sent out returned.

The man carried the same hacksaw Samael held. The thing clattered to the ground as Samael sank to his knees before the mess of feathers. He planted his elbows on the tub and folded his fingers together. *"Sub tuum praesidium confugimus."* He closed his eyes as he prayed.

Once his entreaties dried up, Samael projected himself and Harut's wings to Arcadia, leaving the rest of the horror for the humans to clean up. This Heavenly Plane was an empty world of white and echoes. He held Harut's wings in his arms as he approached the last living Throne. Ophanim stood in her blinding universe.

"Sister." Samael presented his load as if displaying a treasure. "I'm sorry to disturb you."

Ophanim's solid white eyes reflected Samael cradling Harut's crumpled wings. "Harut is dead?" Her arms fell. "I remember sculpting those wings."

Samael's head bowed in reverence. "They are beautiful wings."

"This is the third dismemberment this year." Ophanim emptied Samael's arms, her eyes studying the feathers. "Why did he do this?"

"He wanted revenge." Throughout history, many angels have given their wings for the ability to make their own decisions. Gabriel's angels kept their corrupted Scientia, while Harut gave up everything that made him an angel.

"You're distracted." Ophanim's head bent as she held Harut's wings to her chest, resting her cheeks against the feathers.

"It was his last mistake, his only mistake. Can this outshine his good life?"

"No, Samael. He will return to the earth with the nobility he lived his life. I will use his wings to make something as beautiful as him. In the end, he will be here." She turned back to him. "Now, hold these."

With the burden returned to his arms, he thought of human parents. Of how they often sacrificed all their passions to enrich their children's lives. Was this why the heavenly planes remained vacant? They'd given everything beautiful to humans, leaving emptiness.

Ophanim's eyes drifted shut. The mother of angels threw her arms forward, grabbed air and pulled it to her bosom as if digging in the sand. She shook her head, pushed the air aside, and reached out again. "Here," she said, pointing at nothing. "I will make his wings into a basin in the Pacific Ocean. A place where there is only peace."

She dug at the air with one hand, patting imaginary walls as if digging the moat of a sandcastle. She lay both her hands against her invisible structure and furrowed her brows.

They stood like that for a while. Samael's body itched with unfamiliar emotions. Finally, the Throne held out her arms. Samael passed her the wings. She smoothed them, the knobby knuckles of her fingers curled and uncurled as she pressed one feather or another.

The wings became smaller, the feathers and blood and bone smoothing together into the consistency of clay. She formed a flat bowl from the clay wings and then massaged them into place. Time froze and bent as she worked, the craving for perfection palpable in the air.

When she finished, Samael fell to his knee with an angel salute.

Ophanim stepped forward, resting her hand on his forearm until it lowered. She caressed his cheek. "The day I do this for you, I will create a grand abyss."

Chapter 12

Lex

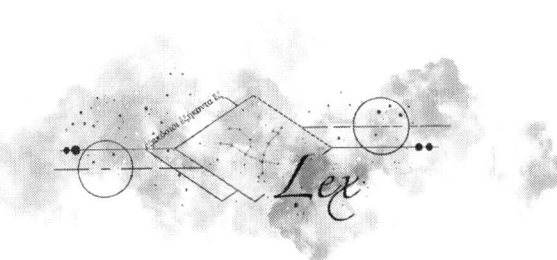

Lex woke to the sound of breathing, a calm presence beside her. Her face throbbed with the ache of old hurts. She didn't open her eyes; she didn't feel Abaddon's presence, but no angelic presence would be welcomed, and she knew that's what sat next to her. A false safety emanated from it. The flimsy comfort she recognized as angel-borne peace lingered in the space between them.

Images flared and flashed in her thoughts like broken glass. A knife glinted in the foreground of her mind. She breathed in deep, replacing the image with the smell of dryer sheets and cotton candy.

Her fingers shook as she reached for her face, the tips caught on delicate gauze. The flesh underneath felt heavy and unattached, as if someone had sewn a slab of meat to her forehead. It hurt less than she thought it should. Her body trembled with suppressed pain. She knew whoever sat beside her was keeping it at bay. She didn't think she'd survive without an angel or a hit. Lex knew herself. She had no pain tolerance. The last few years of her life, she'd lived blissed out of her mind. She had no space for discomfort.

Lex blinked. Her eyes burned. At first, only blurry light translated to her brain, and then they focused on the white bandages covering her forearms. Red bled through in several spots. She prodded the line and hissed. She needed to figure out where she was and how she'd survived. Her heart raced as she felt around the twin-sized mattress under her, intent on escape. If only she could see.

"Abaddon is not here." The treble voice did not belong to her angel.

She blinked and blinked. Her eyes protested but finally remembered their job, bringing a blur of pink into focus. Hot pink and princesses decorated every inch of the walls. Someone had covered her with butterfly-print sheets that felt more like plastic than fabric. The chill morning air against her breasts informed her of her nakedness. Many years as a drug user made her adept at waking up in random places, but she'd never found herself in a room like this. Lex pressed her lips together so she wouldn't ask her question. She didn't think she'd ever speak again. The lump in her throat was too large, the hate in her heart too much like a bomb. She craned her neck to find the liar who promised safety. She'd never be safe again.

Gabriel sat next to her on a little girl's pink throne. He wore cream linen slacks and a black button-down. He'd placed a deep part in his raven wavy hair. The smell of his gel mingled with the smell of her unclean body. From head to sandaled foot, he seemed more manicured than polished.

"Good morning."

Lex sat up, trying to shove the mosquito net canopy from around her. Claustrophobia strangled her.

Abaddon! He'd strangled her too.

"Abaddon can't hurt you now." Gabriel reached for the net, but Lex yanked it away.

Lex glared up at Gabriel in his ridiculous chair. She didn't want his help or anything to do with him.

He laughed. "No one will hurt you while you're under my protection."

She snorted. She needed his protection like she needed the clap. Angel pain control, yes, she'd take that for now, but protection? He can go ahead and fuck himself. She fought the mosquito net. Who knew what this dickhead's protection would cost her. She didn't care to know, tearing the net from the ceiling, and threw it at his feet. Her lips curled back. She didn't need another fucking angel in her life.

"I'm not like other angels, *cher*."

Stop reading my mind, asshole. Lex leaned against a dresser, her blood rushing to her head. She pressed her cool hand to her forehead, dropping the sheet on accident, revealing her breasts.

Gabriel held up his hands, turning his head away from her like some kind of gentleman. "I can't help it. You think loudly."

She grabbed a snow globe and threw it at the angel with all her strength.

He caught it.

Fuck you.

She stomped to the closet and discovered the wardrobe belonged to a preteen. Thankfully, she was short. She found the stretchiest dress hanging and pulled it over her head. The bright yellow skater left most of her thighs bare. She couldn't guess the size. She knew nothing about children.

The spiral started with the freedom of being clothed. Plans took form in her head as she set limits on how far she would go to get high. They'd expect her to do more than she used to, with her pretty face no longer a currency she could rely on. She held her stomach as it rebelled against the idea of selling her body. She shoved her fears aside and savored the memory of her eyes rolling back in her head. Of finding peace.

"You don't want to travel that road."

His words stopped her in her tracks. She looked up at Gabriel's unimpressed face, the casual way he lounged there, inspecting his nails.

Lex cracked her knuckles. This man had been her last stop before Abaddon skinned her face. He didn't get an opinion about how she'd survive this.

He crossed the room and opened the door. "Can I get you something to eat?" He gestured for her to exit. "This isn't my home, but I think I can figure out where the kitchen is."

Great job changing the subject, asshole. She wanted him to look at her and see how useless his protection was. She closed her eyes against the tears. This angel didn't deserve her tears.

"I was wrong to let Abaddon take you."

He took a step toward her, and she held up her hand.

"I see you. I see what I've done."

"Stop." Lex choked on the word. It came out wrapped in sandpaper.

"That's why I brought you—" his explanation stopped when Lex lifted her fists and came at him—hammering his chest.

Victim Defender, she learned the term at rehab. It explained her fit of rage now. Her unquenchable anger.

She ignored the pain as she screamed, her fists pounding against him. Tears and snot and spit streamed down her face. Her wordless shouts were hoarse and carried all the hate she held for Abaddon.

Gabriel waited. His hands lifted in surrender when she finished.

She ducked away from them, knowing that with one touch, he'd immobilize her, whether physically or emotionally.

"I wouldn't." He swallowed hard, ducking his head as he studied her. "You're not done. Hit me."

Without further encouragement, her fists landed on his chin and his abdomen. Her hands fell away, only to fly up to grab his throat. She squeezed even though her fingers didn't fit around his neck. She searched his face, hating the compassion hiding under his dark brows.

Her fingers cramped, and her wounds oozed, so she let go. She stepped back, wishing she was big enough and strong enough to kill every angel.

Her palm met his cheek.

I hate you all!

She slapped his other cheek.

Gabriel caught her hand before she could scratch his face. He pulled her against his chest until she had no choice but to lean into him and catch her breath. She hated him, but she didn't hate this. Being held . . . When was the last time she'd let someone hold her?

He lifted her from the ground as if she weighed nothing and brought her back to the bed. He knelt beside her. "I know there is nothing I can say to make this better, but I'm sorry." He ran his fingers through his disheveled hair, his regret written on his face with downturned lips and brows.

She rolled away from him and covered her face with her hands.
Go. Just go.

Chapter 13

Wylie

Wylie stared into her living room with apprehension. "Did you clean the carpet?"

Rosa turned to where Wylie had leaked crimson all over the floor.

"The apartment manager hired a company to do it. There was a lot." Rosa rubbed her arms, crossed the room, and placed a vase of roses near the window. She stood back, narrowed her eyes, then readjusted the arrangement. "You've gotten more flowers in four days than I've received from Jose in the last ten years."

Wylie sat on her bed. "Don't blame your husband. It's the headgear." She tapped the plastic splint that held her nose in place. "Maybe your problem is fashion."

"Sure, sure. You look a lot cuter with your face covered like that." Rosa snorted as Wylie threw a pillow in her direction.

It fell at Wylie's feet, her laughter falling short too. "How's Lupe?"

"Mama wants to come to see you now that you're home. She wanted to see you before then, but you know . . ." She picked up the pillow and sat at the foot of Wylie's bed. "I hope you know she didn't visit because of me."

"I'm glad she didn't come. She's dealing with enough already. We all are." Wylie's attack brought Roberto and Dean's murder back to the surface.

"Did the police say the attacks were related?"

Wylie had already considered it. Her mind spun with theories, and the hospital stay prevented her from trying to work it out.

"The cop who took my statement yesterday said the two incidents seemed unrelated." She didn't believe him, though. She knew better. Everything was connected. The attacks, the healing, the killing, the things she refused to think about because she may just lose her mind. The thoughts spiraled.

Rosa broke the silence. "And what about the doctor?" She leaned into Wylie, a grin replacing the serious topic of the moment before.

"What about him?"

"He was sleeping in my chair when I got there yesterday." Rosa slapped Wylie's leg again. "Wasn't he at your housewarming party?"

"No," she said. "I mean, yes." A smile snuck onto Wylie's face. "But, no, I'm not ready."

Rosa nodded, her lack of response a sign of solidarity. "Are you sure you'll be okay by yourself?"

"I'll be fine. Thank you for all of your help."

"*De nada, chica.*" She bent over and kissed both of her cheeks. "Call me if you need anything."

Wylie waved goodbye and waited for the trauma of being alone in the place where she'd nearly died. The fear of attack didn't move her as much as the probability she'd murdered someone. She groaned as she stood, her body resistant to being vertical. She pulled out her laptop and settled at her kitchen table. She would have to learn how to control it after she figured out how she did it. It didn't matter so much when she suspected she nudged her patients in the right direction for healing, but murder? She saw those blue eyes every time hers closed.

She googled 'real witches.' The first three links were Christian websites. They described witches and their 'evils,' quoting the Bible. A YouTube video showed a psychedelic slideshow, the narrators whose only experience with magic included puffing the Magic Dragon. Next, she read two historical descriptions of women who followed their passions and burned at the stake. Not much help there.

An hour later, and six clicks into Wikipedia, she learned more than she would ever need to know about necromancers. Annoyed, she slammed her laptop shut. Researching this way was like her patients deciding they had a genetic disease because WebMD said so.

She checked her windows to ensure no one watched before pointing at her closet door. "Open." She swished her wrist like she imagined Madam Mim from the *Sword and the Stone* would. Nothing happened. Magic made no sense. How could opening a door be harder than commanding a person's lungs to forget their job? Or was this God-stuff? She wished she'd paid more attention when attending mass with Lupe.

Soon her face throbbed, and her shoulder shouted its displeasure. She thought about healing and how she'd helped so many these past months. Closing her eyes, she focused on her injuries—the torn tendons in her shoulder, the broken cartilage in her nose, her cracked ribs. Wylie waited for the familiar pain in her chest, a signal that told her the healing had worked, but her face continued to throb, and her aches remained where they belonged. She groaned in frustration.

I need a drink, or some pain meds, or both.

As if on cue, her phone belched and danced on the table. Sliding the lock screen, she read the text.

> **DAVID**
> Just got off of work. Need anything? Dinner?

> **WYLIE**
> Tequila!

> **DAVID**
> Got it. Do you like Chinese?

The phone buzzed, and she sent a thumbs-up emoji as she dug through her hospital bag for pills.

Normal-people clothes next. She'd worn none since adding the sling to her wardrobe. She looked in her drawer of shirts. None of them had those shoulder buttons she'd grown fond of. Maybe she'd start with something easier.

The jeans challenged her, but in the end, she triumphed. The bra —*impossible*. After several failed attempts at snapping it with one hand, she tossed it aside. The doorbell rang as she tried the top.

Shit!

She pranced around, failing to shove her limp arm into the sweater. The pressure of leaving David waiting on the doorstep increased her clumsiness. A sharp pain zinged from her shoulder to her hand, and she abandoned the sleeve, leaving it flopping at her side.

She ran to the door and pulled it open. David stood there. Chinese food hung from one arm and tequila under the other. His expression froze, and his eyes darted over her disheveled appearance.

"Um, hi." His lips tightened against a smile. "You look… better."

She understood why laughter danced in his eyes. Her hair stood on end in a static mess, her fly down, and she leaned to one side to compensate for her injured shoulder.

"It's not funny." She glared.

He shifted everything to one arm and flattened her hair with his hand. "There, that's better."

"I guess you can laugh as long as you help."

"If you'd adopt my haircut, you'd never have to deal with static hair." He followed her into the apartment.

She returned the favor, rubbing his scalp. "How often do you shave? I don't think I have time for all that."

He smirked and ducked away, setting his bag and bottle on the kitchen counter. "Where's your sling?" He asked as he pulled her empty sleeve.

She reached above the sink to grab two shot glasses; her wardrobe malfunctions her last priority. "Shots first."

"Fine, one shot, and then we get that sling back on you."

"Two shots." She didn't drink on the regular, but she believed in biannual therapeutic binge drinking, and she only had two days left to make it happen this year.

He held up one finger before twisting the cap and poured the brown liquid into the shot glasses.

She held hers up. *"Salud!"*

Their glasses clinked, and she poured the whole thing down her throat. David took a sip. "I know nothing about tequila. I thought I picked a good one, but it tastes horrible."

"Oh, c'mon." Warmth blossomed in her throat and chest.

He tossed it back and poured another. She held her glass up again, waiting for him to provide the toast.

"To healing."

"To healing." She tipped her head back and swallowed.

"Sling time. I'll help." He rubbed the top of his head, a smile on his face. "Amy worked hard to put that shoulder back together. She wouldn't be happy if she knew you weren't wearing your sling."

They made it to the hall before Wylie pulled David down for a kiss. "I missed this."

"I don't want to hurt you." His arms cradled her against him, leaving a kiss on her forehead.

Her lips found the collar of his shirt and paused as she breathed in his cinnamon scent. The headiness of the moment spun around them as it brought them closer. Without music, they swayed.

A dance. They danced. The kind middle schoolers did behind their teachers' backs. His hands found her waist—closing the space between them.

She looked up.

He leaned down.

Their eyes closed.

Their lips met, and they kissed with abandon. His fear and her confusion mingled to make a storm of tongues, lips, and hands.

Her soul sighed in relief as she inhaled his breath. "Thank you," she said as their passion simmered. "Before we met, I was drowning. You helped me past it. You brought light back to my life." Something Wylie didn't understand flashed across David's face. A frown? Before she could linger on it, he leaned in to kiss her again.

"I'll always be here, Wylie." Their slow dance continued until she couldn't keep her eyes open. He ran his thumb down her cheek. "Let's get that sling on before you fall asleep."

It lay in a pile on her bed, deserted during her wrestling match with the bra. He helped her to sit on the mattress, and the romance fell away as they played their parts in that nurse-doctor choreography of mechanical intimacy and getting things done in the least painful way. Everything went smoothly until Wylie caught David's hand and pressed it to her breast.

"Dr. Godwyn, why do you keep looking up at the ceiling?" She kissed his wrist.

David knelt in front of her, placing himself between her legs. His hands came around her waist, slid to her hips, and then rested on her thighs as he kissed the swell of the breast she'd offered him. "I was trying not to do this."

"Why?" Her good hand pulled at the top button of his shirt.

"Because you're hurting, and you're tired."

The button released, and her fingers traveled down to the next, loosening it with difficulty.

"It's okay." Her hand glided to the third button. Between the ibuprofen, the alcohol, and David's presence, she felt better than she'd felt since Christmas. "I'm okay."

He caught her hand. "You're not okay." He kissed her palm. "Show me where it hurts."

She laughed, but when she saw the seriousness that furrowed his brow, she pointed to her shoulder.

He kissed a trail to the injury and rested his cheek there. His fingers brushed her nipple. "Where else?"

She pointed to her opposite side, where she had three fractured ribs.

His chin slid across her skin, his eyes watching her for any sign of pain. He framed her side with his large hands and his lips feathered across the yellowing bruises the man's boot had left. She felt the wetness of his tears before she saw them. "David." She pulled at his arms, wanting to comfort him.

"No, Wylie, let me take care of you." His breath chilled the wetness he'd left behind. "Where else?"

Wylie pointed to the bruises around her throat. His nose and lips alternated the job of making a path between her breasts to her throat.

"This never should've happened." One hand found her hair, the other, her chin. He tilted her head back and kissed all the pain away.

She shivered with his touch. David made a choked sound as he settled near her ear. "Where next?"

"My face."

She closed her eyes as his hands worshiped her cheeks and forehead. With gentle fingers, he massaged away the swelling before kissing her.

"Lay down with me." She spoke against his lips.

"I don't think we should." His hand grazed her sling.

"I want you to hold me." She buried her face in his shoulder, needing him. "Can we cuddle?"

He smiled, those lips burning a place in her heart. "That sounds great."

The sun shone through the slats of Wylie's window. Now and then, people walked past, casting shadows, interrupting dust motes as they floated in their morning dance. For the first time since the attack, she awakened pain-free. She reached for David but found him sitting on the edge of the bed, holding his head in his hands.

"David?" She squinted through the light to find the same pained expression from last night disrupting his handsome face. "Is everything okay?"

"I have something to tell you."

Confused, Wylie sat up.

She flinched on the inside, a sudden fear replacing the spell of lust and peace he'd kissed into her skin the night before.

He stood. "Are you hungry?" His arms folded. "We skipped dinner last night. We should probably eat first." He turned to the kitchen.

"Wait." Wylie scrambled out of bed, his anxiety creeping under her skin. She caught his arm. "What's going on?" When he answered with silence, she searched his face, imagining the worst plausible explanation for his guilt. "Tell me."

"I've been hiding something from you."

God, he's married or has an STD. "You're scaring me."

"I want you to know I didn't have a choice." He scrubbed the top of his head with his fingers. His trip to the kitchen became him pacing in front of the bed like an apologetic puppy.

Wylie sealed her lips against her questions, her mind doing the opposite of her mouth. It shouted, begged, and threatened. She needed David. She needed him to be good and honest and all the things she'd imagined him to be. "Just say it already."

"Sit down, and I'll tell you everything."

Wylie climbed back on the bed, wishing she had a translator to read the volumes of thoughts which slumped David's shoulders and bowed his head.

He sat beside her. "You're not human."

Laughter bubbled in Wylie's throat as she convinced herself David, the serious man, was messing with her. "You're joking."

"Look in the mirror." He pointed to the one above her dresser.

"Why?" She let out another nervous giggle, a shard of doubt impaling her relief.

"Please, just humor me."

She walked over to the piece of furniture and leaned into it. Her face almost touched the glass. *Holy shit!*

Bright purple-and-green rings no longer traced circles around her widened eyes. She peeled the now-loose splint away from her nose, discovering it was half the size it'd been the previous day. Her hands went to her sides, palpating her ribs; nothing, not even a twinge. The Velcro straps of her sling crackled as she removed it, reaching for the sky. Yeah, it still ached, but not bad enough to wear the contraption.

"What the hell?" She watched David sit down. "No, seriously. What the actual hell?"

"It has nothing to do with hell."

She'd tried healing herself last night, but it didn't work. She narrowed her eyes at him. "You did this with all that kissing." She covered the smile on her face, feeling insane.

"Kind of. We did this together."

"But how?" She traced her tawny nose. The overwhelming need to laugh, or cry, or shout made her hands tremble.

"You're an angel."

She snorted. "I'm sure you say that to all the girls." She looked at him from the corner of her eye as she prodded her cheek, which lifted with a confused smile.

"I'm being serious." He folded his arms. "You're an angel."

"So, like cupid." She couldn't stop her giggles. She preferred this explanation to her witch theory, but had she believed in the supernatural before he gave one? Only half-heartedly. She stumbled as she turned to him.

He caught her and pulled her to his chest. "No, Wylie."

She leaned into him, his touch peeling away the humor she'd guarded herself with.

"You're like the biblical angels who strike down nations and fight ancient wars."

"An angel," she said, her eyes unfocused, seeing scenes from movies like *Moses*. "Bullshit."

"Wylie." His hands ran down her back.

"Then where are my wings?"

His hands stopped near her shoulder blades, where wings would originate. "You'll have to find them."

"What does that mean?" Her mouth opened and closed, then opened again. "Okay, let's pretend I believe you. How long have you known?" David's Adam's apple bobbed, and Wylie pushed past him to the kitchen when he didn't answer. "We should eat. When did we eat last? We should have eaten before all this." She gestured at the world around her. "My appetite is in the shitter now. Maybe coffee." She filled the silence with nervous chatter. All the while, her legs threatened to drop her to the ground. He'd convince her if she stopped talking. She filled her coffee pot with water, poured it into the machine, and decided to sit. Seconds later, she collapsed in a dining chair as white stars clouded her vision.

David leaned against the counter. Concern turned all of his features down. "Are you mad?" As if circling a wild beast, he carefully slunk to the chair across from her.

"It depends. Are you fucking with me?" She leaned her elbows on the table. He acknowledged the strangeness she'd ignored for so long. She felt sloppy and not quite ready for change.

He scrubbed his face with his hands. "God, I'm so serious right now. I wish I weren't the one to tell you, but I couldn't lie to you anymore. Not now that we . . ." His voice trailed off.

"Fucked?" Hysteria bubbled up in a laugh. "Not now that we've fucked, right?"

He blinked. "What we have is more than fucking."

Her vision blurred as her eyes glassed over. "That's what I thought until you confessed to knowing what's been happening to me and keeping it a secret."

"I care about you."

"You tricked me."

He shook his head. "You're angry, and I deserve it, but I didn't have a choice."

She blew out a breath, and a chasm stretched out between them. Could she ever trust him again?

"There's more."

Wylie steeled herself, very aware of the temptation to lay her head on the table and close her eyes. "Tell me."

He put his hand out, a peace offering.

"David, I can't."

His hand dropped. "Angels have a connection to humans in every story. Angels are protecting them, testing them, or delivering their prayers. But why would these powerful creatures care about humans? Why don't they take over the world?" He let his questions linger in the air, his head dipping down as he caught her eyes. Both his intensity and his words caused her to sweat and shiver simultaneously. "It's because God encased every angel's soul in a human." He squeezed her hand. "I'm your human."

She snorted and folded her arms, guarding her chest, guarding her heart. "Yeah, right." She searched his face.

His brow furrowed, and his frown deepened.

"You're serious?" The panic and the question increased the pitch of her voice. "Tell me you're messing with me." She leaned away from him, her heart racing, her mind searching for an explanation. She knew with all her being she'd healed people with her mind for over a year now, but this? The explanation made her question everything. "David, you already got me into bed. You don't need to make up stories."

"I know you feel it, the tug between us." He moved forward in his seat. "It's why being together helped you heal. I'm your charger. I'm your power. It's how I relieve the pressure on your chest. Remember, like with Jane?"

Wylie's jaw dropped. "How did you know?"

"An angel told me what to expect. I think you did most of the healing on the day of your housewarming party. It's the main reason I stayed. I saw it in your face, how much it drained you. I knew you needed me."

"You mean you didn't stay because you wanted to kiss me?" Wylie covered her cheeks with her hands.

"That was a bonus." David smiled, a sad half-smile, telling Wylie he had more to say. He locked his fingers together and looked down at his hands. "They call us muses. My father was one, and so is Jane. She's 'Uncle' Sam's muse. It runs in the family. Our job is to ground angels to the earth. I'm the part of you that exists within the limits of time. When you used your Scientia, your powers, you felt that pain." He rested his hand on his chest. "When we see each other, it transfers onto me. With my sister, with your patients, with the two angels you killed..." His mouth snapped shut as her head jerked up.

"So, I killed them?" Her heart sank. Suspecting she'd murdered someone and actually murdering someone was two different things.

She rested her head against the cool table. It felt too hot and too heavy. She held back the urge to vomit as tears dropped onto the wood. She'd taken a life, no, two. *Fuck!* Self-defense? Revenge? There was no good excuse. She would never be the same. She blew a wet, shuddering breath against the table. What if they could have prevented it? What if she'd known what she was and what she could do? No one had to die.

She closed her eyes, unable to look at David's face. "How long have you known?" The words were garbled and nearly impossible to get passed the lump in her throat.

She heard his chair shove back and then his pacing. "We moved here because of you. I didn't have a choice."

Wylie remembered her first day back at work, being introduced to him, the stern-looking young man. She respected him for his quick decisions and his kind bedside manner. She remembered running in the rain and falling into his arms. Of telling him about Roberto's death. He'd already known. He'd know about all of it. And if the men she'd killed had been angels, then he must know why. Why they'd done those things to her and her family? She sat up. "So, the man who murdered my husband and child was an angel?"

He tensed. "Yes."

"Did you know him?"

"No."

"Do you know why he did it?"

Silence.

"Tell me." Her words matched the blank slate of her face. "I need to know. I deserve to know."

"Wylie, I'm human. I don't know enough to understand it."

"Why?"

"I'm new to this, too."

"Bullshit!" Her fists came down on the table. "Why were Roberto and Dean killed?"

His body froze, his eyes distant.

Wylie stood. "Tell me."

"I think they needed you. On your own. You, without your family."

She sucked air through her teeth as if he'd stabbed her. "Needed me on my own? As if my three-year-old son and loving husband were nothing but baggage?!" David flinched. Rage straightened her back, and she clenched her fists. "Whose side are you on?"

"What do you mean?" He looked lost with his brows raised and his mouth slightly agape.

"It's a simple question. Are you on my side or theirs?"

"Wylie, there are no sides." He came to her and rubbed her upper arms.

She pushed his hands away. "There've been sides since the moment an angel killed my family." She met his honey-colored eyes. "Whose side, David?"

"Yours, always yours. I'm your soul, Wylie."

She stiffened, fighting the peace his presence brought her, even in her anger. "What does that mean?" The mere thought of walking away from the promise his words brought scared her more than his lies of omission.

"It means when you're hurting, I can fix you. When you're lost, I can find you." His hand hovered next to her cheek. "We may not have chosen this, but at least we're not alone in it."

Wylie planted her hand on his chest, and if it weren't for the heat that filled her every time they touched, she would've pushed him. She should push him. Instead, his warmth melted the anger that lined her face. Her fingers glided to his neck. "Alone?" The contrast of her ochre skin against his seashell-pink tones mesmerized her. "I was never alone before you came." She lifted her thumb to the cleft in his chin. "Why do I want to hurt you right now?"

"Wylie, I—"

"No, David." She pushed her forehead into his chest, her arms snaking around his neck. "Let me think for a minute." She wanted to hate him for hiding the truth from her. From delaying her understanding of what had happened the night her husband caught bullets with his back as he tried to save their child. Wylie's cheek rode the rock of his chest as his lungs filled, listening to his heart. Her eyes scrunched closed as she breathed him in.

She hated him and needed him in equal parts, and maybe it was because she thought so much clearer with her body against his. She'd noticed it long before now. The more she touched him, the higher she flew. Soaring in those positive emotions she'd stamped down until they barely broke the surface anymore. He'd acted as caffeine in the middle of the night, Xanax when panic hit her, and pain relief when everything else failed. "You should leave."

"Wylie, please. I didn't mean—"

Raising her hand to stop his explanation, she looked him in the eye. "I can't think with you here. You broke my trust. You lulled me into this false sense of security, but I should be mad. I need to be mad right now."

His shoulders slumped, and he nodded. "I never wanted to hurt you."

"David, go." She could only keep her tears at bay for a little longer.

"Everything that has happened between us. Everything I've said. It's all been true."

She turned her head. The desperation in his voice made her wince. She couldn't look at him. Her front door opened and shut, and a low wail escaped her lips.

Chapter 14

When Wylie stopped crying, she itched to get out of her apartment. She didn't know where she'd go, but her feet needed the sidewalk. Ready to pay homage to the pavement gods, she shimmied into her leggings and headed to her closet for her distance shoes.

Wylie never found the shoes. She didn't recognize the first box she pulled down. She discovered the lid covered in a collage of Mod Podged pictures. She'd never seen it before but suspected her mother-in-law of placing it there.

Guadalupe, you're the real angel. The box smelled like Roberto's cologne. With greedy hands, she reached for an envelope. Holding her breath, she freed the fragile contents.

>The sound of rain reminds me of you
>It is the tangible sound of my emotions
>When I am with you
>When I am without you
>Like a million drums
>Tapping out the rhythm of life
>Como mi Corazon
>Cuando veo tu sonrisa
>Como mi alma
>Cuando tengo tus besos
>Like the tears
>At night

Like my tears

The familiarity of Roberto's scribbled hand made her breath catch. Written on a Starbucks napkin, a darkened ring cut through the poem. The stain came from a cup, a cup his lips had touched. She kissed the mark.

In the envelope remained the pressed stem of a dandelion. She'd spent the wish the day she received it in the mail. Back when Roberto and her lived states apart as they decided if the fires of love were worth all the damn compromise. The dandelion hadn't survived the whirlwind of the last decade, and neither had the man, but his words —they'd live as long as she did. She missed her poet husband.

She reached for a white stockinet. A nurse had tied a piece of rainbow yarn into a bow at the top to make a hat. She pressed it to her nose, trying to imagine the smell of Dean as an infant.

My boys.

Matching hospital bracelets, a birth announcement, tickets to Ozzfest, another poem, and, *oh* . . . a moan escaped her lips. Roberto's wedding ring.

She thought she'd buried him with it on. She slid it onto her thumb, cherishing the feel of the cold metal. The gold band matched the ring that hugged her finger. *Roberto, you weren't supposed to take this off.* She lay on her side, twisting the ring around her thumb. Around and around. Just like her mind.

The box distracted her from the problem at hand: angels. She wished her best friend were there so she could ask him what he thought, and that's when she decided where she needed to go. Wearing Roberto's ring on her thumb, she pulled on her old shoes and stepped out of her apartment with her earbuds at a deafening volume.

Her feet hit the ground to the beat of the song.

Angels.

Holy hell, I'm an angel.

Calling herself one was as unbelievable as hearing it from David. Her thighs burned as she met her first incline and entered Millionaire Mile. Emerald elms and scarlet oaks lined the historic streets, separating the pedestrians from the ultra-rich. Seattle's founders settled here. Thinking of their ghosts brought her back to Roberto and what he'd say. He'd ask her if there'd been clues in her childhood.

There were none. Not a single clue. If anything, she experienced the opposite. Life gave her family nothing for free. Nothing fell into place because they wished for it. Her mom and dad adopted her as an infant, working hard in blue-collar jobs. Her adoption was their remedy to their empty nest syndrome. Linda and Adam's unspent love needed a child to invest in, and they chose Wylie. They did the paperwork and started over. Wylie confronted her mother when she figured it out. The memory was colder than the howling wind as she crossed the University bridge— the frigid air crisp in her lungs.

Her parents raised her to be active and smart. They raised her to be confident and kind. She was lucky they'd lived to their eighties. They stayed long enough to see her wedding. Mom even made it to Dean's first birthday. What lesson did they leave her with? To make good choices and work hard for her dreams to come true.

Over a night of tequila and angels, everything collapsed.

HONK!

Her skin attempted to jump off her body as a man in a forest-green Subaru lay on his horn. Halfway through an ignored stop sign, the man's bumper inches from her.

"Asshole," she mouthed, gathering her wits and moving out of the way. Back on the sidewalk, her heart slamming in her chest, she raised her middle finger, hoping the man would catch it in his rearview mirror.

Adrenaline tinged her thoughts with panic. Her feet regained their rhythm, and her quickened pulse made her fingers throb.

Her heart screamed while she summed up her life in memories as she ran up one last hill. Roberto's hands on her hips as they danced. Dean's chubby-cheeked smiles as he giggled under a barrage of belly raspberries. The way her heart mimicked a run when her foot rested on David's as they watched a show with Jane.

She crested a hill and ran into Calvary Cemetery in search of her husband. What she found instead was a man on one knee before

Roberto's gravestone, his hood pulled up. His eyes were closed as he faced the sky, a pair of human-sized dove wings folded at his back. Wylie's foot caught a rock, and she went down with the velocity of her running pace, skidding over the rocks on hands and knees. She rolled onto her bottom and looked down at her palms. They hurt, but they weren't bleeding.

The man crouched in front of her. "Are you okay?"

Her head lifted, and moss-green eyes met hers. "Uncle Sam?" His face was all wrong, maybe twenty years younger than it'd been on Christmas Day. The lines had vanished, along with the gray hairs at his temples.

"My name is Samael."

Wylie scooted back, her hands skidding along the rocks as her bottom dragged. "What do you want?" She held up her hands defensively.

Samael flinched. "I'm not here to harm you."

"Then, why?"

"David told me what he did." His jaw twitched. "I thought you might have some questions." He put out his hands for her to take. "I know how you like to come here when you think."

Wylie stared at his offered hands. The magnetic pull she'd felt the first time they'd met reverberated under her skin. She took them, and he lifted her to her feet like she weighed nothing. They stared at each other for a beat before Wylie let go. Her mind rushed back to the problem at hand. If this man with shoulder-length hair and powerful jaw was "Uncle Sam," then he was someone she shouldn't trust.

"I thought David hated you."

He raised one of his prominent brows. "David told you about that?"

She nodded in reply. "So, Jane is your—" Wylie stopped to think of the word David used.

"My muse." Samael completed the sentence for her.

"And that's also part of the reason David hates you?"

"Partly. Yes." Samael replied through gritted teeth.

Noticing his stiffened shoulders, Wylie changed the subject and gestured to Roberto's grave. "What were you doing?"

"Come, I'll show you." Taking her hand, he pulled her to where she'd buried her husband and son. He sat, and his calloused fingers combed the grass. "Sit."

The pull between them intensified, and she did as she was told.

"Now, press one hand into the ground and give me the other."

Again, she complied without deciding to.

"Close your eyes." His warm fingers interlaced hers.

Behind the blackness, her brain churned with visions of Roberto with Dean on his shoulders. A hum traveled from his hand through her body and down her other arm into the earth. Dean looked older. Roberto wore his hair longer than he ever did in life. He smiled up at her. His ring around her thumb burned, and she jerked her hand free of Samael. The circuit broke, and daylight blinded her as her eyes opened.

She touched the wetness on her face and looked at her glistening fingers. "What was that?"

"We visited them." Samael turned his head, looking into the horizon.

Wylie's face crumpled, her hands coming up to cover the bittersweet knowledge that they were happy in heaven. She'd hoped they would be, just like everyone else that lost someone hoped, but witnessing their wholeness and their safety was more than she'd ever expected to experience. "This means the world."

Samael grunted and shifted where he sat. "I come here when I miss them."

"You miss them?"

Samael nodded, turning to look at her. Without his wings, he passed as a human. "We loved them, Wylie. We all loved them. Dean was a miracle. The first child to be born from an angel. The heavens rejoiced the day he entered the world and mourned when he left us."

They sat in silence, her mind racing in circles. The Seattle sky threatened to cry with Wylie as a chill wind swept past her. She shivered, disbelief making her more numb than the cold.

"Say I believe you, then answer me this: why did an angel kill them?"

"It's not what you think."

"It's not?" Her voice took on an edge. She wanted to believe him. Being an angel would be so much easier if it were true.

"It's hard to explain." He stood, offering her his hand again. "I could show you?"

Wylie ignored his outstretched hand. "Show me what?" But even as she asked, she had a terrible feeling she knew what he meant.

"There are angels who could take you back and show you what happened."

She hugged herself. This time, the coldness settling over her had nothing to do with the weather. It cut through her running tee. "No, never, just tell me."

Samael sighed, shrugging off his jean jacket and placing it over her shoulder. "There are rebel angels. Angels that don't like you and what you represent."

"And what do I represent?"

Samael's jaw ticked. "You represent the end of the world."

An explosion sounded behind him. Wylie let out a cry of surprise and Samael dove on top of her. Covering her body with his, just as he'd done for Jane. The broad planes of his chest stole her breath, and not because of his weight. Without thinking, she ran a hand down his arm, appreciating his build. She lifted her eyes to find moss-green ones staring back. Behind him, the sky lit up with red starbursts. She cleared her throat, "It was a firework." She'd forgotten about New Year's Eve. A group of teenagers gathered at the cemetery's edge with sparklers and paper bag-wrapped bottles.

Breaking eye contact, Samael sat back on his heels and pulled Wylie upright. "I thought—"

"You thought someone was trying to explode me." Wylie pulled the lapels of his jacket tighter around her shoulders. "Am I in danger?"

"Hmph, this is why David was told not to tell you. I'd hoped to eliminate the threat first so you wouldn't have to worry."

"Leaving me in the dark almost got me murdered." The anger

returned, redirecting it at the angel before her. "If I'd known to be worried, my family may still be alive." And for the millionth time, she wished she would have stayed home that night. "I would have stayed home that day."

"And there would have been one more death that night."

"I don't need you to make my fucking decisions."

Samael gripped her shoulders and squeezed until her red-rimmed eyes met his. "I will tell you what my superior told me." His head dipped down. His breath brushed her face. "It was not your fault."

Wylie yanked herself free and tossed the angel's jacket onto the ground. "You don't know that." Two steps back, her breaths became gasps. "You. Can't. Know. That."

He folded his arms. "I can."

Tired of all the lies and secrets, she bolted, running into the setting sun. Her only goal was to sprint so fast that she couldn't think anymore.

Chapter 15

Lex

Gabriel arrived thirty minutes ago, but Lex refused to see him. She hadn't spoken since she'd screamed at the bastard weeks before, and she didn't plan to do so now. The angel waited in the living room. Lex didn't care. The fucker could wait for hell to freeze. Being a nice angel didn't change the fact he was an angel, and she suspected his niceness was all an act.

Two knocks sounded on her door. "Let's talk."

She'd locked the fancy clear door knob and planted herself on the pink throne of the child's room they'd given her while she recovered. The safe house belonged to a large family of muses Gabriel had freed from their angels with some mysterious power. She heard it was a painful process with lifelong side effects. It all made her think of a cult. They talked about him like he was some kind of muse savior.

The doorknob rattled. "I have a gift for you, *ma petite rêleuse*."

She crossed her eyes. Fuck him and his sexy French.

"I will kick the door down."

Lex's grip tightened on the arms of her throne.

With a crunch, the door caved in. The metal lock jingled as it hit the wood floor. Gabriel patted his hair and took a deep breath through his nose. His usual smile returned when he stepped into the room. "Hello, Alexis." He lifted his hands with an innocent shrug.

Lex glowered at him. The angel stood a foot and a half taller than her, which meant she needed to be a foot and a half angrier.

He set his finger to his temples. "I'm a friend. There is no need to be angry."

Leave me alone, douchebag.

"C'mon, hellcat, I have a gift for you."

She folded her arms, rested her head against the chair back, and closed her eyes. The angel would fuck himself before she'd budge.

"I see how it is." He removed his jacket, folded it, and lay it on the bed.

She squirmed as he unbuttoned his collar and then the cuffs of his sleeve, rolling them up his muscular forearms.

"Excuse me." He bent over her and grabbed the arms of the chair, sliding it away from the wall. "I'm not going to touch you. I can tell you don't want that. But you need to see what I've brought, so we're doing things the hard way." He raised one brow. "Ready?" He didn't wait for an answer. He rounded the chair and lifted it.

Lex held on tight, worried the neanderthal would drop her. *Put me down, you fucking bastard!*

His low chuckle tickled her ear.

It's not funny, asshole. She lifted her feet onto the chair, preparing to spring off.

"We're just heading outside, *cher*. Please don't jump." He carried the chair out of the room, through the hall, and to the front door where one of his men stood ominously. "Open it, Todd." The man opened the door, and Gabriel carried her into the sunlight.

She covered her eyes; she hadn't left "her" room except to use the restroom. The fresh air felt so good in her lungs, even if she tasted the exhaust of his running limousine. He placed her before the passenger door and tapped on the window. Abaddon's head lifted, and a trickle of dried blood left a trail from his mangled nose to his ruined mouth. His head turned, and their eyes connected. He wore his Vietnamese flesh. Lex wondered if his original features reflected her ancestor's faces or the other way around. His broad nose and double lids, dark skin, and black hair filled Lex with nostalgia for the homeland she'd never visited.

"You don't look at her." Gabriel pointed away from Lex, and Abaddon's head snapped forward.

Lex peeled her fingers from the arms of her chair. Color returned to her knuckles. Rage and fear fought each other with knives in her belly. Rage won. How dare they? She stood, knowing that if Abaddon could hurt her, he would have by now. She glared at Gabriel. Why would he expose her to this sack of shit? She shouldn't be surprised, but a tiny part of her had hoped he was different.

Gabriel's eyes softened. "It's not what you think, *cher*. I promise he will never hurt you again."

Ignoring Gabriel, she took a hold of the plastic chair and swung. It smashed into the vehicle, vibrating in her hand with each impact. The Scientia under her skin rushed to her hands and leaked into her weapon. Soon, they left dents instead of scratches. Placing the chair next to the front wheel, she climbed onto the hood and lifted it. She roared at Abaddon and raised her weapon above her head. The glass shattered, raining down on Abaddon with a hundred slices.

A slow clap brought Lex out of her frenzy. Gabriel stood where she'd left him. He nodded with a half-smile. "Did you know that glass was bulletproof?"

Her eyes settled on Abaddon. He bled from multiple cuts on his face and forearms. She resisted the urge to scrabble off the car and into his arms. She touched her raw forehead to remind herself why she'd never do that again.

"What would you like for me to do with him?"

Her chest heaved, and she raised her arms to open her lungs. "Kill. Him." Her ravaged vocal cords managed two words between pants.

"Come here." He put out his hand to help her down. She took it and jumped. His other hand caught her hip to stabilize her as she landed. He escorted her to the other side of the sidewalk. "Do you want him to suffer?"

"Alexis, don't do this to me," Abaddon begged. "Remember, you're my good girl. You wouldn't—"

Lex turned to Gabriel. *Make it hurt.*

Gabriel smirked and lifted his hand. "I warned you, Abaddon. We treat our muses with kindness." He fisted his hand and Abaddon crumpled into himself. Bones snapped as he wailed.

Lex watched, fighting the small part of herself which still

loved him.

"Tell me when."

At first, Lex didn't understand what Gabriel meant, but then one of Abaddon's eyes popped out and his screams turned into wild gurgles. *Do it.*

Gabriel rotated his wrist, and Abaddon's neck snapped. "Todd," Gabriel called over his shoulder. "This one is going to need water on it. We don't want the bastard coming back."

"Yes, sir."

He turned back to Lex, "Can we talk now?"

She couldn't talk. She'd tried, sitting in the princess room. The sounds she made didn't belong there. Her voice only came out as a high-pitched scream or raspy grumble.

"Let me rephrase. I want to make you an offer."

She looked at the door of the house Gabriel carried her from. The place was too homey, too perfect. She felt like a stain inside that cookie-cutter house. With Abaddon gone, she had no reason to hide. She walked past Gabriel's ruined car with Abaddon's unrecognizable body and down the long country driveway.

The exhilaration of freedom drained from her with every step. She'd just watched her angel die. He was dead. That was the last time she'd see the beautiful face he'd made to remind her of her mother's homeland. He'd never . . . What the fuck did he ever do for her? She was lucky he hadn't killed her. She was still unclear how she'd escaped him and ended up with Gabriel.

"You exploded."

Exploded?

"You brought down half a block."

She picked up her pace, uncertain of what to make of this information. The fucker was about to peel her face off and she'd *exploded*. She didn't think she'd be able to use the Scientia. There was nothing about being able to in the old family journal, but she'd felt it coursing through her when she broke that windshield with a plastic chair.

"I felt it. That's exactly what you did. The question is, how?"

Other than her scars and her voice, she didn't feel different. The ever-present buzz of power grew stronger and maybe that was the cause, without her angel drawing the Scientia off of her, it had nowhere else to go. The wind cut through her dress, but it didn't hold the icy touch Portland wind carried. Maybe she would stay in this state until summer. If she did, she needed to call her father and tell him she was alright. He probably thought she was using again. It hurt her to imagine his heartbreak. He'd saved her from strip clubs and alleyways, hospitals and halfway homes. How much more pain could the man take? These ruminations made her want to give him a real reason to be heartbroken. She palpated the veins on her arm.

"Why waste your abilities on such a life when you could work for me?"

She'd spent most of her life serving a higher power, she wasn't interested in trading her old one in for a newer model.

Gabriel snorted but said nothing, instead he pulled out a pack of cigarettes and lit up. She didn't have to see it to know what he was doing, the sound of the pack opening, the flint wheel, the flame, and his relieved inhale. She felt his Scientia relax; heard his footfalls slow.

The fucking angel's dress shoes clicked while her bare feet whispered across the pavement. This angel could have passed for a human in every way. Not like Abaddon, whose arsenal of emotions included anger and vengefulness to caring, and not much more. Abaddon could have talked Lex into anything, but Gabriel didn't seem interested in pandering.

"I want to help you learn how to use your new powers," he said, filling the silence between them.

A sharp stab in the bottom of her foot interrupted her plans to ignore the man. "Argh." She hissed and took the injured foot in her hands. She saw a speck of black under her skin and laughed. It felt like a fucking two-by-four.

"Here, let me help." He went down on a knee, without a thought for his suit, and opened his hands to her expectantly. "Angels may not be able to heal muses, but I can pull out a splinter." He looked up at her through his dark lashes and gave her one of his killer smiles, his cigarette hanging off the side of his lip.

She tried not to focus on what his smile did to her insides while she used his shoulder for balance as she set her foot in his hand. Then as punishment for confusing her, she took his cigarette. She took in a puff, her head lolling back.

"Lexy—can I call you Lexy?" He didn't pause for her response. "Why don't you come with me and see the compound? You can decide what you want to do there." He lifted his brows, listening for her thoughts.

Lex frowned at the part of her that'd already caved. *How long do I have to decide?*

"As long as you need, *cher*." He adjusted her foot in his hands and narrowed his eyes at the offending object. "Now, count to three."

One. Two. Fuck!

Lex was sitting on a rock with the last of Gabriel's cigarette between her lips when the Hummer limousine arrived. She'd never been this close to one before, circling it before she entered. This left Todd holding the door and Gabriel leaning against the vehicle, watching. Once inside, she lay flat on the leather, belly down. The seats were so soft she wanted to swim in them. She might as well swim in a pile of money.

So far, what she'd seen of Gabriel's wealth led her to believe the asshole was the bad guy.

Gabriel barked a laugh and slid a seat closer to Lex.

Todd's head whipped up, his hand going for his gun. Gabriel tapped the side of his head and pointed at Lex.

Todd nodded and leaned back into his nap.

People are going to think you're crazy if you keep reading my mind.

"At least they won't think I'm the bad guy."

Lex nuzzled her face into the leather. *Only bad guys spent this much on a car.*

"What about Batman?"

She shrugged and looked out the window. *Where are your gadgets?* She imagined Gabriel in leather and forced the image out of her head as her body heated.

"I don't need gadgets. I have wings."

Lex rolled her eyes.

"They are better than gadgets, *ma petite rêleuse*." Gabriel followed Lex's line of sight out of the window. "So, what do you think of Baton Rouge?"

Lex wiped the sweat from her forehead and reminded herself this was winter weather.

"We're almost home." He leaned back, his arm resting along the back of her seat.

Her blinks slowed until her eyes stayed closed, and sleep claimed her.

Lex felt a hand remove the locks that hung over her face. "Lexy." Her name spoken with that velvet voice had her pressing her thighs together.

Her eyes fluttered open, confused. She stared at the leather seats. She wiped the drool off her cheek as her brain caught up with her body. *This is Gabriel's Hummer.* She leaned back. *And that's Gabriel.* Her body jerked up in surprise. She'd been using his thigh as a pillow. Lex scrambled to the end of the bench seat, her eyes finding the wet patch of drool on his pants. Her cheeks flushed, and she squirmed in her seat.

Gabriel offered a soft smile, "Nothing a bit of water won't take care of, *cher*. You were so peaceful; I didn't dare move." He pointed at the building he lived in. "We're here."

Todd opened the door and held out his hand to her. She shook her head and stepped out unassisted. The place looked the same as she remembered—miles of manicured lawn, a mass of enormous buildings with parapets. Gabriel came to her side, his elbow out for her to grab.

She slept in his lap, why not get a little more handsy? Her fingers curled around his forearm, her palms zinging with the touch.

A smug smile bloomed on the bastard's face, so she pinched him and laughed when he side-eyed her.

"Let's get you settled, *mon cher.*"

Through the gravel and up the grand stairs, they found a room full of angels waiting for them.

The chatter in the room stopped as they entered. Lex's hand dropped and turned into a fist at her side, her eyes landing on a vase near the front door. She could use it as a weapon.

"Not that vase, hellcat, it cost more than the car." Gabriel reached under his jacket and pulled out a gun, handing it to Lex. "This would work much better, anyway." He lifted his chin and addressed the angels. "This is Alexis. She's considering a position here as a consultant."

Binah, the one angel Lex knew in the group, broke into laughter. "And is hellcat her nickname? Because it's perfect for her and I want one next." She walked up to Lex and put out a hand. "Welcome back. You look different." Binah smirked at her scars.

Gabriel stepped in front of Lex and took Binah's hand. Lex couldn't see over Gabriel's shoulder but she heard the angel gasp in pain.

"Hands off. No one touches our Alexis. No one speaks to her without my permission." Another gasp, accompanied by a sickening crunch. "Have I made myself clear?"

There were "yes, sirs" and "yes, Gabriel" and one "of course." Lex flushed. Some primal part of her was very attracted to his protectiveness. She rubbed the gun between her hands. The cool metal warmed under her touch. Maybe she could trust him.

The angels before her stood at attention, their respect for Gabriel obvious in the way they squared their shoulders for him, and in the way they gathered for him. She'd never seen so many angels in one place. Their jobs were pretty solitary from what she'd understood.

Gabriel returned to Lex's side as he checked his watch. "I rarely have such a big welcoming party, but we need to plan a business trip we're taking later tonight."

Now? Not that I care. She held back her thoughts as her body screamed for him not to leave her yet.

"Yes, unfortunately." Gabriel gestured at Binah. "You know Binah, she's my . . . for lack of a better term, my spymaster. Oh, and she also thinks she's funny. Please, let me know if any of her jokes are a little too offensive."

Lex lifted her chin, her eyes meeting Binah's. Lex had no problem letting the bitch know herself. She showed the angel her middle finger with a grin and a glare. She'd treat this moment like the streets. Gabriel inspired her. She couldn't scare them as he had, but she could act batshit crazy. Everyone took a pause when faced with a bit of mental instability.

"And that." Gabriel pointed at a tall angel with a cherubic face. He was all baby cheeks and blond curls. "That is Leliel. He's an archangel and a new recruit. He's leaving now. Right?" The boy nodded and then disappeared.

"And those two are Jophiel and Zuriel."

Lex wondered if the two had posed for any famous artwork throughout history. In their muscle beaters and board shorts, it was hard not to notice every ridge of their bodies.

"They are brothers and old as dirt, but you'd never know because they're both goofballs."

They saluted her with smirks on their faces. "Oh, and they read minds."

Shit!

Their smiles widened, but neither said a word.

Even as Lex's cheeks burned, she winked, not dropping her façade for a second.

"Todd, can you show Lex to her rooms?"

Todd tried the elbow thing.

Lex's eyes narrowed. *Don't even fucking think it, Todd.* She raised her brows and waited for him to show her the way.

"Goodbye, *cher*. When we return, I'll give you a proper tour of the place."

Like I give a fuck, Gabriel.

"Rest well, *ma petite rêleuse*."

Chapter 16

Samael

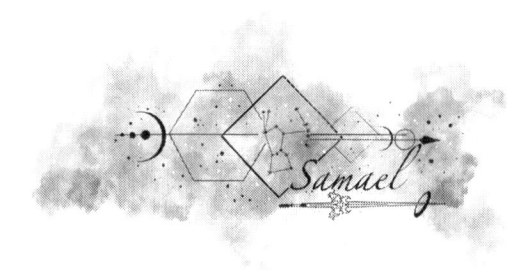

Sweat slid down Laoth's female face. She lunged low, her leathery wings twitched as Samael blocked her blow. Their steel clashed and she gasped.

Samael advanced, bringing his sword down, again and again, sending her into defense as she fell back a step at a time.

Her arms shook as her blade held off Samael's onslaught. "*Skitr!*" Laoth's sword clattered to the ground as she tripped, landing on her bottom. She shook out her hands. "I hate practicing with you, by the way."

"Earlier today you said practicing with anyone else was too easy." Samael sheathed his blade and reached for Laoth.

"It wouldn't hurt to let me win." She glared at him as she took his hand.

"It would." He pulled Laoth to her feet.

"*Bacraut.*"

Samael barked a laugh. "You and your Ostmen language. They knew how to make words profane."

"It's true." Laoth picked up her blade, a sly smile on her face. "We were known for much more."

"True." Samael returned to his side of the circle.

Laoth wiped the sweat out of her eyes, leaving horizontal mascara lines across her face. She caught her breath. "I don't have any new answers for you. For the last six months, I've watched the area. I can't get in."

"What about those who come and go?" Samael raised a brow.

"They're mostly muses and know as little as Brandon does." Laoth found her place and stretched her shoulders.

"I understand Gabriel's separating them from angels, but what's the point of keeping them so close? He can't possibly need all their Scientia."

She switched arms, her wings acting as a counterweight for her stretch. "Maybe we can get closer to him through politics or money. I'll have to talk to a Power."

"Mariam is in Louisiana. She might be a good contact." He thought of the angel and how she always wore mature female faces. "You remember her. She's one of the oldest Powers in the area. I believe she's a nun." Her influence in the political spheres of New Orleans allowed Mariam to plant ideas in all the right ears.

Laoth rolled her eyes. "Why would a Power choose to be part of a religion anymore?"

"Rome will never stop being Rome, sister."

"Touché."

"And then there's Dumah. Virtues are always helpful." Samael rubbed his temples, feeling a human ache his body adopted. "I spoke to her just yesterday. She's a reliable resource. Have you spoken to her?"

"Not yet, but I will."

"I'm heading back to Seattle after this."

Laoth's head snapped up. "But I need you here." Her hands rested on her hilt. "I can't do this alone. Gabriel is raising an army to prevent the apocalypse. We need to be prepared."

"Wylie is the Apocalypse. There's no point in this unless she's safe."

"Have you considered that her death might be what needs to happen?" Laoth's wings spread as if in emphasis.

"The prophecy—"

"Means nothing to angels with freedom."

"Laoth, I trust you to discover their plan without me." Samael shook his head as he crossed their circle. "Your petulance must stop."

Samael placed his hand on her shoulder. "You're my most trusted Archangel. And also, my cleverest. I have faith in you."

Laoth looked away. "You just want to return to Wylie."

"She will fight this battle, not us old creatures with our silly words. We must protect her until she comes into her power." Samael gave her his back as he returned to his side of the circle.

"She can protect herself," Laoth scoffed. "Wylie's already killed two of my brothers."

"She didn—"

"*Geysa!*" Laoth launched at Samael, her sword in her hand before she finished her command to fight.

Samael spun and parried, his blade appearing where it had not been an instant before. The song of their swords ricocheted off the walls.

Laoth's blade ran across Samael's bicep, drawing a red line on his white shirt.

Samael hissed, his eyes widening, and he dodged a blow, smacking Laoth with the flat of his sword as she fell forward with the force of her attack.

Laoth spun and charged.

Samael ducked under another assault, this time bringing his sword down, burying the tip into Laoth's foot. She screamed, and he lifted his sword, striking her chin with the hilt. The force brought her off the ground.

"What was that for?" Laoth touched her bloody face.

Samael's ragged breaths stopped as his mind caught up with his body. His sword clambered as it landed beside him. "Laoth, I . . ."

"You're changing, and I bet it's Armageddon causing it."

Samael wiped the sweat from his forehead and looked at it glistening on his fingers. He'd never allowed this body to sweat before.

"Gabriel has the same effect on his followers." She spat blood on the ground as she stood. "Are these two making angels more human?"

Samael placed his wings between his friend and himself.

"The things she can do as an untrained angel are astonishing. It's time she came to the Heavenly Planes and learned her place."

Samael shook his head as he found another emotion swirling in his gut. Shame. He felt ashamed. He should prepare God's army for the last days, not watch Armageddon. Not make his friends bleed.

"At least consider it."

"I will, but first, I must see my muse." And with gritted teeth, he admitted it. "I think Wylie affects me more when my Scientia is low."

"It's up to you, but if she changes you like this, I could teach her . . ."

"No." Whether Laoth heard his response, he'd never know. He projected himself to Seattle and appeared in the park across the street from his muse's apartment. He followed the lines of the building with his eyes, searching for her window. *David's home.* He'd wait until he left to get any closer.

Why did he, an ancient being, need to listen to that man? He'd led men into battle in the morning and buried them later that day. He deserved more respect. He'd punished men who'd ordered the death of millions. He'd watched the lives of prophets brighten the world and fizzle out. But here he sat, growing wet with rain as he waited to gain the energy he needed to fight.

Only for Jacob's sake did he ignore David's disrespect. Missing his former muse didn't stop him from regretting the oath he took to protect the man's children. Samael would do anything for Jane, but David, the man-child, would be his burden for a lifetime.

Samael looked into the bruised sky and shook his head. He'd been alive for too long. His job was an endless chess game, placing each precious piece in its most proficient square, only to sacrifice it in the next move. Commanding his brothers and sisters became more difficult the closer they got to the end. They'd lost so many because one man could not withstand temptation.

Some events have irreversible effects. They start as innocent as snowflakes, delicate and fast to disappear. Unless they learn to stick together, gathering power and momentum as they grow into an avalanche of war and genocide, changing the trajectories of every being on earth. This mission started with such an event. The day Adam and Eve left Eden for the earth.

Samael stepped before his fellow Dominions, approaching the most sacred of angels. He bowed so low he lay on his belly. "Great Seraphim, I volunteer to bring our humans back." He spoke to the floor, dirt on his lips, his face touching the earth. Behind him, his equals held their right forearms over their eyes in reverence.

The four Seraphim formed a row, their feet shoulder-width apart, their arms folded across their chests. They stood sentry before the wooden door springing from the ground, solitary in a field of flowers. The wood panels rose forever, reaching straight into the heavens, with no sign of what force held them in place.

The Seraphim spoke at once.

> "Dominion Samael,
> From the water, she will rise
> Born of Death
> Raised in Love
> Above her, her white horse
> He will find her
> She will break him
> Beside her, the red one
> He will wake her
> She will hate him
> Before her, the black horse
> He will protect her
> She will save him
> Behind her, her pale one
> He will betray her
> She will forgive him
> Angel, Fallen, human, Muse
> They will gather
> For she is Armageddon
> The entrance to heaven"

Samael had found her after millennia of searching. He knew God always meant for him to be her white horse. He'd assumed she hid, living as a human of average position. He didn't realize she was yet to be born until the power exchange between her muses. The terrifying realization amplified his urgency. Angels were not born. Thrones made them. Carving them out of the earth, not carrying them in a womb.

He'd botched his first meeting with Wylie. He wondered if the healer would fight for his cause. And if she did, would he have enough energy to fight at her side?

Samael stood when he saw David walk his bicycle out of his apartment's parking garage. He waited while David climbed onto his bike and pedaled away, so he could get closer to his muse.

Crossing the street, he stopped short of entering the building. Footfalls from the park, too soft to be a human's gait, stopped him.

"Who dares follow me?" Samael said, knowing an angel, even a lesser one, would hear his words if not his thoughts. Muffled slaps sounded as the being retreated.

A towheaded angel sprinted away. He turned to check behind him just as Samael appeared, his outstretched arm stopping the male by his throat. He folded his wings around the younger angel as he yanked the male's corded neck, crushing the blond's head against his side.

"Who are you?" The boy's magic felt like a cat's tongue against his skin. Samael loosened his grip, opening his wings and leaning away from the swell of corrupted Scientia.

"I'm Leleil."

"Why are you here?" Samael let go and stepped back in disgust.

Leleil flicked a blade from his sleeve and lunged.

Samael caught the male's arm and squeezed, glaring at the insignificant weapon.

"Do you not know who I am?" Samael pulled the dagger from Leleil's hand. "Your little pocket knife won't hurt me." He turned the blade on himself and planted it in his abdomen.

They looked down at the hilt where it stuck out of his stomach. Leleil's eyes widened with disbelief. Samael smirked.

"Don't come at me with your silly toys." He pulled the blade free and tossed it into a puddle. "Who sent you?" Samael ran his hand over his wound and gripped the back of the angel's neck, leaving a handprint as he pulled their foreheads together. "Why are you here?"

Leleil's eyes narrowed, his dripping hair their only barrier. "Gabriel will put your monster out of her misery. Wylie will die."

A jolt of fury ran down his spine at the sound of her name. His body moved faster than his mind could follow. With his hand still holding Leleil's neck, Samael wrenched the angel up and planted him face-first into the ground. Water splashed up around them. The mud welcomed Leleil as Samael straightened and stomped on the angel's back.

Samael fought to contain his rage. With a quick upstroke of his wings, he flung the rain that enveloped him away in irritation. He reached down to pull Leleil back to his feet. The male gasped, his face dripping with clumps of grass and dirt. Samael forced his thoughts into Leleil's mind.

Brother, tell me why you're here, and I will return you to our Throne for an honorable rebirth.

"I only answer to Gabriel. And he will snuff out that blasphemous freak you call an angel." Spit flew from his mouth. "He will pull off her wings and eat them." Leleil shared the image of a man in a suit tearing off Wylie's wings with a heel planted on her back as he pulled.

Fury unglued Samael. Every muscle in his body tensed. Before he could stop himself, he'd flung the male backward, sending him flying toward the street.

The windshield of a bus caught the body, shattering the glass. The bus swerved. Horns blared as multiple cars crunched their noses under its long carriage, lifting it onto its side and pushing it forward. Metal screeched and sparked as the asphalt grated against the pile of totaled vehicles. Horns blasted, car doors opened, and cries filled the air.

Samael rocked on his heels, shocked. He'd lost control. Trembling, weak, he stared at the horror he'd caused with his anger.

He stumbled into the accident, the smell of gasoline and death making him dizzy. Children cried, women wept, and men wailed.

An accusatory rain pelted him as he climbed the side of the bus. He found hands reaching skyward under a busted window. One at a time, he lifted the humans to safety. Jutting glass bit into his arms, and his blood rained.

Sirens approached as he cleared the path. He jumped into the bus, and debris crunched under his boots. He followed the sound of heartbeats, scanning the wreckage. One at a time, he handed the first responders the wounded, sending them up with prayers for forgiveness. Each survivor added another drop into his overflowing bucket of guilt.

One:

A woman in her seventies shook as her tiny form folded into him.

Two:

An unconscious teenager whose bike helmet saved him from being scalped

Three:

The driver.

He was the hardest one to retrieve. Slumped over the steering wheel and buckled in, he sat unmoving. Leleil lay dead, the top half of his body tangled with the driver and the steering wheel. The young angel's eyes stared up unblinking, his face fixed in terror.

Samael turned back for the bodies without heartbeats, checking between each seat. He leaned against the metal ceiling as he went. Finding none, he climbed over Leleil's body and out of the bus, heading to the closest car. Intent on finding more injured, he flinched when a female EMT tapped his shoulder.

She looked him over. "Sir, this way." She waved to an ambulance. He raised his brows.

He looked down at himself. Between the dagger and the glass, the day had torn him to shreds.

His hesitation turned to acceptance as she reached out to take his hand. "I know you're confused, but please come with me. We'll take care of you."

He looked up and found the floor his muse lived on; Jane was no longer home. Another prayer to God rattled about in his mind: *Please let Wylie be at the other end of this ambulance.* He took the human's hand and followed.

Chapter 17

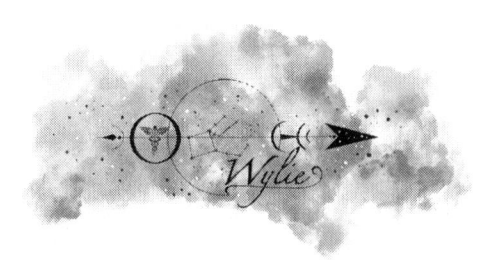

At 12 p.m., Wylie's phone rang. "Cherry Hill Hospital" popped onto the screen.

"Hello?"

"Wylie, it's Mary. There was an accident on First Street. A bus took out a bunch of cars. And then there was a shooting at Eastlake Park an hour later. We're up to our necks in beds. I've called everyone. I know you're on medical leave, but if you can work, we could use the extra hands." Mary broke some major rules by calling Wylie while on leave, and she could guess why. At least three ambulances had screamed past her apartment in the last half hour.

"I'm on my way."

"Thank you."

Wylie jumped off her couch, pausing *Hocus Pocus*, and pulled on a pair of scrubs. Lights off, door locked, and outside in less than ten minutes. She snuck in through the ambulance-only entrance behind a man on a gurney. Nurses ran up and down the halls, while providers sat in front of screens staring at imaging and labs. Beds lined the walls, and a collection of moans filled her ears.

Mary power-walked past Wylie and then spun around. "Oh my God, thank you for coming." She dumped three clipboards in Wylie's arms. "Clock in later. Can you triage these three?" She started walking away before she finished her sentence. And then over her shoulder, "You look great. That makeup covers those bruises well."

Wylie dropped her bag and coat just inside the nurses' station and looked over the charts as she headed to 2B. Large enough for one bed, they used the decontamination room for prepping the newly departed for the morgue. She'd seen it occupied by a living patient once. Showerheads lined the walls, and a drain sat in the middle of the lime-green floor tiles.

She opened the door, and the clipboards clattered to the ground.

"Fuck." She stumbled back. Samael sat cross-legged, his eyes sealed shut, his bared chest covered with bleeding cuts, a pair of gigantic wings filling the space behind him.

He opened his eyes to the sound of her clumsiness and followed her gaze. An eyebrow lifted. "Are you okay?"

"I'm sorry." She picked up the boards. "I don't remember them being so big."

His hand held pressure against a larger wound on his abdomen. "I need my muse," he said with a grimace.

"I'll call David."

"No, please don't inconvenience *the doctor*."

"He's here. I'll just text him." She pulled out her phone and sent a begrudging message to the man who'd stalked her, slept with her, and then told her she wasn't human. "What happened?" she asked, reminding herself that an angel was bleeding out all over her ER.

"A bus rolled. A shattered window cut me as I lifted people out of the wreckage." He leaned forward, curling around his injuries.

Wylie didn't buy what he was selling. Maybe because she didn't trust him yet, or because he wouldn't meet her eyes. His wounds seemed consistent with his story, but the color of his face and his racing heartbeat made her think of shock. Some scrapes wouldn't cause this. Samael didn't look like the type of guy who would faint at the sight of blood. "Are you injured anywhere else? You look like you might puke."

He shivered and closed his eyes. "I'm fine. I just need my muse."

"Can I look closer at that cut?" She pointed at the gauze and pulled on her gloves.

"Wylie, I'll not let a human stick a needle into me. I just need to see Jane."

A knock sounded at the door, and David entered. Red splotches marred his face on his cheeks and scalp. He pulled a metal tray behind him. "Mary said I might need this." He parked it in front of Samael's bed.

David frowned as he hovered over the covered suture tray. They glared at each other. Their resentment sucked the air out of the room.

"David, I need to see your sister." Even with the pallor of a fish, Samael's voice rang with a demanding tone, one that spoke of years of disappointment.

"Then go see her." David's fingers curled around the instrument tray.

Samael lifted the soaked gauze he held against his abdomen, and blood gushed out. "David Jacob Godwyn, this is not a game. I'm too weak to heal."

"We're done helping you. That includes Jane." Ignoring good sense, David raised his voice at the large, wrathful-looking angel. "I know you caused this. There are six dead people out there." He pointed at the door.

Samael's eyes widened. He pressed his palm into his forehead. Wylie's stomach cramped at the statement. Both because of what he said and how loud he'd said it. Security would have investigated the raised voices if they weren't in a room sealed like a freezer.

"Wait." Wylie stepped in front of the slow-moving train wreck that was the two of them. "David, don't you think Jane would want to see her injured 'uncle?'"

David's head whipped in her direction. "Don't you remember how tired Jane was after he visited on Christmas Day?" He pointed at Samael with his chin. "He did that."

"She's my muse."

"And she's my sister." David shoved the tray aside, all of its instruments singing songs of metal and violence as they crashed. "Let's stop pretending. You don't care about Jane. You just want her to heal you. Why would you come here? Wylie is not yours, either." He jabbed his finger at Samael. "Wylie doesn't want to be your hero. She wants her baby back! She wants her husband back!"

Wylie's eyes watered from the impact of the accusation.

"I'm sorry. I don't have time for him. You're an adult. You decide how much control you'll give this angel over your life." With that, David marched from the room.

Out of habit, Wylie walked over to pick up the scattered instruments, chest emptying until hollow. She froze when Samael spoke.

"I've imagined meeting you for most of my existence." He shook his head. "Neither of our meetings met those expectations. Allow me to pay you the respect you deserve."

Without explaining further, he swung his legs off the bed and used one hand to steady himself. Her nursing instincts sent her in his direction, ready to catch her fall risk of a patient. He held his hand up, signaling for her to stop. Gritting his teeth, he came down to one knee.

He lifted the back of his forearm to cover his eyes. His reverence was lost on her as she watched blood drip down his torso.

"Armageddon, I've looked for you since the original sin."

Awe, and maybe even love emanated from him in waves. He waited for a response, unmoving.

For the first time, she noticed his face and body. He impressed her as much as the feathered display behind him. He seemed endangered and picturesque, with his bowed head like antique artwork mounted too close to a fire.

This angel has no ill will toward me. She felt it. Felt it in her bones.

His sandy-brown hair shone under the fluorescent lights. His chiseled physique belonged on the cover of the smut novel at her bedside. Even in his pain, he held his chest high. The precision of his bizarre salute placed tension in all the right places, showcasing his strength. He was pretty in a masculine way. But it was his innocence which persuaded her to have compassion.

She felt like a priest standing over him. Compelled to lay a blessing on his head, just as Guadalupe's priest did during Mass. Her hand landed on his raised forearm before she could stop herself.

Big mistake.

Her good intention made his needs disappear. He sucked in a breath through his teeth as color returned to his face. His wounds scabbed over and then vanished. She felt her strength flowing into him and flinched away from the sudden energy loss.

Beside her, a lion the size of a car ripped the heads off of men, one after another. She ducked away, only to find an angel with wings made of ice hovering above her. David dangled from his hands by his throat. With a sickening crack, the angel snapped David's neck, dropping his body.
"No!" *She raised her hands as he fell.*

Collapsing backward, she caught the wall as the vision of death flashed before her eyes. Her hands came to her chest, cradling the now-familiar pain of magic. Unable to speak, she stumbled from the room. The images strobed in her mind as she found the closest bathroom and emptied her stomach into the toilet.

She never went back to 2B.

Wylie stripped off her scrubs, showered, took two naked tequila shots, and climbed into bed, defeated. Trepidation and losing her energy to Samael caused her chest to ache. Almost dying, being a murderer, being an angel, not feeling alone, and then losing it, and all in a single week.

She rolled onto her belly, shoved her face into the pillow, and screamed as hard as possible. Her neck tightened with her frustration, her throat burning with the release.

She regretted letting David inside of her. She regretted trusting him. She regretted feeling comfortable. Those happy moments made the sadness coming for her even more daunting.

Knock, knock, knock!

She sat up in bed, squinting in the darkness, her reflexes hindered by a wave of dizziness.

Knock, knock, knock!

Exhausted, she pulled on her robe and stumbled to the kitchen. She fisted a knife before heading to the door. Through the peephole, David peered at her as he rubbed his fingers over the stubble on his scalp. She could feel him, the way his nearness changed the air in her lungs, feeling her, the way he stared at the door as if he saw her.

He rested his hand where her heart would be if no barrier lay between them. She opened the door, showing him her down-turned lips and bloodshot eyes.

"You left me alone with him." She hid her knife behind the door.

"I'm so sorry." His brows came together as his honey-colored eyes beseeched her. His hands went to the door frame on either side of her. He smelled of hand sanitizer and cinnamon. She did her best to resist his warmth. She wished she could hate the wholeness radiating between them. The memory of her broken trust held her at bay.

"Go home."

He flinched. "Wylie, I can feel you need me. As a muse if not a friend. You're running on empty. He took too much."

The verbal confirmation of her fatigue brought her back to her body. She hunched her shoulders with bone-deep weariness as the door frame held her up. Her body ached with flu-like lethargy.

"David, I can't be around you." But she wanted to. Every cell of her being wanted to pull him out from the streetlamps and into the dark so she could heal in his arms.

"I understand." He turned and strolled to the curb, where he sat. His legs looked too long, his knees coming up too high. He'd locked his bike to the chain-link fence behind him. Such an awkward pair, resting in the nighttime mist, both meant for more important things.

"What are you doing?" she whisper-screamed.

"It will work. I don't have to come inside. I can't leave you like this." He closed his eyes and rested his head in his hands. "Go back to sleep, Wylie. It will all be okay."

Wylie groaned in frustration. This wouldn't work. He's been lying to her since they met. Even if he wasn't the mastermind of all this craziness, his lies of omission hurt. The foolishness and shame cut at her, emotions she didn't have before she met him.

But he'd helped her too. The safety of his presence while she slept in the hospital bed. The sweetness of a decorated home for Christmas. A stranger's hug in the rain. *You don't have to do this alone. There are no words.*

She took a deep breath and left the door wide open. She headed to the kitchen and heard the front door click shut behind her as she replaced her weapon in the butcher's block. Without moving, she listened to the shuffle of his feet on the carpet. Even the way he shuffled to the living room sounded repentant.

He waited until she returned to her bed before sitting on the couch. He leaned forward, and she closed her eyes, not wanting to look at him.

Roberto spun Wylie in a circle for the hundredth time that night. She felt the blisters forming on her toes with every click of her high heels. Back in his arms, they continued their dance.

Bachata music blared in the background, lights flashing against the dance floor with every beat. Their sweat mixed as his face touched hers. He stole another kiss, his forearm wrapping around her back, tucking her into him.

The song stopped with the brassy blare of a trumpet solo, the light strobing out around them. It took him a minute to let her go, and when he did, she drank in his handsome features. His black hair matched his bottomless eyes. His golden skin gleamed as they caught their breaths together. He tasted like tobacco, mint, and tequila.

"Let me get you a drink, mama." His Spanish accent clipped the words, his genuine face so inviting. She smiled and nodded, afraid that if she spoke, she'd say all the wrong things. He spun her once more and led her to the bar, her hand in his.

"Dos cervesas y . . ." He looked down at her. "What would you like?"

She leaned over the bar, his presence giving her courage. "Y caballito de tequila, por favor." The bartender winked, but her dance partner raised his brows. They were the first Spanish words he'd heard her speak.

"Se hable espanol?"

"Si, un poquito." She covered her mischievous smile with her hand. "I learned the necessities, like 'Where's the bathroom?' and 'Can I get a shot?'"

The bartender slid the shot to her. "Salud!" Both men watched as she tipped her head back, clapping when she slammed the glass on the counter.

Wylie did a tiny curtsy, blushing. Her dance partner smiled, grabbed his beers from the bar with one hand, and led her to the corner of the club, his hand on her back. Another song thrummed, and bodies moved to the music. She watched, hypnotized, soaking up the foreign seduction of the place.

"What's your name?" he asked, leaning close so she heard him over the din.

"Wylie, and you?" She saw the future in his eyes.

"Roberto." He winked, resting his hand on her arm. "I'm so glad I rescued you earlier," he said, referring to when she sat alone at the tables where girls waited for a partner. "You're too pretty to be alone." He winked before leaning in close to kiss her neck.

The dream left her breathless, as if Roberto's flirtations teased her for the first time. Her neck felt naked without his lips.

You're too pretty to be alone.

The phrase spun in her head, over and over, until one word haunted her: *alone.*

Before her husband, she floated about as an independent girl with the loneliness of an only child. Roberto saw the emptiness and endeavored to fill it.

Without him, she'd buried herself in the solitude of her mind.

Tears filled her eyes. *I don't want to be alone anymore!*

Roberto wouldn't want this for her. And if the roles were reversed, she wouldn't want it for him. Had he visited her dreams to give her permission? To remind her kisses could happen before trust?

Before second-guessing herself, she slipped out of bed and covered the few feet between her and David. Her nakedness was revealed as her robe trailed behind her.

David slept sitting upright. His head bent forward. Wylie settled beside him, feeling him wake with a start. He took a shaky breath, his hands curling into fists in his lap. His body opened, his thighs falling apart, his chest rising. Only his eyes remained closed.

Wylie's dream emboldened her. She didn't need to be alone. She placed her foot on his shoe, feeling her heart flutter. His hands opened and closed but remained in his lap, his face pinching in concentration.

"David."

"Yes?" She heard his sleepy voice in her lower belly.

"Do you also feel tired like Jane does after 'charging me?'"

"It's not as bad. I think because you're still partly human."

"I'm done being mad."

"You are?"

"I am." She placed her hand on his thigh.

"And what does that mean?" His hand took hers.

"It means no more secrets. Complete transparency, no matter how difficult you think it may be for me to hear it." She rested her head on his shoulder.

"Promise."

A car drove by, and light flashed through the slats of the window shades, highlighting her peaked nipples.

He kissed the top of her head. "You're naked."

Her teeth vibrated with his voice. "Yes, I am."

"For me?"

She smiled. "Do you see any other bald-headed, honey-eyed, sexy doctors around?"

He rubbed the top of his head. A smile snuck onto his lips. "But I'm the worst." His free hand moved as if possessed, cupping her breast.

"You are?"

"I hated myself for every day I didn't tell you." He kissed her ear. His teeth, oh his teeth, they trapped the lobe.

She traced the inner seam of his slacks.

"Hmm." His hands captured her face, and he took her mouth with his, placing passionate apologies on her tongue. "I . . . thought . . . you . . . hated me too," he said between kisses.

She answered by draping herself over his lap and wrapping her arms around David's neck. "Will taking me to bed convince you otherwise?"

He lifted her to her feet and followed suit. There was the push and pull of kissing and walking and kissing and bed. Finally horizontal, their limbs tangled. Tender, aggressive, wordless expressions of attraction guided their hands, their mouths, their hearts.

She wasn't sure who had fallen asleep first. She just remembered smiling at the pounding of her heartbeat in her bruised lips: *thump, thump, thump.* The ghost of their kisses lolled her into more dreams.

Chapter 18

Wylie

They sat on the rooftop terrace of David's apartment. It spared them the rain, but not the wind. Wylie curled closer to David. Guilt turned her shiver into a frown. "I feel bad visiting your place and not hanging out with Jane."

David rubbed Wylie's arm. "She's down there getting ready for a New Year's Eve party. She doesn't have time for us old people."

Imagining Jane at a party lightened Wylie's mood. "That's exciting. I used to love parties, but nowadays, I'm a dud."

"Maybe you're not going to the right ones." He winked.

"Becoming a mother tamed me." She opened her mouth to laugh but pinched her lips between her teeth as her joke fell flat.

David squeezed her thigh. "You're still a mom, Wylie."

She pinched her eyes closed, ready for a new subject. She gestured at the flashcards in David's lap. "Let's start."

He nodded, fanning the pile out. "This is everything I've learned about angels so far. Hopefully, you can read my writing."

"I love that you put it all on flash cards." She kissed his cheek.

"A friend is helping me compile this information." He rubbed his temple. "Her angel is abusive, and she's trying to figure out a way to separate herself from him."

"Abusive?"

He nodded. "Physically abusive."

Wylie winced. "I thought angels were supposed to be good."

"They all have a job. Those jobs help humanity. They're good at those." He snorted. "But angels are more machines than humans. They care for nothing but meeting their goal."

"And your friend told you this?"

"I've witnessed it. Samael claims to have loved my father, yet under his watch, my father wasn't just burdened. He was murdered." His nose crinkled with disgust. "Can you imagine, not even twenty-four hours after giving birth, my mother was going to the morgue to identify her husband?"

Wylie remembered seeing Roberto's face disappear as a stranger zipped his body bag closed. If she'd become pregnant the night Roberto died, would she have been able to raise the child without him? She lifted her eyes to the skyline. Fog crowded the building, obscuring her view. Could she hold an infant in her arms and not see Dean? The family she always dreamed of was ripped away from her in moments. She didn't think she could ever be part of a family again.

The tin roof of the terrace sang as the sky opened and hailstones fell. Ice bounced and rolled to their feet. "That's strange." Wylie stood and moved toward the railing. Samael appeared before her, and she bumped into his chest.

"Wylie, don't move." He spun around, pulling her behind him and under his wings. The feathers pressed her into the hard lines of his back.

Wylie resisted her instinct of self-preservation and attempted to duck away from him to see better what was going on, but Samael held her fast.

"What the fuck are you doing here?" She barely heard David over the falling ice.

Samael didn't answer him. His head turned to a female angel who landed beside him. "There's four of them, brother. What's the plan?"

"I'll take Gabriel. You capture one of the others. The last two can die."

The black-winged angel with neon green hair ducked her head and grinned at Wylie. "So, we're winging it." She straightened with a cackle.

Samael grunted, and Wylie caught hold of his shirt.

"I'm Laoth, by the way." The female ducked down again, searching for Wylie between Samael's feathers.

"Not now!" Samael barked.

Laoth stuck her tongue out at Wylie and saluted the back of Samael's head.

"Wylie! Come out!" A male voice Wylie didn't recognize called out to her. His nasal Cajun accent was made evident by how his mouth formed around his T's.

"Leave this place, abomination!" Samael's growl rumbled through her.

"Who the hell are you?" David's voice came from beside her.

Wylie fought her way to Samael's side to find a male version of herself standing untouched by the wind, ice, and rain. He drew a puff from his cigarette. Wylie froze as she looked into her obsidian eyes on a stranger's face. Her raven curls flew with the wind from his roots. Cheeks and chin, all hers, but covered with a manicured beard. Their resemblance was almost identical.

Both taller and broader than her. Their biggest difference was his wings. They were as alive as the surrounding storm: all ice shards and mist. "I have no business with you, muse. I'm here for my sister." He held out his hand. "Come, Wylie, it's time for you to join your family."

Sister?! Wylie wanted to answer him, tell him he was no brother of hers, but staring at the mirror image of herself told her otherwise.

She looked to Samael for an explanation, but he shook his head with a snarl. "Gabriel."

"Come with me, and I will bring you to Roberto and Dean."

Wylie's knees threatened to give way at the proclamation. "What?" She took a step forward.

Samael caught her wrist. "He lies."

Gabriel laughed. "He's right. I lied. Angels can't go to heaven."

Wylie's eyes widened, his breath catching. "What?"

Gabriel sighed, clearly annoyed with Wylie's ignorance. "*Frangine, cher*, let's not waste time with insignificant details. You'll be dead by the end of the day. Should we destroy this city to make it happen, or will you give yourself up?"

"You'd destroy Seattle to get to me?" Wylie took another step and Samael yanked her backward, holding her against his chest.

"I'd destroy most things to end you." Gabriel took another puff and tossed the rest of his cigarette into the wind.

She didn't believe him. She couldn't believe him. "But why? You just claimed to be my brother."

"Your twin."

"My blood. My only family."

Gabriel scoffed. "Don't be sentimental. It's not like I haven't wanted you dead for years now."

Wylie didn't need the male to say it. His upturned face and sly smile told her enough. Rage coursed through her. She fought Samael's hold. "You killed my son."

"I hired someone to kill you." Gabriel lifted his sleeve and studied his watch. "More than once. But you know what they say, 'if you want something done right . . .'" An angel landed behind him. "So, let's get this over with." He straightened his arm as a third angel appeared at his side.

Wylie's mind became a canvas of hate. She didn't give a fuck that she'd just met her brother, *her twin*. She wanted to rip him apart. "You killed my so—" In a whoosh, an angel dropped beside her and grabbed David. His feet dragged on the ground as he fought the midnight-skinned female, his arms and legs swinging.

"Aah, Binah, just in time. I'm growing bored."

David let out a gurgling sound as Binah's forearm squeezed his throat.

Wylie remembered her dream. Her heart slammed in her chest. She couldn't let him die. "Let him go!"

David's head slumped forward, his whole body limp.

"I'll make you a deal, Wylie." Gabriel gestured to the guardrails. "You jump, and I won't have Binah toss your boyfriend over."

Binah draped David over the guardrail. Her teeth were stark white in her sadistic grin.

"No!"

"No!"

Both Samael and Wylie shouted, his arms loosening their grip. Everyone's eyes whipped up to Samael, whose stoic demeanor had cracked. Wylie used the opportunity to rush forward. She didn't know what she'd do. Water splashed beneath her feet as she sprinted to David. She crashed into Binah, who dropped David on the ground and caught Wylie by the waist, flipping her over the guardrail. She heard the ring of her shoe as it smacked into the wrought iron, then nothing but wind.

Rain cut her, and air refused to enter her lungs. Her ears popped as she raced past the windows.

And just when she thought she'd hit the ground, her back slammed into something hard, emptying her lungs. Blackness surrounded her, and so did wings.

"Breathe!" a male voice barked.

Her eyes opened, her mouth opened, and her lungs opened, but nothing happened.

"Damn it, Wylie, breathe." The chiseled lines of Samael's face came into focus. "You're turning blue." Without warning, he dropped her legs and swung her around to face him. His large hands pinched her armpits as he dangled her.

She gasped. "Fuck." With that, she realized she was no longer falling but flying. "Oh shit, motherfucker."

He pulled her back to his chest, but she continued her profanity as the slow beat of his wings came to her attention. "Wylie." He squeezed her until she silenced. "Calm yourself."

Hysteria boiled out of her mouth along with her words. "I almost died. I just fell off a building. And David. What happened—"

"Wylie!" The firmness in Samael's voice shook her. She focused on his its sound as he spoke. "I need you to wake your Scientia. To do that, I need you to calm down. Open your mind. Find the power you use to heal people. Focus it on your back. Think of wings. Make them real."

Wylie took a deep breath, pushing aside her questions and followed his orders. She searched for the gnawing discomfort that so often lived in her chest. When she found it, she poked it. The pain grew until it met the barrier of her skin.

She opened her eyes to the green grass shade of his. He couldn't fight them and hold her. An unspoken question lingered between them.

Fear couldn't exist next to the pain of this power. Nothing could. Wylie rested her hand on Samael's cheek. "Do it."

He grimaced, seemingly warring with his thoughts. His eyes caught hers for what felt like the last time. "Find your wings, Wylie."

He let go and dove away, meeting the first angel with such force lightning flashed. Dazed, she watched her magic streak like a tail as it followed her path downward.

Find my wings?

A boom reverberated through her body as the angels clashed again. This time, she lost consciousness.

A voice woke her.

"Mama, Mama. Fly. Fly." He lay in the snow, his cheeks rosy as his arms and legs flapped. "Fly." His tongue showed as he pronounced the 'L.' His pudgy finger pointed at Jinx, who soared in the sky on a broom.

Roberto scooped him off the ground and swung him around, peppering him with kisses. "This is how you fly, mijo."

Love. The sensation superseded the pain she'd harnessed as the world came back into focus.

Muscles loosened as peace churned like lava through her veins. The fall stopped, and a shout ripped from her throat as a blaze shot from her back. Flames crackled in her ears, and a wall of protection took its place behind her, heating her with primal memories.

Her wings opened wide and snapped forward. Clouds evaporated with each beat. Her clumsy flight continued until her body trembled, and her mind refused to work. She didn't have enough control to land. She just needed to make it to Lake Union. The water beckoned her. Just a little further.

Chapter 19

Wylie

Wylie woke up with a jolt. "Brother!" Her muscles and hormones mimicked the moment her eyes locked with his. Those eyes. His hair. She had a brother, and he'd hired the men who killed her family. It hollowed her chest. Ragged gasps followed. Her body shook with cold and adrenaline. She lay in the fog of it. Still drenched from the storm he'd created.

Brightness burned her eyelids. She held up a hand, flinching as she risked a peek. A sterile white gleam surrounded her. Holding her neck, she sat with a grimace. The shooting pain which zinged down her shoulders meant she was alive.

"David?" Her voice echoed off the vacant walls. *Is he safe?* She remembered how he looked crumpled on the ground.

She stretched, and her hesitancy bloomed into curiosity. Yes, her hands still shook with a backdrop of fear, but an overwhelming vibration of safety emanated from the ground. The place felt alive, a blank slate, odorless, colorless, and built out of a razor's edge, its sharp lines holding everything together. Cinder block walls held bare concrete floors and low ceilings apart. A few coats of white paint covered everything but the linear light bulbs above.

"Samael."

She rubbed her arms.

"Samael?"

She stood and steadied herself against a wall. Smoothing the singed tatters of her jeans, she tiptoed to the doorless threshold. She wore no shoes and her shirt was more of a bib than a blouse; the back of it had burnt away.

She leaned into the hall and counted fifteen doorways.

This couldn't be heaven. *That would be disappointing.* God wouldn't be into harsh lighting and hard lines? *Would He?*

She went back to the center of the room and sat down cross-legged, tapping her fingers on her knee. Her bladder soon demanded her attention.

"Samael." She waited for a beat and ran to the exit, projecting her voice into the hallway. "Samael!" She started the pee-pee dance.

She heard a male grumble and swung around to see Samael in all his naked glory.

"Whoa!" She covered her eyes. While she appreciated the perfection of his body, including the circular tattoo in the middle of his chest and the constellation that dotted his ribs, she didn't need the temptation. "Umm, bathroom?"

"You still need to void?" he asked, confused.

She nodded, pinching her legs together.

"We don't do that here." He shrugged.

"Okay?" She clenched her teeth, changing tactics. He needed to see the panic on her face. She held a hand out, covering his nakedness from her view. "Take me somewhere where we do those types of things."

"Are you sure?" His eyes trailed down her body to the apex of her thighs. "Angels don't do that."

She crossed her legs. "I am. I'm so sure." She shifted her weight from one foot to another.

"Okay, fine, you can do it there." His eyes stayed trained on her.

"Are you a pervert?"

"Angels don't do that either." He lifted his brows.

She laughed, peeing a little as she did. "Turn around."

He did as told, and even though his wings faced her, she went to the room's corner for privacy. She did her business and then ripped off the lower leg of her pants to dry the urine that splashed on her calves and dropped it on top of the puddle to cover it.

She straightened. "Okay, I'm done."

Wylie caught her breath when she realized he looked different. He stood taller, wider, and built on a giant frame. His green eyes reflected all the seasons of foliage.

A hint of a smile twitched on his otherwise stoic face, and she remembered how light she felt in his arms. How his biceps felt under her fingertips. How his . . .

"What?" Her cheeks grew hot, and she pushed her frizzy hair away from her face.

"That was very human of you." He leaned to one side, raising his brows at the camouflaged mess behind her. "Your shame is very human too."

Their gazes locked, and she squirmed at the intensity of it. "I'd rather be human than impolite."

He stepped back. "I didn't realize you expected human customs to be upheld on an angel plane." He looked down at himself. "I assume that means you'd like me to wear clothes?"

It was her turn to clear her throat. *No, thank you.* "Yes, please."

"Follow me." He left the room. She fell into step behind him, her eyes studying his wings. The tips dragged on the floor behind him. Creamy white feathers glistened with a gold sheen as he moved. They touched the ceiling and tickled the walls on either side. His glutes peaked out from below, where his feathers parted.

"Is David safe?" Tearing her eyes away from the view.

"Yes, Gabriel was there for you."

"How long has he been trying to kill me?"

"Two years."

Wylie massaged her temples. "How many times?"

"A dozen."

"Fuck." She couldn't wrap her brain around it. Her brother, her one blood relative, hated her enough to want her dead. "Why?"

"There's a prophecy. You have a great destiny. A destiny he doesn't want you to fulfill."

She blew out a breath. "Am I safe here?"

He grunted in the affirmative.

"This is a Heavenly Plane?"

He grunted again.

"What does that mean?"

"The Heavenly Planes are available for angels to, you know, do their heavenly business." He paused and tossed a smirk over his shoulder. "The planes stack on your world like a deck of cards. This is Ludus." His feathers ruffled as if to point out their surroundings. "This is where we train new angels to blend in with humans." She followed him into the room.

Multiple bars ran across the back wall. From modern and traditional to formal and casual, the garments hung, first in order by type and then in order by color. A black summer dress with poppies caught her eye. She could dance. The idea of wearing clean clothes excited her that much. Two open shower stalls took up opposite corners.

"Thrones make angels. We never have a childhood. We come into being as adults, knowing our mission." He grabbed a pair of sweatpants and pulled them on. They hung low on his hips. It would be a crime to cover more of his cut abs than necessary. "As a new angel, this class was tough for me. I could never understand the use of covering one's body." He grabbed a shirt. "I learned my lesson after my first sunburn." He raised his eyebrows at her, his face serious.

"What?"

"It's funny."

"What's funny?" she said, confused.

"Angels don't get sunburns." He grumbled to himself. "Never mind."

Samael's shirt pulled on as if he didn't have wings. The fabric passed through them as if great holograms grew from his back.

She pointed behind him. "How'd you do that?"

He shrugged. "They don't exist on this plane, just like on earth."

"What do you mean? Your wings, those giant feathered things, they aren't here? In this room?"

"More like neither of us are. We exist outside of time. The constraints it places on earth do not affect us." He stretched the collar of his shirt. "Have you heard of astral projection?"

She blinked. "I'll have to Google that one."

"It doesn't matter. You've been doing it without knowing your entire life. We can always talk about the mechanics of it later." He pulled down the floral cotton dress she'd been eyeing earlier and handed it to her. "This is the one you wanted, right?"

She cringed as she reached for it. *He can read my mind too?*

"I can. Many of the stronger angels can."

Forgetting their Philosophy 101 debate about existence and caves and Plato and shit, she palmed her forehead. Before she could stop herself, the image of his ass popped into her brain.

She recognized Samael's I'm-not-going-to-smile half-lip-raise. "I will take your appreciation of my body as a compliment. Can we return to our discussion?"

"Just turn around." She waited for him to turn and peeled off her ragged clothes, folding them in a pile. She pulled the dress on, enjoying the crispness of it through the layers of dirt she wore.

Samael turned back to her. "If it makes you feel better, I also appreciate your form."

Her cheeks flushed. "It does not." She changed the subject. "Before we have any more discussions about angel stuff, I want to talk about my family."

He folded his arms across his chest. "I said to you before, all we ever wanted to do was protect you and your family." He shook his head and sat on the ground. He gestured for her to join.

"Then why? Why did they die? How do I know I can trust you?" She swallowed the sting in her throat and took her place next to him, holding her head in her hands. She squeezed her eyes closed, unable to breathe as she remembered the smell of blood and Dean's lifeless face. "Show me," she whispered.

She opened her eyes to find Samael giving her a questioning look.

"You said you could show me what happened. How they died. I want to see." She had to know. She had to see who her brother had sent and why they killed them instead of her.

He hesitated, his lips turning down in a frown. "If you're ready, I'll take you to see the death of your angel child and your muse."

His words snuck up on her; she jerked her head in confusion as she turned toward him. "My muse?"

"Roberto."

"Wait, what?"

"Your husband, he was your muse."

Wylie looked at him in disbelief. "Are you saying he knew about me being an angel?"

"No, David is your first muse to know what he is. The other two had no clue."

"The other two? What are you talking about?"

"Your adopted father and your husband."

"Now, hold up." She stood. "What are you saying?"

"I'm saying when your father died, Roberto replaced him. And when Roberto left . . . You seem upset."

Her nails scratched her scalp as she pulled her hair. "There's a whole list of reasons why what you're telling me is upsetting." Roberto and Wylie's relationship had always been so organic, so natural. They fell into each other's arms at the end of each day with dreams of bills, work, and mundane human things. How could their romance be related to this world?

"What I'm telling you is the truth."

"I don't care about the truth!" she shouted. "I just want my family back." The tears splashed down her cheeks. She closed her eyes and failed at slowing her breaths. Nothing she knew of the world was real. Not even her relationships with her family. And now she had a brother—one who'd hired her husband and son's murderer.

She thought back to his cruel smile, the coldness behind his gaze. The things he'd said to her burned through her. And then she remembered the worst revelation of all. Her throat filled with a groan as a fresh wave of tears filled her eyes. "Tell me Gabriel lied when he said I could never be with them again?"

Samael remained silent for a moment, his face clearing with expression. His back straightened as he approached her, his hands landing on her shoulders. "I can't." He bent down as he studied her face. She could see the sympathy swirling in his gaze behind his tight-lipped façade. "You can't. None of the angels can."

"Why?" Her heart wrenched. "Why?" She rubbed her chest, trying to remove the pain from the wound he'd inflicted. "How do you know?" The hiccups of sobs shook her. "How do you know?" Her hands landed on his chest as she begged him with her eyes.

"I'm sorry."

She rested her head against his chest and soaked his shirt with sorrow. Time folded between Wylie and her shock, even as her heart raced with desperation.

Samael took her hand, keeping it in his. "So human." His eyes softened. "I'll take you to see what happened to your family, Wylie. But first, you must rest. It will not be easy." Samael's palm came to her forehead. "Here." His voice rattled with kindness. "This will help."

Something transferred into her. Her limbs let go of their anger, her face relaxed, and her lips tingled as laziness settled over her. "What did you do?"

"I blessed you."

She shivered at the sound of his voice. "Hmm?" Her eyes closed of their own accord. Her body leaned against Samael, the hard planes of his chest becoming her pillow as sleep took her.

Chapter 20

Samael

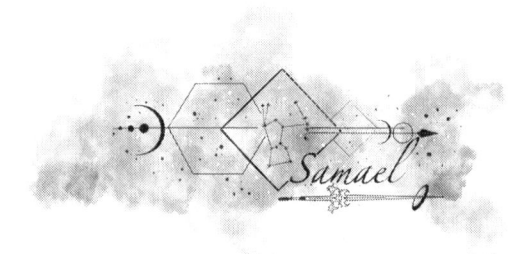

Samael settled Wylie on the floor, arranging her limbs with gentleness. He pushed her wild hair from her face. The tenderness caused warmth to dance along his skin. His fingers paused, and he stroked her ear, his Scientia covering her as he breathed in her womanly scent. A grunt of frustration at himself passed over his lips. He should be figuring out how to protect her from her brother, not staring at her sleeping form.

Gabriel. The angel fought like a devil. If Wylie hadn't led them over Lake Union, Samael and Gabriel would have destroyed chunks of Seattle while they battled. They met each other blow for blow. Samael had never felt so challenged in his life. But the fight ended quickly. When Wylie landed like a shooting star in the water below, Gabriel's wings blinked out, and he followed suit, crashing down like an icy meteor and landing in the water not far from her. Samael had a choice. Wylie or Gabriel? Save the girl or finish off his enemy? There was no question about who he went for.

He left the room, the anger he'd harnessed during the fight returning as he sought out Laoth. The Archangel was neck deep in the job she'd started before Wylie distracted him. Laoth sat on a backless metal rolling chair behind a female angel as she hummed *Love Me Tender*.

While Dominions chose a form and kept it, not all angels enjoyed spending eternity with the same face. Laoth changed her hair and features every time he saw her. The tight cut she wore as she worked matched the stern look on her face.

"Every time I'm near your muse, I end up singing Elvis for weeks," Laoth said as she looked up at Samael. "At least our friend here enjoys my singing."

Their victim sat straddling the back of a dining room chair, her feet bound to its legs. Her naked toes curled in pain, the only sign she lived. A tube ran from her forearm to a bag of fluid hanging on a pole beside her. A constant drip flowed into the line, ensuring her wounds wouldn't heal.

Laoth smacked her cheek. "Speak."

"Of course, I love your singing, Valkyrie." Binah's head lolled onto her shoulder, her blonde strands tumbling down to her cuffed hands. A trace of a smile appeared on her face.

Laoth tugged her hair. "Flattery won't work on me." Beside her, a tray of metal instruments glistened in the light, brandishing their red stains with pride. Laoth reached for the scalpel. "But it might work on the Dominion." She looked up at Samael. "What do you think?"

Binah's eyes opened, her Scientia extending. Samael breathed it in. Binah had once been a Power, but now only corrupted Scientia filled her, making her a living blasphemy. He recognized the slant of her eyes, her flawless ebony skin, and the fullness of her mouth from the silver screens, the news, or both. Samael spent most of his time handling Archangels like Laoth. Powers, who spent their days pretending to be human, did not follow the same militaristic creed that Samael and his subordinates did. No, they lived lives of fashion and treachery. Ruling countries and backing monarchies as they spent centuries undercover.

"Here's what I've learned so far: she's old." Laoth ran her finger down Binah's spine, a smile on her face. "I mean that in the nicest way possible, jelly bean." She looked up at Samael. "No young angel could regenerate the pieces I've cut off of her with the speed she has." Laoth leaned into Binah's back with one hand as she moved the other with short, delicate slices. "I open her up, separate a muscle from its origin, and as I grab a clamp, the damn thing reattaches. That's why I started the IV. Let's see her do anything with a liter of fluid in her." She threw the scalpel on the tray. Blood left her hands sticky.

"I can see that." Samael eyed the red polish of Binah's fingernails. He'd ripped her arm off during their fight the night before. "When did this arm grow back?" Samael asked as he studied the perfection of the new extremity. She'd done better than her brothers in arms. The two males were now in Arcadia with Ophanim. Laoth dispatched them both.

"I was showing off for the Viking warrior." Binah let out a cry as Laoth applied pressure with her thumbs.

"Samael, I believe this angel is flirting with me. Can you remind her I have not traded my soul for free will?"

"Angels don't flirt." Samael raised his brows.

"You'd. Be. Surprised." Binah punctuated her words with moans and grimaces.

Laoth clicked her tongue and wiped at the white bones she'd uncovered in Binah's back. "There." She reached for the welding helmet and torch. Helmet on, torch lit, Laoth leaned against Binah, shoulder to shoulder. "Last chance. Why build an army? How does free will work? Why the muses? Pick a question, any question."

Black tears fell from her smudged eyes. They left lines pointing to her quivering lip. "I came here for you, Laoth."

"Remember, I asked you nicely first." Laoth shrugged and lowered the flame.

Their captive's screams sped along the walls in deafening echoes, the room broadcasting the pain Laoth conjured.

The sizzle of the torch stopped, and Laoth pushed up her visor, her face scrunched against the smell of scorched flesh. Smoke floated, thickening the air with the oily heaviness of burned fat. "Samael, have I ever shown you the original rune system we created?"

Ignoring Binah's heaving breaths, Samael folded his arms and walked around to see her back. Burned into the bone lay black runic writing. "I know you're partial to Latin, but their letters don't hold the same power as runes do."

"What does it say?" Samael asked.

Laoth reached for her scalpel and turned it on herself, drawing it along her palm. Blood pooled up to the surface, and lifting her hand, let it drip onto the script. "My name." Laoth smiled. "Did you hear that, Binah? I'll always be inside you."

"I'm sure that comforts her," Samael said, allowing himself a half-smile.

"Boss, always trying to make a joke."

"And never successful at it, either. I tried my sunburn one today. No luck."

"I know how to cheer you up." Laoth turned off the IV. "Here's some Latin for you." She slapped Binah's open back with both hands. "*Sanaret.*"

Binah shivered as her body knit itself back together with Laoth's ancient command. "That's more like it, Valkyrie."

"Oh, we're just getting started, jelly bean." The Archangel left a line of blood across her forehead as she wiped away the sweat. She turned to Samael. "We haven't tortured anyone together in centuries. I thought I'd try something Raphael told me about. Watch this." She squeezed her hand into a fist, and Binah's screams returned. "My name is inside you, jelly bean. Now I decide what you feel." Laoth's fist loosened. "Now, speak."

Before the Archangels of the Louisiana brigade formed, Laoth served as a male Viking Commander. She specialized in torture, inventing novel forms many countries continue to use today.

Laoth snickered as she drew a painful sketch on Binah's back. "Talk."

"Okay. Okay." She gasped as Laoth stopped. "He separates us from our muse by connecting them to himself."

"How?"

"I don't know."

Laoth spit on Binah's wound. "You're pissing me off." Laoth fisted her hand, activating the part of her victim she'd written her name upon.

Binah screamed. "I don't know!"

"I guess not." Laoth shrugged. "What makes your Scientia smell like shit?"

Binah panted, her eyes screwed closed as she gritted her teeth. "It happens because of the division. We only get half. The rest stays with our muse."

"What are your guys doing in the compound?" Laoth wiped away the fresh blood again.

"No. No. No." Binah struggled against her bindings. "I could show you."

Samael and Laoth looked at each other, a silent conversation occurring between them. Samael rounded on Binah, with Laoth following. "You'd take her to the compound?"

Binah nodded.

"How do we know this isn't a trap?" Samael crouched down in front of her.

"Take me hostage. Gabriel would speak to her. He wouldn't compromise my safety."

"No one in this room believes you." Laoth wiped Binah's tears, leaving red smears across her face.

"It is true. I swear by my wings."

Laoth barked a laugh. "You betray me, and I'll take more than your wings."

Samael stood, pinching the bridge of his nose. Could he sacrifice Laoth for this cause? Time passed, and the buzz of the fluorescent lights filled the space words did not. Samael thought of Wylie, peacefully sleeping, and the prophecy and wondered how far he'd go to protect her. No question arose in his mind. He'd follow her to the end of time2 and back.

"You shouldn't do this alone," Samael said, turning to Laoth.

"I've seen worse, old friend. I'll find you in Seattle when I'm done. *Pro summum bonum.*"

They gripped forearms, and Samael's Scientia embraced his truest friend. "*Pro summum bonum.*"

Laoth closed her eyes, her form changing until she became the businessman with the Rolex. She returned to the back wall and palmed the saw Gabriel had gifted to Harut. She rested the blade against the base of Binah's wings and, with a nod, cut the female's bindings. With the saw slung over her shoulder, she grabbed Binah's upper arm. "Let's go for a ride, jelly bean."

They vanished. Samael continued to stare at the space she'd occupied. A puddle of IV fluid leaked at the same speed he pushed away his doubt.

Lex

When Gabriel said rooms, Lex imagined an attached bathroom. What she found instead was a lavish king-sized bed in room number one, a similarly sized bathroom, an office, and a random room with a fireplace and random chairs. She sat in each, glaring at the flames in the fireplace as they cooked her.

"There is no password on the computer. We ask that you keep our location confidential for safety reasons. There is also a landline if you need to call your family." Todd pointed at the study, ignoring Lex as she poked at the fire. "Dinner should be up in a few hours. I'll leave you to yourself. If you need anything, just dial nine and pound."

Lex didn't look up as Todd exited. The thought of room service returned her to the motel room, the pain, and the shower. She traced her ruined top lip. No one would recognize her with this fucked up face. She tugged her septum ring, thinking. Maybe she should call her dad.

She walked into the office and sat in front of the desk. The phone and the computer competed for her attention. Her hand trembled as she reached for the receiver. She couldn't. She couldn't handle the sound of betrayal in his voice and the hurt in her heart at the same time. And then there was the fact he may not recognize her ruined voice. Taking the mouse instead, she opened a browser. There were three emails from David.

Lex,

I told her! And you were right. She was pissed I lied to her. I get it, but I'm not in charge here. I'm feeling pretty impotent. Do you have any advice? We all know I'm new to this. I don't think it helps that she's not a normal angel. I'll have to tell you more later.

My sister thinks her angel is her uncle. We both grew up calling him that. After my father died, my mother insisted on being uninvolved in that world. Speaking of my mom, she's a pain in the ass, but at least she means well.

Any news about your tattoo? I'm off to work.

Looking forward to hearing from you.

David

Lex,

I didn't hear from you yesterday. I hope all is well.

Let me know if you need anything.

David

Lex,

I hope I'm not bugging you. I'm worried. Your sponsor called me today. I'm your emergency contact. She and your dad are looking for you. I hope everything is okay.

David

David,

I'm alive! Long story. Can I call you tomorrow? I'll need your number again. My phone didn't survive the last few days.

L

She'd slept deeper than she had in years. The bed had to be made of clouds, or marshmallows, or both. Her dressers were stocked with yoga pants, sports bras, socks, and panties, with attached tags. Baggy t-shirts with band names filled another drawer. She suspected the shirts had once belonged to Gabriel. They smelled like him, even after being laundered.

A knock sounded on her door.

She ran to the door and cracked it open.

A large man stood on the other side, his hands behind his back. "Ma'am, Gabriel is requesting your presence."

Lex nodded and stepped out of her room. She followed the man down the hall until she didn't know how to return to where she started. He opened a door for her and shut it after she entered.

Gabriel sat at a large desk, his black curls tied back and suit crumpled. Lex held back the smile the sight of him brought to her heart. He waved her over.

Rough night?

"You could say that. You?"

Lex thought back to the slice of heaven they made her bed of, the clothes in her drawer, and the computer. She swallowed her gratefulness, the angels owed her this much. Anyway, the asshole had a big enough head already.

He smiled. "Take a seat beside me." He set down his pen. "I have a quick meeting, and then I'll give you a tour."

Lex shrugged and crossed the room, sitting in an armchair against the wall. Again, she wondered at the man's intentions. Why would he invite a broken muse to a business meeting? Why did he smile at her like that? *And fuck you if you're reading my mind.*

Gabriel snorted as the door opened. In walked a fucked-up Binah and a black-winged angel with a saw resting on his shoulder. Lex wondered what the hell was going on.

"All in due time, *cher*," Gabriel said, his eyes never leaving Binah and the stranger.

The male pulled a chair from the wall and set it before Gabriel's desk. "Sit." He pulled Binah into the seat and stood behind her, settling the saw against Gabriel's desk. "I thought I'd return this. I meant to put a bow on it, but I was too busy playing with jelly bean here." He lifted his gaze to Gabriel and grinned. "So, how was your swim last night?"

Lex tensed. She had a sudden itch to kick this male's ass.

"Refreshing. Tell me, how is good ol' Harut?" Gabriel's words spoke volumes, maybe because they came with a heavy dose of Scientia.

The Angel's brow creased, and wrapping Binah's braid in his hand, he lifted the saw and cut it loose. He tossed it on the desk and pressed the blade against the base of Binah's wing. "I should show you how it feels to lose a friend that way."

Gabriel's and Binah's eyes connected, and Binah nodded.

"Do it." Gabriel steepled his fingers. "If that is what is needed to get you on our side, then Binah is willing."

Lex's hand covered her mouth. She'd never seen such loyalty before. She saw the same shock in the male Angel's wide eyes.

"Well?" Gabriel picked up Binah's braid and gestured at the saw with it. "What's the holdup?" A flood of his Scientia filled the room again.

Laoth circled Binah and sat on the corner of the desk. "I'd be impressed if I hadn't witnessed your sister fart more Scientia in her sleep."

Gabriel slapped the desk twice and leaned into a laugh. "This one is funny, Binah. No wonder you thought she'd work well on your team."

Binah nodded, a grin on her face. "You should hear her sing. She's also very good at tickling. Right, Laoth?"

She? Lex raised her brows.

"Well, since the cat's out of the bag . . ." Laoth shivered and shimmered until her body transformed into that of a voluptuous woman.

"So, what do you want to know? I'm an open book." Gabriel centered the braid on his desk and checked his watch when Laoth did not respond. "No rush."

"What's the catch?"

"Catch, no catch. You may decide to work with us once you hear me out."

Laoth's features hardened. "Do I look like a traitor?"

Gabriel's eyes appreciated Laoth's body, and Lex decided she didn't like the way he looked at her.

"No, you look like a beautiful woman who would do anything for her brothers and sisters. I think you'll find you may serve them better by working with me."

Laoth's annoyance showed on her face in a flash. "Why all the muses?" She gritted the words through her teeth. Lex wondered at her thoughts. She looked like a junkie saying no to a free hit.

"If we can free the muses, we can free ourselves."

"But you aren't freeing them, are you? You're tethering them to you."

Lex's mouth gaped in shock for the second time. She wondered how much Scientia Gabriel could tap into.

"I am."

"Why?"

"It's the only path to free will which leaves angels with some of their Scientia intact."

Laoth snorted, unimpressed. "So, you're making an army of weakened angels."

"Does Binah seem weak to you?" Gabriel folded his fingers together. "I'm making an army of free angels, and just as we've seen with humans, freedom can motivate us to do more than anyone expects."

Laoth paused for a moment, her face contemplative. "And this free army . . . what do you plan to do with them?"

"War, of course. Do you want this world to end? Can we just let all of angelkind blink out of existence?"

"So, you want to fight against God?"

For the first time during the meeting, Lex saw Gabriel become irritated. He rose from his seat, placing his hand on the desk. He leaned forward. "What God? You, of all people, should know what atrocities angels do in the name of God."

Laoth tightened her grip on the hacksaw. "Don't pretend you know me, young one."

"I know you," Binah interjected. "I've sent you into battle on behalf of mankind many times, *ceannfort*." Lex almost broke her neck, turning to Binah.

Laoth narrowed her eyes, shooting from her seat and back to Binah. Her free hand shot out and snatched Binah's hair. "You'd go from sending me into battle to being this child's pet?"

Lex balled her hands into fists, uncertain why she felt a sudden protectiveness over Gabriel. Her Scientia flickered over her skin. A knowing grin overtook the male's face. Lex shook out her hands, annoyed with herself for not having better control of her emotions. She raised her chin, daring him to say something about her giving a fuck for all of a second. He winked before turning back to Laoth, who stared into Binah's eyes like she was reading her soul.

"I was once a child." Gabriel tapped his desk. "Do you know whose stories graced my bedtime hours? Stories of Laoth the Valkyrie, and Samael God's first, the angel of death. Do you know what those stories taught me? Laoth never loses. She loves victories more than morals. Being the best means everything to her."

Laoth remained silent.

He continued. "Ugh, what a bore. So bound by duty, unable to see the bigger picture. Nothing like the Valkyrie of legends. Loyalty to your brothers and sisters is more important than misplaced duty." Gabriel stood and moved around the desk. "What an honor to have met you on the battlefield." Gabriel held out his hand. "Give me a chance, and I can show you why you should be on the winning side of this war, *chérie*."

Laoth remained silent, studying Gabriel's outstretched hand before laying her fingers on his palm.

He folded his thumb over and kissed her knuckles. "You've made the right decision."

Chapter 21

Wylie

This time, when Wylie woke, no harsh light burned through her eyelids. She lay on a damp softness. Moving her fingers at her sides, cool strands of grass weaved between them. Her lashes fluttered open, and her eyes caught sight of the most beautiful sky she'd ever seen. A cloudless heaven expanded forever; the gilded daylight kissed her cheeks. The smell of honeysuckle floated in the air.

Once, while in Mexico, she visited Monte Alban, an ancient indigenous ruin. She'd lain on a stone bench and stared into the sky, amazed by its sheer magnitude. Only such a view could dominate that magnificent place of temples and stone staircases.

She sat up and the world somersaulted twice before she fell back. She closed her eyes against the grove of pines which lined the top of the hill. Mashing her fists into her eyes, she swallowed the acid rising in her throat. White dots of daisies drew circles on the inside of her eyelids.

"You need your muse." Samael's voice came from nowhere until she heard him crouch beside her. His hand landed on her bare collarbone, and the dizziness halted. She risked opening her eyes. "Traveling the planes takes a lot of energy. We just came from Ludus to Elysian, another Heavenly Plane." He sounded concerned, but he looked glorious with the sun framing his Angel outline.

"Why are we here?"

"To see the Seraphim."

"The ones who will take me back to see Roberto and Dean . . ." She couldn't say it. She couldn't even think about it, but she had to do it.

Samael nodded. "They aren't far from here." He pulled her to her feet, his touch gentle. "Hold my hand, and I will give you the Scientia that you need."

She held on for dear life, her fingers dug into his forearms, afraid the plane would spin away if she let go. They walked into the trees. Time passed and her concentration went from staying upright to the calloused fingers engulfing her own. His hand led to a thick arm and a strong shoulder. Neck to chin, cheeks, and brow. All of him chiseled and squared. From his sandy hair to his straight back she drank him in.

She shook her head, her mind searching for safer topics. The woods provided some. The dappled sunlight left beauty marks on the ground. Birds chirped, a breeze blew, and a branch caught her foot, tripping her.

Samael's free arm shot out. He caught her by the shoulder and righted her. "We're almost there."

His words caressed her like the wind. For a moment Wylie wished she'd studied linguistics. She wanted to discover every land he'd lived in by his lilting vowels. His grass-green eyes remained averted as he righted her. Samael found his former pace, pulling her along. They emerged from the trees into a clearing. The ground under her feet was both soft and sharp. Twigs and moss caught at her toes and ankles.

Before them, a tall, wooden plank rose into the sky forever. As they drew closer, she realized a massive door acted as a splinter in the horizon. No knob announced its doorness, but large, iron hinges lined one side.

"These are the Seraphim, the God's Guard. They are the keepers of the doorway to Heaven. Please be respectful." He pointed at the four preteens standing before the Jack-and-the-Beanstalk-sized door. "Whatever you do, do not touch the door. It will kill you."

Samael pulled her close, emphasizing the importance of his last statement. His lips touched her ear. "Follow my lead."

He let go of her hand and fell to his knees before the boys. He bowed so low he lay on his belly. "Great Seraphim, I volunteered to bring our humans back. And I've brought you Armageddon." His head stayed bowed.

Wylie fell to her knees too, but more from lack of balance than to show respect. She reached for Samael like a blind woman, searching for bare skin. She found some at the nape of his neck, her fingers curled in his hair as the spinning slowed.

"Samael," said one boy.

Too tired to care anymore, Wylie leaned her forehead against Samael's back.

"You have come to ask a favor." The third child smoothed back one of his wings.

"Samael, stand," the last boy said, his eyes narrowing.

"Bring her to us." Their voices sounded at once, a chorus keeping to a cadence of syllables.

She shook as Samael turned to face her. His big body bent over as he created skin-to-skin contact by placing his forehead against hers.

Trust me. He pushed the thought into her head as his hands cupped her cheeks. A heady calm filled her.

She closed her eyes. "Thank you."

She breathed out a tired sigh and let Samael lift her into his arms and carry her to the Seraphim.

The smallest one rose to his tiptoes and craned his neck to better see her. "You have come here so we may take you back in time." His childish voice pierced her.

She looked over their shoulders at the oak door. Her family was on the other side. The thought made her chest implode. "I wish to see the truth of my son's and husband's deaths."

Samael tightened his hold on her.

"There's no doubt in your mind?" The four boys spoke in unison, their wings touching as they moved closer. "You cannot give it back."

All the questions that kept her up at night would finally be answered and she would have a new reason not to sleep. "Yes, I'm ready."

Samael set her on her feet, and the oldest Seraphim took her hand. "Beautiful Armageddon, so much you will be responsible for."

"Witnessing your son and husband's martyrdom will be the first step to fulfilling your destiny. Are you ready?" They were speaking together now, their voices high with youth. The beauty of their falsettos calmed her heart.

"Behind you, your pale horse; beside you, the black one." Their voices crescendoed as the sounds of wind threatened to mute their words. Her clothes and hair lifted, flying around directionless. "Above you, your white horse. Before you, the red one. Oh, sweet Armageddon, so much you will be responsible for."

A static charge ran down her arms as the hands on her shoulders disappeared. Something snapped in her brain, like the rubber band of reality giving way, and her eyes opened wide in panic.

Rose-colored eyes met hers. "We're here."

She shivered as he dropped her hand. Her feet landed on the ground, and she swayed as her body once again took responsibility for her full weight. The Seraphim before her stepped aside, his wings no longer blocked her view and a neat living space appeared.

Home.

The familiarity of the scene made her legs itch for action. She attempted to walk, but try as she might, her legs would not move. She opened her mouth to shout a warning, but no sound passed her lips.

"This is not your time and place, Armageddon," said the oldest Seraphim. He intertwined his fingers with hers. "We must observe."

They stood before the sliding glass door the murderers left open. The softness of the new carpet curled between her toes and cushioned her feet. Smells that were forever lost filled her nose. Like Roberto's worn cologne, the special way his body transformed the pine and musk into an intoxicating cocktail.

Glass and metal rattled behind her. Unable to turn, she waited, listening, stilling herself as she forced all of her emotions back into the cage that was her ribs.

"Behind you are two humans. They have come for you."

The sound of the door sliding open did not prepare her for what followed. They walked through her. Malice burned along her spine as they passed.

Dressed all in black, they continued into the hall. The first man stopped at the door of her room. His silver hair gleamed in the moonlight. His hand lifted to the knob. The long gun slung over his shoulder looked out of place in her apartment. With a backward glance and a nod, he entered her room.

Shouts, furniture breaking, a toddler cried from the room across the hall. "*Hijole!*" Roberto crashed out of their room and bounded into Dean's. The shock of his wild brown hair and his naked fear had her fighting the bonds of time to no avail.

The gray-haired man returned to the doorway, his gelled part still perfect, his clothes unaffected by the struggle. "Check the bathroom for the woman. I'll check the kid's room. She's supposed to be here."

"Roberto was such a good man." The Seraphim stepped in front of her, blocking her view. His hands came to her shoulders as she tried to see past his many pairs of wings. "Men like him should give you purpose."

A squeal from Dean sounded as the wood shattered. "She's not here."

Dean cried. "Mama! Mama!"

Baby, Mama is here. Wylie groaned.

"Shut that kid up."

The hands tightened on her shoulders. "You can save husbands and sons, wives and daughters. You're the place of gathering." The God's Guard stepped aside, revealing Roberto coming down the hall towards her. Blood dripped down his chin from his mouth, mixing in his beard. Dean clung to his father, his legs wrapped around Roberto's waist, his arms holding his neck. He buried his face in Roberto's shoulder, muffling his cries.

Her whole being vibrated, breathing forgotten as the deepest fear a mother could know drowned Wylie.

"We can leave now," the angel said as Roberto stumbled into the living room. The silver-haired man followed behind with his gun raised to her husband's head.

"What do you want?" Roberto adjusted Dean in his hold.

"Where's your wife?"

Roberto's lips parted, and his eyes searched the room, but no answer came.

The butt of the gun crashed into the back of Roberto's head, making him miss a step and fall into the reading chair in front of him. Dean screamed, his arms flying out as if to steady them both, as if his tiny body could stop their fall.

The chair cracked under Roberto's weight, and he toppled sideways, smashing its twin as he fell. On the ground, he clung to Dean, struggling to put himself between his son and the man with the gun. Inconsolable, Dean fought to breathe between the cries that passed his tiny lips—round cheeks framing a mouth wide open in terror.

A kick landed on Roberto's back. "Shut that kid up, or I'm putting a bullet in his head." A second kick found Roberto's leg, and he grunted, gritting his teeth. Wylie's husband moved from all fours to standing with a shudder of discomfort. "Shh." He smoothed Dean's hair. "Can you sing with me?" Dean shivered with a sob and nodded his head.

Roberto bounced in place. "You are my sunshine . . ." A child's voice soon joined his tenor. Roberto employed their trick to help Dean calm down with his usual patience.

Their eyes.

Their matching garnet eyes shared all the love and comfort a family can create in three years of skin-to-skin and heart-to-heart. Her boy sang, even through hiccups and leftover tears.

Roberto moved to the fireplace, finding the furthest spot from the man with the gun. The Seraphim left her, appearing beside them, one hand finding Dean's back, the other finding Roberto. The angel wrapped his wings around her little family and for a split second, her husband's eyes raised to the glass doors where she stood. Their eyes locked as he sang the last lines of the song, and she felt an unspoken *goodbye* warm her.

"Shut the fuck up. I can't think," said the younger man as he returned to the living room. "If she picked up a shift, she'll be home in about an hour."

"Shit." The older home invader kicked a broken chair and pulled his phone from his pocket.

The Seraphim returned to Wylie's side, pointing to the hallway. "The angel who is about to appear there is Marut." He pulled her body against his. "It was his duty to protect you."

The younger assailant entered the kitchen and opened the fridge. The bastard pulled out a gallon of milk and drank from the jug, then dropped it on the ground with a laugh.

"You will recognize Marut." The Seraphim dropped his arm.

"So, I guess we have no choice. We wait." The older man put one hand through his shiny hair and, moving across the space, lowered himself onto the couch. He trained his gun on Roberto. "You stay right where you are."

The younger man wiped his lips with his sleeve and leaned back into the fridge as if perusing a store shelf. "Maybe we should have done this at the hospital." He slammed the door, a bag of grapes in his hand. He popped a few into his mouth. "She's always there." Tossing the grapes on the counter, he searched the cabinets. "Where the fuck do these people keep their sweets?"

"This family is under God's protection." A voice came from the hallway. The twin of the angel who attacked Wylie just a week before stepped into the moonlight—tan with a long beard and blue eyes. The man didn't fit in their hall. Behind him, black wings spread wide.

"*Dissulto.*" The younger assailant flew backward and slammed into the microwave. The appliance and the man crashed to the ground.

The silver-haired man ducked behind the sofa, shooting with abandon. Roberto swung around, pulled Dean into a ball against his chest, and crouched. Bullets smashed into Marut. His teeth gleamed as his lips pulled back.

"*Dissulto.*" The couch flew into the wall. It crushed the silver-haired man. The gunshots stopped.

The young man pulled a knife from a drawer as Marut appeared beside him. He grabbed the man's shirt and pulled him head-first over the island, guiding his skull onto the tiled floor. With a crunch, his neck bent backward under the weight of his body.

Panting and a moan. She recognized that sound. She'd heard it while in the throes of ecstasy. Never in pain. Marut came to her husband.

Marut pulled out his phone. "I need you now."

Samael appeared next to him. "How?"

"Humans, we never expected him to send humans." He gestured at the human he'd left crumpled on the ground. "Can you take care of the body? I've got Roberto. Wylie should be here any second." Marut pressed his palm to Roberto's forehead, and he fell silent.

"He's dying," said the Seraphim. "Dean is gone, in heaven, at peace. But Roberto, he refused to leave you." Bile filled her mouth and tears ran down her cheeks.

"With mercy, Marut took your husband home before his time." The boy angel pulled her into his arms, blocking her view, but his angel's peace didn't touch the horror. "Roberto would have died on an operating table hours after you found him without Marut."

She heard the front door open.

"Good morning, boys."

Shoes bounced in the entryway closet.

"Boys?"

And then blackness.

Chapter 22

Lex

"That went well." Gabriel spun his desk chair to face Lex. "What do you think?"

She didn't know what to think. She'd learned more about angel politics in the last hour than from anything written in her mother's journals. She folded her arms. *Why am I here?*

"Because I want to earn your trust."

She chuckled as she played with her septum ring. Did she trust anyone? No, the last person she trusted died under a desert sun years before. When her brother died, she'd locked her trust away so no man or angel could influence her. Her eyes leveled with his. "My trust is not for sale." She winced as the words slid past her throat like sandpaper. A lightning bolt of pain shot up the fresh scar as she frowned.

"*Mon cher*, I wouldn't dare put a price on your trust." He leaned forward and rested his hand on her thigh.

Her breath faltered, and his touch burned. In a good way.

"Here, let me help with that." His fingers squeezed.

The pain melted away, but the heat of his hand on her thigh lingered. She narrowed her eyes, and he raised his brows innocently. She glared right back.

"There." The bastard knew what he was doing. "Let's get started on that tour."

He showed her the theater, the library, the indoor pool, and the gym. Last, he showed her to the underground rooms. "This one is yours." He flipped on a light. "It's blast-proof. You can come here to practice anytime you like. I've never seen a muse—" He mimed an explosion, sound effects and all. "So, I'm afraid I can't do much more than provide a space for you."

Lex rested against the wall. Her eyes were on Gabriel's back and a smile on her face. Her trust wasn't for sale, but other things were. His hands clasped behind his neck. She admired his defined shoulders, the way they strained against his shirt. He'd left his jacket in the office, and with him facing the other direction, her eyes traveled downward, enjoying the view.

"Are you ready for me to show you back to the gym?" He smirked over his shoulder, his ebony eyes as hungry as hers.

Lex dropped her smile as he turned around, her brows furrowed with confusion. *Why the gym?*

"I think it will help you control your Scientia." She held still as he devoured her body with his eyes. Every nerve ending came to life, sending goosebumps down her arms as their gazes met. "Plus…" he paused as unadulterated heat filled the space between them. His voice lowered. "You look like you work out."

Her fists clenched when he leaned in. She needed to keep her hands to herself. They shared a breath, and she shivered, stepping back. Lex had spent half her life dancing for money. Sexual tension made all the difference when it came to what kind of tips she'd collected, but this charged energy between them was something different. And she hated him for it.

She backed away, advancing into the gym. She reached up, her fingers running over the pull-up bar. He was right. She'd always exercised. As a child, she'd competed in gymnastics. As an adult, she danced a pole. Since her overdose, she'd been trapped at her father's house, but she still took the time to keep fit. She'd never know when she'd need to use her body to earn money.

What are you looking at, asshole?

"You."

Why?

He gave her a lopsided smile. "I'm flirting with you."

It started then, the game of cat and mouse. Every day, when he joined her in the gym with his board shorts and fitted tee, she allowed herself to watch him. They worked out in companionable silence, the atmosphere around them thick with a wanting that grew with each passing day. She appreciated his built shoulders and got lost checking out his ass, imagining touching those places with her hands. She didn't bother to hide these thoughts. She'd caught him doing the same, and Lex made sure to live up to the exhibitionist she was. Bending at the waist instead of the knees, flexing and pointing with every action, laying herself out for his viewing pleasure. Her skin was electrified when she caught his heat-filled gaze on her ass as she stretched, his bottom lip caught between his teeth.

Lex's cold shoulder melted under the heat. She wanted to know him. To know the man behind the big boss façade he wore around the others. And then she reminded herself he was an angel, her enemy, and useless at meeting her needs between the sheets. She knew how angels worked. They were interchangeable with Barbie and Ken dolls. Angels had all the equipment but none of the functionality. So, she enjoyed the view as she pleased and never did anything more than fantasize.

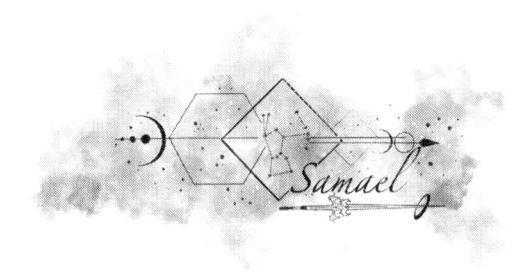

Samael

"She needs you," Samael said to a red-eyed David as he barged past him into his apartment, an unconscious Wylie in his arms.

David shut the door behind them and followed in a rush. The moment she came within reach, his fingers grazed her cheek. The color fell from his face. "What's wrong with her?"

"She's drained dry." Samael stumbled, leaning into the couch. His nostrils flared as he breathed his muse in. He needed her. "Jane's here too. Good. Sit."

David did as told. Samael set Wylie on his lap. He shifted her limbs to make her comfortable and went to Jane's bedroom door. He leaned against it and slid to his bottom. "How long were we gone?"

"Twelve hours." David's hands lingered in the air, hesitating inches from the bare skin of her arm and neck. Instead, he reached for the blanket on the back of the couch and pulled it over her. "I thought she was dead. I woke up on the roof alone and thought you were both dead." He rubbed his neck where a mark remained from the attack.

Samael's arms braced the door jamb. He gritted his teeth and groaned, his eyes closing. "I gave her too much of my energy. I was afraid she'd die."

She flinched awake, her heart rattling against her lungs. A blanket covered her, like a Band-Aid on a bleeder. A blanket couldn't fix the ache in her bones. A blanket couldn't settle the acid boiling in her belly. A blanket couldn't stop the sound of the dying—the feeling of being a murderer.

David's hands ran over her arm, a tempo to base her breaths. "You're home," he said over and over.

But he was so wrong. She'd just left her home, which had stopped existing the moment Roberto took his last breath. And she could have lost David too. The realization put desperation in her hands as she reached for him. She needed him alive. She needed him safe.

"David." Maybe his light could outshine her darkness?

His eyes filled with apprehension. He nodded once, his face smoothed by understanding, and rocked them onto his feet. She wrapped her arms around his neck. The stinging of her eyes turned into sobs. Grateful to be with him but drowning in a truth she hadn't been prepared for.

He shouldered his bedroom door open and kicked it closed behind them. His Adam's apple bobbed as he sat, and Wylie steadied it with her lips. She buried her face in the softness of his cinnamon-flavored throat and soaked it with tears. She'd almost lost him. He could've died.

"Wylie, you're home." He caught her hands and held them against his sides until their tremors stopped.

"David, she was going to kill you. I thought you'd die like everyone else."

They reached for each other. His hands came to her hair, tangling themselves there. Hers snaked to his back. Their teeth clicked together. Their noses battled for position. Gasps and pants competed as he chased the memories away with kisses, and Wylie confirmed his existence with hers.

Drawing him into her, she wrapped her legs around his hips, and they rocked against each other. His hands slipped under her dress and cupped her ass. The delicious feeling of his jeans against her nakedness overtook any other sensation. With his guidance, her fevered movements became something softer. His arms found their way around her again.

She moaned a cry into his mouth, and he swallowed it. He whispered to the skin below her ear. Her skin tingled as he worshiped her, saying prayers to the muscles that held her head up even when it felt impossible. Venerating the pulse, which brought oxygen to her "beautiful" mind.

Some words she caught over the sound of her heartbeats and hot breaths, others she felt burning against her skin. Physical aches melted away as his muse magic took hold of her. He healed her with his words, his touch, his very presence.

His hands followed the curve of her spine. His fingers caught the hem of her dress, and he lifted it over her head. His eyes went first to her breasts and then to her pregnancy-scarred tummy.

He placed her on the bed. Her legs hung off the edge. Her feet rested on the floor. He leaned over her and weaved his fingers with hers, steadying them as he persisted with his whispers. He told her stomach and thighs the same secrets he'd told her neck. Her toes curled, grabbing at the soft carpet.

It occurred to her, as her back arched, this man touched her, held her, and moved against her as if they'd done this dance a million times before. In her bones, she felt it: they completed each other. A feeling she never thought she'd find again. Two parts of a whole being joined: angel and muse.

He traced the curve of her hip, her waist, her ribs, and then settled at her breast, finding her nipple with his thumb and forefinger as his mouth coaxed her leg to rotate, his hand guiding her knee onto the bed. The apex of her thighs opened to him. The coolness of the air and anticipation sent a shiver up her spine.

He moved up her body, taking the unattended nipple in his mouth. His fingers drew a slow, deliberate line down the center of her being, and she cried out. His warm fingers drew masterpieces against her inner thighs. Their kisses grew long, and just when she'd forgotten the intentions of his hand, one of his fingers entered her. Catching her groan with his mouth, a second finger followed.

She clung to his arm, riding his hand like a virgin, unintentional movements making her thrash under his ministrations. His thumb found its place on her clitoris, and fireworks went off in her head.

"David."

"Yeah?" His response came with raised brows and dreamy eyes.

"I want you . . ." Her hands slid to the waist of his pants. He didn't respond, his brows coming together in concern. She ran her fingers along the length of his hardness, communicating her desires with touch.

He shivered and pulled back to meet her eyes, his fingers leaving her empty. "Yes?"

Pushing her face into his chest, she blushed. "I want you inside me."

Wylie's arm covered her face as he rolled onto his back beside her.

"I can't. I want to. I thought I could, but I can't." His hand brushed her shoulder, and she flinched away. "We need some boundaries first."

"Boundaries?"

"I keep thinking about being dragged by that angel. How easy it would have been for her to end me. I have people that rely on me. I need to think."

"So, what were we doing just now?" Her hands returned to shaking. This rejection, on top of everything else, might break her. "You're giving me whiplash."

"I wanted to comfort you."

"So, you gave me a charity fingerbang?"

"Wylie." Her name cracked in his mouth.

She'd discovered after falling from the sky that her life's path followed a prophecy, which left her to question every choice she ever made. Did she love Roberto because of the man or because he was her muse? Did it matter? "I used to think I made my own decisions, but I'm finding that we have control over nothing. This . . ." She took a deep breath and reached for him. "This is something we can control. I can decide to feel passion instead of grief."

"We're feeling these things for a reason. We feel fear because we are in danger and sorrow because we are hurt. I don't want to cover this up. I want to fix it."

The force in his words blinded her. They burned like an accusation. She pulled her hand back to her chest. "What are you trying to say?"

"I'm your soul. I can't eat, shit, or breathe without doing it for your existence. At least give me some time to figure things out."

"Are you saying you need space?" She shot from the bed and searched the ground for her dress.

"Wylie, I have to protect myself. My mother, my sister, I'm the only one they have. How do I take care of them if I'm dead?"

Her fingers caught the cloth of her discarded dress, and she whipped it over her head. "Of course, David, you know best."

Samael

Samael shot to his feet and bound forward in search of Wylie. Someone was hurting her. His hand landed on the door to David's room. Whispers hissed on the other side.

"I can't eat, shit, or breathe without doing it for your existence." The edge in David's voice cut Samael as surely as it cut Wylie. He had the sudden urge to break the man's neck.

He covered his ears; he had no control over her. He didn't want to hear them or smell what the two had done in that room. Their swirl of emotions overwhelmed him in ways he'd never experienced before. Something about her and David alone together made his chest hurt. The way David held her as if he owned her. How Wylie relaxed into the man's arms. Their human empathy allowed them to understand each other in a way he never could. It also allowed her to know him in the biblical sense, something Samael and his siblings were not made to do.

When her muse and son were murdered, Samael arrived at the site to remove the body of the human Marut had dispatched. He stayed to observe Wylie's reaction. He suspected her proximity to the veil would reveal her powers, but in the end, he saw her at the peak of her humanity. Useless to help her, he'd squirmed, uncomfortable with her sorrow. He remained useless now.

He should assign someone else to her care. How many times had he almost lost her? At every turn, he'd made mistakes since he'd found her. For the first time in his existence, his power and his strength weren't adequate. This anger wasn't God's wrath. No, it echoed the emotion that had him throwing young Leleil at a bus.

He paced the living room, debating who he should trust with her care. His energy now returned. Nothing kept him here, but could he leave her? He was her white horse, and she'd broken him just as the prophecy predicted. Why else did he have the itch to crack open his rib cage and give Wylie his heart?

David's door swung open, and Wylie ran out. Her face was wet with tears; the smell of sex followed her. Samael glared at David as Wylie smacked into his chest, his arms wrapping around her.

"Let's go," she said, and then Wylie's mind spoke to him. A single word broke through his barriers without his allowing the communication: *Now!*

He folded his wings around her and took her away.

Chapter 23

Lex

Lex squatted down and then jumped. *Twenty-five, shit.* Squatted down and jumped, *twenty-six, fuck*, exploding into the air with each burst of her thighs. At rep thirty, she wiped the sweat from her eyes as she caught her breath.

She hadn't been at the compound for long, but she already felt like she owned this gym. Every time her traitorous heart reminded her of the needle, she came here. A place where she could grit her teeth and prepare for battle. Somewhere she could exert herself hard enough that sleep would find her at night. There lived a secret part of her that knew with her face ruined she'd need to use her body to support her habits if she ever decided to use again.

She closed that part of herself down as she caught her breath, instead enjoying a little eye candy. Gabriel leaned back in a chair, his legs crossed at the ankles, staring down at his phone. What would it feel like to put her fingers through his hair? To bite his lip? To sit in his lap and touch the hard planes of his chest?

Gabriel's lazy smile lifted his cheeks as she turned back to the mirror. Their eyes met through the glass, and her breath caught. He stood, his smile becoming wolfish, and strolled to her. Each step was calculated, his obsidian eyes never leaving hers. "Have you been practicing?" He shoved his phone into his pocket.

Practicing?

"You know." He mimed an explosion. "Boom!"

She held a snort in. *I have, but I'm going to have to quit if I ever see you do that again.*

He raised his brows. "Are you talking about the sound effect or the —" His hands flew up with another fake blast.

Both.

"Hmm." He lifted his shirt and itched his six-pack. Lex licked her lips. Her hands wanted to replace his. Gabriel smirked. "I have some business to attend to outside the compound. Would you like to join me?"

Where? Lex asked his abs, her eyes trapped.

His smile grew. "Seattle."

I really shouldn't. She forced herself to walk away, heading to a treadmill.

"Lexy, should I have someone look in on you while I'm gone?" He leaned against the mirror, facing her.

She pushed a few buttons, starting her run at a sprint. She watched him watching her in the mirror. She didn't need checking up on. What she needed was a cold shower. His carnal gaze was directed at her ass. This time, she smirked.

He reached in front of her and pushed the up arrow twice. The treadmill's elevation increased, and his grin shifted to the right as he watched her body transform.

"I'm going to miss you."

She ignored him, making herself believe his words did not affect her. *You're coming on strong today, asshole.*

He pushed himself off the wall and stood beside her as she ran. "I'll be thinking about you biting my lip."

She choked, smashing the red stop button.

He laughed and walked out of the gym.

She sent his retreating form images of him roasting on a spit as she restarted the treadmill.

Wylie

Mirrors lined every wall of the room. Ludus' fluorescent lights screamed with brightness as they protested their wire cages. Wylie stood facing Samael, her chest constricting. "How can I be this thing you claim I am?"

Samael lifted his hand as if to touch her face and stalled as their eyes met. She saw doubt in his gaze for the first time. She saw pain and questions, and the foreignness of it acted as a speed bump in her spiral. Were they spiraling together?

She wrapped her fingers around his wrist. "I don't think I can survive this."

His eyes anchored her. His hands came to her waist. "Wylie." The surrounding whiteness faded with the sound of his voice. "Hold on to me." His forehead rested against hers, and her world became the green of his irises.

She did as told, running her hands up his arms until her fingers took hold of his sleeves. Soon her breaths came in time with his. Air eased into her lungs, her heart slowed, and her grip loosened.

"I want to understand better." Samael still held onto her as if she would blow away. "Close your eyes and show me."

She immediately realized what he meant. She closed her eyes. Her whole body tensed as she forced all the pain into one place.

Boot to back, screaming Dean, the silver-haired man.

A moan escaped her.

Marut's chest catching bullets as he tried to save her family, the etch-a-sketch experiment that killed him.

It all suffocated her. Samael's grip tightened on her waist, reminding her she wasn't alone. She pushed on.

Her in scrubs, teeth bared as she compressed a chest.

Can any good deed make up for murder?

David on the other side of the room, giving orders. She'd ruined his life. *Jane in a wheelchair. Jane's hug. Jane smiling at her brother. David's heels dragging against the rooftop. The sound of him choking. Her face on a male Angel. His taunts. The ice wings that rose behind him. The man who ordered her death was her brother.*

Her legs gave way, and Samael held her against his chest as she cried because that was all she knew how to do anymore. She was somehow this powerful angel with this huge destiny that had done nothing but break things. In her sorrow, she'd lost everything. The part of her that was good. The part of her that was loved. She needed to regain control. But she was just so exhausted. She needed to find out what being an angel meant for her. And maybe along the way, she'd forgive herself. She struggled to keep her eyes open.

"Rest, Wylie. I'll be here when you wake," Samael whispered in her ear.

She accepted his words as permission and allowed herself to slip into oblivion.

When her eyes opened, Samael cradled her in his arms, sitting on the ground with his back against the mirror. "I'm ready to be an angel."

"Hmph." The sound rumbled through her. His pulled her close. His wet-with-sweat hair hung into his face.

"Teach me."

Samael grunted. "Why?"

"I'm tired of being dragged along for the ride." She rested her head on his chest, knowing she should feel uncomfortable or embarrassed, but they'd written songs about being held by an angel, and none of them did the feeling justice.

Wylie felt Samael's gaze on her and lifted hers to meet it. His brows met as if contemplating whether or not this was a good decision before he nodded. "Okay." He lowered her onto the ground next to him. "It will be difficult."

"I'm tired of things happening to me. I'm ready to change that and stand my ground against Gabriel. Show me how to be an angel."

"You will start here." He pointed at the mirror opposite them.

Red patches rimmed her eyes, and her lips showed two shades lighter than her skin. "Here?" She looked away so she wouldn't see the slump of her shoulders or the silent uncertainty in her jaw.

"Yes." He got to his feet and put out his hand for Wylie. "Let's find your Scientia."

"You think I can do this?" She let him pull her up.

"I know you can." His wings appeared behind him, his chin lifted, and his confidence seeped into her in waves.

"Am I feeling what you feel?"

"You're feeling a fraction of my faith in you."

She covered her cheeks with her hands.

"We're going to find your wings." He turned her to the mirror. "Mirrors are a focal point for angels. Like water, they ground us in time and space. Wylie, you're going to look into the mirror and find your wings."

Wylie's tension lightened as she studied Samael's serious face. If he believed she could find her wings, she would adopt some of his faith and try.

The Dominion grunted in approval. "Now, look at yourself and repeat after me." He waited for her to focus. *"Veni Angelus—"*

"Veni Angelus."

"—da mihi Scientia." Samael's wings opened with his words.

"Dammm—wait, what?" She rolled her shoulders. "Dameatia."

"—da mihi Scientia."

"Dummy entia." Wylie shook her head. "I'm so bad with languages. If we can't do this in English, can we do it in Spanish?"

His wings lowered. "It's Latin. The older languages hold more power. Modern languages are diluted and lazy." His hands found Wylie's shoulders. "It means: Come, angel, give me knowledge."

"Say it again." He squeezed her. *"Veni Angelus."* He waited for Wylie to murder the words with her crappy American accent. *"Da mihi Scientia."*

"Da mihi Scientia." She folded her arms. "So, what does it mean?"

"Imagine you're calling to the angel inside of you. The part of you with fiery wings whose only care was to direct fighting away from civilians."

A nervous laugh bubbled up. "That happened? I'd convinced myself I dreamed it."

"You were magnificent." He ignored the skeptical tilt of her head and focused on himself in the mirror. *"Veni Angelus, da mihi Scientia."* As he spoke, his wings came to life at his back, their gold glittering as they spread wide, nearly touching the walls on either side of the room. His warm light ate up the fluorescent brightness.

The heat in the air intensified until Wylie was sure she would melt. The burn of his presence converged where his hands rested. The familiar heat reminded her of the wings she'd donned as rain and chaos swallowed her.

"Now you," he said. His aura receded, and his wings disappeared.

She shook her head and concentrated. *"Veni Angelus, da,"* She mumbled the next two syllables. "Scientia." Nothing happened.

"Let's try together. We will chant it. Put your hands on mine. Concentrate on my palms. Imagine your wings coming from where my hands meet your back."

She rested her fingers on his, where they curled over her shoulders and looked at her reflection.

"Veni Angelus, da mihi Scientia."

"Veni Angelus, da mihi Scientia." At first, Samael's low voice dominated the chant, but as Wylie became confident in the words, her voice grew in volume. She stared into her eyes. Their blackness matched her brother's. Her brother.

The anger started to boil in her belly. It rose to her chest, splashing against the cage of her ribs and flowing into her voice. Her lips lifted from her teeth, and the Latin burst from her mouth as if through a microphone. The lights flickered as flames exploded from her hands. She charged her reflection.

"I hate you!" The glass shattered as her fists landed like hammers. Ludus shook, and the lights above burst into sparks and smoke. Pain and blackness devoured her.

Miles of people chanted. "Armageddon, Armageddon." Wylie leaned against the door to heaven. With a cry, she became an inferno, her fire engulfing the door. They burned away, and the throng of humans ran through the ashes into the beyond. Angels hovered above, watching as the humans left them behind.

Wylie forgot the dream before she woke.

Chapter 24

"Do you think she's ready for all that power? Look what she's done so far."

"This is not up for debate, Laoth."

"Then she needs to have a cap. No more dead angels because her panties are in a twist."

Samael grumbled as Wylie peaked around him, hoping the two voices she heard weren't talking about her. She recognized neither angel. The warehouse-sized room they argued in did not belong in Ludus, with its soaring ceilings and gray walls. A steel pillar dominated the space, with a wooden platform surrounding it. Scorch marks climbed the metal column.

"Samael, I wasn't expecting you yet." The click of high heels punctuated an angel's southern lilt. The thin female with green hair folded her arms and disappeared.

"Dumah, I've brought our guest." Samael stepped aside.

The angel that remained caught sight of Wylie and dropped to a knee without caring what her thigh-length skirt did. She lifted her forearm to cover her eyes. "Armageddon." Her bald head gleamed as she bowed. Her flawless umber skin glowed next to her white cardigan.

Drawn to touch her, Wylie folded her arms. She'd never forgotten the vision she'd had when Samael saluted her this way.

"The mirrors won't work for Wylie," Samael said as Dumah rose.

"She's been human too long, hasn't she?" The female pulled Wylie into an embrace. "Don't you worry. We can fix this."

Wylie smiled at her own awkwardness. This angel felt so familiar.

"I'll return for her Catharsis." Samael lifted his chin. "I must speak to Laoth now."

"Indeed, brother, I think you should."

"But . . ." Wylie's eyes widened as she realized he meant to leave her.

"You're in excellent hands." He nodded once and disappeared.

Wylie stared at the empty place he'd just occupied. How could he leave her? How could he introduce her to a second angel and then leave her?

"Let me show you around." Dumah clapped her hands, her wide smile reassuring. "That stage is where your Catharsis will take place."

Catharsis sounded either painful or perverted. She wasn't sure which to hope for. Her eyes found the pillar again, her head tilting back as she followed it up. A fan the size of a car spun around the column's origin at a slow clip. They'd built this room to contain a large fire. Bleachers lined the wall on the other side of the platform. *Fire with an audience.*

"I'm guessing from your blank stare that Samael told you nothing."

Wylie shook my head.

"Bless his heart."

"Bless his heart?"

"I'm an angel. I can, 'bless his heart.'" Dumah hooked her arm with Wylie's. "This way."

Wylie decided to like her before she saw the art lining the cinder block. Painting after painting depicted flames, with small writhing figures at the center of all the orange, red, and yellow. Some held bound victims. They leaned against their restraints, their arms behind their backs, their heads lifted skyward. Others showed their curved shoulders as they clung to the stake, their hair alight.

Oh my God, they're going to light me on fire.

Wylie's legs stopped working, and her knees gave way. Her breaths came in staccato pants as the fear of being burned alive climbed up her throat. Thousands of paintings covered the wall, the columns and rows an uneven reflection of fire's chaos.

"Those can be quite shocking." Dumah squatted next to Wylie, whose hands had found her knees. "But they are beautiful, aren't they? Would you like to see mine?"

"What?" Wylie's voice came out in a whisper.

Without ceremony, she hauled Wylie to her feet. "Tartys paints these." Dumah steered her back to the door. Too shocked to run or fight, she followed. "There. That's me." Dumah pointed just above their heads.

It would have been striking. It would have been beautiful if a pyre didn't loom behind her. She knew what standing in those flames did to a person. She'd seen burns. Third and fourth-degree burns blackened bones and sucked hydration from their victims. Skin peeled back, fat sizzling as it followed gravity, muscles stretching tight like rubber bands. Wylie's skin tingled as it prepared to crawl away.

She moved closer to the painting of Dumah. "You can tell our Angel types by how the fire burns. She draws a circle around the flames. "See how mine burns low and wide? That's a sign of a Virtue. Look at that one." She points at the one next to hers. "That's Azazel. He's a Power. When Powers burn, there's always lots of smoke. It makes sense. That's how they got that smoke up their asses." She winked.

Wylie leaned in. Her fingers lifted to touch the thick valleys of acrylic color.

"Go ahead, touch it." Dumah stroked the painting. "And then step back, and you'll see surrender."

Wylie resisted the urge. Maybe she didn't touch it out of politeness for Tartys or respect for the burning victim. Maybe she was afraid. Afraid the pain would transfer to her through her fingertips. As if burning to death could be catching.

She looked down at her hands. Her healing hands, but also ones that belonged to the mind of a murderer. Yes, she deserved to burn. She thought of Susan's description of Marut's death. With a slap, her entire hand covered Dumah's painted form, sweaty palm and all.

Peace.

Wylie's apprehension drained away. She stumbled back. One foot after another until the entire collection came into view. The art's second meaning emerged. She gasped. Finally, she saw more than death and carnage . . .

Surrender.

A city of dancing angels crowded the wall as flaming wings wrapped around them. Their faces contorted in the ecstasy of freedom.

Chapter 25

Wylie

"This way." Wylie jumped when Dumah spoke. The angel guided her past the morbid stage and into a duplicate of Wylie's living room.

Dumah sat on the coffee table, smiling as Wylie dove onto the couch.

"How did you do this?" Cushions muffled Wylie's voice.

"When you know the right angel, you can do anything."

Wylie rolled onto her back and stared up at the industrial ceiling. "Why did you do this?"

"I wanted you to feel comfortable. Sometimes it takes a Virtue to know the importance of comfort."

"Thank you."

"Do you need to rest?"

"No, I . . ." She rubbed her temples. "What's a Virtue?"

"I'm a Virtue." She put her hands on her hips and struck a pose. "We rule the seasons, the ebb and flow of time, the rising and setting of the sun, the moons, the stars." She gestured at the ceiling as if a sky existed on this plane. "We all have our specialties." The smell of chocolate and roses filled the air. "My skills lie in manipulating hormones and moods. Some people call Virtues like me the Lady in Red, because of my monthly visits."

Wylie's uterus twinged with a crampy confirmation.

Dumah's eyes narrowed. "What are you thinking? It's strange. I can't read your mind."

She squirmed under the Virtue's scrutiny. "Samael can."

"Samael is more powerful than I am."

"Can he read yours?"

"If I let him." She smirked.

"Wait, you can control it?" Wylie leaned forward.

"It takes practice, but yes." Dumah put her hands on her hips.

"So, how do I do it?"

"Samael told you about how angels project themselves. Right?"

"Yeah."

"It works the same, but instead of projecting our bodies, we project our minds." Dumah tapped the side of her head. "We can practice later."

"Wait. I want to make sure I'm understanding you correctly. You create a decoy brain?"

"Pretty much, but it doesn't always work. Strong angels, like Samael, can see through it if you're not careful."

"Strong angels like Samael? What makes him different?"

"His angel type."

"What's Samael?" David's flashcards popped into Wylie's head. She wished they'd had time to look at them. *David*. She sat, crossing her legs. Regret pierced her heart.

"Samael's a Dominion."

Wylie blinked, ignoring her frustration with David to return to the conversation.

"They are God's generals. They only answer to the God's Guard."

She remembered the Seraphim and how Samael kneeled for them, how he basically laid on the ground. "No shit?"

"Oh yeah, he's my boss's boss. The guy is stupid powerful."

Wylie's cheeks reddened.

Dumah glanced up at Wylie through her long lashes. "It's funny. Out of everything I've told you, you question Samael's place."

"It's just, he's wasted a lot of time helping me." Wylie ignored the way Dumah frowned at her words. "So, what kind of angel am I?"

"That's why you're here." Dumah gestured to the mural of burning angels.

"Is there another way to find out without barbecuing me?"

Dumah huffed a laugh at Wylie's description of the Catharsis. "Unfortunately, since the mirrors didn't work, this is the only way." Dumah gave her a contemplative look. "The decision is still yours. You don't have to do it. But remember, you will never be able to use all of your powers without it." The sound of her heels echoed as she paced the length of the coffee table.

Wylie frowned. "You've all pointed out how human I am. I can't even use my wings. What if I'm not an angel, and you guys kill me?"

"That's what the Catharsis is for. It separates the two. On Ludus, we spend all this time ensuring our angels know how to be human. They practice wearing clothes and socializing. We even do some training on modern technology. We're militant in our training, and by the end, they need a reminder of who we are. This is the graduation." She smiled. "We don't have to train you to be human. You're already an expert. You've been playing with humanity your entire life. It's time for you to graduate."

Dumah stopped moving. "Watch."

Wylie stood as Dumah's skin tone lightened into the sun-kissed color of antique lace. Her image flashed and her body morphed.

Wylie's hand came up to cover her mouth. Samael stood before her with a grin she'd never seen before on his face. Barefoot and shirtless, Dumah's skirt stretched tight over his hips.

"Samael presents himself in a body that reflects his angel strength. And the stuffiness of his personality." Samael's deep voice sounded too cheery as Dumah smoothed her skirt. "Your body tells a story of a strong woman who can fit toddlers on her hip and lift the fallen off the ground."

Dumah ran her fingers through her hair, the strands lengthening and curling as she combed them. Her hips widened, her shoulders narrowed, and the shape of her eyes pulled up and out. Her skin took on Wylie's earthen hue.

"Okay, now that's just creepy." Wylie circled Dumah, taking in the finer details she missed. Like the scar on her left knee from a tumble she took while running and her laugh lines.

Dumah raised her arms and pranced about with more confidence than Wylie ever had. "Look, I'm gorgeous like you." She giggled as she did a figure eight with her hips and then, with a blink, became herself again with that near-twilight skin and red lipstick. "This is your chance to become the angel you were meant to be. What do you think?" The Virtue pushed one of Wylie's curls behind her ear. "Should we scrub your humanity off with a little fire?"

Wylie shivered. Would the pain be worth it? Could she survive it? Could she survive without it?

Gabriel's smug face entered her mind.

"When can we start?"

Lex

Lex opened the door. Gabriel stood on the other side, handsome in a navy three-piece suit. "Wow." He put out his hand for hers. "You're gorgeous."

For the first time, she realized why she never shook hands. The gesture always reminded her of Abaddon, how he'd spun her around and called her a "good girl." But Gabriel wasn't Abaddon; he'd revealed enough of himself to show her how different the two angels were. She rested her fingers on his hand. He squeezed them lightly and rested them on his forearm. His chin lifted in the virile way of a proud man.

She wore a long-sleeved black dress that barely covered her ass and matching four-inch heels. She knew she looked good, though it'd all fallen apart when people saw her face. The broken tattoo on her forehead, interrupted by a spider web of scars, competed with the pink line which bisected her nose and mouth. She didn't know what to do with makeup anymore.

"We will meet with Laoth, and then I'll project us to our destination." He looked her over, starting with her legs. "Are you sure you're ready for this?"

She nodded.

He stopped. "But, first . . ." Lex caught her breath when he leaned down and kissed her temple.

The sudden display of affection confused her. His lips lingered there before moving to her ear. "Your scars are one of the most beautiful things about you. You're a survivor. A fighter. If anything, they're the reason I'm drawn to you."

Lex pulled back with a jerk. Her eyes narrowed as she looked for the lie in the black depths of his eyes. But all she found was the hunger she'd always seen. Except now, it looked a little more like admiration. For the first time in God knows how many years, Lex felt . . . *seen*.

She desperately wanted to believe him, but she needed to keep her guard up. He was an outstanding actor. She'd witnessed how he manipulated the angels who followed him, how they were all ready to fall at his feet. So, Lex responded the way she always did.

Sure thing, asshole. No one wants to look at this fucked up face. I know what you're looking at and they're not for you. She gestured at the low 'V' of her dress.

He didn't take the bait. Instead, he offered her a soft smile. "One day, *cher*, I'll show you how much I want you. Starting with those lips."

He smirked and continued down the hall, leaving her more confused than ever.

Gabriel turned into his office, and Lex hurried to catch up. Laoth paced in front of the desk. She stopped as they entered, huffing as she leaned on the desk. Lex took her spot next to him.

"You're here already." Gabriel straightened his cuffs, his smirk ever-present.

The polished desk screeched as Laoth dragged her palms over it. "You're lucky I don't know you well."

"And why is that?"

Laoth's eyes flicked to Lex and back to Gabriel, her smile matching his. "Because I'd tell you to fuck off, but I'm far too respectful for that. Unlike some people."

Lex refused to fall for the bait. She sent her thoughts toward the task at hand. *Why was she here?*

"I'd advise against that."

"And that's why I didn't try my luck. Well then, let's get started." Laoth pushed herself off the desk. "There will be four of us there—Samael, myself, and two archangels, Madoc and Ariel. No one is to be injured except for me. I can handle most things, but let's not try decapitation or dismemberment."

Gabriel pulled a file from the top drawer, tossed it on his desk, and steepled his fingers. "Lex, you'll want to see these."

Lex came to lean on the opposite side of the desk from Laoth.

He pulled out six photos. All the angels appeared as men. They presented themselves as large and muscular, too handsome to be human.

Lex knew these were for her. Gabriel could have pushed these images into Laoth's head. She'd have to remember to thank him later. Or not, she rolled her eyes. *This guy.*

He tilted his head to hers, the only sign that he'd heard her. "These angels have all asked for free will. I've offered to speak to them as a group at this Italian restaurant." He pulled a post-it off the front of the file.

"I know four of them." Laoth pointed to a blond and three brunettes.

"They are all known for murdering at least one of their muses. I'll separate them from their muse and signal you I'm done." He turned to Lex. "You leaving the building will be my signal. You'll return to our point of entrance and wait for me."

"I'll try to engage you before Samael, but that may not be possible. He's upset about you killing Wylie's muse and the baby angel."

Gabriel shrugged.

"Speaking of, do you know where the human bastard you hired to do the job is?"

"I don't. Binah did the legwork with that one. Why?" His fingers interlocked with each other.

"He might be useful if I'm going to gain Wylie's trust."

"Have you spoken to her?"

"No, my first time meeting Wylie in person was when you first met her. I don't get what the big deal was. I mean, she fell off that building like a potato." Laoth shook her head in disgust.

Gabriel turned to Lex. "My twin sister is pretty famous among angels. They call her Armageddon. They expect her to end the world. I'm just hoping to cut her off at the pass."

Lex narrowed her eyes. *Does she live in Seattle?*

"She does."

She didn't let herself think of David. Instead, she thought of the six muse murderers. "What will happen to these angels?"

Laoth cringed at Lex's painful rasp. "They will be tortured and disposed of." Laoth gathered the folder. "I read minds too, not as well as him." She pointed her thumb at Gabriel. "But I'd rather work a little harder to read your mind than hear that creepy voice again."

Lex jumped as Gabriel's fist landed on the desk. "What did you say?"

"Never mind." Laoth looked at her watch. "I should go. Samael's waiting." With that, she projected away.

Lex couldn't look at Gabriel, suddenly too embarrassed. Her hand held her throat. Now more than ever, she wondered why an angel like Gabriel would want to give any attention to a broken muse.

He reached for her. "Do you want to talk about it?"

She shook her head.

"Then, come here." He opened his arms.

The fuck?

"There are only a handful of angels who can project a human. It's difficult and could be . . ." He shrugged. "A little dangerous. The closer you are to me. The easier it will be. So, come here, *rêleuse*." He patted his lap. "It's also better I leave you here in a seated position. I don't want you falling over."

Wait, we're leaving my body here?

"Trust me. It will be a fun adventure."

She stepped between his legs and peeked at him from under her lashes before sitting on his knee.

"Closer." Gabriel wrapped his arms around her waist and slid her against him. "That's better."

Hey, asshole, you get me killed, and I'll haunt you for the rest of your life.

"I have no doubts about that." He rested his chin on her shoulder. "Okay, hellcat." He squeezed lightly. "Are you ready?" He projected before she could answer.

Samael

Samael and Laoth met with two archangels in an empty warehouse. Laoth's hard work had finally paid off. Her debrief included the six leaders of Gabriel's army who would be at the restaurant across the street. A God-light flashed six times, whitening the window and splashing its brightness onto the street. They'd wanted to wait for Gabriel to turn the angels, knowing that in their weakened state, there would be less cleaning up after this ambush.

Samael narrowed his eyes as a muse left the restaurant. He'd only seen her back, but he recognized her Scientia as old and familiar. She walked with a strange combination of confidence and uncertainty. Her thoughts were masked by Gabriel himself. Samael would look into her later.

The plan was simple. Laoth and Samael would project into the space, while archangels, Ariel and Madoc, entered from either side of the building. The goal would be to take prisoners.

Laoth picked at her teeth with her dagger as she leaned against the windowsill. "Ready to clean house?"

Samael grunted; he was in a poor mood. Leaving Wylie with Dumah affected him more than he cared to admit. The pent-up energy had to go somewhere. He'd go into this mission weaponless and looking for brawls as if busting his knuckles on someone's face would cure his infatuation.

Madoc unfastened Joyeuse, Charlamagne's lost sword, from his back while Ariel rechecked the multitude of firearms attached to her body. "Ready," they replied in unison.

These were Laoth's soldiers, so Samael awaited her command.

"Pro summum bonum." Laoth raised her forearm to her eyes.

"Pro summum bonum!" Samael projected with the exclamation still in his throat. He landed behind Gabriel, who sat at the head of the table of traitors. Samael wrapped his arm around the unsuspecting angel's neck and lifted him with his forearm.

Gabriel disappeared, reappearing behind Samael. His foot came down like a sledgehammer on the back of Samael's knee, and he shoved the gold-winged angel onto the table.

The table broke apart under him. He projected before hitting the ground. The Dominion touched down facing Gabriel, his feet apart, his hand extended. He caught hold of Gabriel's throat, and their eyes met.

Wylie's eyes.

Gabriel struck the inside of Samael's elbow and kneed his groin at the same time. Samael lost his grip and crumpled forward, crashing into Gabriel and taking them both to the ground. A gunshot rang out, followed by another, and another as the two angels grappled, teeth bared. Elbows, knees, and knuckles found their homes as they fought for dominance.

Samael sat on Gabriel's chest, a volley of blows landing. The ground shook with each blow, his Scientia pounding into the male as hard as his fists. The bastard would suffer for what he'd done.

A dagger materialized in Samael's hand, drawing blood before Samael could stop himself. The silver of the blade shone bright against Gabriel's ochre skin. "You're coming with me."

A shot rang out, and next to him, Laoth grunted as she caught a bullet with her shoulder. She crashed into him, and they went down together.

The Dominion freed himself to discover Gabriel had projected out of the building. He could be anywhere. Laoth panted as she held her arm. Their eyes met. Samael growled, turned to the angel who'd shot his friend, and charged with fists full of frustration and the smallest spark of doubt in his heart.

Chapter 26

Samael

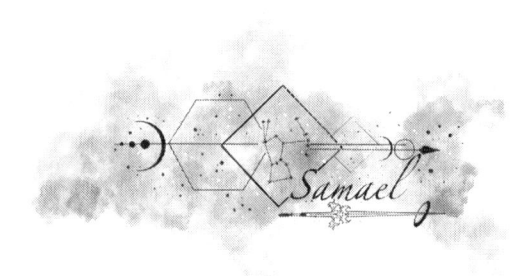

Days later, Samael joined his fellow angels on Ludus to celebrate Wylie's Catharsis. He sat with the Dominions, unable to focus on anything happening around him. Raphael leaned in with more of his usual sarcasm, but Samael heard nothing, felt nothing. Lines creased his forehead in a perfect mirror image of Wylie's. Drawn by her vulnerability, he listened for her thoughts. Nothing. Silence rose between them like a wall, a barrier she created. Dumah had taught her well. His hands gripped the bench on either side of his thighs.

"Samael, brother, what do you think?"

He thought she was human, and maybe he was becoming human too. If she died, he might go along with her.

Raphael's hand rested on Samael's shoulder. "I've never seen you so distracted."

"Of course I'm distracted." Samael's knee bounced, his eyes still on the stage. "She's the one."

"So you've said." Raphael folded his arms and shrugged. "I've yet to see proof."

Samael scowled. Raphael always knew how to get under his skin.

"I heard she has a twin." Raphael raised his brows as Samael's head jerked up. "You have to know even among angels word gets around." He snorted. "Maybe, she isn't so special after all."

"What do you know of Gabriel?"

Raphael's head fell back as he laughed. "His name is Gabriel? Really? Talk about a lack of originality."

"You're trying my patience."

"And you're coming close to offending me. You should know better than to think your growling has any effect on me, *brother*."

Samael turned back to Wylie, frustrated. After dealing with Laoth all these years, he should be immune to Raphael's antics. Sending his Scientia out, he absorbed every detail about her, how the white cotton gown puddled at her feet. How her wild curls swallowed her shoulders. How her fists clenched and unclenched.

"No bindings?" Raphael spoke the words as Samael thought them. "At least she's brave."

Most angels opted to be tied to the stake, either to help save face as they suffered or to prevent them from running. Both Dominions shook their head. If most angels couldn't handle it, how would she?

"This is going to be a disaster."

"Raphael, if you don't shut up, I will deliver your body to Ophanim once this ends." Samael breathed in Wylie's Scientia. She would survive this test. Every angel did.

More angels attended than she'd expected. Every row was filled. Some wore their wings, blocking the view of those behind them, while others sat naked, their bodies slick and a perfected version of humanity as if they'd coated themselves in baby oil. Those who looked like ordinary humans stood out from their counterparts. Their rounded physiques and sallowness contrasted with the glowing majority.

Skin tones of the rainbow dotted the audience. Eyes like jewels and hair of every color and texture gleamed under Ludus' harsh light. In the front sat nine men and women, their mouths set in grim lines and dressed in plain sleeveless tanks and board shorts. The Dominions loomed larger than the others, taller, harder, and meaner as they glared into the eyes of those who dared to look in their direction.

She searched the faces of those before her and held the gaze of a few she recognized. Roberto's second cousin, her third-grade teacher, and an ex-coworker among them, but nothing prepared her for finding Jinx and his mother. She pushed her back against the metal bar dominating the center of her stage and thought of Dean.

She stared at Jinx. Had he been Dean's Guardian? He wore an encouraging smile, his little boy nose and chubby cheeks reminding her of Dean. Thinking of her son made her arms feel empty. Her back and hip ached for his weight. She'd thought she was healing, but witnessing their death had reopened her wound, and now in between Dumah's constant teaching, she tried to stop the bleeding.

"Are you ready?" Dumah sounded more confident than she looked. "Good, good. Let's get started."

Dumah walked away, swaying on her ridiculous heels. The angels fell silent as she hopped over a pyre surrounding the stage. She spoke, but Wylie's jumbled brain could not separate the swooshes of the ceiling fan from the announcement.

Fire burst from the woodpile, and her heart crawled into her mouth. The flames licked at her feet. The heat alone was unbearable, yet the flames had yet to touch her.

You are my sunshine. She closed her eyes and thought of how brave her husband had been when he sang to their son. She could be brave. She would come into her angel powers and prevent other families from suffering as she did.

My only . . . Soon, the words fought their way out. Her volume increased as the flames grew closer and hotter. She shouted at the angels with her singing voice. Sweat poured down every crevice of her body, and her skin tightened.

She paced the stage as streams of smoke crawled skyward, waiting

—a lifetime of waiting. A haze filled the air, the heat traveling past her to the ceiling fan. Her eyes stung. Dizziness from lack of oxygen squeezed her ribs. The rubber of her boots slipped and stuck against the hot stage. Her bones stiffened, but she needed to keep moving, or she would run.

She cried in pain when her shoes melted around her toes, boiling her feet. The mess of rubber and flesh took one more step before she fell to her knees.

She screamed. Her dress caught fire. Agony dug deep where the dress lay tightest against her skin.

She fell on her belly when her hair went up. Her body rolled of its own accord. Her cheeks and ears bubbled, sloughing away. The smell of cooking meat joined the sound of sizzling fat.

The stage collapsed, and she fell into the great maw of the inferno.

A cheer filled the air somewhere beyond her death.

Buried in flame, her body numbed in patches. Involuntary jerks became exclamation marks to her inability to draw in breath.

Choking on terror, she realized: *I'm dying.*

I'm human.

I'm human, and I'm dying. Gabriel won.

She'd close her eyes if she had eyelids. *Let it end.*

End.

Her tether to life broke free with one last zing of pain.

Like lightning against the backdrop of blackness.

Relief replaced all the beating and breathing organic material required. Released from her human container, she became the peace after a climax. Her heart took a break in her chest and enjoyed the stillness.

Alone.

Her memories hummed in her periphery.

My boys.

The syllables twirled around her.

Dean.

A name called with a voiceless song.

Roberto.

An echo from the chasm they left behind.

"Wylie." Samael's voice broke through the still, and she wondered if she'd imagined it.

"*Wylie!*" This time he was in her head. Louder. Clearer than he could ever speak. "*Push through this.*"

I... I can't ... It's too hard. I'm not the one.

"*Yes, you are, Wylie. Remember, I have faith in you. Remember all the good things you've done. Don't let them stop here.*"

She wanted to remember, she did.

Mama!

The blackness froze solid around her.

Mama!

Dean? Where are you, baby?

Fly.

I will, baby. Mama will.

She pushed away from the simplicity of freedom and grabbed hold of what was left of her physical shackles.

You can do this, mi amor. *You're not alone.*

Roberto's voice was what she needed to remind herself of who she was. Dean's mother. Roberto's wife. A nurse. An angel. Armageddon.

Piecing together the details that imprisoned her now boundless mind, she focused on the place she belonged: her body.

Her blood came first. The vessels connected the rest of her body to her heart. She drew all four chambers with her mind, tempting them into action.

First, the upper right. Then, the lower. Half of a heartbeat sounded. The left side took a turn. The song of her heart set the tempo as she strung together nerve cells, sculpted bones, and weaved muscles.

Elated with her work, she rode the waves of her heartbeat. Rocking in the ocean of life.

She quickened in the darkness as she made her organs. Her lungs and brain and skin. Molding herself as if from clay, she formed each imperfection from memory. Her body, the body she chose for herself, felt more alive, more vibrant than past versions of her. A new and subtle ownership blessed her curves and her largeness, her age, and her scars.

Lastly, her soul remembered its wings.

Her eyes opened, staring through the flames at the monstrous ceiling fan, the sight distorted by fire. She climbed out of the ashen pit, savoring the feel of muscles moving over bones she'd made herself.

She looked out at her audience; the fire danced around her. Ludus shifted, and the inferno remembered its place, climbing her back and forming her wings.

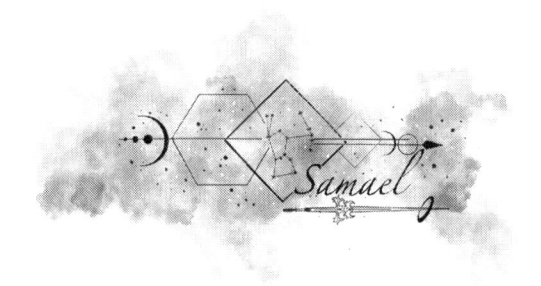

Samael

The room quaked, and paintings fell from the wall like raindrops sliding down a window. A chorus of gasps filled the air. Samael's damp clothes dried in a flash of heat that burst from the stage. Samael's back itched as silence swelled behind him. Waves of emotion emanated from the pit. He absorbed a wife's love, a mother's acceptance, a daughter's forgiveness, a caretaker's empathy. All emotions angels witnessed but never experienced. He opened himself wider. Each wave a caress, as if Wylie's Scientia cradled them.

A divine being stood on the stage. Her body appeared bare and perfect in its detail. Her black hair cascaded down her naked back, and her arms lifted. Fiery wings opened wide. Spanning the stage as they danced with flame, dark embers rained from them. Samael crashed to the ground, his knees landing on the concrete so hard his teeth rattled.

"I am Armageddon." She rose into the air.

A crack reverberated, and Ludus returned to itself. Angels fell, and limbs tangled as Wylie's spell released them. Samael shot into the air as her wings extinguished, his eyes on her falling form.

He caught her, her familiar warmth giving his lungs permission to breathe.

Wylie smiled, nuzzling his chest. "Did you see that? I have wings."

Chapter 27

Lex

"*I* brought lunch."

Lex startled. She lay in a puddle of sweat. Her eyes closed. Her mind swam in the place between dreams and memories. She stared up at the low gym ceiling. Gabriel's face obstructed her view.

"Did you miss me?" He poked her forehead.

He left two days ago. *Maybe.* She rubbed her arms. Her sweat and the cool breeze from the fan had her body hair standing on end.

Gabriel set down his paper bag and shrugged off his jacket, pulling it over her shoulders.

You don't want to do that. I smell like ass.

"That's what laundry detergents are for."

You don't know shit about laundry.

"I don't?" He ran his fingers through his hair as he sat beside her, his suit wrinkling at the edges. "I brought sandwiches. I made them myself."

She pictured his fancy suit against a backdrop of stainless steel and mess. She didn't know how they let him into the kitchen.

He rolled up his sleeves and reached into the bag. "People let me do what I want." He handed her a sandwich.

She studied it. *Peanut butter? What, are you two years old?*

"Two and a half, so at least six months your elder."

Lex laughed before she could stop herself, blushing as his smile widened. She'd a lot to think about since Gabriel fed those bad angels to the opposition. She was at a point where she wanted to stay and live this life of helping muses and freeing angels. But was her willingness real, or was she just attracted to his power? His body? The security of this place?

Gabriel shifted his body closer to hers.

She shook her head and poked at the Gucci sunglasses that hung out of the front pocket of his jacket. *How'd you get all this?*

He crossed his legs and pulled his shoes off. "It's a long story, *cher*. And I'm a boring guy."

Lex smelled something sour as she brought the sandwich to her mouth. She pulled the slices of bread apart and frowned. "Is that a pickle?"

He looked up. His thick brows met. "You don't have to do that for me." He placed a finger over her lips. His finger lingered a little too long. "I missed you."

Is that why you ruined this perfectly good peanut butter sandwich with a pickle?

Gabriel laughed. "You caught me." He pulled out his sandwich and sank his teeth into it. His nostrils flared, and his eyes rolled back. "Mm." The pickle crunched as he chewed. "You've got to try this."

She poked at her sandwich. *Who does this?*

"You're lucky I didn't add onions and mustard."

Gross. She shook her head as he took another bite. *Private thought here...*

Gabriel rested his half-eaten sandwich on the paper bag and plugged his ears as he finished chewing, a grin plastered on his face.

Close your eyes too.

He followed her command. Her eyes ate him up in a way she never allowed herself. The easy way he took up space with his long limbs and muscular physique. The way the left side of his mouth always crept toward a smile. How his clothes were made in foreign places by people with expensive names. How some of his curls refused to stay slicked back with the rest of his hair.

He reached out and rested his hand on her fingers, his eyes still closed. "When are you going to let me kiss you?"

She scoffed in reply. *Kiss me? I thought we were being serious. You know as well as I do, angels don't kiss.*

"I told you, I'm not like other angels."

Yeah, I know, you eat fucking peanut butter and pickle sandwiches. Newsflash: humans don't like them, either.

"A human taught me about the pleasures of peanut butter and pickle sandwiches. Growing up, my best friend ate them every day."

He's probably as much of an asshole as you are.

His ever-present smile slid from his face as his eyes focused on something across the room. "He's dead."

Lex flinched, wishing for once she had a damn filter. *Shit, I'm sorry.*

Gabriel pushed back one of his stray curls. "Don't be. He's not." He turned to her and nudged her knee, the upturn in his lips returning bit by bit. "I'll forgive you if you try the sandwich."

Lex studied the sandwich before taking a small bite with an upturned nose. She held her breath and chewed, doing her best not to ask the obvious question.

"What?"

She swallowed and lifted the sandwich to her mouth.

He poked her in the hip. "Ask me."

You grew up? She took another bite.

Gabriel rolled his eyes. "You don't believe a word I say, do you?"

What gave me away? She fluttered her lashes at him.

He huffed a laugh, shaking his head. "If you don't believe me, ask Todd. We grew up together, too." Gabriel crossed his legs at the ankle. "He's a muse as well. Not my muse. Léon, the sandwich guy, was my muse." He rolled his sleeve up another inch. "I grew up deep in the bayou. Our small community was a mix of proud Creole muses and transplant muses seeking asylum. I could go on for days on how we got there, but it's easier to say we ended up there the same way everyone else in Louisiana did."

Lex thought about her mother and her birth rite. Being a muse had ruined her life.

"Not many angels spend most of their lives surrounded by muses. I've grown protective of them over the years. My father's an angel—"

Lex's jaw dropped.

He shook his head. "Not my blood father, but he raised me as a father would have. He kept me hidden for most of my childhood, and when my muse died, he opened the world to me. I traveled. Got a gentleman's education using the languages I'd learned. He let me have a human coming of age."

The gym fell into silence as Lex finished her food. She folded Gabriel's jacket, tossing it into his lap, and stood, stretching. *I can feel how sad you are. Is that normal?*

He laid back, his arms reaching above his head. "You think loudly. I emotion loudly. Believe it or not, Lex, we have much in common."

She touched her toes, avoiding his eyes. *Like what?*

"Like, you lost your childhood to studying. The only goal you ever had was to fulfill your destiny. Like someone important to you died as you became an adult. Someone you would have died for. Someone who you believe deserves this life far more than you. Like now, you find yourself with more power than you ever imagined, and you're ready to turn it on your enemies."

Lex followed the lines of his furrowed brow with her eyes, plopping onto a bench as her hands shook with shock. *How do you know all this?*

"I'm guessing at some of it, but Abaddon told me the rest. The angel was quick to answer questions. He told me about John."

Lex remembered how 9/11 became her brother's calling, how she'd been high when John died in the desert. She shook her head against the sting in her eyes and slid to her knees, her hand finding his arm. "How did Léon die?"

Gabriel found her eyes. "Here's my last truth of the day." His hands found his jacket, and he twisted the fabric in his fists as he spoke. "He sacrificed himself so that I could have all of *this*."

Lex flinched when he sat up.

Gabriel's face paled. "I'm sorry, kitten. I'm not good company anymore." He moved to stand.

Wait. Don't go. I'm not afraid of you.

He stood anyway, pulling on his stinky jacket.

When he turned his back, Lex jumped to her feet, wrapping her hands around his middle from behind. "Please, don't go," she whispered to his back.

"Why?" His body tensed under her hold.

You confuse me. Her hands dropped, and she circled him. Her eyes rose. *You share things like this with me. You spend this extra time with me and show me parts of your world. You look at me like you want to . . .*

"Like I want to eat you?" His fingers ran down her arm and then his thumb traced her cheek.

Don't get me wrong, I enjoy the attention, but where's this all going?

"Where do you want it to go, *cher*?"

Lex wanted to go everywhere with him. *You're a fucken' angel.*

"And?"

I know your junk doesn't work.

"Lex."

I call you an asshole at least once a day.

"Lex."

Not to mention my face.

"Stop!"

You stop. You're driving me crazy. She showed him what her nights looked like with her mind. The way she tossed and turned as she imagined him on top of her. How, in her frustration, her fingers slid between her legs.

She didn't see him move. In an instant, his hands were on either side of her face. Gabriel cut off Lex's gasp with his mouth, his lips on hers. Lex moaned, holding onto his shirt, meeting each stroke of his tongue with her own.

Gabriel pulled back, his forehead resting on hers, their breaths becoming one. "I'm sorry, *chèr*, but I've wanted to do that for so long. The sight of your fingers between your thighs stole all my control."

She came to her toes. Her hands rested on his chest.

He laughed when she bit his bottom lip.

She'd never kissed someone while they smiled.

Can you? Her fingers traveled over his ribs to his hips. *Can we?*

Gabriel moaned as she traced the line of his cock through his shorts. "I told you, I'm not like other angels." He ran his nose along her ear.

I'm going to need you to prove it.

When Wylie woke, she felt too dizzy to open her eyes. She lay on a bed. Her fingers traced the mattress as she breathed in the smell of her laundry soap. *I'm home.*

"Samael?" Her voice cracked as her bed careened to the right.

"I'm here." His hand found hers. "David should be here soon, too."

"Is he angry?" A long pause followed her question, and she opened her eyes.

Samael sat on the ground beside her, a frown on his face. "When is that boy not angry?"

"What do you mean?" Her palm felt slick against his. He didn't reply, but she knew his thoughts. Or rather, his emotions. They danced along her new skin, boiling out of him and into her. Frustration and tenderness. Relief and confusion. "You know I can feel you now?"

Again, no response. His lips flattened as he squeezed her hand. "We must do something before your muse arrives." He stared out the window as he spoke. Samael swallowed hard and adjusted her hand in his so he could kneel. His grass-green eyes met hers. "When the Thrones first made me, they performed a ritual that dampered my power. They did this to all Dominions. The ritual made it less dangerous for those around us as we learned to use our Scientia." He rested his other hand on her collarbone. "I want to do it for you. You'll still have to be careful, but you won't kill someone with a daydream or take a chunk out of the earth when you get mad."

She nodded as he spoke, remembering what Dumah said. Her mind raced through one dangerous scenario after another. "Okay, I understand, but do we have to do it now? I'm so tired."

"It will be easier to do it while you're weak."

She took in a fortifying breath. "What do I need to do?" Her heart wobbled in her chest as a wave of Samael's fear hit her.

He released her hand, and her world turned upside down. "You do nothing. I will make it quick." He stood, his face a blank mask. "This will only hurt for a minute." Without further explanation, he climbed on top of her, his thighs straddling her hips.

She gasped at the contact.

"I'm sorry." His hands dove into her chest.

The immense pressure brought a groan from her throat. "Samael?" She mouthed his name and dug her heels into the bed. She grabbed his wrists and pulled, fighting. Fire burst from her like a match meeting oil. Painless flames came with the hysteria that gripped her.

Her throat burned.

The bed burned.

His clothes burned, but he held steady.

Illumina, custodi, rege, et guberna." The words forced their way inside of her, joining his fingers where they fluttered and twisted between her spine and her ribs. Samael's wings appeared, a light emanating from him growing brighter and brighter. The world flashed white.

"Amen."

She gasped as his hands pulled free.

Light and flame and pain disappeared.

She turned to the side and vomited bile as she ripped at her throat. *He left something inside of me.* She clawed and clawed and clawed at the fullness.

Her head fell back, the fatigue finally quenching her panic. "You hurt me?" Her throat shredded the words.

Samael stared at her, his face pale, his eyes wide. "It shouldn't have been so hard. I didn't want you to be afraid. I thought if I just did it. If I . . ." He froze on top of her and shuddered. "If I . . ." His hands, he held them aloft as if they didn't belong to him. "If I . . ." Blood dripped from them. "If I did it quickly, there'd be less pain." The drops landed on her singed bed, adding red to the black.

A sob rattled her body as the edges of her world blurred. She reached for him.

A knock sounded, and the front door opened. Samael vanished and reappeared on the other side of the room, his hands clean, his clothes fresh, his shame polluting the air.

"Again?" David's raised voice filled the studio as he walked through the entryway. "This feels worse than last time." He rounded the corner. "Oh, my God." David rushed to her side, his hands and eyes inspecting her.

She shivered at his touch, her arms still aloft. She'd reached for Samael and got David instead.

David glared at Samael.

Dammit, what has he done?

It started as a trickle.

There's no escape. We're fucked. We're so fucked.

Her relief disappeared as his thoughts flooded her mind. His rage mingled with Samael's shame.

"Stop." Wylie cringed and leaned away from him, their skin-to-skin contact breaking. "Stop." She placed her fists against her ears, trying to block out what she heard and felt. His anger and unease pushed against her. She didn't have room for anything else.

"She's hearing your thoughts." Her hands muffled Samael's voice.

David recoiled. He shook his head, turning to Samael. He launched himself at the angel. "What. Have. You. Done?" David emphasized each word with a shove.

Wylie watched the violence in slow motion. When David lifted his fist, she sprung off the bed with the wild movements of a spinning top, directing herself at him. She staggered forward and they clambered to the ground with a series of thuds.

She landed on top of him. Her chin smacked against his chest. His face turned away from her, his forearm covering his eyes. He did not move as she wrapped her arms around him. "Please, David, please." She cried into his shirt. "Please."

She closed her eyes, listening to his heart for a moment before rolling off of him. Her bed creaked behind them and Wylie imagined Samael sitting down.

"I deserved that," Samael said.

With difficulty, Wylie pushed herself up and clambered onto her bottom. Scooting against a wall, She wiped her eyes.

They stayed like this for a while, in their own heads, forced to share the small space. She sorted through the emotions in the room, separating hers from theirs. Samael hunched, his eyes staring into nothingness, his body dominating her twin-sized bed. David—she looked away. She couldn't bear to look at David.

"What did you do?" There it was again. David hurled his question like an accusation.

Samael and Wylie lifted their heads.

The red splotches around David's eyes betrayed the tears he'd covered moments before.

"You're not—"

"Shut up, Wylie. You don't understand." He climbed back to his feet and dusted off his slacks as he turned to Samael. "What have you done?" He pointed his finger.

"You don't understand, do you?" David turned back to her, his face a scowl. "He's using you." He pointed at Samael, disgust scrunching up his nose. "The almighty, all-knowing angel doesn't comprehend what it is to be human!" Spit sprayed from his mouth with the force of his words.

"This is not Wylie anymore. She was the epitome of what you angels are supposed to protect. And now . . ." He ran his fingers over his scalp, his hands shaking. "She can't be human again. Angels can't have children or husbands. Angels don't have careers, or friends, or love."

He took another step toward Samael, leaning over the angel. "Congratulations. You've turned her into a weapon."

Wylie caught her breath and Samael rose. They stood chest to chest, David's tense cyclist body dwarfed by the Angel as his golden wings revealed themselves.

Wylie turned away from them, frustrated by their machismo, her eyelids growing heavy with exhaustion. She didn't have the energy to break up another fight, let alone watch one. She needed sleep. The pressure in her head subsided when she closed her eyes. She reached for the peace of her Catharsis and used it to shield herself from their hate.

David's body curled around her, trapping her under the bedcovers. Though clean, she could smell the places where the mattress had been charred. Street lamps glowed outside her window as she soaked up his cinnamon presence. He held her arm, his thumb drawing circles over her skin. A foreboding tainted the gentleness emanating from his still form.

"David?"

"Yes?" His breath moved her hair.

"Why do you hate angels?" She'd dreamed about the question. Her mind didn't want to forget its importance.

Silence.

Silence and hatred.

She fought to get out from under the blanket. David moved off the bed as she headed to the closet.

"I'm going to go." She felt his shock just as much as her own. It felt like a shove to the back. She folded her arms.

"Don't." He stood.

Her hand trembled as she reached for a shirt. "You would've taken the power too."

"What?"

"If someone hurt Jane, and you had a chance to make things right. I know you, you would have sacrificed anything to do so."

David stepped behind her. Her body called for him and so she leaned against his chest. His arms wrapped around her. They rocked.

"I don't hate you."

She pressed her lips together. "But you hate what I am."

"You look more angel than human now." His breath caught. "You feel more angel than human."

She agreed with him. She couldn't remember when she felt the urge to void or eat last. No one could call her dirty even though the angels barbequed her hours earlier. Her palms sweated out of habit. She stepped out of his hold. "This is who I am."

"I should ask you why you don't hate angels." He searched her eyes. "Your husband is dead because of them."

"Stop." She backed away. "You don't understand."

"Your son died."

"No."

"Your family is gone because . . ."

"David!"

The room's temperature increased to an uncomfortable degree, and David stumbled back.

"Get out." The heat grew. The edges of the posters on the wall curled.

"But . . ."

"Get! Out!" The place between her shoulder blades itched. A static buzz hummed at her fingertips.

"Wylie?" Droplets of sweat fell from David's forehead. The candles on her dresser melted into a swirling puddle.

A pressure in her chest grew, sending currents down her arms. Her eyes widened as flames flickered to life in lines along her forearms, following the path of her veins. Her anger became dismay as she lost control.

"David, go!" She gritted her teeth as he took a hesitant step away. Like holding back vomit, she knew something hot threatened to erupt from her hands. She followed him as he retreated, intending on getting outside. "Run!"

He didn't run. He went into the bathroom. The sound of water followed.

"Wylie. Come."

She did as told, too consumed by the fire to do much else. David backed behind the toilet as she jumped into the tub, submerging her arms. Water sprayed into the air as her head fell back and she released a blast of heat. The water boiled. Steam rose.

David paused at the door.

Neither of them spoke as her head rested against the tile.

"I'm afraid of losing you." David sat on the toilet.

"For the first time in two years, I don't feel broken."

He touched the tub and flinched away. He ran his fingers under cold water without saying a word. He looked away. His jaw twitched. "I thought I was helping with that."

Wylie's hands yearned to touch him, but she didn't trust them.

"You have helped me so much, David." She sniffled. "But you can't do it all. Comfort and healing aren't the same."

David stood. His arms folded. "I wish I could've been enough." He turned his back.

"I'm sorry."

David shook his head. "I can stay with you for a while. You know, wait for things to settle," he said with his back to her.

"Are you angry?"

"Wylie, I'm always angry." He blew out a breath and sat back down on the toilet. "What a mess."

Beads of sweat ran down Wylie's face. "David, I haven't stopped needing you."

He answered with a half-smile.

Chapter 28

Samael

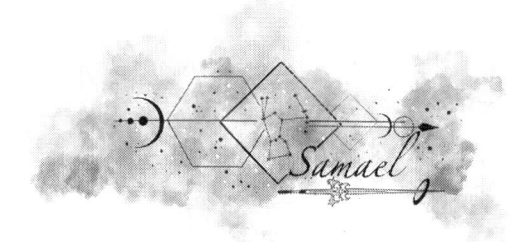

Samael and Laoth stood on the corner of North East Sandy and North East Davis. They'd already waited thirty minutes in the rain as they watched customers of Voodoo Doughnut Too wander in and out of the bright pink building. At two in the morning, the building's traffic continued at a regular clip. Samael found his sense of annoyance heightening with every non-angel who passed him.

"You will take over Wylie's training."

Laoth raised a brow. "She's a handful. Do you really want to do that to me?"

"You were right, I'm getting too close to her."

"Did you just say I'm right?"

Samael grunted.

"Fuck, Samael, that's a first. You mind saying it again?"

A growl reverberated in Samael's chest, and Laoth let out her usual cackle.

"Just messing with you." She punched him in the arm. "You really are changing. But all joking aside, brother. I never lost faith in *you*."

The wind blew a swirl of petals past them. Samael smelled Gabriel's expensive cologne before he saw him.

"Lex, look, it's my two least favorite angels." The male voice came from a flowering plum tree. Gabriel leaned against the trunk with a short woman of Asian descent. Her eyes bore into Samael with an accusatory glint. Her purple hair hung down to her breasts, and pink scars marred her face.

"We've been waiting thirty minutes for you, brother," Samael spoke just above a whisper. "You'd think punctuality would be important to a rebellion."

"You can call me Gabriel. I'm not your brother." Gabriel possessively ran a hand down Lex's arm. "I may have been distracted."

The woman blushed as he flipped the lid of a pink box reading "Voodoo" and poked around inside. Gabriel wore a plaid button-up shirt and torn jeans, a fedora holding his curly hair at bay. The Angel smiled through his disrespect as he crossed his legs at the ankles. Samael could not read his emotions or his mind, even though he seemed human.

"I'm surprised you didn't try to interrupt us during dinner." His smile became a grin.

"Don't worry, we can stop by for a meal any time," Laoth said.

"I'll have to remember that next time I feel like getting punched in the face." Gabriel shook his head and turned to the woman behind him. "Right, Lex?"

The woman nodded, her hate-filled eyes trained on Samael.

Gabriel lifted a finger as if to pause the conversation and chose a doughnut from his box.

Samael straightened his back and rolled his head on his shoulders. "Is this why you came? More games?"

Gabriel ignored the warning and took a bite; powdered sugar dusted his shirt as he closed his eyes and nodded his appreciation. "I swear, this is the only reason to come to Portland." He spoke while he chewed and then laughed. "It's funny I have to come all the way here for some good Voodoo." He leaned into Lex. "I got the pink one for you, *cher.*"

You're an asshole. Lex's thought came as clearly as her voice might have and Samael remembered a boy that reminded him of her.

"Oh, I'm sorry. Would you like one too?" Gabriel held out his box, interrupting Samael's thoughts.

Samael glared, but Laoth grabbed the biggest and shoved half the thing in her mouth.

"Whoa!" Laoth spoke around the bite. "These *are* good."

Samael huffed in exasperation.

Laoth shrugged. "What? They are." She carried on chewing.

"There's a lot of gossip coming from your side." Gabriel licked his fingers. "I heard you guys lit my sister on fire the other day. You all should be ashamed. My sister and I feel pain like humans."

Laoth and Samael shared a look and with it, she used her mind to show Samael all the possible traitors in their inner circle. While Samael's foresight in battle was legendary, Laoth could smell a traitor from miles away.

"Why are we here, old one?"

"I'm here to offer an invitation. An Angel Tribunal will be held, and the Seraphim requested your presence. There must be peace in the heavens before there can be peace on earth."

"Did you hear that, Lex? We've been invited to the party." Gabriel held open the box once more. "Are you sure you don't want one?"

She scoffed, even as she smiled. *You're such a shit.* She plucked the pink one out of the box.

That's when Samael realized who she was. He'd only met one muse lineage who spoke to angels so easily with their thoughts. "You're Doan Thị Dung's daughter. I knew your brother."

Lex stiffened.

"I've met your parents." Samael pointedly studied Gabriel. "They wouldn't want you around the likes of him."

"Then you knew Abaddon." Lex held her throat as she rasped the words.

Samael frowned. "He served God since before your family tree began."

You call it 'served,' I call it committing sanctioned genocide. I think I'm where I belong.

Samael gritted his teeth. "Your brother died for the greater good. What have you done?"

She fisted her hands. Doughnuts bounced on the ground as Gabriel reached for her waist but missed. He felt an untapped Scientia teeming inside her tiny frame.

"She's a bomb!" Laoth barked. The pressure in the atmosphere multiplied.

Samael's wings opened wide as he grabbed time with his mind. Portland froze.

"Laoth, go to Wylie!"

The night flashed white. The blast pitched Samael back. His wings came around him as a shield. Hot pain rippled through him as his human form threatened to dissolve. He projected himself to the closest high point and stumbled as he landed on the forty-story Wells Fargo building. Its modern lines pointed to the heavens.

Staggering, Samael's wings opened with a shudder. Smoke rose in the distance.

"*Merda.*" Thank God he'd contained the explosion with a human reprieve. He opened his arms wide and called with his mind to all the Archangels in the city of Portland. He'd need to hold the city still until Lex's mess was cleaned up. Every muscle in his body already shook. They'd need to hurry.

Wylie

She sat in the tub overnight, her fingers wrinkled and her face itched from her hair frizzing around her cheeks. Her bottom ached from sitting. The more frustrated she felt, the hotter the water became.

I need to think of better ways to blow off steam. Laughing at her joke, she remembered she wasn't human anymore. She hoped this self-imposed unpleasantness would stop if she ignored it. She pulled her hands from the water. She needed to go on a run. She visualized the route she'd take as she dressed, knowing exertion would dim this amplification of her anger.

She grabbed her shoes and burst out the door into the dead of night, savoring the instant temperature change. She'd been hot for too long. A jolt of adrenaline reminded her why flying the old-fashioned way, with sweat dripping and feet drumming against the asphalt, would cure the scalding heat beneath her skin. She plugged in her headphones and fingered through her playlists, choosing a dubstep mashup of "Frozen" by Madonna and The White Stripes' "Seven Nation Army."

She pushed play and missed a step, the sound cutting her to the bone. Stringed instruments thrummed her rebuilt veins. Madonna's voice made her toes curl. She thought she loved music before, but now? Music moved her, one foot at a time. Her first dropped beat brought tears to her eyes. Her legs worked through the overstimulation as she jogged down Pill Hill.

The smack of feet behind her had her picking up speed in hopes of losing the runner. Her tail continued at a steady trot.

"Wylie."

She turned at the sound of her name and pulled the music from her ears.

"It's Laoth." A tall blond female came to her side. "Samael sent me to check on you."

Wylie couldn't speak; she ran too fast.

"Don't slow us down by trying to say anything. Let's keep running."

Laoth took the lead.

Wylie studied the sidewalks and brick walls. The broken glass sparkled like glitter under the sunshine that escaped the clouds. One of her feet landed on a fast-food packet and the sauce squirted against the wall. The smell of Tabasco filled the air. Its sharp tang burned her eyes and blazed through her nasal passages. Even the city's bad smells captivated her. The scent of secondhand tobacco, thickened urine, and the gasoline-oil-rubber cocktail rushed past them. All complex, distracting her with their stories. Rich with the aroma of humanity.

"You like this shit, don't you?" Laoth waved her hand at the concrete cradle that swallowed them. Wylie opened her mouth. "Again, don't talk. Samael sent me to train you. I saw you running and I thought we'd start now."

"Yeah?" Wylie huffed the word between breaths.

"Yeah." Laoth turned to her, running backward with ease. "Now, follow me." Her foot landed in a puddle and mud splashed on their shins. Wylie followed her into a greenbelt, over a trail, and through a skate park. "You're about to fly. The key is to use your wings, or it will hurt." Without breaking at the bottom of the hill, Laoth ran up a ramp and jumped into the air. Her wings opened wide and she glided until she landed on her feet at a sprint.

Wylie ran with too much momentum to stop. She gritted her teeth and jumped. A sickening crack announced her landing as her ass hit the ground and she skidded into a faceplant.

"Oh, shit. That must've hurt." Laoth ran to Wylie's side and continued to jog in place. "Time to try again."

Old Wylie would have said "no" and picked up an extra shift at work so she wouldn't have time to deal with it. New Wylie wiped a trickle of blood from her forehead and used the anger she felt at Laoth to make herself move. She took a minute to shake it off, and then the glow of the streetlights marked her progress as she sprinted in a wide circle and up the ramp.

The second time she crashed and burned hurt more than the first. She got up slower, wiping the blood from her nose this time. Her anger peaked again and the drips sizzled and instantly clotted as they met her hot skin. She marched to the ramp. She rolled up her sleeves and started again.

"What the fuck am I doing wrong?" Wylie's skin itched painfully from all of her healing wounds.

"Nothing." Laoth shrugged. "Maybe you just suck at being an angel." She pulled a dagger out of thin air and started playing with it, twirling the blade between her fingers.

"That's not helpful."

"Then take it up with Samael." Laoth looked around the park and then slapped her forehead. "Oh brother, he's not here."

Wylie limped back to the ramp, thoughts of arson playing in her head. Did she suck at being an angel? Yes, yes she did. She thought back to the things she'd done well. How her successes came from the ground up. She thought of the last time she'd used her wings. Of stacking the pieces of herself back together.

This time, when she jumped, she didn't rely on her new Angel body to know what to do. Instead, she built her wings from scratch, starting with the flame.

She burst into the air like a fucking phoenix. Exhilaration sent her soaring into the clouds; her fire was so hot steam replaced the moisture around her. She pushed herself, her wings finding limits as she discovered the freedom of flight.

"That's what I'm talking about!" Laoth shouted from just below her.

Wylie froze at the sound, nearly falling from the sky.

"Landing is harder than flying, so prepare yourself. I don't want to hear you bitching when you land on your face again. Follow me."

Wylie marveled at how clearly she heard Laoth's words with all the wind rushing past her. She landed on her feet, taking a few quick steps before crashing down on her hands. She laughed.

"This is just the beginning. One day soon, you'll fly and use your flames however and whenever you want." Laoth crouched down, her eyes on Wylie's disjointed movements. "What do you think? You ready to learn? No more setting fires or *accidental* killings. Next time someone dies at your hand, you'll have planned it." She winked before booking it back up the hill. Wylie sprinted after her with no hope of catching up.

Chapter 29

Wylie

"Samael?"

The angel leaned on Wylie's kitchen counter, his forehead against the cabinet. His limp wings blackened at the tips.

She rushed to him. "What happened?"

He held his hand out, gesturing for her to stop. Burns marred his alabaster skin, his arms raw and red, his lips cracked.

"I met your brother today."

"Why?" She couldn't keep the betrayal from her voice.

"Hhm." Samael hung his head.

"You need Jane." Wylie pulled her phone out, ready to call David.

"Don't." Samael cringed and jerked forward. His teeth glistened as his lips parted in pain.

"But Samael..."

"I just needed to see you." A groan escaped his mouth, embarrassment seeping out of him.

Wylie reached for him. She smoothed his feathers with one stroke and then another. Her magic sought his pain and pulled, like untying a shoelace.

Samael sighed, sagging forward as his burns healed. "I'm sorry." He looked down at his perfect skin. "Why help me when all I do is fail you?"

With his beautiful face restored and his pain eased, a swirl of emotions bubbled to the surface. When Wylie felt his shock, she wondered if these emotions were new to him. She combed his feathers with her fingertips. They danced with the intensity of the contact.

Intimacy on a level she'd never known warmed her cheeks. Similar to the moment her patient trusted her. He let his guard down, and she knew him on a base level. He exchanged his faith for her compassion. Piles of words lay unsaid between them. Thousands of years slid from Samael's shoulders.

"Laoth will take over your training."

"She said as much." Wylie leaned forward, her cheek resting against his gossamer wing. "But why?"

His shoulders bunched, a punctuation to his silence. "Because you cloud my judgment."

Wylie's heart jumped at his admission. No reply came to her head. How did she cloud his judgment?

"Dumah will be here soon. I will stay with you until you finish your Catharsis."

"I'm not done?" Wylie shivered. She couldn't go back into the flames so soon.

"You've found your wings. Now you must become one of us."

"What does that mean?" She stepped back, giving Samael his space or maybe taking it for herself.

"Our Throne will give you a gift, and Dumah will reveal your angel type."

"A gift?"

"It's more like arts and crafts for angels," Dumah said from the living room. "You will need to collect a few things first."

"Why are you both being so cryptic?"

"Because you won't believe us if we tried to explain it." She clapped her hands. "Now, I'll go over your Catharsis results while you gather a few items." Dumah plopped on Wylie's bed, and Samael leaned against the wall.

"So, we're going somewhere?"

Dumah nodded with a smirk on her face. "Think hiking clothes: long sleeves, jeans, boots if you have them.

"Fine, I'll change clothes." She pointed at Samael and swirled her finger in the air. "You know what to do."

Samael turned around, more pensive than usual.

Wylie dug through her drawers.

"You know that fun question, what three things would you grab if your house burned down? That's what I need you to collect. These are items that you would want to carry with you forever if you could."

"Like my wedding ring?" Wylie asked, fingering the piece of jewelry as she spoke.

"Exactly. Now, while you do your thing, let's talk about your flame." Dumah sighed and lay flat on the bed. "The wide base had me thinking of the Lesser Angels. Guardians and Shadows, especially. But the height, well, that was a Seraphim-quality fire. I've never seen one myself, but they are well-documented. The smoke was minimal, but what I did see was lighter than the Powers. The truth is. I don't know what you are. And the prophecy doesn't give me a clue, either. I've never been stumped before, so this is quite embarrassing."

"It sounds like I'm the defective one." Wylie pulled a shirt over her head and headed for her jewelry box. She'd put Roberto's ring and napkin poem in there. She also took the gold chain her in-laws bought Dean when he was a baby. "Are these okay?"

"Perfect."

"Tell me you guys aren't planning to burn my apartment down."

"We won't." Dumah sat back up. "Make sure you grab a heavy coat. It's going to be cold. Think snow."

Wylie handed her special items to Dumah and added an extra layer to her outfit before adding a jacket. Samael still faced the other direction, his head resting against the wall as if he could fall asleep standing up. "I'm ready."

"Okay, Samael will get you as close as we can." Dumah reverently handed the items back to Wylie, and she zipped her things into her coat pocket. Dumah vanished.

Samael opened his arms, and without a word from either, Wylie walked into them. He pulled her close, and she rested her head against him. In a blink, the icy wind cut through her.

Dumah stood under a tree where the snow was less deep. A male angel Wylie didn't recognize laughed beside her.

Samael released her and fell behind Wylie as she joined the two. "Raphael, brother, thank you for coming."

"Of course, anything for Armageddon." Raphael took Samael's hand in a rough handshake. "I brought a shield." He pointed at a steel shield. "Stole it from a Prince of Darkness during the Crusades."

Samael pulled a sword out of thin air. "This is a part of me. Ophanim made this blade when she made me. No other Angel has carried it. She's named *Kushima*." He held the blade out for Wylie, who took it with both hands.

"Always the showoff." Raphael lifted his shield from the ground.

"Wylie, you will hold your gifts as they bless you, and then you will meet with Ophanim to forge them." Dumah gestured to the Dominions.

Between the cold and the strangeness of the moment, Wylie found herself speechless. She managed a nod.

Samael rested his hands on Wylie's shoulders and brushed his lips against her forehead, where they stayed as he spoke. "May this weapon travel the planes with you as a companion and protector. May God guard you with it. May it never fail to make your enemies bleed. *Domine, benedic et protege familiam meam, Amen.*" The cold disappeared as the weight of the sword eased. Samael breathed in deeply before stepping back. She had a hard time not following him.

Raphael held up the shield. "Rest the sword atop the shield." Wylie did as told, wanting to tell these big males that she didn't know a thing about weapons. "Now you hold them." She cradled the shield in her arms, the rounded side down, the sword balanced on top. He lifted his hands to the sky, then holding her cheeks, he kissed each one. "May this shield protect you." He rolled his eyes. "*Domine, benedic et protege familiam meam, Amen.*" The shield warmed in her hands.

"Now, Wylie, take these blessings and join Ophanim." Dumah leaned forward and spoke in Wylie's ear. "This is where I will ask for your blind faith one last time."

Wylie looked around her, feeling blind already. She could still be in

Washington, judging by the pines, peaking out under the snow. But she also could be anywhere in the world.

"We're on Mount Saint Helens. Ophanim waits for you in the volcano's belly. Close your eyes."

Wylie did as told, her heart drumming.

"Reach for her Scientia with yours. And reform yourself next to her, in the same way you did with your Catharsis."

She gritted her teeth as she reached. At first, she thought the feeling of being buried came from the volcano and then realized it came from a living being. The angel felt like sand falling from between her fingers, mud between her toes, and snow landing in her hair. She reached for the center of that feeling and rebuilt her body—organs, muscles, nerves, and on and on. Sweat pooled in every crevice, and her fresh skin burned. Orange glowed through her eyelids. She risked opening them. She stood on an island in an underground crater full of lava.

An ethereal angel stood next to her. The female was at least seven feet tall with milky white irises. "It is an honor to meet an angel I did not make." Ophanim held up a breastplate. "I also have a blessing for you. Stack your gifts on mine."

As if in a trance, Wylie rested her shield and sword on the breastplate.

"Now take your memories and say goodbye. They will never look the same again."

Wylie unzipped her pocket and set Dean's necklace and the napkin on the pile but changed her mind when she pulled out Roberto's ring. She could not say goodbye to it. She slid it on her thumb and placed her own wedding ring on top.

"Now, hold."

She took her gifts, and Ophanim rested both hands on Wylie's head. "May you never forget their faces as they guard your heart and head. May your dancing and fighting become poetry. May you wear your halo and know the truth, decide correctly, and hear God. *Domine, benedic et protege familiam meam, Amen.*

"Now, you must do the rest. With your hands, you will forge your gift. Kneel."

Wylie dropped to her knees, her body not registering the danger her brain screamed of.

"Push your Scientia into your hands and lower your gifts into the fire."

She concentrated on her hands, allowing those flames she barely kept at bay to come to life. She pushed every part of her Scientia in her hands, and on instinct, her love for her boys joined the surge of power. The earth rumbled as the breastplate met the lava and shook as the sword submerged. It was like shoving her hands into the earth. She used all her strength to do so. Tears evaporated from her eyes as the gifts melted away. The heat didn't touch her, but the loss did. The mountain mourned with her.

"Now," Ophanim shouted over the earth's grumbles. "Pull it out now."

Wylie reached for something, anything, and was about to give up when the tips of her fingers grazed something hard. She pushed further into the lava until she almost kissed the sludge. "I got it."

Ophanim pulled her back.

Wylie fell back, her fingers curling around something warm and hard. They called it a halo, and that is what it was. A gold ring, too large to be a crown. Geometric patterns matching her wedding band were etched into it. Three larger diamonds floated in a constellation of smaller stones. She placed it on her head, and a rush of confidence filled her.

"This will be the only weapon you will need in this fight. You will use it, and you will use it correctly because it is made of your husband's words, your son's beauty, and your eternal promise." With her words, a warmth hugged Wylie's torso. The breastplate appeared over her coat, hugging Wylie like a second skin. Roberto's words were carved into the leather, and a gold chain lined the collar.

"Thank you." She hugged herself, feeling the warmth of her family's love.

"Now, return to Samael before he comes for you."

Chapter 30

Lex

"Mm." *That was fun.* Lex slipped her hand up Gabriel's bare chest. Her teeth caught his bottom lip.

"Which part?" Gabriel asked, his lip still trapped.

Lex's hand came up to Gabriel's face as she kissed him. *I don't know. It's hard to choose.*

"Oh, yeah?" Gabriel rolled onto his side and pulled a handful of Lex's hair.

"Ouch." She giggled and pinched Gabriel's nipple in return. They wrestled for a moment, sharing warm kisses and filling the room with laughter. She'd moved into the compound four months before. They'd shared a room for a month now. The two of them fit together like they'd finally found a home.

As if choreographed, the pair rolled onto their backs, catching their breath. *What about you?* Lex's lashes danced as she turned to him.

"No contest. It has to be how you shouted at me with your brain." Gabriel smiled.

You're such a dick. She pulled his chest hair.

"Don't you start that again, *ma petite rêleuse*."

What does that mean?

"I don't want to say."

She ran her finger down his ribs. *Tell me.*

"It means 'my little grump.'" Gabriel's lips quivered as he held back a smile.

Lex's body shook with laughter. *You asshole.*

"That's me."

She curled into his side as the laughter died away. *Are you ready?*

"I think we are." Gabriel kissed Lex's shoulder. "I know you're worried. Don't be. I'll be fine."

I just wish I could go. She traced his ear with her finger. *Imagine what I could do in a group that size.*

Gabriel laughed, his hand finding Lex's breast. "It's on another plane. I'm not risking taking you there."

Lex took his hand and bit his thumb.

"Ouch. You're ruthless."

Speaking of ruthless, what about your sister? Will you kill her?

Gabriel stroked her cheek. He hesitated before replying. "I can't."

Lex sighed. She didn't want him to come home with Wylie's blood on his hands. Not if she was David's angel, as Lex suspected. Wylie's story and David's angel's story sounded the same. Growing up human. Not knowing what she was. His confession that they'd slept together.

Gabriel's fingers traced down her sides. "You know her muse?"

I do. She didn't want to tell him any more about David. She didn't want to hurt her friend, but he would be better off without her. *Why can't you kill her? Wouldn't that solve all your problems?*

Gabriel gave her a hard stare. "If I tell you the answer to that question, you will know my biggest weakness. Do you want that responsibility?"

She responded by turning to him. Her hands cupped his cheeks, and she kissed him long and slow. *I want to know everything about you.*

"And I can trust you not to tell your little muse friend?"

You can. She wouldn't mix those worlds. She cared for them too much to pit them against each other.

He pressed his forehead into hers, his eyes squeezing shut. "Remember my first meeting with Laoth? That time she brought Binah home with a hack saw at her wings?"

Lex nodded, wondering where this was going. *Yeah.*

"Well, I discovered the night before that Wylie's powers are linked to mine. If she dies, I die."

She pulled his mouth back to hers. *Then she can't die, because I like you too much.*

He pulled her close. "I like you too, hellcat."

Thank you for trusting me.

"Just don't use it against me when you're angry."

She pinched him and enjoyed the sight as he laughed. She'd never been so happy in her life. She could not come up with one childhood memory or a moment when Abaddon spoiled her that felt as good as this moment. She didn't want it to end, but Binah waited.

She checked Gabriel's watch. *I better go.* Lex slipped off the bed and pulled the blanket to Gabriel's chin. He needed all the sleep he could get.

"I'll see you soon, *rêleuse.*"

From the door, she blew him a kiss. He caught it, his eyes still shut.

She pulled on her gym clothes and tiptoed out of the room, enjoying the coolness of the hallway. She'd never lived somewhere with an air conditioner. She walked at a brisk pace, becoming more excited with every step. When Gabriel first offered to have Lex train with Binah, she'd jumped on the opportunity. She wanted to be useful, and while the compound had plenty of jobs, she didn't see herself working at a desk or in the infirmary. She'd spoken to Todd, who encouraged her to train for a guard position.

Lex knocked on a pair of tall oak doors.

"Just in time." Binah held the door for Lex, her red lipstick blanching her porcelain skin.

Lex held her belly as entered the room. Her nerves settled in her stomach.

"Since I don't read minds, I invited a friend." Binah closed the door. "We should probably learn some sign language. Believe it or not, I speak eight languages. What's one more?"

Lex nodded until she noticed the woman in a pantsuit lounging on the other side of the room. Laoth's Louis Vuitton heels rested on top of a grand oak desk.

She waved, her gold Rolex at her wrist glinting in the light, her blue braid clashing with the oranges of the acrylic painting hanging on the wall behind her.

Lex folded her arms, following Binah further into the room.

"Long time no see." Laoth came out from around the desk and put out her hand.

I don't do handshakes.

"She doesn't do handshakes?" She dropped her hand and smirked at Binah. "Jelly bean tells me Gabriel gave you Abaddon like other men give their girlfriends flowers."

Lex had no intention of taking the bait. She pointed at the pink line that started at her chin and turned her lips into a Picasso nightmare. *We all know angels give strange gifts.*

"I also heard your dead great-great-great-great-grandfather was the first one to get your special tattoo?"

Lex narrowed her eyes at Binah, who shrugged and sat on one of the couches that lined the walls. *He was Chinese. I'm Vietnamese. For fuck's sake, I'm not related to the guy.* Lex rolled her eyes. *Dumbass.*

"God, she's a bitch." Laoth flopped into Binah's lap, her legs hanging off the couch. "How did Abaddon spend so long with you?"

"She's the boss's girlfriend. We don't talk to her like that." Binah palmed the side of Laoth's head. "Sorry, Lex. Somehow, I forgot how much of an asshole Laoth is."

"Who ever heard of angels having girlfriends?" Laoth continued without missing a step.

"Don't play dumb. It's one of the main reasons you want free will." Binah winked at Lex. "She doesn't have it yet. We're planning a big coming out party after the Tribunal."

Let me guess. I'm not invited.

"She's just so loud." Laoth plugged her ears for emphasis.

"You're a dumbass." Binah flicked her. "Be nice to the muses."

"I'm not used to working with so many muses. But you are, right, Lex? Isn't that Gabriel's kink?"

Lex caught Binah's eyes and shook her head. *No more,* she mouthed.

"What? Is it weird sharing your boyfriend with every other muse in the building?"

"Go fuck yourself!" The sound that came out of her was monstrous. Lex kicked the couch, some of her Scientia leaking out with the blow. Wood split and the furniture sagged, sending Binah and Laoth sliding into the edge.

Laoth jumped to her feet. "I'm not impressed with your theatrics." She projected behind Lex and grabbed a handful of hair. "I'm tired of you human scum thinking you deserve anything from us." Laoth bit Lex's ear, drawing blood.

Binah appeared in front of Lex and pulled the muse behind her back. A sword appeared in her hand, and she leveled it at Laoth. "No one touches Alexis."

Laoth raised her hands. "Oops. I forgot." She winked at Lex before projecting away.

"I'm so sorry." Binah spun and reached for Lex, who flinched away, her hand cupping her ear. "I thought she'd be helpful. She's just nervous. She's giving up everything for this cause."

Lex held up her middle finger, brandishing the only sign language she knew before walking out.

Wylie searched the crowd for Laoth's pink hair. She'd worn an unfamiliar face every time she'd seen the angel over the last few months. Today Laoth had divided her Pepto-Bismol locks into pigtails, with skin darker than Wylie's.

"You weren't joking when you said pink hair."

Laoth rolled her eyes. "How's work been? Have you cooked any humans lately?"

Her medical leave ended somewhere in the middle of everything. Returning to the hospital had been a blessing and a curse. Maybe because she returned as an angel. Maybe because she almost forgot about the stabbing that caused her to take said leave in the first place. She'd been back to work long enough now that she was back into her routine.

The job gave her time to think. Falling into her familiar role, nothing could phase her while she wore scrubs. As she held pressure against a half-amputated ear, *I'm an angel.* She'd plug in the leads for an EKG, *I have a twin brother.* She held back someone's hair as they vomited, *his name is Gabriel, and he wants me dead.*

Each epiphany hit her when she directed her concentration elsewhere. Her brain did her a kindness with this misdirection. It worked better under stress. Running for twelve hours and collapsing onto a soft mattress afterward did her good.

But those short stints were her only chance to sleep. Laoth trained her during her free time, spending Wylie's nights off at her apartment, teaching her how to control the heat in her hands and the sensitivity of her mind, all while drinking large quantities of tequila. Wylie enjoyed the well-deserved comradery, even if Laoth was rough around the edges.

"You haven't lit anyone on fire, have you?"

"No, but with this mind-reading ability, it makes it difficult not to. At least it only works when I touch someone's bare skin. This girl wears her gloves for everything now." She pulled out the chair across from where Laoth had been sitting.

"No, don't sit. Follow me." The angel headed for the exit. "We have a date for the Tribunal. The plan is to push the world's pause button at midnight in Moscow. It will be the day of the March equinox. The largest population of humans will be sleeping at that time. With the humans taking a brief reprieve, angels can leave their posts and participate." She pushed the door open. "We will stay close to our muses as we try to build our Scientia. I won't be able to visit as often. You should do the same."

"The same?"

"Stay close to your muse." She raised her eyebrows when Wylie sighed in response.

David confused Wylie. She didn't know how she could see someone so often and miss them so much.

"Is there a problem with your muse?" Laoth shut the industrial door.

"No, no." Wylie frowned.

"Your muse has one job, and that's keeping you strong."

"My muse has many jobs: caretaker, physician, pain in my ass." Wylie followed Laoth down a narrow alley. A spring mist still clung to the corners of the building as the sun worked to reach its zenith.

"Come here."

Laoth placed her hands on either side of Wylie's head, and their foreheads met. This was part of the routine, too. It felt like someone stuck a taser to Wylie's face and turned it on high. Bands of white-hot pain held the inside of her skull together. Laoth promised the more they did it, the easier it would be for Wylie to control her power.

"Shit." Wylie wiped at her eyes.

"You're such a pansy."

Angels fly, fight, disappear, and on and on, she still felt pain when she didn't have to. "No, I'm useless."

Laoth jabbed Wylie's side with her elbow. "You sure are."

"Fuck you." Wylie batted Laoth away.

They faced a dumpster, and the smell of garbage encased them. "Now what?" Wylie lifted her hand to her nose.

"His name is Stephen."

"Who?" Wylie's heart raced as she saw the serious line on Laoth's mouth.

"Your silver-haired man." Laoth folded her arms behind her back. "I found him."

"What?"

"I've seen him in your thoughts. I showed my friend his image." Laoth tapped her head. "And she knew him. She's looked for him too. I will help you, but first, you need to prove you're ready." She gestured to the dumpster. "Write his name there."

Wylie had plastered the silver-haired man's face over the interior of her mind. She thought of her husband and child's murderer as often as some people prayed. Her thoughts ran in a thousand directions as she pulled her sharpie from her breast pocket and jumped when Laoth's hand connected with the back of her head. "Not with that, you idiot."

Wylie's flames sprung to life. Dropping the marker, she fisted her hands to stop them from shaking with the wrath that burned through her veins.

"Easy." Laoth lifted her hands. "I want you to burn his name there." She pointed at the dumpster. "With this." She held up a finger.

This angel body's biggest challenge was controlling emotions. Laoth told Wylie angels have little to no emotions, which was her problem. The new Wylie felt too much. Laoth thought it was funny. She enjoyed pushing Wylie's buttons.

"Snap out of it, Wylie. You have fifteen minutes left of your break." Laoth planned this: Wylie's anger, the time crunch.

Reaching out, Wylie's finger connected with the metal. She bit her lip and scorched an 'S' into the green paint. The smell of the contents became a cacophony as they cooked together.

"T," she said as she finished the letter. The trash caught fire with the letter 'H.' Boiling fluid leaked from the corner.

"Pull it back."

The swirl of anger in Wylie's mind muffled Laoth's command.

The dumpster rattled against the hospital wall, and Wylie sucked in a breath, trying to dampen the heat. "N. There, I'm done." The announcement came as she took several steps back. The blackened splotches were unrecognizable.

"Well, that's a dumpster fire." Laoth cracked her knuckles. "You better head back in. I'll take care of this."

Laoth clapped her hands as Wylie entered the building, her cheeks rosy with both heat and embarrassment. A security guard passed Wylie with a raised eyebrow and a pack of cigarettes in his hand.

"Shit!" He shouted as Wylie rounded the corner and picked up speed.

"Code Red alert, external alley, north exit. Code red alert." The announcement came as Wylie joined a group of nurses at the nurses' station.

"Damn smokers," Mary said. "I bet a cigarette got flicked into the recycling again."

Wylie shrugged, her hands still shaking with excitement. "Maybe it's electrical?"

---

*L*ater that morning, Wylie strolled through the dairy aisle at the Safeway on Eleventh and paused in the yogurt section.

She compared the sugar content of the Greek yogurt options—no question about it. In the past, she would have purchased the plain option, even though it tasted like ass-cheese.

She stared at a vanilla-flavored tub, licked her lips, and tossed it in the cart. No more ass-cheese yogurt for her. Her new body craved satisfaction more than fuel. Now she understood why Laoth always brought fried chicken when she stopped by for their lessons and why Dumah settled for nothing less than wedding cakes for dessert.

"Wylie?"

She didn't recognize the youthful voice. The corners of her lips lifted as it cracked over the 'ie' in her name. She turned to find a be-pimpled teenager. He stood an inch or two taller than Wylie, a handsome jock who looked familiar.

"Yeah?" she answered, trying to place his sandy-blond hair and square jaw. His grass-green eyes brought recognition with a gasp. "Samael?"

Teen-Samael smiled, his pearly whites gleaming in the fluorescent light. His expression puzzled her. Samael wasn't the smiling type.

"Yeah," he said, blowing out of the corner of his mouth to push the hair off his forehead. His easy stance and longish hair felt out of place on the Dominion, whose frowns were often half-smiles in disguise.

"You seem different," Wylie said, doing her best not to roll her eyes.

"Yep. Definitely different." His cheeks turned red. "I mean, with the lack of inhibitions and the mood swings, I look foolish." He rubbed at his cheeks.

"So?" She wanted to send the boy-Samael to boarding school for violating the sacred ritual of grocery shopping. She pushed her cart until she arrived at the tubes of raw cookie dough. "Why are you *dressed* like that?"

"Um . . ." He giggled, one of those awkward pubescent trills which sounded wrong at its lower timber. "It's the only way I can spend time with Jane. I have, like, four classes with her." He blinked hard at the cookie options. "I need to gather as much Scientia as I can."

"Oh, well, that makes sense. I'm guessing David doesn't know?"

"That douche? Hell no." The words spilled from his mouth, and he slapped his leg and laughed again.

She snorted. "Be nice."

He shrugged, his letterman jacket bouncing up and down on his shoulders. "High school is the true battleground. I'm barely surviving four classes with those heathens." He reached for a roll of double chocolate chip and tossed it in her cart. "Building up my Scientia is worth it, though." He ignored her look of annoyance as he tossed some peanut butter cookies in there next.

He lifted his chin to her cart. "Can I grab some milk for those cookies?" He grabbed a gallon before Wylie could respond. "Anyway, I've got things to tell you."

She turned back to her cart, pushing it around the corner. Its little wheels squeaked in protest.

"We have a week until the Tribunal." His voice lowered. "I just wanted to run over what to expect because you won't see any other angels until then."

Wylie frowned. Blocking her thoughts, she grabbed a box of Oreo cookies, sending them to join their raw siblings in her cart.

"When it's time, Laoth will come for you."

"I'll stay with her during the Tribunal?"

"Yes, you'll be with her brigade. I think you'll like them." He reached across her and grabbed a bag of chips, holding them to his chest as he winked. "I've asked Dumah to stay with you, too. They'll protect you if Gabriel shows up."

"An entire brigade? How many angels is that?"

"I think there are four thousand Archangels in Laoth's brigade."

"Shit. Thousands?" Wylie stopped in her tracks. "To protect me from one angel?"

"Your brother is like you. Powerful. The God's Guard hopes he'll be better behaved while surrounded by all my brothers and sisters."

"Please don't call him that." The cart handle melted under her hands, and her teeth ground together as her mind reached for the reins of control.

A loud *pop* sent her ducking behind Samael. The top of the bag of chips had blown open under the force of his chokehold. With a shrug, he reached in and pulled out a handful. "You're not the only one who doesn't like the guy."

She walked past the chips, the bags expanding from the heat waves coming off her as she went. "Then tell me why he's invited."

"Because he's an angel, and we shall hear every voice." Samael trailed behind her as her speed increased. "There is always a possibility we can bring our brothers and sisters he led astray back to the light."

She spun around, and he walked into her. "And you think they deserve forgiveness?" Her body vibrated, but she kept it in.

"Everyone deserves forgiveness, and it's our duty to give it."

The soda cans beside her burst, spraying in all directions. She gritted her teeth against the pain as she forced her fire to stay inside.

"Wylie?"

A swelling crowd of grocery shoppers whispered as soda flowed over the tiles.

Home!

BAM. The thought brought her to the rhododendron bush outside her apartment. She marched around the side of the building as she wondered what she'd done to deserve the stabbiness of her new landing spot. She wished she'd brought the Oreos with her.

Samael, big Samael, waited at her front door. Nighthawks called each other, announcing the sunset, as Wylie glared at his silhouette.

"That was a mess," Samael said, his muscular arms folded over his chest.

She rolled her eyes. "No biggie, I'm sure you'll forgive me. I should've killed a few babies while I was at it since you angels are such a lenient lot." She glared up at Samael, expecting a retort, but instead, she found his head turned as if she'd struck him. "Fuck it, just move. I need to get inside and order dinner since all my food is at the grocery store."

"Wylie." His eyes burned into her, his mouth falling open. "Please."

She released a sigh, her anger still bubbling over. She opened the door and directed him to enter first.

He stalked past her before turning to block her way. "Show me."

Wylie held them up in her hands. Her Scientia buzzed under her skin, threatening to surface. How dare they invite the man who wants her dead. The man who would have seen David thrown off a building. Who sent the men that killed her child and husband. She gritted her teeth in an effort to keep her temper at bay.

Samael took her hands and ran his thumb over her palms. "Your Scientia is not your enemy." He pushed her hand against her chest. "If you must be angry, use it. Let it out."

Her finger curled in on themselves. She couldn't. She didn't want to hurt him. She closed her eyes to the innocence on his face. "I can't control it, Samael. I'd burn the world down."

"We will teach you to control this." His confidence bled from his skin to hers. His Scientia pushed against her, enticing the power inside her in licking waves as if calling for hers to join it.

Her resolve evaporated. Her flames welcomed him like kindling, curling around him. "Samael." His name came out in a whisper.

"Let it out. Let it all out." He pulled her to his chest and wrapped his wings around them, his breath soft against her ear. His magic cocooned her own in an embrace as strong and kind as his hold. With a rumbled word from Samael, complete silence pressed against them.

Their eyes met, and he nodded. Her nails bit into his shoulders, and her throat shredded with a scream as she became an inferno. His arms tightened around her, and he hummed, absorbing all of her hate, her fear, and her fury.

Chapter 31

Wylie

Laoth pushed the door open.

"Who's there?" A man in the center of the room straightened, his back to them.

"Don't let him see you sweat." The angel shoved Wylie inside. "Have fun."

"Bu—" Wylie turned back to Laoth, only to have the door slam in her face. She let out a frustrated sigh and returned her focus to the man. His gray hair glowed under the warehouse lighting, and she recognized it instantly. Her hands trembled, revenge sat mere feet away, but could she hurt someone?

Flashes of the night when she lay in bed and imagined the death of her family's murderers repeatedly reminded her she already had. She'd killed an angel. The thought stoked her courage further. This man had turned her into a murderer. He'd taken her innocence, and now that it was gone, was it worth clinging to?

"Binah, is that you?" The tail end of the question was a high pitch whine. "It's been two years, is your boss still pissed at me?" His head swung from side to side as he failed to see over his shoulder.

Wylie leaned against the wall. This man deserved to be tied up and frightened. She doubted she'd do much more than that. Her heart tapped out its beat as fast as Wylie's mind raced.

"Hello?"

She took a shaky breath and circled the man, hoping she exuded confidence. Let this man believe she'd take his life. He deserved much worse. "Hello, Stephen."

He'd received a blow to the head, and dried blood left a trail down his face. She should be wiping it, not planning ways to hurt him further.

The man blinked up at her. His brows rose as his eyes focused. The blood crusted on his cheek and flaked off as he laughed. "You're that nurse. What are you doing here, sweetheart?"

Wylie's fists clenched. "I'm here to hurt you."

His laugh became a snort. "Hurt me? You couldn't hurt a fly."

"Hurting people takes more creativity than practice." Her voice sounded steady as she quoted one of Laoth's nuggets of wisdom, though the urge to run away had her shuffling in place.

"You know, if you untie me, we can pretend this never happened." He worked his hands against the ropes, a smirk on his face. "Honey, do us a favor and pick up an extra shift."

She flew from standing in a stew of insecurity to a fiery hand on his cheek in seconds. He screamed as his flesh sizzled. Then gasped when she pulled her hand away. Sweat poured down his face. The nurse in her raced through all the steps it would take to fix his wound, listing the supplies, counting the hours and days spent on bandaging and healing and bandaging again.

"What the fuck did you just do?" He panted, his shoulders jutting out as his arms strained.

"I burnt you, Stephen." She tilted her head. "And I'm going to do it again." The man looked like a young grandfather. He wore a ponytail and had tan lines on his driving arm.

"Fuck you."

He felt wrong. She didn't know if it was his missing emotions or out-of-tune reaction. She pressed her finger into his forehead. *Instant regret. Instant satisfaction*

Stephen yowled, sliding toward her as he shook his head, unable to escape her touch. Wylie shivered and pulled away.

"What is your full name?" Wylie held tight to the flames, which threatened to burst from her skin.

"Fuck you." The man's face scrunched up in nearly the same way it had when he'd kicked Roberto.

"Okay, Mr. Fuck-You. Did that hurt?" She traced her finger along his sideburn, and the smell of burning hair filled the room. Smoke rose between them.

"What the fuck are you doing?" His eyes bulged as Wylie cupped both his cheeks in her hands. Hoarse screams fell from his mouth. His eyes rolled back in his head.

She replaced the sight with Dean's tear-stained cheeks. No one made her baby cry. She blinked back tears of rage.

"This isn't fun." Wylie rubbed her greasy fingers together, looking at the flesh that clung to her palm. "It's pretty gross if you ask me." Patches of his skin rolled and bunched as she wiped them on his pants. "You disgust me."

"What are you?" Snot and drool blended as he gaped at her flaming hands. "What are you doing with your hands?"

"Sending you to hell."

She lifted her hand, and he leaned away. "It was just a job." His swollen face oozed, and he dropped his ear to his shoulder to dry it on his shirt. "It was supposed to be you that died. Then that big guy showed up . . ." His eyes darted from one side of the room to the other as if it could happen again. "We were just trying to protect ourselves."

"By spraying bullets around my apartment?" Wylie dug her heel into his foot, eliciting shouts of pain each time. Once. Twice.

Again.

"Stop!"

And again.

"Stop!"

"Tell me your name?"

"What? Who?"

Wylie moved to his level, her eyes locking with his. "I want to know your name before I kill you." Spit from her shout landed on his ruined face, and she squeezed his thigh, leaving a hand-shaped burn on his jeans.

"What are you?" Stephen grit between his teeth.

She slapped him. "Tell me."

"It's Stephen Peterson." His shoulders shook with sobs. "I don't want to die!"

A ringing filled the space between Wylie's ears. "Stephen Peterson, look at me." She lifted her arms, allowing her wings to come to life. "I'm an angel, and I'm here to punish you."

"I was just doing my job." He whined like a child. "Have mercy. I was just doing my job, and everything got out of hand." His shaking shoulders shrugged. "Things got out of hand."

Got out of hand?

Got out of HAND!

Wylie's heart birthed an explosion, the pressure so intense it lifted her from the ground.

"God, no! PLEASE, NOO!"

Her top lashes met her bottom ones as her flames covered her. "Never again!" A wet squelch announced the silver-haired man's detonation. A mist of boiling blood hovered in his place. Her crimson revenge showered down on her.

She stared at the empty chair, her breath coming in pants as the blood congealed on her skin.

"Oh my God, Wylie, you exploded him!" Laoth's cackle echoed off the concrete walls.

"Did I?" Wylie clutched her chest. It burned as it twisted against reality. "I killed him?"

"Girl, you killed him with a capital 'K.'" She snorted. "What a mess, I mean. I don't think I've ever made a mess this big." She spun, her hands open, catching red drips from the ceiling.

"How..."

"Don't worry about it. Come here." She grabbed the nape of Wylie's neck and pressed their foreheads together. "After seeing that, I wonder if we've done this enough."

Wylie gritted her teeth as her body convulsed. Drool formed in the corner of her lips. Her body leaned into Laoth as she finished.

"Gross." Laoth held Wylie at arm's length. "I'll clean this up, but first, I'm going to drop you off with your muse. You don't look right."

The "no" never made it past Wylie's lips. Laoth dropped her in

David's room, disappearing before the man stirred under his sheets. The bedside alarm read three a.m. in neon red. Wylie swayed in place, afraid to touch anything.

"Wylie?" The whites of David's eyes glowed in the room's darkness.

"David, I . . ." Wylie lifted her hands as if the blood explained everything.

He came over the foot of his bed in a rush, his arms catching her just before her legs gave out.

She moaned as their skin touched, his muse magic easing the trauma beating against her heart. His amber eyes captured Wylie's, and everything else fell away.

"You're covered in blood. Are you hurt?" His fingers searched for signs of an injury, her sins transferring onto him through stained fingers.

She shook her head. "Not mine." She pushed his hands away. She didn't want to expose him to this.

David pulled her close. He wore only boxers, and though Wylie's shirt stuck to his bare chest, he coaxed her against him. "Come, let's get you cleaned up."

She listened to his rapid pulse, hating herself but was too weak to resist the attention he showed her. Taking her hands, he led her to his ensuite and then into the shower.

Wylie welcomed the shock of the first spray of cold water. Red swirled around the drain. The smell of Stephen's blood and David's cinnamon enveloped her. She held onto her muse as if he could slip away at any moment.

"Lift your arms." He pulled her shirt over her head, her breath halting as his knuckles brushed her ribs. Soap ran over her skin.

"I killed him." Wylie wobbled, and he pulled her close again. She clung to him, her face buried in his neck, too afraid to see his reaction.

"Who?"

"Stephen Peterson. The man who came to my apartment and . . ." She squeezed him tighter. "He said it was an accident, and then he shrugged. Please don't hate me, David, but he shrugged. He said, 'things got out of hand,' and then he shrugged. I didn't mean to hurt him, not that time. I'm just like him."

"Shh." David smoothed Wylie's hair. The water rushed over them as he held her. "I have faith in you. You're a good person who saves lives. Don't discount all the good you've done."

"But, David—"

"Stop." He lifted her face by her chin. "If we were at work and someone died, what would you do?"

She opened her mouth but couldn't speak.

"You'd clean up. You'd chart. You'd debrief with the team. That's what we're going to do. I'm going to clean you up. You're going to write this all down, and I'm going to call Samael back here. We'll figure this out."

"I wasn't with Samael."

"You were by yourself?" His hands ran over her shoulders.

"No, she. She. She said she would clean it all up after she dropped me off here."

"I still think we should call Samael."

"I don't think he knows about this." Wylie's body quaked with shock.

"I see." He rested his hand on her cheek. "Let's get you cleaned up."

She nodded. Her hands went to her pants, but her fingers refused to work.

"Hold on." He unzipped her fly. Her jeans came down with several hard jerks. She braced her hands on the glass wall of the shower.

Stepping out of them, she returned to David and pressed her body against his. She rested her lips on his chest and closed her eyes as his fingers worked a lather into her hair.

The soap slid down her back in feather-like strokes. "Nothing else matters, Wylie. The hospital, the angels, the world." He tilted her head back, rinsing her hair with careful concentration. "You and my family are all I care about."

He pulled her against him so tight her lungs lost room for air. Her body bowed as his curved around hers. "I should care that you showed up in my room covered in blood." His hardness stiffened against her belly, his boxers the only barrier. "I'm ashamed that I don't. I don't care because you're the kindest, bravest, most compassionate person I know."

Wylie answered by slipping her tongue past her lips and tasting the water running down his chest. He hissed, his hands framing her face. Their mouths crushed together. She moaned.

Her nails found his back as he pushed her into the wall, his hips rolling against hers. "David." His name, a gasp.

He pulled away, and her heart ached from the last time he'd done so.

But looking down, she realized he was freeing himself from his boxers.

"Turn around."

She did as told, her nipples burning against the cold glass as his hand slid down her ass and between her legs, their bodies flush. She rose to her tiptoes when his finger entered her. Something not quite a word escaped her throat.

"Can we?" His lips against her ear. His cock against her hip.

"Yes." She whimpered as his finger left her empty, and he lifted her leg.

"You feel so good. I've missed this." He lined himself up against her core. "I want you in my bed." In contradiction to his words, he pressed into her, barely entering. "In my bed, now."

Her back vibrated with the rumble of his groan as she wiggled against him in protest.

"Please."

"Wylie." His hips lifted, and he pushed another inch into her.

Her body shook as he paused again. Her core burned with his intrusion.

With a growl, he pulled himself free and spun her around. He pushed her into the shower wall and lay claim to her mouth, lifting her by her ass. His cock slid between her legs, so close to where she wanted it.

He left the shower running, water creating puddles as he carried her to his bed. His lips never left hers as she undulated against him.

With reverence he sat, his gentleness not matching the urgency of the kisses he branded into her neck. She wrapped her legs around him, reached between them and, holding his length, lowered herself onto him.

The room lit up as flames licked her body, but for the first time, the fire engulfing her wasn't there to harm. Consume, yes. Burn, never. "David," she gasped, wanting to hold him with her fire. "Are you okay?"

Steam rose from his still-wet chest. Light flickered across his face revealing only hunger. "I know you'll never hurt me." His hands encircled her hips, guiding her until she found a rhythm. She held onto his shoulders, the fire an extension of her pleasure as it feathered against him.

Chapter 32

Lex

Angels have controlled humans for too damn long. Lex lay on her bed, her head resting on Gabriel's shoulder, her legs tangled with his.

"You could say it's the other way around." He lifted a bunch of her hair, inspecting it before poking her in the forehead with the tips. "What reward do angels get for helping humans?"

Lex waved his hand away, turning her head so Gabriel wouldn't see her smirk.

We aren't debating about peanut butter and pickle sandwiches.

"You're right." He kissed the top of her head. "We're talking about freedom."

What if freedom to me differs from what you call freedom?

"I don't think it does."

Then why do you keep all these muses here?

"Why do you think they're here?"

She leaned away from him so she could see his face. *There's lots of gossip. I don't want to believe most of it.*

"When I separate an angel from their muse, the muse remains attached to me." He blurted, his forever smile dimming. "That's what would have happened to you if you hadn't had that tattoo. Abaddon would have got freedom, and I would have tied myself to you."

She removed herself from his warmth, sitting at the side of the bed. Her stomach was cramping. "Remember the first time we met, and you called me Abaddon's 'tithe?'" Her voice rasped over the words. She studied the red patterns on the rug under her feet, her fists pressing into the pain in her middle. *Is that what you're doing? Collecting our Scientia so that you can become more powerful?*

His hand touched her shoulder but fell away when she flinched. "There is so much of this life I don't have a say in, Lexy. So much of it is destiny. God has chosen for me."

Lex closed her eyes. "Why do you do it?"

"I'll tell you everything, but not like this."

The bed shifted under her, the covers rustling as he moved off.

Naked, he knelt in front of her. "Can I touch you?" His hands hovered over her shins.

She nodded, studying his face. His seriousness transformed it. He looked younger. Some would interpret how his thick brows turned down as anger, but his forever smile hid that part of him.

"Before I was born, angels believed the only way to gain freedom was to cut off their wings." His fingers wrapped around her calves. They slid up and down as he spoke. "But doing it that way left angels powerless and soulless. A shadow of their human counterparts. I can separate a muse from their angel by tethering the muse to myself." He paused, his charcoal eyes finding hers.

Is this why you feel, like—she gestured at the surrounding air—*so fucking much? Do you keep their Scientia?*

"I don't need their Scientia, Lex. I'm not boasting when I say my power has proven to be boundless." A shadow of his smile returned as he leaned forward and kissed her knee. "But I'm flattered you think of me as being 'so fucking much.'" He kissed her other knee. "I try to leave the angels with as much Scientia as their muse can spare."

Shit, Gabriel. What do you do with the free muses?

"We're at war. Sacrifices must be made." He rested his hands, palms up, in her lap. Relief smoothed his brow as she set her hand on his. "As for the muses, you could be the solution. Do you have any idea how many muses I'm linked to? How many I'm responsible for? There are some days it feels crippling."

She squeezed his hands.

"Hellcat, I didn't bring you here to save you. I brought you here hoping you'd save me."

Wylie opened her eyes to find herself in a familiar meadow dominated by an infinite door. "Samael said there would be lots of angels."

"There will be. This is Elysian. I thought we'd take a pit stop before heading to Arcadia. The Tribunal will be held there."

Wylie moved close to the door. "Where's the God's Guard?"

"They are at the Tribunal. This is the only time this door is unguarded." Laoth elbowed Wylie. "This is as close as I get. I'll give you some privacy, fifteen minutes?"

"What do you mean?"

"I mean, you're always bitching about missing your family. Here's your chance. Open the door. Say 'hi.'"

"But Samael said—"

"Samael says many things, but God seems to think you're an exception to most of them."

"But..."

Laoth projected away before Wylie could finish her reply.

Her hands braced her chest, working like splints for her broken heart. Her shoes caught in the grass as she crossed the space. Leaning forward, her forehead rested against the wood. A buzz emanated from it, rattling her teeth.

"Roberto?"

The buzzing crescendoed in response, bouncing as if to pronounce syllables.

"Berto?"

The whirring response could have been her name. She circled the freestanding door, the back an exact duplicate of the front. She placed both hands on the door and pushed. The soft buzz became a pulse like a taser, burning her hands, her chest, and her face. Those bands Laoth left in her brain stretched taut. Wylie gritted her teeth and burned back, flames jumping from her palms. *Fuck you, door! Let me in!*

With this push, she willed her wings to assist her. Flames burst with a crackle behind her as they opened wide. The muscles of her arms ached, but the door held fast.

"*Veni Angelus, da mihi Scientia!*" she shouted as she pushed.

CREAK!

The world around her trembled as the door opened. She swung around, worried she'd be caught. She remained alone, on her own, with an ancient door that opened after all.

She cupped her hand around her mouth and shouted into the crack. "Roberto."

"*Mi amor?*" The answer took her legs out from under her, her husband's rich tenor sending her to her knees. The sound soothed the scars his death had left behind.

He slid his hand through the slit, and she took it, resting her face against the crack, peaking through. Beyond the opening, she found a tuft of salt-and-pepper hair and an ebony eye surrounded by wrinkles. "Roberto?"

Age spots adorned the back of his hand. He pushed his face into the crevice, the thickness of the door keeping their faces from meeting. She squeezed his fingers and settled on kissing them. Her tears soaked their hands. "I've missed you so much." She slipped the ring from her thumb and back to where it belonged.

"We've missed you, too."

She traced the smile on his face, memorizing it. "Our boy, he's a man now." He kissed her hand, speaking against her fingertips. "You'd be so proud of him. We're so proud of you."

"They told me I'd never see you again."

Now, his hand found her face. "You see me every day." He ran his thumb over her lips. "Every time your heart sings, I hear it. You touch a sick child. I feel it. You smile, and I smile, and there's no end to how we imprinted ourselves onto each other." He cupped her chin in his hand. "Each raindrop that touches your skin is a kiss I've sent you. Each ray of sun a caress. You're not alone." His hand slipped from hers. "*Te amo.*"

Elysian swayed, and Wylie jumped to her feet, her shoulder and hands desperately shoved against the door as it closed.

"I love you." She leaned against the door. Her hand traced the crevice of the jam. She desperately wanted a few more minutes. She had too many unsaid words. Her fist half-heartedly slammed into the wood.

It slammed back.

A lightning bolt sunk its teeth into her, sending her flying.

Her muscles contracted, her back arching, and the sickening feeling of burning alive raced through her veins. Her tongue lolled as it worked in her mouth, and a chain of popping connected her ears as the bands broke apart one at a time.

Lying flat, she stared up at the impossible sky.

"Wylie? You're alive?"

Wylie jolted at the sound of Laoth's voice. Yes, she was still alive, but damn, did she hurt.

Chapter 33

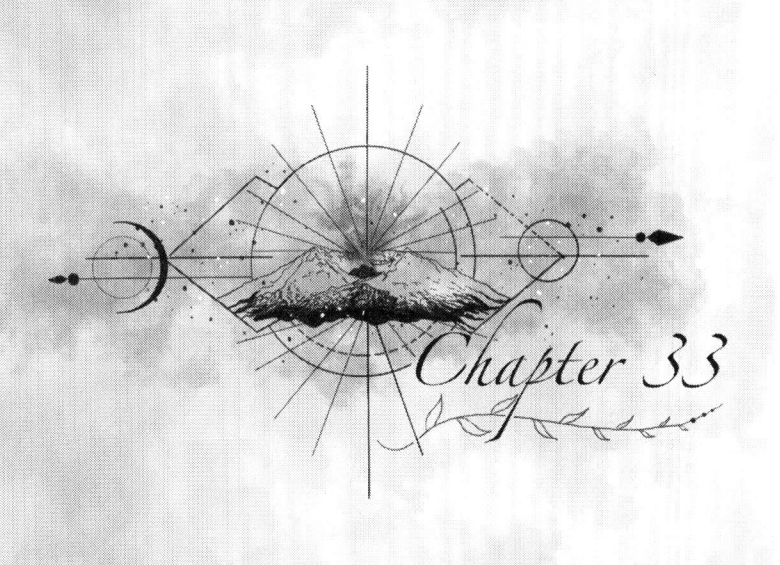

Samael

Moscow's cityscape shone with lights at midnight. Samael stood on the roof of Moscow State University. Considered one of the Seven Sisters, Stalin financed it in 1955. Each sister tower allowed full visualization of the city from its spot at the city's perimeter. Stalin meant to use his circle of towers as a pinnacle of defense in the post-war era, but the tower's current occupation had a much more important use. Education.

Samael could feel the hum of energy from the youth who enchanted the halls below him. The vitality of the city filled his chest. With the fog settled, the blurred colors of lights emphasized the landmark structures of the ninth most expensive city in the world.

"Hey, Sam." Raphael clapped his shoulder. "Are you ready?"

Samael grunted at Raphael and turned to the other Dominions, his arms opening to them. "Let's do this."

The last worldwide human reprieve felt fresh in Samael's mind. The memory of sharing his Scientia with his fellow angels enthralled him. They would create music with their souls. Melding their skills together to become a winged orchestra.

The Dominions joined hands, creating a circle. No need for words between them. They spoke with their minds, calling their Skilled brethren. They breathed in the night.

Together they breathed out, their Scientia speeding away from their circle in pulsing tidal waves. The Skilled Angels posted around the city caught the Dominion's power and forced it to spread. They used their voices to tether their Scientia to the net and cast it further.

Sending it out of Moscow and into Tula and Tver, Ryazan, and Kaluga. Each Skilled Angel projected their combined power to the next angel and then the next as they created the tapestry of the reprieve.

The chorus of angels sang out, matching the pitch of the wind and the rumble of thunder. The crescendos and dissonance mimicked the world around them. Their harmonies flowed from the Dominions. Though some voices rose to take precedence with the same soprano wails of a violin or baritone thumps of a drum, each angel's mouth produced a perfect blend of melodies.

Scattered masses of humans froze in time as angels' voices clung to them like comforters, tucking them in. The angel choir did not imitate nature as they sang their humans to reprieve. They were nature.

Samael stepped onto the Throne's Plane, his ears still full of angel music. Pride for his kind replaced the lingering worries of organizing the Tribunal. Ophanim had transformed Arcadia from an open expansion of white to a landscape of every tone of rust, bronze, and ivory.

A great organic stadium took up more space than Samael knew existed here. While the sky remained an empty white, rock formations towered for miles around him, creating a bowl of steps as far as the angel's eye could see. Ophanim and her sisters used sliding glaciers for millions of years to create the natural amphitheaters of North America. The last Throne put together the landmass before him in a few days.

"There is enough space for ten thousand times ten thousand here." Her white eyes swept across the expanse.

"Yes, sister, there is." Samael kneeled before her, raising his arm. "We are grateful."

"They will fit, and they will hear." She smoothed his hair. "The limestone eats the whispers and repels shouts, so those angels brave enough to raise their voices will be heard. And those who are not will be silenced."

Below and around him, thick layers of white, snow-like rock quarreled with its quarry siblings and won as it dominated the land. Still, on his knees, he found himself wishing angels sang for each other. That they could raise their voices in something other than duty. He wanted to hear how Ophanim's creation could carry a song. How all the living angels would sound with their voices raised as one. He closed his eyes and allowed himself to dream of such a moment of defiance.

"The other Dominions are here with their first group." Ophanim's voice woke him from his reverence, and he stood.

The first angels to report to the Tribunal scattered amongst the rocks as they arrived. The other Dominions escorted the Lesser Angels to Arcadia.

Samael stood guard as each new wave arrived, watching over their most treasured angels. The Lesser Angels' powers were too precious to be spent on the human's reprieve. Their Scientia was meant for their humans and their humans alone. Back on earth, the Skilled Angels spread the reprieve. The last to leave earth would be the Virtues. They'd join the rest once they finished sewing together one end of the blanket of song to the other.

Hands on his hips, he relished the wild essence that developed over lifetimes of human interaction. The Lesser Angels took all shapes and shades. They took the forms of household pets and paper pushers, of gang members and transparent ghosts. Many wore their halos openly, and most dressed in black or white to honor their loss. The sight of jeans and cell phones had him wondering, and not for the first time, if angels influenced humanity or vice versa.

The Skilled Angels would arrive in the robes and armor befitting their stations, but for now, Samael appreciated the simplicity of the Lesser Angels.

His fellow Dominions trickled in behind their flocks. Each caught his eye as they surveyed their surroundings.

We're here, brother. They reassured him.

His shoulders fell back. His breaths eased as he supervised the last Tribunal. This emotion he knew. He loved them. He loved all of them. This was home.

The moment the Archangels arrived, the Dominions gathered. It was time to prepare for battle. They fell in line behind Ophanim. She showed them to a private orange grove where the God's Guard waited. The Seraphim knelt in a circle. Their lips moved with a silent prayer. Their multiple wings entangled with each other'S. They looked lost without the door of heaven as their background. The Dominions kept their distance, apprehension apparent in their stances.

"Let us prepare." Samael gave his siblings a curt nod and unbuttoned the top four buttons of his shirt. With gritted teeth, he reached into the tattooed circle on his chest. He growled as he pulled his halo free. Around him, his fellow angels did the same.

Samael placed it on his head, the gold blending with his hair. The weight of it atop his head steadied his heart. Secure in his mission, He called forth his armor. He used the plain leather and brass breastplate he'd worn when fighting with the Spartans in the Peloponnesian war. He did this out of pure sentiment. His helm and gauntlets came from a young smith in Michigan who traveled from state to state selling his wares at fairs. Laoth had discovered the boy in her wanderings and recommended updating his ancient armor.

He placed *Kushima's* sister at his side, hung his shield from his back, and waited. The Dominions dressed in silence. An air of apprehension swirled among them, and their eyes took turns sliding toward their elders. The God's Guard had promised news. What could be worse than the pending apocalypse? Samael frowned. No good would come from this day.

The Seraphim rose, one after the other, their movements slow and disjointed, as if in pain. The Dominions formed a line as the Guard approached. Shoulder-to-shoulder, they saluted, forearms to face. Their eyes stayed covered as the God's Guard paced before them.

"We must leave you."

The Dominions dropped their forearms in shock. Samael noted how the perpetual teenagers somehow looked older than the earth. Maybe it was the haunted look in their red eyes.

"You'd leave us now?" Raphael's tone inched close to disrespect.

"God does not want us to be present when Wylie triggers the apocalypse."

"What does that mean?" asked Beburos, the youngest of the Dominions.

"We will die," said one.

"Hours?"

"Days?" Another added.

"What does it matter?" The tallest guard shook his head.

"We must convince the rebel angels to return to the fold so that we may unite during these arduous times." The Seraphim sang this last part like a dirge and walked away, returning to their prayers.

The Dominion's armor glinted as they turned to each other.

"Well, that sucks." Raphael shouldered Samael, their gauntlets clicking as they met. "Did you know about this?"

Samael shook his head. He'd expected bad news from the Seraphim—but this? How would he or his brethren speak to God without the Guard? Who would watch His door?

Samael sensed the uncertainty around him and stepped away from Raphael to raise his fist. "I'm honored to enter the last leg of this journey with you at my side." Samael met his fellow Dominions' eyes. "*Persta atque obdura.*"

"*Persta atque obdura,*" they repeated in unison.

Samael lifted his chin when an angel in the shape of a child approached at a run. "I'm the second to last to arrive. My Virtue sister will follow shortly."

Samael nodded. "Please, find Wylie. She may need your support today."

The Power lifted his tiny brows but did not voice his concern. With another bow, the child angel leaped into the sky.

"Is it time?" Raphael gripped the hilt of his sword.

Samael tied his hair on top of his head. "It is indeed."

Chapter 34

*D*umah and Laoth sandwiched Wylie as the moving mass around them grew. Wylie easily guessed which Archangels belonged to Laoth's brigade. They all wore fur-lined capes and face paint. Their faces went from greeting with grins to growling with annoyance in volatile intervals. Other than the halos, which most angels wore like crowns, there was no floating luminance to be found, and no one carried a weapon or a shield as she'd expected.

As Wylie turned to Laoth to ask why, a child-shaped angel landed on their boulder. Using her hand to shield her eyes against the brightness of the blank sky, she made out his familiar shape.

Jinx smiled down at her.

"Wylie." His tone carried the same excited note as the rest.

The sound engulfing them dampened as Wylie realized who she stared at. He sat behind her smelling new backpacks, crayons, and bubble baths. He stretched out his knobby boy legs and boxed her in with his teal wings. His feathers visibly twitched as they settled into an ornate quilt behind him. "It's nice to meet you in person."

"You're a Guardian Angel, aren't you?"

He smiled a sweet smile, and his wide eyes asked a wordless question as he leaned into her.

She turned and lifted her arm so he could cuddle her side. "I've always wanted to do this."

"You're not my angel, though."

"No." He lifted his short fingers, catching her hand. He traced her palm and then played with the indent where her wedding band had once been. "But I'm here for you now."

His calm warmed her. She recognized it. The calm had once put her to sleep on the couch while Dean watched Jinx's adventures. The bustling continued, but they sat in a circle of peace, both thinking about the same rambunctious toddler. Soon they shared images of Dean's wild hair and chocolate eyes. His belly laughs and full-body expressions.

"You know, he's all grown up now." The mom in her reached up to re-part Jinx's hair, the brown strands moving between her fingers as if they belonged there.

"That's what they do."

Happiness, body heat, and memories.

"Sisters, Brothers, it is time to begin." A disembodied voice brought Wylie back to the present.

The loud buzz of the crowd vanished, and Jinx squeezed her hand.

Laoth stood. A bold crimson line divided the cyan paint covering her face. Black surrounded her eyes, and her electric blue braids fell down her back in a tangled mess as if she'd already been fighting. Hundreds of angels scattered throughout the rock formations joined her in her proud stance. At once, they lifted their fists.

"*Oppmeskohmet!*" Laoth's voice carried the full power of her Scientia.

"*Ad Signa!*"

"*Attention!*" The commands came at once from Laoth's equals, turning the air static.

Wylie's breath caught as thousands upon thousands of angels rose to their feet. Their heads snapped forward, their bodies straight.

"*Bida!*" Veins bulged in Laoth's neck, her teeth shining in two straight rows as she conjured a shield out of thin air. Her soldiers did the same. Shields appeared, and knuckles whitened as they gripped their handles. Their stances squared, and their ranks closed in. Wylie sat in the epicenter of an army.

"*Il ya duna!*"

A roar deafened Wylie. The Archangel's closest to her let out wild growls while other brigades shouted uniform *Uurahs* and *Uukhais*. She held tight to Jinx as she fought the urge to escape.

Horns sounded, and a contingent of angels rose from the ground. The one in the middle beat his chest until silence fell upon the crowd again. "The God's Guard," he announced.

The warriors, along with the robed and plain-clothed angels, knelt in waves, holding their forearms over their eyes, as their power release rushed over her like morning sickness. The Scientia compressed the air, and Wylie reminded herself that this was how angels showed reverence.

Jinx patted Wylie's leg as the angels stood. "Don't worry. Archangels like to show off." He tilted his head up to look at her. "Putting you in the middle of a brigade may have been overkill on Samael's part." His smile melted Wylie's tension away.

Four short figures with auburn hair and far too many wings springing from their backs walked into the amphitheater's center.

"Are those..."

Jinx lifted his finger in a shushing action, his eyes ahead. Samael and the other Dominions formed a loose circle of defense around the boys, hands near the hilt of their swords.

"Stand." The first Seraph waited as everyone stood. He faced the multitude behind him. "We will begin this gathering by introducing Armageddon."

"Wylie," said the second Seraphim, the littlest one. She remembered him with a familiarity she didn't feel for the others. Wylie stood in response to her name. Thousands of heads swiveled in her direction.

"And Gabriel."

Wylie stumbled back at the sound of her brother's name. Her eyes darted around as she searched for him. Somehow, she'd convinced herself that the man wouldn't come.

"Sister and brother." The third Seraphim opened his wings wide and with two quick beats, took flight. "The end is nigh. These are the angels who will guide us through these trying days."

"We've heard this before." A man in a crimson robe spoke to the surrounding crowd, his voice loud enough for all to hear.

A flash blinded Wylie as the angel dissolved into... W*as that salt?*

"We will welcome you to speak, but now is not the time." He directed his remark to the salt.

"Armageddon is here, and we will be tested," the God's Guard spoke at once. "Lines have been drawn. We have gathered today to beseech those who have left us." The two shorter Seraphim joined hands. "Remember who you are. A Throne made you to follow God's will, not your own."

The crowd rippled as angels fidgeted.

"Many of your siblings will die in this war." They paused, flapping wings took up the space between revelations. "This is not only a judgment day for humans. It is *our* last days, as well." Their voices threaded in and out, and each Seraphim opened their wings in emphasis.

A slow clap echoed around the amphitheater as a man bearing wings alive with flowing water burst into the sky. Wylie's stomach sank. She recognized herself in his movements and coloring. Her fiery wings burst forth as if in answer. Angels behind her dodged the flames, hissing. Jinx grabbed her arm, and Dumah yanked the other.

Not yet, Wylie. The young Seraphim spoke in her head. *The more angels die here, the fewer humans die on earth. When all is lost, remember your home.*

Gabriel continued to clap as he made low circles around the perimeter of the gorge, a smile on his face.

"Sister!" His voice exploded over the sea of people. "Did you hear that, *frangine*? I think they want us to play nice." His water and ice wings glistened as he lowered himself onto an outcropping emptied of angels as he neared it. "I think we should play either way."

Wylie's arms caught fire, and those who held her jumped back. She'd kill him, and she didn't care how. She didn't know how to fight, but kamikazes didn't have to. They just needed the element of surprise.

"Your friend Samael invited me. Almost didn't come, but I couldn't miss this. The angels have a new chosen one, and it's my sister. What a surprise! An honor, really."

"Fuck you." Her wings spread wide, and she lunged off her perch. Her eyes focused on her brother.

Gabriel opened his arms as if waiting for a hug.

She flew.

Halfway to her mark, something crashed into her side. Her breath caught as thin arms clamped around her waist. She hit the ground hard, rolling and tumbling until she hit a tree trunk shoulder first. Oranges rained down around her, their smell joining the metallic taste of blood in her mouth.

She rolled onto her back. Jinx lay in a smoking pile next to her. "What did you do?"

"I stopped you from getting yourself killed."

Once the sting of the crash lightened, Wylie checked that her halo remained secure, jumped to her feet, and rushed to the edge of the orange grove.

"Wylie, we have to get back to earth. I'm not strong enough to carry us both. Tell me you know how."

Wylie shook her head, squinting. The angels remaining faced the center of the amphitheater, and Gabriel continued to speak, though she couldn't make out a word he said. Her wings reappeared.

"Please." A small hand wrapped around her fingers. "Please don't go." Jinx looked up at her with tears in his eyes. "Please."

The blank sky opened, and sleet formed a curtain between her and the angels.

Samael

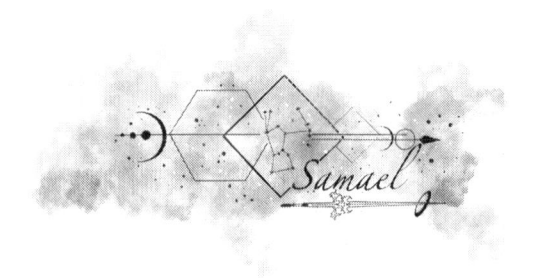

Samael closed ranks with his Dominion siblings.

"It is time we make our own decisions!" Gabriel's voice boomed over the sound of splashing water. "Today, the Seraphim have given you a choice—and yes, you're free to choose—but I beg you to ask one of your own before you make your decision." Gabriel gestured to an Archangel who'd broken from her battalion to take flight.

His gut clenched as his oldest friend stepped forward. She offered him a knowing smirk before addressing the crowd.

"I'm Laoth. I've served under God for many millennia, and I can tell you one thing for certain. Wylie is not an angel. She's the enemy of angels." Her Scientia spilled over, and her eyes reconnected with Samael's. "It is not too late to choose life."

Why? He pushed the question into her. Her gaze became icicles, turning her into someone he hardly recognized.

The question is, why not, brother? The word brother felt like poison in his mind. *You're infatuated with duty, and it has made you weak. You've lost sight of the bigger picture.*

And what's that, Laoth? Turning your back on God?

Victory, you fool! Her eyes flashed with anger.

Samael's gaze hardened. *I look forward to seeing you on the end of my sword.*

"Fuck you," she mouthed back.

"Laoth is a leader among you!" Gabriel's shout broke through the crowd's shock, ending their whispers. "She came to me seeking freedom. Will you?" Gabriel grinned. "This will be your first decision. I vow to reward you for making the correct one."

The Seraphim stood back-to-back behind Samael. Knowing the Guard expected to die here and now, he made a vow of his own. While he stood, no one would touch his elders.

"Those who will follow me, show yourselves!" Gabriel raised his sword arm, his eyes on Samael, his smile never faltering.

Palpable shock clogged the space between raindrops as, one after another, Angels thrust their blades into the sky. The silver that cluttered the air did not end. Faces of angels Samael had trained, advised, and protected twisted in rage as they roared their betrayal. Never had he received a more catastrophic wound. His sword burned his hands as if to protest the deaths of these brothers and sisters.

Gabriel turned to Samael, offering him the half-smile of a businessman before his face turned to stone.

"Attack!"

Samael's shield appeared as three angels came at him, blades first.

Joints jarred as the Dominions cleaved their way through their enemies—shields, pain, and swords. Gore joined the rain as the Seraphim let loose their power. The heads of the rebels burst in twos and threes as they succumbed to the God's Guard's wrath.

Beburos fell first. His body was trampled as rebels filled the space he'd just occupied. The Dominions fell back, their circle holding steady, though the rebels outnumbered them by the hundreds.

Time passed in a blur of death and feathers. Samael ignored those who attempted to fly over them to get to the Seraphim. His most loyal Archangels covered the space. Limbs fell from the sky as angel comrades tore each other apart, the leftovers crashing down in a tangle. The Generals fought with efficiency. Both their bodies and their minds were well-honed weapons.

"Samael!"

Samael lifted his head as Gabriel projected before him.

"Step aside." Those who fought for Gabriel retreated, turning their swords outward. They faced each other in the eye of the death storm.

Samael pointed his sword at Gabriel. "Die!" The Dominion's cry was strangled as half of his circle turned their blades on themselves. Burying them in their bellies.

Gabriel opened his fists, and the angels fell to the ground. "Step aside, old ones. I wish to speak to the God's Guard alone." Gabriel lifted his hand and thrust it downward. Three of the six remaining Dominions dropped to their knees, their bodies following the motion of Gabriel's gesture until they lay prostrate on the ground.

Samael charged.

Gabriel deflected his sword.

Once.

Twice.

Thrice.

A sharp pain sent Samael stumbling into Gabriel. He looked down in time to see a flash of silver withdraw into his abdomen. *Someone stabbed me from behind.* He staggered, his body turning as his shield arm rose against a second blow. Raphael's eyes met Samael's, his lips flattening out. Gabriel stepped past them, heading for the God's Guard.

"Raphael?" Samael's voice broke. His brother, the only other angel to walk the earth as long as he had, had stabbed him in the back.

Raphael's blade left a line of blood across Samael's cheek.

"Why?" Samael half-heartedly blocked, nearly forgetting why he fought in the first place. Distracted, he didn't see the blow coming until Raphael's shield crashed into the side of his head. He fell, landing on his back.

"We didn't have a lot to choose from." Raphael's panted breaths broke his words into syllables, and his advances paused.

"Why him?"

Raphael smirked. "Who do you think trained him?"

A head landed on the ground. Its cherubic face rolled into Samael's shoulder. Empty red eyes stared at him. "No!" He scrambled to his feet. Over Raphael's shoulder, three boys held up their hands as Gabriel advanced on the Seraphim.

Thud and roll.

Samael threw himself at Raphael with billions of years of strength.

Thud and roll.

"Move!" he shouted.

Thud and roll.

Raphael's sword slid across the ground, his eyes widening as he ducked behind his shield.

Samael's blade came down with the killing blow, but before it could land, Gabriel caught it with his steel.

Gabriel shouldered his way between Samael and Raphael. "Go, Father, I will finish this."

"*J'suis fière de toi.*" Raphael's parting words drowned in the cacophony of the battle.

I'm proud of you.

Laoth landed in front of them in the orange grove, loose tendrils of her blue hair plastered to the sides of her face.

Jinx sighed. "Thank God you're here." Jinx took Wylie's hand. "You know I wasn't made to fight."

"I do." Laoth drew her sword. Her nostrils flared as she flashed her teeth in a smile.

Realization dawned on Wylie, and her heart sank. She recognized the expression. Laoth made that face before pouncing. She grinned like this when one of her insults would cross a line.

"I think you're facing the wrong direction." A nervous laugh shook Jinx's thin shoulders.

"I think you're on the wrong side." She weaved her blade through the air, passing it from one hand to another.

"Wylie, find Dumah." Jinx raised his hands, placing himself between Laoth and Wylie.

"Jinx, do you want to die for her?" Laoth raised her brows, her mouth twisting.

"Run!" His command joined the sound of thunder as his body transformed, growing bigger. Black fur covered him, and muscle built on muscle. Jinx snorted, his back leg kicking up dirt.

Despite the anger in her veins, Wylie obeyed and turned into an all-out sprint. *That bitch.* Wylie welcomed this angel into her home and trusted her with her insecurities and fears. She'd put up with her rudeness. Her feet screamed to run faster, but her brain begged her to turn around. The desert floor grabbed her sneakers, and it took all her will not to stop. She wanted to make Laoth hurt for every moment of embarrassment she'd endured under the angel's tutelage.

The thousand pounds of bull at her back was the only thing between her and the Archangel she'd once called a friend. The earth rumbled under his hooves, knowing she only ran for him.

"Fuck." Wylie slid to a stop as Laoth appeared before them.

Jinx's fur grazed her arm as he lowered his head and charged.

Laoth conjured a shield, holding it tight to her chest as she waited. When Jinx's snout reached her, she sidestepped and dragged her blade along his ribs.

His momentum carried him forward, his legs becoming disorganized as he spun a wide circle and rushed at her again. The scene seemed to move at a crawl before Wylie. Laoth's sword slashed Jinx's horn and then plunged into his side. The tip of his horn bounced on the ground as his legs buckled, and he slid to Wylie's feet on his belly.

"NOOOOOO!"

Wylie fell to her knees. Her hands went straight to the puncture wound between his ribs. Her flames cauterized them as her wings came alive. The surrounding wetness evaporated, and her clothes dried. Jinx continued to bleed from an unknown source. Blood created a moat around them, and Jinx returned to his child form.

Wylie pulled him to her breast and wailed. His head lolled back, his eyes staring into forever. She held Jinx as she held Dean, and she pressed her lips into their curls, her hands gathering and gathering. She tasted blood and saw spots. Her heart threatened to implode.

"I hoped the door would kill you." Laoth wiped her sword on her pant leg before sliding it into her scabbard. "Imagine my surprise when that fucker opened up."

Wylie shook her head, pulling Jinx closer. "I hate you!" Her body shook as she screamed. Her hands arranged and rearranged his limbs. She trembled with terror and rage, and that place somewhere in between, before the brain knew what to do with all the hormones.

"Humans are so ugly when they cry." Laoth's fingers found Wylie's hair, and the angel yanked her sideways.

"Laoth!" A female voice brought Laoth to a pause.

"Binah. Look what I have." Laoth ignored the white-winged angel and lowered herself to speak in Wylie's ear. "I've been adding layers of caps on your powers for weeks, and it looks like I didn't need to. What a waste of wings."

"Laoth. Don't make me tell you again. Gabriel's sister is off-limits." The angel held up her hands, her ebony skin glistening in the rain.

"Off-limits? Who isn't off-limits?" She gestured at the fighting. "All of this will be over when she dies. Tell me Gabriel doesn't see this?" Laoth shook Wylie by her hair as she spoke, and Jinx fell from her arms.

Something inside of Wylie cracked with the rough handling. Anger seeped past the sorrow. Her fingers wrapped around Laoth's hand. "Let go."

Laoth's eyes widened in surprise before she let out a blood-curdling scream. The angel's flesh melted under Wylie's touch as the crack inside her widened. Raindrops paused in their fall. Everything she'd held back since becoming an angel escaped her mouth in the form of blinding light. It filled the plane, blanking out all Ophanim's work. The pain broke like a fever, leaving nothing but wrath. When color returned to the world, Wylie wore her breastplate with her husband's poem imprinted in gold.

Laoth fell on her ass, her sword vanishing. The Archangel's cockiness slid away.

"I remember sitting like this in my living room." Wylie patted the floor with her still-flaming hand. "We drank tequila."

Laoth scooted backward as Wylie got to her knees. "Binah! Jelly bean! Help!"

"I confessed my hopes to you." Wylie's fist bounced against her breastplate as she stood, ignoring the other angel as she flew away. "You mocked me." Wylie memorized the fear in Laoth's eyes and closed her own. "You mock every human." She collected the sensations of hurt she'd taken from her patients. "You don't deserve to be an angel." Wylie's palm slammed into Laoth's forehead, shoving it into her brain.

Laoth writhed in the mud. But the sight of her torture didn't fix the holes in Wylie's heart. So, she grabbed those too, forcing her grief into her. "This is what you deserve."

Laoth's hands went to her mouth, covering the way it gaped. Tears tracked a steady path down her face, and she wailed. The inhuman sound serenaded Wylie as she stood and reached into the sky for her sword. *Kushima* answered, filling her hands. She swung the blade down. Its flat edge slapped Laoth's shoulder, lighting her up like kindling.

Wylie's body buzzed with the same overstimulation she'd felt after her Catharsis. Laoth slapped herself as she rolled on the ground. Her frantic movements slowed into pained twitches, and her shrieks became bubbling moans.

Wylie felt no remorse. She looked at her and saw Stephen. Gabriel. She saw an enemy. The war in the gorge beckoned Wylie, and she took to the air, intent on ending another life. She found chaos below.

How does anyone know who they're fighting?

She plunged toward her brother. Around him, like a macabre wreath, lay four boys buried in a bed of feathers and blood. Samael darted forward and back. His face screwed up in a grimace. He felt empty to her. Scientia trailed behind him with every move he made. Gabriel conjured shards of ice from the sky and hurled them like missiles. He fought with the same competence as the ancient Dominion before him.

They were so distracted by each other, they didn't see Wylie coming. She sent them to the ground. Gabriel and Wylie tumbled together, a ball of ice and fire. His malice showed in how his corded muscles and sharp bones took every opportunity to leave bruises. She gritted her teeth and dug her nails into his face.

His hands wrapped around her ribcage and squeezed. *"Frangine."* His spit slapped against her face as she reached for his mind. Her vengeful will and dangerous thoughts did not phase him. She couldn't hurt him with her hatred.

He laughed at her. "That won't work on me." His fingers dug in. "You're lucky I don't want you dead anymore."

"You talk too much," she growled.

She held one of his ears in each of her hands, and with her knee planted in his groin, she pulled.

She ignored her ribs cracking. Her left hand slipped, and he threw her off. She smacked into the hard rock face-first, her nose imitating its last break as blood gushed down her throat.

She blocked her face with her forearms, forgetting about being an angel as white stars crowded her vision. The rain pressed down on her with a fresh surge of intensity. Someone stepped before her. Wylie shook the flashing lights from her head and focused on Samael's gold-tinged ivory wings. The surreal sound of clashing swords sent her scurrying back.

Gaping wounds and little nicks alike marred their skin. The two angels clashed with so much force that thunder clapped as their bodies met.

One lost footing because of the other's blow, the first stumbled forward, and vice versa, the cycle of violence fueled by heavy blows.

Wylie spat a mouthful of blood onto the rock beneath her, her eyes swelling shut. A stream of red flowed past her shins. Her narrowed vision followed the river to a pile of angels crumpled on the ground. Their faces contorted into the mask of bad deaths.

Her field of vision opened.

She couldn't count all the bodies.

They die forever.

She looked up as her savior and her brother attacked each other on unstable feet.

There is no afterlife for them.

Wylie thought of all the angel abilities she'd learned. None of them would save the bloody mass of surviving angels, but maybe she could disrupt them?

When all is gone, remember your home.

She closed her eyes, placing her hands flat on the ground. The shouts and screams drowned as she reached past the plane they battled on, straining her Scientia as she found her home. *I've done this before, but could I take them with me?* She took a hold of the earth with her mind, gritted her teeth, and pulled.

Chapter 35

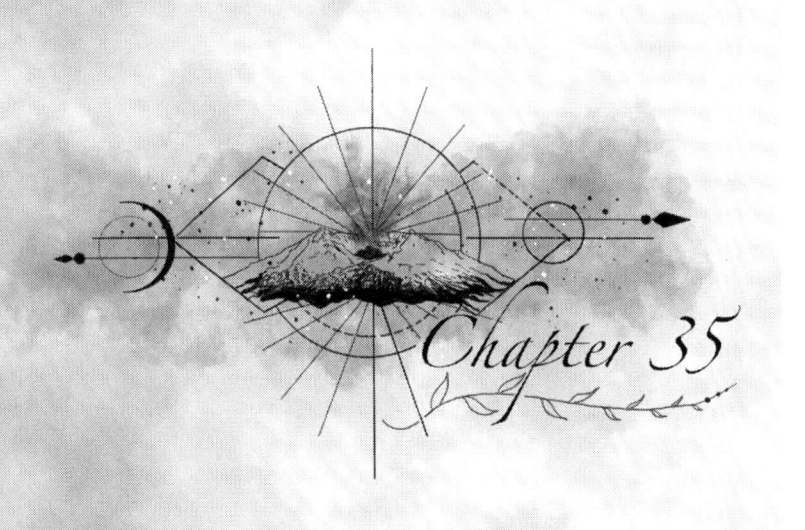

Wylie

Falling

Home. Home. Home.

The fall took hours, or seconds, or days. She expected to land in her rhododendron bush, possibly surrounded by wounded angels. Instead, she slid against the concrete of a rooftop terrace on her hands and knees.

She rolled onto her back as her breathing slowed. Above her, the clouds and fog hid the truth of what she'd done for a few more innocent hours. She knew the blanket of gray covering this city because her heart sang for these clouds. These were her clouds.

Seattle. She thought of Samael and Dumah. She didn't see any angels. She'd hoped to bring it all with her. The entire plane. The good guys, the bad guys, the damn orange trees.

Her head throbbed as despair coalesced there. She permitted herself to cry before she heard the metal security door open. Her eyes snapped shut, preparing an explanation.

I tripped, yeah, I tripped because that one always works.

The crunch of shoes stopped beside her head, and she peeked through her swollen eyelids.

"David?"

He huffed as he lowered himself to the ground and stretched out next to her.

Wylie's eyes closed again, a wave of pain reverberating through her face.

"How did you get here?" he asked.

"I was trying to get home but landed here instead. Wherever here is." She reached up and held her cheek. "How did you get here?"

"This is my apartment building."

David's apartment? Home? Or was David her home?

His hand found hers, and his muse warmth dampened her pain. Their fingers intertwined, and she saw herself through his eyes—her on his bed with her head thrown back—her as she knelt next to a patient and talked them down, her laughing at his kitchen island. "This is the hardest part. When you come back like this. All the things that make being a muse difficult—they're not killing me. If you didn't come home, that would kill me." He cleared his throat. "So, when I saw the angels falling on the news—"

"The angels falling?"

"Yes, they're falling all over the world. What happened?"

Wylie's eyes filled with tears. "I think I saved them." She squeezed his hand.

"We should go inside."

"David, I can't move. I hurt too much. Can we lay here for a little longer?"

The white noise of traffic lulled her to sleep as their silence stretched on. The gravel of the ballasted roof dug into her back. She healed as David held her.

The sky sprinkled its icy tears on them.

A drop landed on her lips, waking her.

Each raindrop that touches your skin is a kiss I've sent you.

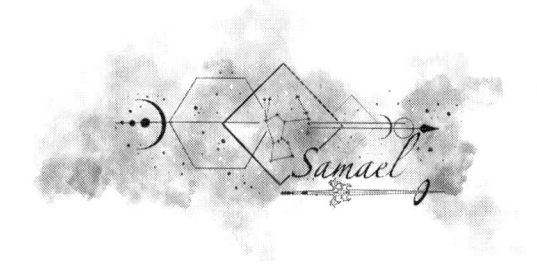

Samael hit the ground so hard dust flew up in a mushroom around him. Too drained of Scientia to prevent all the pain, he curled around his abdomen, where he leaked the most blood. He ground his teeth. He couldn't figure out why he hadn't healed. He took off his breastplate and popped the first few buttons of his shirt before he realized it was wet. The rain left him soaking. With shaking hands, he tore at his clothes. Removing the wetness. A body landed beside him with a squelch. He crawled to it before he noticed it was empty of Scientia. Three more bodies landed as he removed his clothes. He lay flat on his back and waited for the spins and the pain to disappear.

Wylie, what have you done?

"I always dreamed we'd be gone in an instant." A wing protruded from the wall of the bodies. Dumah pushed it flat with her shoulder and tucked it under another lifeless angel's arm. "I imagined the humans would disappear, and then we'd disappear."

Samael grunted, his hand pressed into his abdomen. No longer wet, his wounds had healed the night before, but the place where Raphael's sword exited his body ached. He followed the path of the dead with his eyes. The passage twisted and turned until it ended at the door to heaven. The dead angels piled so high on either side of the door that standing among them felt like being swallowed by a maze.

He couldn't tell who fought behind Gabriel or stood under the banner of God, but he'd helped collect them all so Ophanim could return them to the earth.

Did it matter who'd betrayed whom? He leaned down and forced a leg back into place. "I'm surprised it didn't happen sooner."

"Samael, over here," Dumah called, crouching by a female angel. Samael went through the piles of broken wings and tangled limbs and froze. He recognized the tuft of electric blue hair left pristine on an island of oozing scalp. Dumah smoothed it away from the scalded death mask. An unrecognizable face stared skyward. "As misguided as she was in the end, she was still our friend."

Samael crouched next to Dumah, thinking about Laoth's last words. He covered his eyes with his forearm, seeing Laoth whole again with his eyes closed, imagining her usual smirk and raised brows. "May this last adventure be the victory you always wanted, sister." He closed her eyes, and Dumah patted him on the back when he did not move to stand.

"This isn't the first rebellion we've survived. Don't you remember? We had a good six hundred years when cutting off wings was fashionable."

"And we put a stop to that in 70 AD." Samael lifted the body, careful not to injure it further, and placed it on top of the wall he and his fellow angels had built. Dumah took his elbow, leading him away, clasping it for a beat longer than necessary. Their eyes met. Samael shook his head. "Our body count was never this high, and we had Rome back then. Rome was key."

"There's always America."

Samael snorted, turning back to the job at hand. "I thought I was the one who told bad jokes." They'd made it to the end. *Just one more.* He turned a female angel's head and shoved it between the backs of the dead above and below her.

"What are you going to do about Wylie?"

"What is there to do? Train her." Samael stepped back, his eyes searching for any more out-of-place limbs.

"Look at what she did."

He did. He looked around the living angels. "She didn't do this. We did this. She just tried to stop us. Now let's find Ophanim." He followed the outside wall east. He'd been moving since the blood leaking out of him staunched, gathering the dead and the wounded from multiple continents and bringing them here.

"You can't change the subject. She pulled the Heavenly Planes to earth. What else will she do?" Dumah had handled the humans in Rio de Janeiro, explaining the door and the bodies as well as she could. She'd come back in the darkest mood he'd ever seen.

"Gabriel is just as powerful, except he's well trained. She's our only chance at stopping him."

"If it were anyone else, you would've smote her."

"She saved us." Samael thought of the hundreds of Archangels who'd helped him find and prepare these bodies. How many of them would have died if she'd waited longer? He hated to think it, but Gabriel would've won. When Wylie jumped into the fray, she'd saved him from decapitation.

"It doesn't matter, Samael. You need to teach her obedience. She has an important destiny, but that doesn't mean she can go around rearranging God's creations. The Heavenly Planes are gone."

"I'd expect to hear this from anyone but you. I've seen how gracious you're with her." He quickened his pace.

"I'm not in charge of her. You are. I don't think she knows, and it's not her fault."

"I don't want to be in charge of her." He walked around the corner.

"Why, because she makes you feel?" She smacked into his back.

He stood motionless, his hands tightening into fists at his sides. "She cannot."

"But you . . ." She took a step back.

"Enough." Samael held up a hand. "Let's finish this." He kicked an elbow into place and continued forward in silence.

Ophanim leaned on the mass of bodies, cheek to cheek, with an angel Samael didn't recognize. She swayed, her robes fluttering to her rhythm.

"It's done." Samael folded his arms in reverence.

"This is going to take more Scientia than I have."

Samael caught Dumah's eyes. "My Scientia is your Scientia."

"And mine," Dumah added.

"I'll need more." Ophanim never stopped her swaying. Her hands ran up and down the wall before her.

He'd never seen her earth side. She looked broken. How many of her children died? Mothers aren't built to watch their daughters and sons murder each other.

Samael opened his arms and called the Archangels who he'd tasked to weave themselves with the people of this land. He looked at the door, which now obstructed his view of the Corcovado, Christ the Redeemer. The white statue no longer dominated the sky of this place. Even so, the door looked smaller on earth. The top, visible for the first time, brushed the clouds.

Archangels arrived and immediately lowered their eyes from the maze of bodies. "Ophanim needs us," Samael said, taking Dumah's hand. Soon a chain of angels snaked its way into the trees.

Ophanim took the hand of one of the dead and then took Samael's. They sang. The power of the living angels drove through Samael in a burning rush as Ophanim completed the last rites of their dead, returning them to the earth. The walls of angels became grassy hills, the paths trenches.

Epilogue

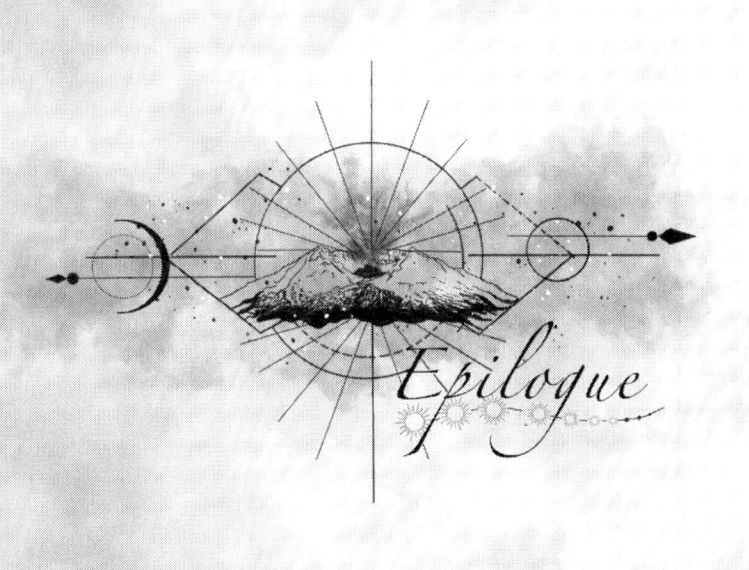

Wylie

Gabriel went public on day two, presenting himself to the masses as a leader among angels. He claimed to provide freedom for angels and humans alike. If Wylie turned on the TV, she'd see him staring back at her. Humans didn't ask the right questions before they trusted him. On day three, religions either denounced him or started funding his movement.

By week two, a mass exodus to Brazil had culminated in tent cities around the door to heaven. Humanity hoarded supplies. The shortages in food and medications occurred around week three. With these new strains on society, people took the law into their own hands, and humanity showed the angels their darkest side.

The hospital couldn't keep up with the traumas. Ambulances delivered two or three at a time. She treated patients in the lobby and the halls. She set up tents and cots in the parking lots and garage as the summer sun beat down on them. She worked twenty-four hours at a time, opening her apartment to coworkers for naps and meals.

"It's a UTI."

"What?" The little old lady narrowed her eyes. "But I didn't even see the doctor."

"I'm sorry, ma'am, there is currently a 12-hour wait to be seen, but your symptoms and urinalysis are consistent with a UTI."

"I had one a month and a half ago." She ran her fingers through her white perm. "But what if it's something worse? Like a kidney stone or cancer?"

Wylie took off her gloves and tucked them in her pocket. In their current disaster, nurses were advised only to discard visibly soiled supplies. "Can I touch your back?"

She leaned forward and pulled up her shirt.

Wylie rubbed her hands together, warming her fingers. She drew a deep breath and rested her hands on the woman's flank. She cleared out the bacteria and soothed the irritation. She couldn't feel a kidney stone, but she could feel the woman's fear. Wylie left some peace behind. "You know, ma'am. I think this is a mild case."

The woman's eyes dilated as they connected with Wylie's. "You're an angel."

"No, ma'am. I'm just a nurse."

Wylie saw the woman off and headed to the emergency bay to get more patient assignments, having discharged all of her own.

"A man in the break room is asking for you," Susan said with a confidential air.

"Who is it?"

Susan leaned in close. "It's that angel from TV. What's his name? Michael. No, Gabriel." She sucked her teeth. "Why does he want to see you? Do you know him?"

Wylie rolled her eyes and walked to the break room. She didn't care about politeness anymore. One foot in front of the other. Wylie's sneakers on tile, bright hospital lights reflecting off stainless-steel door frames. Her heartbeat muffled the patient's moans as they writhed on stretchers parked in makeshift bays along the walls.

Her hand lifted her badge to the security pad. The door opened with a click, and she stepped inside. His presence caused a fever to bloom under her skin, and she fought to keep her fire inside. Her teeth squeaked against themselves. The hospital on fire flashed in her mind. Would the people inside be an acceptable sacrifice if this monster burned with them?

"Hello, *frangine*."

"Have you come to finish the job?"

"The job?" He smiled. "I have no clue what you're talking about."

"Have you come to kill me yourself?"

His thumb ran along his upturned lip. "If I still wanted you dead, I would have done it in heaven." He stood from a metal bench where nurses and doctors mourned lost patients. "I came to clear things up between us."

"Really?"

He chuckled as he shook his head. "We should call a truce." He offered his hand for Wylie to shake, and she folded her arms. He sighed, checking his watch. "The world is fragile right now."

Wylie jumped as he clapped. A massive wave of Scientia escaped him. Alarms echoed through the halls, and a woman screamed. Fear engulfed Wylie. "What did you do?"

"I'm not the bad guy, *cher*." He dusted off his hands as if he'd just gotten them dirty. "You know where to find me when you change your mind."

He walked past her, his shoes clicking.

She followed him but lost him the moment he exited the break-room. The hall teemed with people rushing to exit the building. Wylie ran toward the screams that continued to pierce the air, her eyes searching faces as she passed. A half-naked man walked out of the room where the screams originated, electrodes hanging from his chest, the white cords dragging on the ground.

Turning into the room, she discovered a nurse pointing her bloody gloves in the man's direction. Her mouth gaped open. Tears streamed down her face. A doctor sat on the rolling chair, his white jacket stained red, his head resting in his hands. Another sat on the ground as if she'd fallen.

Liters of blood puddled on the ground around the hospital bed. "We just called a time of death." The nurse's hand landed on Wylie's shoulder, leaving fingerprints there. "He bled out." She squeezed, her eyes trained on the doorway. "We called a time of death. He bled out. He bled out."

Wylie pushed the hand off her shoulder and ran back to the hallway. Patients in their gowns spilled out of rooms. She followed them into the sunlight, joining the stunned exodus of the healed.

Thousands of patients walked out of the hospital that day, all of them healed of their ailments. Gabriel could regrow limbs. She'd made it rain angels. He cured cancer. She'd crashed the Heavenly Planes into the earth. He brought the dead back to life.

And what had Wylie done?

She'd started the Apocalypse.

ABOUT THE AUTHOR

C L Cabrera is a Labor and Delivery nurse and a mother of three girls from Washington state. Her love of writing started in second grade and never stopped. Now, she spends every free moment putting the worlds she made up in her mind on paper.

ALSO BY C L CABRERA

Prologue

Raphael

Lac Des Allemands, Luisiana

1995

Raphael's knee bounced as he held tight to the force field he'd built around his commune. Torn between excitement and annoyance, he sat at his desk as he ignored Alejandra's cries of pain bouncing off the dirt floors of the hut. He'd waited millennia for this, but the being sitting before him and the moans surrounding him ruined what should be a celebration. He steepled his fingers, his jaw tightening as he ignored the demon's thoughts. The Devil family was always so hot-headed. "And you think now is a good time for me to 'pay up'?"

"This baby is the one. The mother is the first to survive pregnancy. I've been providing you with my seed for over a century, and all that time you've promised me a crown. Your Armageddon is almost here. I'm ready to rule hell."

Raphael hated two things most in this world—the ugly sounds of humanity and demons. And now he had to deal with both. The lamplight flickered over the demon's broad face, his square jaw contrasting with his cherubic ebony curls. Raphael held back a scowl as a loud grunt intruded on their conversation. "If the baby survives, I will..."

"No, I've waited long enough. I want this now." The demon stood, his head reaching the beams in the ceiling. "You could not have done this without my bloodline. I waited long enough."

The squeal of an infant interrupted their conversation. A new Scientia rumbled through the earth, bashing into Raphael's force field with such power the surrounding air crackled with static electricity. Alejandra must have delivered. Both males lifted their heads as Raphael's door flung open.

Chloe burst into the room. "He's here!"

"He?" Raphael asked the auburn-haired woman.

"It's a boy." She grinned, and he saw the infant in her mind—pudgy, hairy, and with all the male equipment. "I'm going to go tell the rest." His Muse rushed away, more excited about the baby than he, now that she'd revealed the gender.

Raphael stood, his thick brows meeting. "This changes things. The baby was meant to be a girl." He came around his desk.

The demon stepped in front of the door, blocking Raphael's way. "This changes nothing. You have your baby. Now I want my throne."

Raphael narrowed his eyes. "Move."

"You promised me a throne."

Without touching the disgusting being Raphael waved the male aside, its massive body moving with his will and crashing into the wall.

"We have a blood pact," the demon growled as he found his footing.

Raphael's face smoothed into a blank mask, his mind made up. It was his job as an Angel to protect humans from the vermin. It was time to take out the trash. He pulled his halo from where it hung clipped to his belt and stretched it. He'd break the pact and deal with the consequences later. Now was not the time to start a war with Hell. He hooked the metal around the demon's neck and yanked it back, pulling the demon to his knees. The male's arms flailed. His throat gurgled.

"Hell would be wasted on you." Raphael willed his halo to sharpen as he used it like a garrote to slice off the demon's head. Blood splattered against his face and instant, white-hot pain blinded him. He braced himself against the wall. A moan escaped his lips. His ears rang, and a sudden silence ensued.

He stumbled to the door, swinging it open. The setting sun burned his eyes, and he didn't know his Muse stood beside him until her hand rested on his shoulder. "What happened?"

Raphael heard her words. He heard the rustling of the branches in the wind and a bird that chirped just above him, but he couldn't hear Chloe's thoughts. He reached with his mind for the next Muse and the next. Silence.

His eyes fell on the babe in Chloe's arms. Had he lost his ability to read minds? He shrugged the thought away. The consequences of breaking the blood pact would be worth having this child to himself. Armageddon was the key to everything.

"Can we name him Gabriel?" Chloe asked, her cheeks rosy as she gazed down at the babe's face.

He pressed his blood-covered finger into the infant's hand, and the babe took hold. "A human name for a human angel, *cher*. How fitting."

Preorder Today

Made in United States
Troutdale, OR
01/22/2025